Queen of Diamonds

By

Jae Malone

Happy Reading!
Jae Malone

New Generation Publishing

Other books by Jae Malone

The Winterne Series

Silver Linings (Volume One)
Fool's Gold (Volume Three)

For Erin and Finn

Chapter One

In August 1645, Mary Fuller was hanged as a witch in Bury St Edmunds, Suffolk, accused and convicted by the Witchfinder General, Matthew Hopkins. After several further incarnations, in 2014, her name was Armistice Endor Jenks; she was very much alive and worried about her precious pet ravens, Mélusine and Taliesin, who had not been seen, this time, for three days. Last time they disappeared they had taken a trip to London to visit relatives and friends at the Tower. Mrs Jenks had received a telephone call from the Head Yeoman of the Guard informing her that, on discovering there were eight rather than the usual six domestic ravens at the Tower, he inspected all their leg rings, had found her contact details on two of them and would she please come and pick up her birds; the poor man had seemed more bemused than annoyed. Not relishing the idea of a trip into the busy metropolis, Armistice had paid for a car to collect the mischievous birds and she sincerely hoped they had not repeated that particular adventure; she was not made of money!

"Look, look at them Merlin," she said to her clearly unworried black and white Border Collie, who stretched drowsily on the kitchen hearth rug, "scores of crows, all heading back to their nests which is right and proper but, would you believe it, still no ravens anywhere in sight." Merlin lifted his head, acknowledging the mention of his name and wagged his tail but made no effort to comfort her.

"Oh! You're a great help," she smiled down at the unworried dog. "At least one of us is relaxed."

It was the Sunday before Easter and the bells rang across the village from the small church summoning the congregation to the evening service. Mrs Jenks would not be one of them. She had never attended church services and had no intention of doing so just because it was Palm Sunday. She held her own beliefs and, besides, she had far too much to do in her role as a healer to animals and those who preferred to use her services, to think about going to church.

Steam rose from a saucepan on the black pot-bellied stove in the far corner of the window wall, releasing a strong herbal aroma into the kitchen as it bubbled and simmered in an old black saucepan. Mrs Jenks left the window to check on the contents which she stirred, in anti-clockwise direction, with a large wooden spoon. Merlin sniffed, snuffled and sneezed, twice.

Ignoring the dog and satisfied with how the potion was brewing, she headed back to the window and pulled the curtain to one side. Her dark blue eyes squinted against the vivid golden rays of the sinking sun and she blinked hopefully as two small dots appeared, high above the trees, heading in the direction of Winterne. She smiled. Finally they were on their way home. Her treasured ravens were unharmed and almost back where they belonged. She exhaled, felt her shoulders relax. Relief.

She marvelled at the golden gleam of sunset shimmering on their blue-black plumage while they flew so closely together, their wingtips almost touched. "Brigid be thanked," she sighed, as the magnificent birds descended, skimmed over the treetops in a wide arc to land gracefully on the roof of the garden shed where they hopped onto the window ledge.

As was his habit, the male, Taliesin, immediately hopped inside, leaving his mate alone. Ignoring his calls, she hesitated; the breeze ruffled her feathers as her coal black eyes met those of the woman at the kitchen window. Again he called. This time she chose to join him hesitating just long enough for one last look into the crimson sunset.

Many local villagers called Mrs Jenks a witch and it was easy to understand why. Although she had never owned a tall black hat and her broomstick was used only for sweeping the floor, she was an expert in the use of herbs, had an uncanny affinity with animals and possessed a legendary talent for fortune telling using tarot cards. She also preferred to live alone close to the woods and was rarely seen in the village which only fuelled the speculation and allowed the more imaginative amongst them to create rumours and misconceptions about her.

Armistice Endor Jenks was born on Armistice Day 1918 and was well over ninety years old. She was tall, straight backed, unwrinkled and moved with an agility envied by people half her age. No-one would ever have called her beautiful. She was striking, with a strong handsome face and eyes so dark blue they were almost black, under arching grey eyebrows. She had a long straight nose, a firm jaw-line and a wide mouth often set in a determined line as she concentrated on herbal cures, but could switch to a smile in a heartbeat. She often wore her collar-length, iron-grey hair pinned up or tied back off her face to keep it out of her eyes while she worked.

Those who didn't know her thought she was arrogant but they were entirely wrong. Her few close friends knew her heart was as soft as goose-

down and were privileged by her friendship.

When she did make one of her rare appearances in the village, people either stared or hurried off in the opposite direction, never quite sure how to react. But Mrs Jenks cared not a jot what anyone thought of her, indeed she thoroughly enjoyed her macabre reputation as it kept away the local children, of whom she was not particularly fond. In her opinion, children were noisy, bad mannered, far too boisterous and only became tolerable when they reached her shoulder height, and she was very tall.

In fact it was customary to hear a harassed mother use the ultimate deterrent of 'Mrs Jenks will get you' when scolding their disobedient children, just as their mothers had done; no footballs were ever accidentally kicked into Mrs Jenks' garden.

Had the villagers known just how close to the truth they were, they would have been astounded and probably even more afraid, because Mrs Jenks was indeed a witch, although she had never cast a spell, jinxed or hexed anyone maliciously in any of her many incarnations, all of which she remembered very well. Particularly vivid were those in which she been starved and beaten, tortured with pins being jabbed into her skin or tied to a ducking stool and drowned; her memories of both times she was hanged were particularly distinct.

One person she hoped never to meet again, in any life, present or future, was Matthew Hopkins the Witchfinder General, who had taken great delight in having over three hundred women killed during the trials he instigated in 1645. She shuddered at the memory of his condemnation of her for witchcraft and the satisfaction he seemed to derive from sentencing her to death. It was during her next incarnation she discovered the tables had turned on Matthew Hopkins when he too subjected to the 'swimming test' and executed for witchcraft in 1647. What goes around, comes around, she would say.

Thankfully, those grisly days were long gone and now she enjoyed her life with her cat, her dog, the ravens and her friends Charlie Nowell and the elves. But in truth, her magical abilities had diminished to such a degree over the centuries all that remained were her powers of healing.

As dusk fell, the light dimmed until the long narrow room was illuminated only by the wood fire in the grate, in front of which Merlin was resting, comfortable on the thick hearth rug and made dozy by the warmth. With fires in both the grate and the stove, the room was almost unbearably hot, but Mrs Jenks did not seem to feel it.

On the heavy round table in the middle of the room a cat sneezed.

"Bless you!" Mrs Jenks laughed. "Feverfew a bit strong is it? Never mind, it'll be done soon." The cat, an elegant grey animal with enormous jade coloured eyes, had been grooming himself, licking his paw and

rubbing it across his face. He looked up at the sound of her voice and purred. She moved closer and stroked his head, his purr grew louder and he arched his neck, rubbing his forehead against her hand.

"It's time to light the lamp, Bandit. Look how quickly darkness is falling." Going to the fireplace she stepped over the dog, took an oil lamp down from the mantelpiece and carefully lifted off the glass cover, then holding a long wax taper to the open fire until it ignited, she lit the wick, replaced the glass cover and placed the lamp on the table, away from the cat. A warm glow spread around the long, narrow white painted, room which served as both kitchen and living room.

The ceiling was quite low and crossed with dark wooden beams which, together with the dark furniture, made the room feel smaller than it actually was. This and the heat gave the room a near claustrophobic quality which neither of the animals or Mrs Jenks seemed to notice. Bandit was far too interested in a hairy-legged, black spider as it scuttled about anchoring a huge silvery web between a sheaf of dried flowers on a ceiling beam and the tapestry pole. He continued licking a paw as he observed, through lowered eyelids and biding his time. He would pounce when he was good and ready.

If she had one failing, Mrs Jenks was a hoarder; she rarely threw anything away. Shelves either side of the window and on the two large bookcases were crammed with books on botany or astrology, and every spare nook not jam-packed with plants and herb boxes, had photographs or rolled up horoscope charts squeezed in behind jars and plates. Astrological diagrams and palmistry charts were pinned haphazardly in spaces between the bookcases.

Pride of place above the fireplace was given to a fading tapestry depicting a scene from Greek mythology where white-robed goddesses danced with fauns amongst the trees in a scene of tranquil joyfulness while Zeus watched from above protectively. Mrs Jenks was extremely proud of this tapestry having worked on it herself many years before.

Although the room was messy, Mrs Jenks knew exactly where to find everything she needed, with the exception of her tarot cards which regularly went missing, only to turn up somewhere other than where she absolutely knew she had not left them.

At the far end of the room two doors stood side by side, one was slightly ajar revealing a dark wooden staircase. The other led to a small, neat parlour Mrs Jenks used for the occasional visitor requiring a private tarot reading.

Her treasured birds now home, Mrs Jenks was visibly more content. Passing the stove, she gave the mixture in the saucepan a quick stir then, as she closed the curtains, something drew her gaze to the darkening sky. A

chill breeze blew in through the open window and she shivered, pulling her paisley patterned shawl closer round her neck.

"It's colder than I thought," she said as the cat jumped onto the window ledge. "That wind's coming from the east. The north wind blows cold but nothing good ever gets blown in with the east wind. I have a feeling something's not...right. Trouble's coming," she said, almost to herself.

The breeze blew more strongly making the curtains billow out and she hurried to close the windows. Tugging at the handle of the first window she closed it easily but, as she tried to close the second, a strong gust of wind almost blew the handle out of her hand and she battled to keep hold of it until the wind eased allowing her to pull the window tightly shut.

Stretching, Bandit jumped down from the ledge and disappeared under the red chenille tablecloth. Merlin, disturbed by her struggle with the window, stood up, yawned loudly and padded over to where she stood. She stroked his head. "It's OK Merlin, you don't have to worry...I'm perfectly alright." Apparently reassured, Merlin returned to the hearth rug, flopped down, rolled onto his side and was soon snoring softly again.

Mrs Jenks returned to the saucepan, lifted the lid and stirred the gently simmering potion with a wooden spoon. The fragrant mixture had reduced nicely. She spooned out a little of the liquid and tried it for taste. Satisfied, she put the lid back on the saucepan. "Another half hour and it will be done to perfection," she told the smiling cat who leapt onto a chair and up onto the book and paper strewn table. He stretched his legs, arched his back and sprang over to the sink worktop, almost knocking over a couple of green coloured glass bottles containing a dark liquid. They wobbled threatening to crash to the floor, but Mrs Jenks caught them before they fell.

"Oh do be careful, you silly cat! I'm not in the mood for any mischief tonight!"

The cat made a plaintive mewing sound and nudged her hand with his nose as if asking forgiveness, which he received. She stroked him absent-mindedly and he purred back at her contentedly. Finally, back at the window Mrs Jenks snapped the curtains closed shutting out whatever was worrying her and the cat leapt lightly onto her shoulders and lay across her neck like a scarf, his claws retracted to avoid hurting her.

"Do you feel it, my boy?" The cat rubbed his face against her cheek. "What about you, Merlin?" The dog sat up, tipped his head to one side, his tongue lolled out of the side of his mouth while his tail thumped loudly against the chair leg. "No, it's no good asking you is it, you silly thing?" she smiled at him fondly. "I'll ask the cards."

Merlin lay back on his rug, his tail still wagging happily.

The cat still draped across her shoulders, Mrs Jenks went to a large

dresser near the back of the room. A small bundle wrapped in purple silk caught her eye.

"I can't use them Bandit, they're for Isabel and I haven't blessed them yet. Now where are mine?"

The cat mewed.

Mrs Jenks chewed her lip. "You're sure you don't know where they are?" As she leaned forward to open a drawer, Bandit sprang onto the ledge above and paced up and down, miaowing loudly. Mrs Jenks rifled through the drawer, making more of a mess than there was before, but the cards were not there. She slammed the drawer shut and opened the next one, repeating the process at all four drawers. "Where are they? I used them recently."

Bandit paced the shelf agitatedly, purring constantly.

"It's no good you purring at me, Bandit. It's not helping!" She searched the untidy table, frantically pushing books and packets of herbs out of the way, accidentally knocking a couple of books onto the floor near Merlin. He raised his head and sniffed but, unconcerned, lowered his head and went back to sleep. Bandit dropped onto the floor and headed for a cupboard at the far end of the room. Sitting down at the door he miaowed loudly.

"No, I didn't put them in there."

But the cat's miaowing became more insistent; he scratched at the door.

"Alright, alright, I'll look, but I'm sure you're wrong."

On a shelf at the back of the cupboard, lying face down on a block of oak, were the missing tarot cards spread out in a long line. Small piles of salt in each corner of the block protected the cards from malign influence. "Brigid be thanked! They're here!"

Bandit mewed loudly, rubbing against her legs. "Sorry Bandit, you be thanked as well."

With a loud miaow and a satisfied smile, Bandit leapt back onto the table and waited for her. Holding the pack of seventy-eight cards lovingly, she returned to the table and mixed the pack, selected nine cards at random and set them face down in a square formation, three rows of three, returning the remainder of the pack to the wooden block.

☐☐☐
☐☐☐
☐☐☐

☐

"Nine for the reading, and the tenth, when I close the cards," Mrs Jenks muttered quietly.

First, she selected the central card. "The Priestess, Bandit. That's me,

I'm the enquirer, but you know that anyway. A good start."

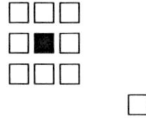

```
□□□
□■□
□□□
```
□

Her next choice was the first card on the top row. "The Empress! She's probably someone's wife or mother? I wonder who she is."

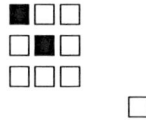

```
■□□
□■□
□□□
```
□

The third card turned over was on the right of the bottom row, giving a diagonal line, from top left to bottom right, of upturned cards. "The Emperor. Hmm. There's a connection to the woman, but how?"

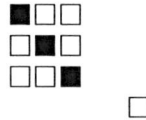

```
■□□
□■□
□□■
```
□

She next turned over the card at the far right of the top row. "The Chariot reversed, Bandit. Quarrels, possibly a defeat, it's above the card representing the man. Hmmm. Let's see what happens next."

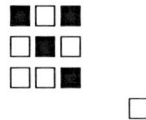

```
■□■
□■□
□□■
```
□

Her next card was the first on the bottom row. "It's The Magician. Hmmm. This indicates a favourable change of position for the woman."

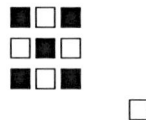

```
■□■
□■□
■□■
```
□

The upturned cards now formed an 'X'. "Now then, the compass points." The next card was in the middle of the top row, at the north position.

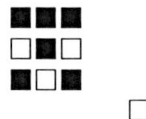

```
■■■
□■□
■□■
```
□

The cat inched closer, concentration creasing his whiskery eyebrows.

"The Moon and it's reversed. I don't like it, Bandit. This shows trickery, deception, maybe hidden enemies. This woman, whoever she is, had better be careful who she trusts." Turning the seventh card, at the south position, she gasped, her hand trembled.

"Oh no! Death reversed! Possible serious loss and painful change and, from its position it's linked to the man again. If it had been the right way up it might have meant new beginnings, but it's a sinister card when reversed."

The cat nudged her hand with his nose. She turned towards him, his eyes locked on hers, he stared intently at her. "Yes, yes, I know you're right. We've come this far and must go on, but this really is quite ominous."

She turned the eighth card, at the west position. "No! This is just too much! The Tower! Disgrace and ruin!" Mrs Jenks clapped her left hand to her mouth, worry lines creased her forehead as she stared down at the cards. Merlin twitched and whined in his sleep, blissfully unaware of the drama going on at the table.

"This portends evil, Bandit. It's linked to the man, but there are two men on this card which foretells sudden and unforeseen calamity. But who are they and which one is it meant for?"

She scanned the cards spread out before her, her expression grave. On the top and bottom rows, all the cards were upturned, only one card in the middle row remained face down, the ninth card, in the 'east' position. The cat edged closer still. Mrs Jenks hesitated; her hand hovering in mid-air.

"I don't want to see this one, Bandit. It's odd too that they're all main cards, the Major Arcana. The cards are usually more mixed."

Bandit looked at the eight cards, and his eyes widened. She picked up the ninth card but, before she could turn it over, Bandit sprang forward, clamped his teeth tightly on it, snatched it from her hand and dropped it over the side of the table onto the floor.

"Why did you do that?" She looked horrified. "You know you can't ignore a drawn card."

Bandit crept to the edge of the table. The card had landed face up, in the

reverse position. Spitting furiously, hackles bushed out like bristles on a broom, he sprang to the top of the nearest cupboard. Mrs Jenks bent to pick up the card and placed it with the others, her hand trembling. "The Devil and it's reversed! True evil!"

A smell of burning reached her nose. "Gwen's potion!" Rushing to the stove, Mrs Jenks found a smelly blackened mess of burnt herbs at the bottom of the dried up saucepan. "Damnation! I forgot all about it."

She was about to run the pan under the cold water tap when she looked again at the charred residue. With a sudden clarity she saw shapes in the cinders. "A black flag and a hawk. More bad omens!"

The cat sloped away into the shadows at the top of the cupboard.

Chapter Two

In the early hours of Easter Sunday, Ernie Rogers, village policeman, hammered loudly on the brass dragon's head door knocker of Winterne Manor, rubbing his cold hands and stamping his numb toes which he thought might fall off when he took his socks off, while he waited, irritably, for an answer. Having started work at ten o'clock the previous morning expecting his shift to finish twelve hours later, he was tired, hungry and thoroughly looking forward to getting home. The day had begun so well, promising an easy shift but it had not ended that way; everything had changed just an hour before he was due to finish and now he had no idea what time he would get to his bed. The events of the last few hours had turned it into a wearisome cold night.

A light went on in the hallway and Ernie moved closer to the door as the bolts slid back and, with loudly creaking hinges, the heavy oak door opened to reveal Dorothy Renwick standing in the doorway.

"Ernie," she smiled warmly, obviously very relieved to see him. "Thank goodness you're here. Harriet's just about worn the carpet away with all her pacing."

"Why's Jonah out at this time of night?" Ernie snapped, storming into the house.

"Jonah? No, he's been in bed for hours," Dorothy declared, puzzled by his uncharacteristic rudeness.

"Then how come I've just seen him in the bushes out the front?" He pointed a little way down the drive.

Dorothy bristled. "I've no idea who or what you saw, Ernie, but it certainly wasn't Jonah. Just because he used to be...well, the way he was...there's no need for you to pick on him. He's much better behaved these days and it would be nice if you'd give him a chance." She prickled with anger at his automatic accusation. They stared at each other, the atmosphere tense.

"Well, who else could it be?" Ernie softened his tone giving her an appeasing half smile, but Dorothy was having none of it. He had forgotten her fiery temper.

"How on earth should I know!" she retorted, closing the groaning door. "It could have been a fox, a...a badger, deer, I don't know, but you have no right to come in here accusing Jonah of...of, I don't know what," she spluttered. "Do you want to go up to his room so you can see for yourself he's there?"

"No, no Dorothy, I believe you. I apologise," Ernie said, withering under the fierce green-eyed glare. "It's just...I definitely saw someone, and it wasn't an animal...that I do know...in the shrubs at the side of the house as I drove up. I'm sorry. Going on past experience I assumed it was Jonah up to his old tricks. I apologise if I was hasty."

But Dorothy's hostile expression remained firmly in place. "I'm sorry too, Ernie, we've got enough trouble without you making more." She barged crossly by him into the hall.

"I know," he said, meekly following. "It's been a long day, but that's no excuse for my bad temper. My shift started at ten this morning but I was in well before that, and should've finished my shift around ten tonight, but with what's happened and being short-handed, I stayed on. It's a pity I didn't get away early like I intended but then all this business at the stables started up. Friends again?"

Dorothy glanced down at her watch; it was ten to two in the morning! No wonder Ernie was cranky. She felt a pang of remorse for snapping at him, and she too spoke more kindly. "Yes, I suppose so, but don't you do that again...coming in here all bluster and accusation. I know Jonah *was* a nightmare, but he's changed since Christmas. He still has his odd outburst, mind...but he's so much easier to live with these days, and you must admit there's been no more trouble...or *accidents*." She frowned. "But I wonder who it was you saw. You're sure you didn't imagine it?"

"No, I saw him...I think it was a 'him', as clear as day. He had a hooded top," he said, as though it explained everything. "I had another look after I parked the car, but there was no sign, probably disappeared into the trees."

"How odd! Perhaps a poacher heading to the woods? But first things first...Harriet's waiting for you. She's fretting no end."

Ernie was relieved the tension between them had evaporated. He was fond of Dorothy and hoped they would see each other more often after he retired in a year or so.

"Speaking of foxes, I nearly hit one on the way up the drive," he said, as they walked through the weapons display, towards the study. "You should've the seen the look it gave me when I braked...talk about a scolding. I hate to think what it would've said if it could talk," Ernie grinned. "Dashing out in front of me like that, it's one very lucky fox I can tell you."

"There's loads of them in the woods; I often hear them barking at night. They've got a sort of high-pitched bark haven't they?" Dorothy replied.

Ernie nodded. "That's mostly the vixens I think. How is Harr...I mean, Mrs Atkins?"

"She..."

A noise on the landing cut her short. Marjorie Seymour, the cook, still tying her pink dressing gown, hair in curlers and clutching a hot water bottle, was hurrying down the stairs.

"Oh dear," Dorothy said quietly as she and Ernie exchanged amused looks.

"What on earth's going on?" Marjorie, red faced and puffing, seemed extraordinarily displeased at being disturbed from her sleep at such an unearthly hour, but spotting Ernie, in uniform, her grumpy expression changed to one of alarm. Stopping beside a gleaming suit of armour at the bottom of the stairs, she looked nervously from Ernie to Dorothy and back again.

"Ernie, why are you here?" she demanded. "What's going on?"

"It's alright, dear, nothing's going on," Dorothy soothed. "Ernie's on nights," she lied. "He's only called in for a cup of tea, that's all." Thankfully Marjorie was too sleepy to ask why Ernie had chosen such a late hour for a social call, and appeared to relax.

"Oh, thank goodness, for a moment I thought it might be something to do with my Stuart."

"No dear, nothing like that. Go back to bed."

"As I'm up I might join you for that cuppa," said Marjorie.

"Erm, no, I don't think that's a good idea," Dorothy lied hastily, but noticing the wounded expression on Marjorie's face she added, "of course, you're very welcome to join us dear, but you know how much trouble you have getting back to sleep if you have tea late at night," Dorothy coaxed , "and you have a busy day tomorrow."

"Yes, s'pose you're right, perhaps it would be better if I just went back to bed," Marjorie yawned.

"Well if you're sure dear," Dorothy gently coaxed and Marjorie turned back up the wide staircase. "Goodnight...don't do anything I wouldn't do," she yawned again as she turned up the next flight of stairs mumbling something about 'strange hours of the night to call in for tea'.

Ernie suppressed a chuckle and was about to speak, but Dorothy shushed him by putting her finger to her lips, pointing upwards. Listening carefully, she waited until she was convinced Marjorie was out of earshot.

"She doesn't know what's happened and I don't want her worrying all night," Dorothy whispered. "She'll only get in a flap. Anyway, you'd better go in now, Harriet's waiting for you and she's really quite anxious.

By the way, I wouldn't say anything about seeing anyone outside; probably best to keep it to ourselves. She's got enough on her plate as it is. You go in and I'll bring you both some tea. I expect you could do with one." She headed towards the kitchen, but stopped halfway and turned back.

"I meant to ask you, how's Alison? How awful this happening so soon after the fire."

"One of the CID blokes from Wells took her to see Doc Brownlow and he sent her to the General Hospital for an X-ray. She's pretty shaken up, as you'd expect, and the Doc thinks her wrist's broken, but she's more upset about Briar going missing. She dotes on that dog."

"Mmm…I know, but you go in and see Harriet. I'll catch up with everything when I bring the tea in." This time she scurried down the hall, down the steps and through the swing door, leaving Ernie alone in the chandelier lit hallway. On the wall close to the study door, was a large, ornate mirror where he checked his appearance. After straightening his uniform tie, he spat lightly into his hand, rubbed his palms together and smoothed down his thinning grey hair. Satisfied he could do no more to make himself look smart, he knocked on the door.

"Come in, Ernie," a female voice called softly.

Turning the handle, he pushed open the door into the cosy, comfortable room. This was where the family usually liked to relax, but tonight Harriet Atkins was anything but relaxed. She paced anxiously in front of the enormous cream plaster fireplace where a warm, friendly fire burned brightly. Her green eyes smiled an uneasy welcome.

Out of habit, Ernie cast a quick, professional eye around the deep red painted walls, taking in the value of the ornaments and paintings which he hoped were adequately insured. The last time he had been in this room had been to break the news of her husband's death just before Christmas. At the time he avoided telling her that her husband himself had set the explosion in which he died; it was not the right time to mention that kind of detail. Harriet soon found out anyway when all the facts had come to light.

"How's Alison, is she being taken care of?" Harriet's voice cut into his recollections. She seemed genuinely distressed by the incident at the stables; her late husband would not have given a damn as long as nothing was taken.

"Well Mrs Atkins," Ernie began.

"Oh, I'm sorry Ernie, please sit down," Harriet cut in. "Dorothy will be in with tea soon, I'm sure you could do with something, considering how long you've been at the stables tonight."

"And then at Headquarters before coming here," Ernie added.

"Oh, yes, of course. It's been a long day for you but what actually happened? We've only had very brief details so far. I'd hoped Alison and

13

Tom would find it peaceful here; they haven't had an easy time lately."

"I know, Mrs Atkins. Awful tragedy…them losing their parents an' all. Terrible. And from what Alison was saying it seems she still feels bad about being away that night," the soft cream sofa sank heavily in the middle as Ernie made himself comfortable, "even though she shouldn't."

Harriet sat rigidly on the edge of the sofa opposite, her hands clasped tightly together in her lap.

"And poor Tom's health has suffered dreadfully since it happened. He was lucky to get out alive but, of course, he'll never compete as a show-jumper again. Life can be so cruel sometimes," Harriet said sadly, staring vacantly into the fire.

Ernie nodded in agreement.

"Sorry Ernie, do carry on," Harriet shook off her melancholy. "I've interrupted you and we've gone off the subject."

"You already know most of it, Mrs Atkins. Like I said on the phone, Alison said she was about to go to bed when Briar started kicking up a rumpus and wouldn't stop, that was about nine-thirty. She and Briar went to investigate. It's a pity Tom was away."

"I know. He's completely devoted to her and rarely goes away, so it's an awful coincidence it happened on this one night when he was away in Yorkshire collecting a very special stallion we've bought from Barney Dangerfield. It's a Hunter, name of Warrior."

Ernie looked puzzled.

"Sorry, I'm talking horse-people language. Hunters are a type of horse, Ernie. It's not a breed, but they're strong, quick and sure-footed. Warrior's a half-Arabian and quite magnificent." Her eyes lit up as she described the horse. "Barney's got a terrific string of Hunters, really good bloodlines and Tom was so excited, he volunteered to collect him."

Ernie listened carefully, memorising details to jot down in his notebook later.

"Have you contacted Tom yet?" Harriet asked.

"No, unfortunately not, and it's a bit worrying. We knew he was in Yorkshire and had a room booked at the Crown Hotel outside Beverley, near the Dangerfield Stables. Alison said he planned to leave about six this morning and thought he'd turn in early tonight, sorry last night," Ernie said, "but he never checked in."

"I suppose he might've stayed at the stables. Has anyone tried there, or what about his mobile?"

"We've tried that, but it just goes to messages, and we tried the stable office too but, at this time of night, it just goes to the answer-phone," Ernie explained. "We even asked the local Force to send someone out there, but they drew a blank too. It's a real puzzle where he's got to," Ernie paused.

"We know he's been there 'cause he got the horse ready for travelling. I can't help wondering if there's a connection between his disappearance and this business here tonight."

"Oh, I think that's unlikely," Harriet answered quickly. "That's your policeman brain working overtime surely." She clearly hadn't considered the possibility that there might be something more sinister behind the incident, "but... it is odd, I must say."

"I wouldn't worry unduly, Mrs Atkins. He's due back tomorrow and there'll likely be some good explanation."

"Yes, I'm sure you're right," she gave a weak smile, "and it's no good worrying about it now...we'll find out soon enough. But I'm going off the track again...please go on."

Ernie had just opened his mouth to speak when Dorothy entered, pushing a small trolley upon which was a silver tea service, three cups and a tin of digestive biscuits. She sat down on the arm of Harriet's sofa and began filling the cups.

"I'm glad you're here Dorothy," Harriet's frown slid away. "I keep interrupting poor Ernie and, now he can tell us together." Harriet's warm smile lit up her green eyes, revealing a glimpse of the beautiful woman she once was before the years with Jeremiah had taken their toll on her health. Ernie took his cup from Dorothy, sipped the reviving brew and began from the beginning, again.

"It seems Alison thought Briar was making a fuss about a fox or badger or something, and didn't really take it seriously...oh, yes, nearly hit a fox on your driveway tonight, just as a matter of interest. Anyway, just as she was convinced it was a false alarm, or perhaps something wrong with one of the horses," he struggled with the cup while he extricated his note book from his jacket pocket. Seeing his predicament, Dorothy took the cup from him and placed it on the coffee table.

"Thanks, dear...I mean Dorothy," he recovered himself quickly, but Dorothy blushed a little. Harriet, giving no sign of noticing, poured herself another half cup of tea while Ernie checked his notebook. "Right then, yes...here we are...Maisie it was, started kicking up a right old fuss, kicking the door and whinnying for all she was worth. Well, of course, Alison went to settle her, but just as she opened the door, it was pushed outwards with great force, knocking her to the ground. She tried to save herself from falling but landed heavily and broke her wrist."

"And she didn't see who it was?" Dorothy questioned.

"No, it was too dark and, in the confusion all she saw was someone rushing by her with Briar in pursuit, but she's convinced it was a man. Our worry now is that Briar's not been seen since. We've got people searching the woods and grounds for her, but it'll be hard finding her in the dark and

Alison's worried sick."

Dorothy nodded. "She must be, poor girl. I don't much care for German Shepherds, they're a bit big for me, but I'll make an exception for Briar; she's so friendly and well behaved."

Harriet broke in. "Ernie, is Meredith still there?" Her daughter Meredith, the stable manager, had rushed off when the call came from a very distressed Alison, and had not yet returned.

"Yes, she'll be there a while yet," Ernie confirmed. "That new vet, Dan Hedges, came up to help check the horses over and Meredith said she'd stay until Briar's found." Under his breath, he added, "one way or the other." Dorothy blanched at his comment. "But on another matter Mrs Atkins," he chose his words carefully, "there's something I haven't mentioned yet. We found some items on the top floor of the barn." Harriet's hands shook making her teacup rattle in its saucer. Dorothy took it from her and placed it on the coffee table beside Ernie's.

"What items, Ernie?" Harriet's voice was husky with apprehension.

Ernie crossed his legs, a tricky task in view of his size, and slid further into the soft sofa. "There was some men's clothing and camping equipment. It seems our man's been camping out in your hayloft. I know you store hay and straw on the ground floor, but Meredith said the top floor's been unused for some time, is that right?"

"Yes. Some of the timbers are rotten...dangerous, but Jerry wouldn't pay for the repairs so we stopped people going up there for safety's sake. I gave strict orders it was to be kept locked at all times," Harriet confirmed. "But that was a while ago and, I have to admit I had forgotten about getting it seen to."

"Meredith said it was taken for granted it was locked so it was never checked, but the lock's been tampered with leaving no obvious signs. It looks like our man's been there for some time."

"But how is that possible...with so many people about?" Harriet looked deathly pale.

"We don't know yet." Ernie hesitated. "Are you alright Mrs Atkins? D'you need a break?"

"No...no, I'm OK, Ernie, please go on." She stood up and walked over to the fireplace and stared into the dancing flames as if trying to draw some comfort there. It's alright Ernie, please go on," Dorothy said calmly, watching her favourite cousin anxiously. Flicking through his notebook, Ernie reeled off the items they had found.

"There was a sleeping bag and blanket, a thermos flask, a bag of dirty clothes, and an old coat. Unfortunately, our chap's clever enough to make sure there's nothing to identify him."

Harriet sighed and continued staring down into the flames.

Ernie glanced at Dorothy who nodded to indicate he should continue.

"There was a Polaroid camera, a pair of binoculars, and…no, no that was all."

Harriet turned to face him. "I'm sorry for getting so upset Ernie, but this is horrible, first Alison being hurt, then Briar going missing. I have a sneaking suspicion this is something to do with Jerry." Harriet sat down next to Dorothy again and, for the first time, Ernie realised how alike the cousins were.

"I've been tying up Jerry's businesses," Harriet continued, "and I've come across some things I'd rather not have known about. Some of the people he was involved with are…dishonest, shall we say, which is why all this chills me to the bone. This incident could be something from Jerry's past come to haunt us." Harriet clasped her hands together nervously. "Whatever has he let us in for now?"

"Please don't worry Mrs Atkins," Ernie began. "We'll station an officer nearby all the time, for a while anyway, and after that, I'm usually around." Ernie's radio crackled into life.

"Yes, John. I'm still at the house. What's up?" The reply was unintelligible to the two women.

"That's great." Ernie gave them the thumbs up sign. "Yes, that's great news. Is Dan still there?"

Harriet and Dorothy exchanged hopeful looks.

"Right, so he's got her now. And Alison knows?" Ernie winked at Dorothy. "Good, that's a relief. Thanks for contacting me. I'll pass on the good news. Mrs Atkins? Yes she's here. Oh yes, John, is Meredith still there? Only Mrs Atkins was asking." Rustle…crackle…crackle. Harriet and Dorothy both strained to hear the reply over the static. Dorothy looked at Harriet and shrugged.

"I didn't make out a word of that," she whispered.

"Thanks, John. See you tomorrow." He clicked the radio off.

"What's happened?" Harriet was on the edge of her seat, excited at the prospect of good news.

"They've found Briar. She's hurt, but alive. She's got a nasty cut on her nose and Dan thinks her right leg's broken. He's taking her back to his surgery where he'll keep an eye on her tonight. If she's alright in the morning, he'll take her back to Alison."

"Thank goodness for that!" Harriet beamed.

"So on that happier note, I think that's all for the moment, Mrs Atkins. The Super's stationing an officer at the stables overnight and we'll be back in the morning with the SOCO's."

"SOCKOS, Ernie?" Dorothy questioned.

"Sorry, it's Police jargon, and people don't always know what we're on about. Not everyone watches 'Midsomer Murders' or 'Lewis' do they?" he grinned. "SOCO stands for Scene of Crime Officers. They do all the painstaking examination of crime sites, take photographs, fingerprints, footprints and the like. Anyway, it's getting late so unless there's anything else, Mrs Atkins." He tried to stifle a yawn behind his big, podgy hand. "To be honest, I'm about ready to turn in."

Harriet shook her head. "No, I don't think there's anything else and thanks Ernie, we've kept you long enough. I'll see you in the morning."

"Right then, we'll keep you updated." Ernie struggled to push himself up from the squashy sofa but Dorothy reached out to help him up.

At the door, Harriet shook his hand. "Thanks Ernie." She looked at the clock on the mantelpiece. "My word, look at the time! It's almost three-thirty. No wonder you're tired," she said with a sympathetic smile. "I'm off to bed too, but I'm not sure I'll sleep much tonight. 'Night, Dorothy, will you show Ernie out please?" Dorothy nodded, and Harriet smiled amiably as she left the room. Ernie made to follow her out, but Dorothy reached the door first and barred the way. Checking to make sure Harriet was heading upstairs, she shut the door again preventing the policeman from leaving.

"Ernie Rogers, you're not fooling me. You're hiding something. Come on, out with it!"

Ernie looked dismayed. "It's police business Dorothy. You know I can't tell you everything…"

"Well you'd better, because I have to protect this family and I'll not have Harriet hurt again...and I can tell when you're hiding something." Determined to have her way, Dorothy fixed him with a relentless, green eyed stare. "What are you not telling me?"

"OK, you win, but keep this to yourself, alright." Beads of perspiration appeared on his top lip and temples which had nothing to do with the warmth of the room.

"Meredith and I found some stuff in the hayloft she didn't want her mum to know about." He withered under Dorothy's stony glare. "There were some polaroid photographs of the Manor and guide books on local buildings and their history." He seemed reluctant to say more but Dorothy made it clear she wanted to hear it all. "Then there were the newspaper cuttings."

"What newspaper cuttings?"

"Well you wanted me to tell you everything," he snapped, "and I'll get to them in a minute. What worried C.I.D. was that every entry in the books relating to Winterne Manor had a ring drawn around it, plus the photos were of members of the family, and they were recent." He looked directly into her eyes. "There were some of you too."

18

"What?" Dorothy cried aloud before lowering her voice to a whisper. She opened the door a few centimetres and peered out into the hallway ensuring no-one was about, then satisfied, closed it again very quietly. Leaning against the door, she turned to face the very tired-looking Ernie. "You mean someone's been close enough to take photos of us all!" She ran a hand over her forehead as she moved away from the door toward the fireplace. "Now you're scaring me." She looked back at him, pacing to the hearth and back. Ernie wished he hadn't told her. He knew she would take it badly, worry about it. Why hadn't he thought up something else?

"And what about these newspaper cuttings?" Dorothy asked quietly. "What were they about?"

"Atkins' death and the memorial service, all of them. But don't take on, m'dear, we're keeping an eye out for this bloke, and we'll get him. We're checking our records for Atkins' known associates, and any information we can find can be crossed-checked against ours. We'll find him, don't you worry."

"You really believe this is linked to Jerry?"

"Probably, but don't go fretting now. We've got a good team working on it and we'll get to the bottom of this." Ernie took her hand and patted it in an attempt to comfort her. "You know whoever he is…," the thought suddenly occurred to him that more than one person might be involved, "or they are, it's likely they've been watching the house for a while."

"Make it worse why don't you?" Dorothy let out a deep sigh and finally opened the door to allow Ernie out of the room. "Well, thanks for being honest with me, even if I didn't like what I heard." She was tense, worried. "And I won't tell Harriet what you've said but," she pointed a finger at him, "from now on you're not to keep anything from me. You're not to hide *anything*. I need to know exactly what's going on. Do you understand, Ernie Rogers?" Shocked at her own volume, she quickly lowered her voice. "For Harriet's sake I need to know what's going on. This has been an awful upset for her, so soon after Jerry's death, useless article that he was." They had arrived at the front door.

Ernie turned to face her. "I know, Dorothy, dear," Ernie gazed at her warmly, "but don't worry, we'll solve this without causing too much upset and, don't forget, I'm here if you need me."

Dorothy opened the door slowly and a little less widely, trying to avoid the loud creaking. The cold air bit into them as Ernie took out his car keys, she touched his arm. "I'm sorry I shouted at you. I suppose I'm just a bit wound up. Are you coming up for coffee in the morning, about ten-thirty?"

"That's a promise and you never know I may have an update for you." He smiled, turned away down the steps and crunched over the gravel driveway to his car. Dorothy waved goodbye and, as the door groaned as she closed it, she made a mental note to get Stuart to oil the hinges. The lights in the hall went out as Ernie started up the engine and the Manor was once again shrouded in darkness as he put the car in gear and prepared to drive off.

A movement in the rear view mirror caught his attention. He turned to look through the rear window. Nothing. There was nothing there, just silent starlit darkness as he drove around the circular green to the main driveway. "The old imagination's playing up again, Ernie. It's probably time to retire," he muttered to himself as the car glided passed the long dark line of trees, just as the moon appeared from behind a cloud creating mysterious shadows. He shivered. Something still told him he was being watched. "I'll be glad to get home," he said out loud, keeping his eyes fixed on the road ahead, deliberately avoiding looking at the trees.

As the car headed towards the gates, Claptrap pulled down his hood and emerged from the shrubbery. He had been hiding in the bushes when the policeman arrived and skulked in the bushes when he went inside. He heard the quarrel between the humans and quite enjoyed being the cause of it, he found it funny, but he was not there for his amusement. The elves were worried about a stranger they had seen in their woods and Claptrap volunteered to spy on the police investigation. He recalled their previous leader, Jimander, had despised Jeremiah Atkins, but now they were both dead. Was it possible that Atkins was causing trouble from the other side of the grave? Claptrap wished Jimander was still alive as now they could do with his wisdom and leadership. Claptrap sighed sadly and turned away into the undergrowth. It was time to head back to the elves cavern and report in.

Chapter Three

For Sam and his parents, Jane and Steve, Easter Sunday lunch meant going to his aunt and uncle's cottage, and Aunt Cathy had also invited Sam's friend, Jenny, who lived next door.

While Cathy and Jane were in the kitchen preparing lunch over a glass of wine, Charlie and Steve sat either side of the blazing log fire in the living room, arguing about a referee's decision in the previous day's football match between Chelsea and Bristol Rovers, with a pre-lunch beer.

Sam and Jenny, bored stiff listening to conversations about sport or neighbours, took Cathy and Charlie's enormous Mastiff-Labrador crossbreed dogs, Benny and Bjorn, out into the garden. After chasing around for a while, Sam undid his jacket to cool down and, Jenny, sounding very much like his mother, warned him he would probably catch a cold if he took it off. She had taken to fussing over him ever since he suffered injuries in the explosion in the cave shortly before Christmas. Jeremiah Atkins had managed to kill himself in the blast but no-one had any sympathy for him, after all he had been up to criminal activities and set the dynamite himself; it was his family they felt sorry for.

Thankfully Sam's injuries had not been too serious, amounting to a broken left arm and wrist, concussion, and severe bruising. Having been knocked unconscious when the roof of the cave collapsed, he had no knowledge of the elves dragging him out of danger with just seconds to spare and the tunnel closing completely. The resulting headaches and nausea gradually eased and his bones mended, but he still had the occasional dull ache in his left forearm.

"Come on, you two," Jenny called as she ran ahead of the dogs through the garden gate, into the field beyond. Bjorn, the older dog, accompanied Sam, jogging sedately along beside him while Benny hurtled after Jenny, stopping only to roll on his back in the long damp grass before springing onto to his feet and racing her to the bottom of the field. Watching her sprinting along with Benny in front, a feeling of contentment flowed through Sam.

Over Christmas, while Sam and his father recuperated from their respective injuries: Jane and Cathy had grown close again, and Sam's friendship with Jenny had blossomed, but he still expected to move back to Nottingham in the New Year. But Harriet Atkins had other ideas. She offered Steve a job to begin overseeing the repair of the damaged tunnels and once that was completed, on the continuing exploration of the cave network. There was a rent-free cottage on the Manor Estate included in the offer, and that proved far too good an opportunity for an unemployed engineer to reject.

In addition, Sam's mother had been ecstatic at the chance of staying near her only sister. Only Sam objected. After his initial resistance to moving to the village, Sam had been much happier there than he had thought he would, even though he had faced life-threatening dangers. Not only had the village provided him with the most exciting time of his life, he had made some good friends; but it was not home, it was not Nottingham. For a while he had become quite morose, aggrieved that his efforts at trying to keep up with his Redlands School work had been for nothing, and he would have to work doubly hard to catch up on the St Merriott's work; the GCSEs were due next year.

For the next couple of weeks he barely spoke to his parents, shut himself away in his room for hours at a time, blankly refusing to talk to anyone; not even Charlie could talk him round. But, there were times when he was alone, when he wondered if he was being unreasonable, but that just made his mood worse.

Knowing he might have pushed things too far, but having no idea how to back down without looking stupid, just made things worse and he found it difficult to face anyone, especially the elves who he knew would just laugh at him. His filthy mood continued into the beginning of the new school term, when everyone around him became sick of being snapped at and that included Jenny, who gave him a wide berth after he bit her head off just for asking him how he was.

Thankfully, his normally amiable personality resurfaced as the logic of staying sank in and, swallowing his pride, he apologised to everyone he had offended. With the help of Mrs Wilkinson, his class teacher and Mrs Tansley, the School Librarian, he soon felt more comfortable about his school work and the mock exams ahead did not seem so terrifying. Settling into village life then followed easily.

Heading into the field beyond the garden, he closed the gate behind him, and a dull pain just below his elbow, made him wince, but it passed as quickly as it had come. Bjorn ran by him on his way to join Benny at the bottom of the field where he was running rings around Jenny.

"Hey!" Jenny beckoned on seeing him. "Come on slow-coach!"

But as he sped up to join her, a movement close to the hedge on his right caught his eye and the blood drained from his face. "Now what?"

Camouflaged perfectly in green and brown colours that blended with the tall, overgrown grass, Piggybait leaned against the hedge, grinning broadly, while Claptrap sat on the lowest spar of the roadside gate, casually examining his finger nails. Fortunately Jenny, busy with the dogs, was not watching Sam and he signalled the elves to stay low, praying the dogs would not sense their presence. As usual, the elves took no notice and ignored his warning, heading in his direction.

"Go away!" Sam mouthed, trying to shoo them away while keeping an eye on Jenny and the dogs. "I'll come and see you later."

This time, they disappeared from view and he relaxed, only to be horrified as two lines of swaying grass moved in his direction proving they were not to be put off so easily. He muttered something very rude.

"I'll be down in a minute, Jen," he shouted, hoping she would stay where she was at least long enough for him to deal with this little problem, or little problems. "I'm just doing my laces up." The grass beside him parted revealing two small smiling faces, totally unconcerned by his anxiety; in fact they appeared to be enjoying it.

"What are you doing here?" Sam whispered, kneeling on one knee and toying with his trainer laces. "You'll be seen."

"It's alright." Piggybait popped his head up to check on Jenny, his hat clearly visible above the grass. "Don't worry, she won't know we're here. Is that your girlfriend?"

"No," Sam blustered, "and take your hat off, it's poking up…she'll see."

"Yeah, it's nice to see you too, Sam. Don't worry, we'll be gone soon," Piggybait frowned, but grudgingly pulled off his green woolly hat, revealing soft brown curling hair that fell to his shoulders.

"We wouldn't be here at all if this wasn't serious, would we Piggy?" Claptrap said.

"But can't it wait?" Sam pleaded, worried sick they would be seen, "I mean this is hardly the best time or place, is it?"

To Sam's irritation, Claptrap casually removed his monocle and examined it, closing first one eye, then the other. "You're right Sam, it's not but this is important…I knew there was a speck of something on the lens." He wiped the monocle on his velvety green jacket before replacing it at his left eye. Sam was sure it had been in front of Claptrap's right eye before, and was about to ask why he persisted in wearing it all when his eyesight was so sharp it would make an eagle green with envy, when Piggybait barked, "Will you get on with it!"

Claptrap ignored the outburst. "Ahh yes, that's better."

Piggybait stamped his feet in frustration at Claptrap's time-wasting.

"Did you hear what happened at the stables last night?"

Sam forgot all about the monocle. "No. Why, what happened?"

"Oooh, it's nasty. Very nasty" Piggybait butted in, eyeing the dogs again, they were closer now, "but yeah, maybe you're right, this isn't the best time, we don't have time to tell you everything now."

"What? You can't tell me something bad happened and leave it like that!" Sam was all ears now. "Come on, what happened?"

"Sorry mate, got to go." Piggybait caught hold of Claptrap's sleeve and began pulling him away into the grass. "Come to the hall tonight, and bring the Chief. It's important!"

"I was just going to say that!" Claptrap exclaimed, indignantly stamping his foot as Piggybait dragged him away.

"Sam, what's taking you so long?" Jenny called, her hands firmly planted on her hips.

"Just coming!" Sam yelled quickly before turning back to the elves. "I'll stay over tonight so I can go with Charlie when he walks the dogs. See you then."

"Sam, Jenny, dinner's ready," Cathy called from the back door of the cottage, just as the elves ducked down into the grass.

"Ooh! Everything happens at once!" he waved back and Cathy disappeared inside. He looked around. The elves had disappeared and not a moment too soon as Jenny was heading his way. Only a slight rippling of the grass betrayed the elves exit from the field. "Phew! Nice timing," Sam sighed. Thinking quickly, he reached down, grabbed one of his trainer laces; they had worn thin with wear and tear and, with a sharp tug, it snapped.

"What's up with you? I thought you were going..."

He held up the broken lace. "Sorry, I was trying to tie one of my laces, but it broke. I couldn't run about with my trainer falling off." Sam put on an expression of pure innocence.

"I was going to race you back to the house, but maybe not," Jenny said, as he knotted what was left of his lace. "I think I've got a spare set indoors."

Sam shivered. Without having the benefit of running about with the dogs, and having left his jacket open, the cold was getting to him. He pulled his jacket more tightly to him, looking forward to the warmth of the cottage.

Jenny shot him a concerned look. "You should do your coat up before you get a chill," she said in a motherly manner, putting her arm through his.

Both dogs panted heavily as they padded up the field, worn out from the exercise, their tongues flapping wetly from the sides of their mouths. Jane appeared at the kitchen window, checking to see if they were on their way

back. At the gate, Sam stood to one side to allow Jenny to go through followed, ploddingly, by the dogs. Closing the gate behind him, he took a deep breath. "Erm, Jenny…,"

"Yeah?"

Sam felt his insides churn. He could not look at her. "Will you go out with me?" He said in a small voice, looking anywhere but at her. "You know, be…umm…be my girlfriend?" Everything seemed to be deathly silent around them, his world stopped excruciatingly still. After what seemed like forever he looked up, horrified to see a dreadful, pitying look in her eyes and wished the ground would swallow him up. He felt as though he would die of embarrassment and wished he had never said anything.

"You know Sam, for a bright fella, you're really quite slow on the uptake, aren't you?" She giggled at the defeated look on his face before taking pity on his agony of discomfiture.

"Why's it taken you so long to ask me out when everyone else's known we've been together since Christmas? Even your folks know." Her warm brown eyes softened and she reached for his hand, grinning at his open mouth and shocked expression. "Close your mouth, Sam, there might be a tractor coming."

Sam stopped impersonating a goldfish and beamed happily as she led him back to the cottage. As Sam opened the back door, the delicious, warm smell of roast turkey and baking cinnamon apple pie greeted them and they realised how hungry they were. Still holding hands, they entered the cosy kitchen, grinning inanely just as Charlie and Steve entered the room. Catching the blissful look on their faces, the men exchanged amused looks prompting Jenny and Sam to let go of each other's hands, but not quickly enough to prevent Cathy seeing the swift movement. To avoid her perceptive look, Sam picked up the dogs bowls and filled them with water for the panting dogs who slurped noisily before padding off to their beds in the hall for a well-earned rest.

The dining table was beautifully laid out with an enormous golden turkey, tureens of vegetables, a jug of gravy, plates, glasses and cutlery. While she busied herself getting everyone settled around the table, Cathy stole another glance at Sam and Jenny, amused at their efforts to hide their new status and delighted they had finally sorted themselves out.

During the cheerful lunch, Benny and Bjorn, although exhausted, were unable to resist the smell of food and sneaked under the table for any titbits coming their way. Charlie pretended not to notice Sam sneaking pieces of turkey off his plate for the dogs, dropping them under the tablecloth when he thought no-one but Jenny was watching.

Agnetha, the tortoiseshell and white cat was attempting to sleep on a chair near to the stove. She opened one eye and scowled disapprovingly each time Charlie's booming laugh disturbed her. Sam wondered where Frida, their other cat, was and guessed she was upstairs sleeping off a hard night's hunting.

"You settlin' in alroight at the cottage, Steve?" Charlie asked.

Sam looked away, trying not to smile at the false local accent Charlie used; knowing that only he and the elves knew how Charlie really sounded, with maybe the exception of Cathy. She had given Sam the impression she knew about Charlie's alter-ego when they had visited him in hospital on Christmas Eve, but she had never hinted at it again, and no matter how often Sam tried to steer the conversation round, Cathy always changed the subject.

"Yes Charlie. It's a great little house," Steve replied. "Harriet's decorators did a lovely job, so good in fact, we've almost forgotten who stayed in it before."

"A den of crime and iniquity," Charlie's periwinkle blue eyes crinkled and his white beard shook as he roared with laughter, "but just 'cause the Atkins gang stayed there, don't mean you'll catch nothin' criminal."

Steve put his knife and fork together, pushed his empty plate forward and smiled at his enormous brother-in-law. "I think Harriet's made sure there's nothing left of them in the house, thank goodness. Anyway, it's time you came up to see it, we're not living out of boxes and cases anymore and you could be our first official visitors. How about next weekend?"

"Fine wi' us an' Oi thought Harriet'd do roight by you," Charlie said, his chair creaked dangerously as he leaned back on it, resting it on two legs. "We do 'ear she's selling 'er 'usband's businesses. Is that roight, Steve?"

It was Jane who answered. "Actually Charlie, it is," she cut in. "Apparently he had some pretty nasty associates and she wants none of it, legal business or otherwise."

Something brushed against Sam's leg and Benny's nose poked out from under the tablecloth as he licked the table leg where a piece of gravy covered turkey had slid down to the floor.

"How do you know so much about her business?" Cathy asked Jane as she put down her wine glass and stood up. "You can tell us all about it while I get the apple pie and custard." At the stove, Cathy put her hands into an oven glove, and lifted out the sweet smelling golden apple pie and set it down quickly on the work top. Jenny went to get the dessert plates from the dresser.

"Well, with Sam at school all day and Steve busy with his job," Jane smiled at her husband, " I was left sitting in a newly done up cottage with nothing to do but housework, feed Portia and look after these two." Jane had collected their cat, Portia shortly after they moved into the cottage and, after a panicky few days, she settled in well to her new surroundings.

"And what's wrong with that?" Steve enquired. "It's a perfectly acceptable occupation for a woman. What do you think, Charlie?" Steve winked.

"Don' you go bringing me into this," Charlie chuckled, "you'll get me into trouble." Charlie's booming laugh disturbed Agnetha and she flicked her tail tetchily, stood up and stretched before lying down again, turning her back on them.

"If it's alright with you, 'Boss', I'll go on now, shall I?" Jane slapped the back of her husband's hand playfully. "Anyway, Harriet offered me a job at the Manor and I start Tuesday."

Cathy stopped slicing the apple pie and looked at her sister in surprise. "Doing what exactly?"

"As her personal assistant," Jane explained, "to help her organise everything with all the lawyers, banks, accountants and so on, and when that's done, with the new ventures she's setting up."

Cathy sat down, the apple pie forgotten and cooling on the worktop. "But she's already got the farm and the stables and then there's the woods that need looking after. Isn't that enough?" Cathy looked at Charlie who nodded in agreement. Sam was concerned at how worried Charlie looked.

"Yes, but these projects will be run by people living locally," Jane tried to explain.

"This sounds exactly how her husband started up," Sam heard a note of suspicion in Cathy's voice.

"No, it's not like that at all, Cathy. There's lots of land around the Manor which could be better used and Harriet wants jobs for local people, and she's increasing the size of the stables to encourage riding and show jumping."

"But she already has Meredith and her team giving riding lessons," Cathy interrupted.

Jane sensed resistance to Harriet's plans. "Riding lessons, yes, but this will be a centre of excellence for coaching show jumping, which is why she took on the Pemburys."

"But doesn't Tom's disability stop him jumping?" Cathy asked.

"Yes," Jane answered firmly, "but he can still ride and he teaches."

"Oh, right," Cathy nodded, "I hadn't realised that." The tension in the air eased a little. "Damn! The pie's getting cold." In her hurry she almost tripped over Bjorn who had moved from under the table and was lying near to the warm stove, close to Agnetha, who glowered at him and hissed the occasional warning, but he stayed far enough away to be sure of avoiding her claws.

"You said she was starting up other new ventures, what sort of ventures?" Charlie asked casually. "Oh yes." Jane replied. "Well, for a start the lake will become a fish farm. There are plenty of people living around the village who will be glad of work. She's already spoken to a few and she'll probably set up a nursery or play centre for the little ones."

Charlie's whiskery face relaxed and his jawline softened. His piercing eyes flashed a hint of a relieved smile at Sam. Thankfully none of these new ventures would impact on his other life. Reassured, Charlie quickly regained his usual affability. "That apple pie looks good, m'dear."

Jane continued talking as Cathy handed out the plates of apple pie and custard to everyone, "Harriet seems to have opened up to me and we had a long chat the other day. She feels responsible for the way Jeremiah and Jonah behaved and wants to try and make amends, but the boy's already doing that, isn't he Sam?" Sam nodded but, out of the corner of his eye, he saw Jenny flinch. He knew she found it hard to forget the bullying she endured at Jonah hands and he wondered how many other people would have even tried to forgive.

But Jane was still talking enthusiastically about Harriet's plans. "She's keen to give something back to the village without changing how it looks, and she's talking about a fund for young people who'd like further education but can't afford it, or a community centre near to the church, and I'm going to help. After all, with Meredith being busy at the stables and Dorothy having too much to do at the house, they don't have time to help, so it looks like I got lucky." Jane smiled and tucked into her apple pie.

Chapter Four

At two-thirty that afternoon, a large white horsebox pulled into the Winterne Manor driveway heading for the stables. The two human occupants had expected to drive straight into the yard, but found their way blocked by a police car parked right across the entrance. On seeing it, Tom Pembury, in the passenger seat, felt his motorway cheeseburger and coffee flip over in his stomach. The driver, Pete Hallett, cursed loudly.

"What the 'ell's this all about?" he moaned as he opened the door and leaned out trying to judge the amount of space between the wall and the offending vehicle and cursed again. "Not a chance of gettin' through there," he grumbled. "Tis a bloomin' nuisance! Can't see the police anywhere or I'd 'ave got 'em ter move. You'd 'ave thought they'd 'ave bin a bit more careful about where they parked. We'll 'ave ter take Warrior out an' walk 'im round."

Pete loved to whinge and being justified made it all the more satisfying. He was a short, stocky man with sparse, wiry grey hair that was seldom seen as he rarely removed his flat cap, but he was not the most observant of people. Busy as he was with grumbling, he missed Tom's grim silence and ashen complexion. "I'd beep me 'orn but it'd scare the 'osses. They don't loike no sudden noises, but I jest can't see no way round. What d'you think Tom?"

Receiving no response, he looked round. Tom was staring, wide-eyed, at the stationary police car. "Tom? I said what d'you think, Tom?"

Roused from his trance-like state, Tom shook his head.

"Um, what? Did you say something?" He nodded towards a plump, red-headed girl, who was mucking out a nearby stable. "If anyone knows what's going on, Kelly will."

Kelly Jones loved to gossip and cared not a bit if the tales she spread were untrue, although generally the consensus was that she was right more often than not. Hearing her name called, she leaned her shovel against the wall and ran over, eager to be the first contact with Tom. There was news and she wanted to see his face when he heard, and she had a bit of a crush on him.

"What's going on Kelly?" Perching on the step of Tom's door, her face flushed with excitement, Kelly could hardly contain herself.

"Hello Tom," she smiled, flirting. "Oh! Hi Pete," she said as an afterthought, finally acknowledging him. "You've no idea, Tom, it's awful." Kelly was revelling in Tom's attention and intended dragging things out as long as possible.

"Well, come on girl! Spit it out, what happened?" Tom barked impatiently, but she was so thick-skinned, nothing was going to stop her enjoying the drama.

"Well," she began slowly, savouring every moment of the limelight.

Tom rolled his eyes, "Oh, for heaven's sake!"

"Don't be like that Tom, I'm gettin' to it," Kelly said huffily. "OK, so, like someone broke in here last night...or broke out of here, whatever. Yeah, like right here at the stables. What d'you think of that?" Her freckled face broke into a grin. "And the police are back here this morning. Mrs Atkins's been here too, seeing how your Alison is."

"Alison? Why? What's happened to Alison?" Tom demanded.

"Oh, yeah, 'course, you don't know do you?" She cast him a look of curiosity mingled with a tinge of smugness. "They tried to get hold of you last night, did you know?"

"I've had enough of this! Get out of my way, Kelly," Tom snarled. She jumped out of the way narrowly avoiding being hit by the door as Tom pushed it open. He grabbed her shoulders roughly.

"Stop messing about! What's wrong with Alison?"

"Stop it Tom," Kelly squealed. "You're hurting me."

She seemed genuinely scared but Tom did not release his hold on her until Pete finally decided it was time to intervene and tried to get between them.

"You didn't oughtta be doin' that Tom. It ain't right."

Pete's voice broke through Tom's rage and he hurriedly let go of Kelly's shoulders.

"Yes, yes you're right. I'm sorry, I shouldn't have done that." Tom backed away, shocked by his own reaction, from the seemingly distressed girl. "I'm sorry Kelly," he said apologetically. "Let's start again. Please tell me exactly what happened."

Kelly shot Pete a look of feigned hurt with a weak, watery smile, and gulped theatrically, wiping the back of a grubby hand across her eyes. She sighed, "OK Tom, I 'cept your 'pology." Beginning quietly, Kelly gained confidence as Tom allowed her time to speak. "Alison's alright and so's Briar now, but they got a bit hurt when this bloke ran away like. Alison's

30

only broke her wrist, that's all, it could have been worse."

"Alison's only done what?" Tom exclaimed. "This bloke! What bloke?" He was finding it difficult to contain his temper with the attention-seeking girl. Kelly flinched and took a step back, treading heavily on Pete's big toe, the one with the in-growing toenail.

"Ow!" Pete's face was knotted with pain.

"Ooooh, I'm sorry, Pete," Kelly squirmed.

Sharon Bartle and Sophie Dennett, who were hosing down the yard, turned to see what the noise was about. Kelly brashly tapped her nose and stuck her tongue out at them. Sharon made a rude gesture back before the two girls hurriedly turned away.

"I'm not wasting any more time on you!" Tom's usually pale complexion turned a shade darker. "I'll find out for myself what's been going on." Impatience and frustration getting the better of him, Tom stormed off leaving Kelly and Pete shocked and open-mouthed as he lurched towards his cottage.

Reaching the end of the stable block, he stopped. Another police vehicle was parked in the lane. This time it was a dark blue van with the police insignia on the front and 'Scene of Crime' in white on the side panels. A sturdy middle-aged woman with grey-streaked hair left the driver's seat and walked around to the rear of the van. Tom ducked down behind a hay trailer and watched as she rummaged around in the back.

From his hiding place, Tom watched as the woman took off her coat, laid it in the back of the van and began pulling on a set of white overalls, right leg first. As she zipped up the suit, she looked around and stared momentarily in Tom's direction. He ducked down further, not wanting to be seen, but the woman was clearly unaware of him. She proceeded to pull white plastic covers over her shoes before closing the van doors and heading off towards the barn. Only when he was convinced she was gone, did Tom emerge from his hiding place and hobble on to the thatched cottage he shared with his sister. The effort of walking quickly took so much out of him he almost fell through the open garden gate, and he was wheezing loudly as he reached the back door.

The three people sitting at the kitchen table jumped as he burst through the door. He had expected only his sister Alison to be there but, on entering, he found Constable Rogers, the local policeman, and a third person, a young, dark haired man Tom had never seen before. He and Alison had been deep in conversation, but they stopped at Tom's arrival. Briar was in her bed under the table, her right leg in plaster. She had big, black stitches in the right side of her nose, and a huge plastic collar round her neck to prevent her scratching or pulling at them. She wagged her tail feebly at Tom, but made no attempt to get up, giving him a look of abject misery.

"Tom! Thank goodness you're home."

Alison ran to hug him but he held her at arm's length. He was shocked at her appearance. Her usually neat light brown hair was tied back in a band and some of the longer strands had fallen out, flopping untidily across her face. Gently he pushed some of the hair back behind her ears and noticed how pale and tired she looked; she had dark, puffy rings under her red-rimmed eyes.

Briar whined and moved a little to make herself more comfortable, a manoeuvre made difficult by the unwieldy collar. Ernie greeted Tom with a friendly handshake, but the younger man fixed him with a cold stare and Tom looked away to avoid the openly hostile eyes. Alison took a tight hold of Tom's arm. He tried to pull away but she held on.

"Kelly told me what happened, are you alright?" he asked. Ernie wondered why he seemed distant.

"I am now, but I've never been so scared."

Detective Sergeant John Harte, observing Tom's reluctance to show affection for his sister, was intrigued by his behaviour, especially by the flash of anger he saw in his eyes as he extricated himself from his better-natured sister.

"Good for you," Tom snapped. "There are worse things you know." Alison blanched and backed away from her brother, giving John the impression she was scared. As Tom limped towards the table his eyes met John's for a fleeting second, but it was Tom who broke eye contact. In that moment, when their eyes had locked, John felt certain he had seen something close to fear or, was it perhaps, guilt in Tom's eyes? Tom took Alison's seat at the table opposite the detective, and turned to the older man.

"I'm glad you're here Ernie, have you found out anything yet?"

"No, not yet," Ernie said. "Our man legged it into the trees. We didn't stand a chance of finding him, it was much too dark."

Alison used her good hand to pull out another chair and sat down beside her brother. Slowly, softly, she began to sob. Ernie reached across to put a hand on her shoulder.

"That's better my dear, Doc Brownlow said you'd cry at some time. It's the shock coming out." A significant look passed between the police officers. "Why don't you go and have a lie down for a while, while we talk to Tom."

Alison shook her head, brushed the tears away from her bloodshot, golden brown eyes with her fingertips and put on a brave smile. "No, I'm alright Ernie, thanks. I'll sleep later."

To ease the tense atmosphere, Ernie decided it was time for

introductions.

"Tom, this is Detective Sergeant Harte." He inclined his head towards the other man who had still not spoken. "He's one of the senior officers leading this investigation."

The plain clothes officer smiled at Alison sympathetically, but turned a penetrating gaze on her brother and his smile slid away. Tom's discomfiture showed as he shifted his eyes from Alison to Ernie then to Briar, pointedly avoiding the other man's gaze. The atmosphere remained tense and it fell to Ernie to break the heavy silence.

"We tried to contact you last night, Tom. Where were you?" It sounded like an accusation. Tom shifted in his seat. It was a few seconds before he answered.

"It looks like I've been caught out." He gave Alison a sheepish look. "I was at a card game until about two a.m.," he wheezed, his breathing harsh again. "I'd settled Warrior before I went out, and it was too late to get all the way back to the hotel, so I slept in his stable after the game."

"That accounts for why the local force couldn't find you," Ernie glanced at the Detective Sergeant, who nodded. Ernie continued, "but in case we need to check. Where was this game?"

A fit of coughing prevented Tom answering but it soon subsided, leaving him drained and breathless.

"At Tom Sutton's, he's the Head Stable Lad at Dangerfield's," he rasped.

"And he'll confirm you were there?" The other man finally spoke, his piercing blue eyes fixed on Tom as if trying to read his face. "Why couldn't we get you on your mobile?"

Tom looked nervously from one policeman to the other.

"Yes…of course he'll confirm I was there." He was flustered, his hands trembled, seemed scared. "And…and…I couldn't get a signal…then my battery died," he added quickly, his voice wavered nervously. "Anyway, why do you want to know where I was?" He tried to sound indignant. "Haven't you got more important things to worry about, like what happened here last night?" He gave another harsh cough.

"Alison," he croaked, "can I have some water please…and my inhaler." He wheezed loudly as Alison took a bottle of mineral water from the fridge, filled a glass, then opened a drawer in the sink unit, found the inhaler and gave them to her brother. Having used the inhaler, soon Tom visibly relaxed and his breathing eased, but still unable to speak, he nodded his thanks to his sister, took the glass from her and swallowed a mouthful of water. He closed his eyes and sat quietly for a moment waiting for the spasm to pass, while the two policemen exchanged glances and Alison stood over him anxiously. After a moment he continued his account of the previous night's activities.

"I wish I hadn't gone at all now. Anyone could have collected Warrior. I shouldn't have offered. I just thought it would be good to get away from here for a while." He looked down at Alison's heavily bandaged wrist, frowned and reached out to give her a hug but John thought, looking at Tom's cold expression, it seemed completely lacking in affection. Ernie noted that Tom still avoided meeting his sister's eyes, and thirty years' worth of experience told him Tom was hiding something and more to the point, feeling guilty. When Tom was ready, Ernie gave him the details of the incident, and Briar's part in it. Tom reached under the table to make a gentle fuss of the injured dog. She groaned and tried to move in her bed, but was hampered again by the uncomfortable collar. Suddenly sitting bolt upright, Tom slapped his forehead with the palm of his hand.

"Damn! Warrior! I've left him in the horsebox." Pulling out his mobile phone, he rose from the table, walked towards the window, quickly tapping out a number. With his back to the others, he had a short conversation, finished his call and returned to the table, looking relieved.

"Well?" Alison asked.

"It's OK, Pete got one of the girls to look after him, and he's being stabled now."

The detective turned to Alison and his previously stern expression softened. "I think that's everything for now Miss Pembury."

Ernie looked away and smiled; perhaps the tough detective had a mellow side.

"We'll head back to the stables but," John glowered at Tom, "if you could be on hand, *sir*," his voice held an edge of contempt. "In case we need to speak to you again?" Tom blanched, and nodded a little too keenly. "Oh, just one more question, sir. Could you not have charged your mobile with the car charger?"

"I…I forgot to take it with me," Tom answered quickly, looking at his feet. "And…yes, of course I'll be around. I'm not going anywhere."

"See you again soon I hope Miss Pembury," the young sergeant said, shaking her hand, holding it just a little longer than necessary.

Alison gave a shy smile. "Yes, I hope…yes I'll be around…you have my number?"

"I certainly do."

Leaving the Pembury's cottage, the two policemen headed for the stables where the Scene of Crime investigator was carrying out a detailed examination of the disused hayloft.

"What do you know about Tom Pembury, Ernie?"

"Not much really. Keeps himself to himself," Ernie began. "He's not at all like Alison. She's a lovely girl, very friendly. Everyone took to her

34

straight away, but not so much to him, although they feel sorry for him. You were a bit hard on him weren't you?"

John shrugged. "Maybe."

"You'll have heard about the fire?" Ernie asked.

John shook his head and slowed his pace, wanting to know more about the Pemburys.

"Well," Ernie began, "they were both into show-jumping and eventing, and about eight months ago, while Alison was away, somewhere up north at an event, I can't recall which one, a fire broke out at their home. Both their parents died...smoke inhalation...and Tom was badly injured. Alison had been celebrating with her team 'cause she'd won first prize, and the local police broke the news to her at her hotel. She was totally devastated, as you'd expect. "

"How did it happen?"

"Well, as I understand it, it was late at night and Tom was asleep when it started. The report says it seems to have been a live coal falling out of the grate in the sitting room that did it. Tom woke with his room full of smoke and tried to get to his parents, but the flames forced him back. His bedroom was at the back of the house and he climbed out onto the conservatory roof, reached for the drainpipe and started shinning down, but the effects of the smoke got to him and he passed out, fell to the ground and smashed his right leg. Tom was the better show-jumper of the two, but after the operation on his leg when they pinned his bones together, he can hardly bend the leg at all, and the smoke inhalation left his lungs permanently weakened, so he can't compete anymore. To make things worse, their father hadn't kept up the insurance payments on the house and they both lost everything, parents, home, the lot!"

"Tough break," John said thoughtfully. "How did he take it, any problems coping?"

John had to wait a moment for Ernie's answer while they moved apart to allow two of the stable girls, leading two saddled horses, to go by.

"Nice to see everything's still going on normally," Ernie said as they moved on again. He nodded towards a young boy who was struggling with a heavy saddle as he headed for the tack room. The boy nodded back and pulled a face.

"That's Alan Davies' lad, you know, the Head Teacher of St Merriott's." But John was not interested; he wanted to hear the rest of Ernie's report on the Pemburys.

"Well, yes, to begin with. He was very unhappy, especially with Alison, poor girl, blamed her for everything, so I hear, probably taking out his feelings of guilt for not being able to save their parents on her, but he seems to have come to terms with it now." Ernie wondered where John's

questions were leading. "Why, what are you thinking?"

"I'm not sure yet, but something doesn't add up. Go on with what you were saying."

"Well, since then it's Alison who enters all the events and Tom coaches her. Of course she coaches youngsters as well and that's why they're here. Mrs Atkins gave them a home and jobs to help them start again. She's setting up these stables as a kind of academy."

"Thanks Ernie, that's filled a gap for me. I've got to see Isabel now, see you later." He was almost at the barn when he walked back.

"Just one thing, Ernie. Tom Pembury used his mobile just now, didn't he?"

"Yeah, why?" Ernie scratched his head.

"Think about it. He'd said the battery was flat?"

Ernie pondered. "Perhaps he recharged it before he came home," he suggested.

"Maybe," John countered, "but you have a look in the stables here and tell me how many power-points you see. Dangerfield's stable office was closed, so when did he charge it up? I'll leave you to think about that one." As John walked away Ernie called after him.

"Well, there you go John. That's why you're the detective and I'm a uniform copper! I hadn't given that a thought!" Ernie chuckled and shook his head.

As John disappeared into the barn, Ernie stopped to talk to two uniformed policemen who had just pulled up in a marked police car. Inside the barn, John climbed to the top of a ladder and made a beeline for a rather portly lady with grey streaked hair. She was taking photographs of a sleeping bag and some clothes. She glanced over her shoulder as he approached.

"Och, it's you. I didn'a ken you'd be here," she growled in a broad Glaswegian accent.

"Hi Izz, love you too," the Detective grinned. "How's it going? Love the white suit, but don't expect it to start a fashion."

"Dinna call me Izz!" Isabel McKenzie, Senior Scenes of Crime Officer snapped.

"Oh don't be so touchy Izz," he grinned. "I always call you Izz."

"Aye, but only because ye ken it irks me," she scowled. "An' ye' ken ah'll nae have disrespect while ah'm on duty. Ah've told yeh a hunnerd times or mair, that's fer airfter wairk." Isabel poked her tongue out at him.

"Very mature, for a nice old Scottish lady," he grinned. "Any progress?"

"None at all and it's a wee bit odd."

"Why, what's up?" John asked.

Isabel did not reply immediately, but she pointed to the sleeping bag, and pulled back the pillow section. As she leaned forward a thick lock of hair slipped out from the pins holding it back, and flopped in front of her eyes. She impatiently tucked it behind her ear.

"Och, ah canna be doin' wi' this. It's fair annoyin' me!" Her hair fixed, she went on.

"See this," she indicated the folded over section at the top, "there's nae hairs on this at all, meanin' oor wee chap is eether bald or wears some kind o' head cover all the time. An' one mair thing. See there." She stood up and stepped carefully over a woodworm riddled floorboard, to a camping stove. "Yeh see this's bin used, but there's nae fingerprints," Isabel frowned. "The pairson we're looking fer is eether fair clever and kens how we wairk an' what we'll look fer tae find their DNA. An' where there should be prints he's eether left none, or they're nae mair than useless smudges." She indicated areas on the wall where there were smeary dust marks.

"What about the clothes?" John asked.

"Aye, they'll get tested o' course, but ah've a nasty feelin' our chap's no gunna gi' up his secrets sae easy, he's tae experienced." She stood up, her hands on hips, frowning at the mystifying lack of evidence available. John examined the loft floor, searching for any little thing that might be useful, which was difficult as there was so much dust, and the floor was still strewn with hay. If they swept the floor they may lose something vital, so the area had been left just as it was.

"You sure there's nothing you've missed, Izz?"

"Och, o' course ah hav'nae missed anythin' yer wee barmpot! D'yeh no think ah ken what ah'm doin'?" she retorted indignantly. "An' dinna call me Izz!"

John grinned, he enjoyed teasing her. "You reckon this bloke's a professional then?"

Isabel nodded. "Aye, he's probably used to dealin' wi' the polis and avoidin' gettin' caught."

"Pity. I'm going to the Manor now, to see Mrs Atkins. I was hoping to give her some good news." John headed for the ladder leading back to the ground floor, and began lowering himself down through the wide gap. He was halfway through when Isabel added.

"Aye, mebbe so, but no today ye'll no. Pairhaps in a day or so when we've had this lot examined in the lab we'll ha' somethin' fer the lady, but definitely no today."

"OK, I'll push off then. See you later, Izz." He was still on the ladder when a broken plastic bucket hurtled in his direction missing him by centimetres, but the "Ouch!" from below told them it had found a victim anyway. John chuckled as he heard a vague, "Och, ah'm sorry!" come from above his head. Exiting the barn, he found Ernie talking to Sophie Dennett, a small mousy girl, one of those Kelly had been rude to earlier. Ernie was taking notes.

"Anything?" John asked hopefully as Sophie walked away.

"No, nothing new," Ernie shook his head. "What about SOCO?"

"No, nothing new from Isabel either," John closed his own notebook, putting it away in the inside pocket of his sheepskin coat. "I'm afraid Mrs Atkins will have to wait for a while before we can tell her anything. See you later, Ernie." Ernie nodded.

John turned back towards Stable Cottage, but was unable to think up a valid excuse to call in on Alison again, so he by-passed the cottage and headed down the tree lined field to the Manor.

John Harte was a good looking young man of average height, with silky dark, almost black hair, which had grown a little too long as he could rarely find the time to get it cut; work and playing rugby took up his days and nights. He had been married, but his job had proved too difficult for his wife to cope with, and they divorced almost two years ago. Since then he had spent even more time working rather than being alone at home. He strolled across the grass picturing the unused hayloft, trying to make sense of the events of the previous evening. Someone would have to have a very good reason to stay in a place like that at this time of year, when the nights were so cold, for who knows how long? John tried to imagine what it must have been like trying to keep warm and dry in that unheated hayloft with the worm ridden timbers and wondered how, whoever it was, managed to slip, undetected, in and out of the stable-yard for what may well have been months.

Of course the newspaper cuttings going back to January did not necessarily indicate the length of time the intruder had been there, and he had to consider this factor may well be something they could dismiss. He smiled recalling the banter between himself and Isabel. She was not known for her friendliness and generally had a 'don't mess with me' attitude. John remembered how frosty she had been when they first met in Bristol three years ago. He was still in uniform when they worked together investigating a series of particularly grisly murders in the Bristol area, and watching her piece the clues together fascinated him to such a degree that he considered transferring to Scenes of Crime, but Isabel had persuaded him to try for C.I.D; she said everyone had their own talents, and his was detection.

The teamwork of the officers involved in that enquiry had resulted in the arrest of two men and the group were disbanded. But Isabel and John kept in touch and both now worked at the police headquarters in Wells.

He cast a quick glance at the trees on the edge of the woods. The trees

grew close together, the area between, narrow, dark and forbidding. Something made him shudder.

He walked on thinking about the impending interview with Mrs Atkins. If the rumours about her late husband were true, it was hard to believe she had no knowledge of his unlawful activities and he wondered what to expect when he met her. He was not looking forward to their meeting, but even so he would be glad to get there. There was a disturbing atmosphere this close to the woods.

Out of the corner of his eye he caught a movement in the long grass between him and the trees. Fleetingly, he wondered whether to check it out, but told himself it was probably only a rabbit, but unconsciously sped up a little. There it was again. There was definitely some 'thing' between him and the trees and moving in parallel with himself. Judging by the way the grass was rippling, he guessed the rabbit, or possibly a fox, was moving close to the ground, but wondered why a fox would get so close to a human during daylight when there were lots of places with full cover. Curiosity overcoming unease, he decided to investigate; that was his job after all.

Just a few metres or so ahead was the tall hedge surrounding the formal back garden of the Manor. Entry was through a high, black wrought iron gate which was usually padlocked, especially at night, but it had been left unlocked to allow easy access for the police during the enquiry. It was this gate John had been heading for when he was sidetracked. Moving nearer to where the grass had been disturbed, he suddenly knew, beyond all doubt, that something, unseen, was watching him. A chill of sheer terror ran through him making him want to run but his legs had turned to jelly, refusing to work. His palms grew clammy, his mouth ran out of spit and he swallowed hard trying to loosen his tongue and work his saliva glands. He wanted to run but he was stuck fast to the ground.

"Pull yourself together man! There's nothing there." He lowered his voice. "If anyone's watching they'll think you're mad!" Hearing a voice, even though it was his own, calmed him. What would he be running from anyway? He recalled feeling like this just once before when searching a dark alley in Taunton for a man he knew was carrying a knife and expecting, at any moment, the knife to come his way. But that had been real, tangible, and he was lucky that time. Two of his colleagues coming from the other direction had caught the man and arrested him before John had found him, or he had found John. But this time he was alone, and this was, well...spooky, not real. His heart pounded. He moved slowly forward. Reaching the point between the oak tree and the long grass, he stopped. A line of flattened grass showed where the 'something' had been. A spine-chilling sensation flooded through him. He was convinced he was being watched, and whatever it was, was close, very close, behind him. He shuddered with a primeval fear and pulled his sheepskin jacket tighter. There was nothing to see except a slight swaying in the shadowy grass, but he felt his skin creep with goose-pimples and the hair stood up on the back of his neck.

"Come on man!" He told himself. "Get a grip!"

Summoning all his courage he turned and almost cried with relief when there was no apparition behind him. He slowly retreated. A gut feeling told him not to turn his back, but it defied explanation. After a few paces of walking backwards, he turned and fled through the gate, gratefully slamming it shut behind him, convinced that, at any moment, some kind of demonic apparition would materialise on the other side. The hairs on the back of his neck were still standing up as he leaned heavily against the gate. He was safe. He breathed deeply, waiting for his heartbeat to return to normal, and his legs to lose the jelly-like sensation before he tried walking.

From somewhere deep in his memory, he recalled rumours of the woods being haunted and a vague tale of a bunch of crooks who were arrested nearby just before Christmas telling stories of an enormous, vicious wolf-like animal that had attacked them. No-one at the station had taken them seriously, but now it did not seem quite so absurd. There was a presence here and it was playing terrible tricks with his imagination.

After a moment or two he felt steady enough to move, and took the path through the herb garden to the kitchen door of the Manor. He did not look back. If he had, he might have seen two small grinning faces peek out from under the hedge, watching as he hurried away. And, if he had still been within earshot, he would have heard their ringing laughter.

Piggybait, the cold and damp ground not bothering him at all, sat down on the grass chuckling merrily as great fat tears of delight ran down his round cheeks, while Claptrap leaned against the gate for support, his small body so convulsed with laughter he found it difficult to catch his breath. Eventually Piggybait recovered enough to speak. "The Chief would never approve you know."

"I know," replied Claptrap, hiccoughing, "but what the eye doesn't see, as the humans say."

Chapter Five

Dorothy opened the back door to find a very pale faced young man whose hand trembled as she reached out to shake it. As this might have been his normal condition she pretended not to notice, even though she was rather perturbed.

"You must be Sergeant Harte," she said, smiling a welcome. "We were expecting you. Can I take your coat?"

"No it's OK, thanks, I'll keep it on." He hugged the tan coloured sheepskin coat closer to him as if his life depended on it. He kept glancing nervously over his shoulder into the garden which Dorothy found quite puzzling. She too found herself looking into the garden but could see nothing unusual, no-one hanging about; she was mystified by his strange behaviour. Then, quite suddenly, he surprised her by seeming suddenly very eager to get inside and brushed past her into the house after taking just one more peek outside before she closed the door.

Once inside, he reached into his coat pocket and produced his police identification card but it was put away again so quickly she barely had time to see it; he seemed very distracted.

"This way," she said, watching him closely. "Excuse me, look I'm sorry, I have to ask…are you alright? "Only you look like you've seen a ghost or something. Come in and sit down."

"I…I'm fine, thank you, I…just need to ask you a few questions." He turned and walked ahead of her, through the narrow, tunnel-like vestibule the family used as a cloakroom. Several anoraks, waxed jackets and raincoats hung on rows of hooks on the walls above neatly lined up wellington boots in assorted colours and sizes, some with stable mud clinging to them, and two pairs of clean and shiny black riding boots. Dorothy moved ahead and guided him through a second door into the warm kitchen where the flames of a bright fire danced welcomingly in the open grate. Another, rather heavily-set woman was peeling potatoes at the sink unit. She looked up from her work as he entered, looked away, then did a

41

double-take and gave what he took to be a friendly smile.   Glad of the normality, his irrational fears melted away and his tension eased.

"Marj, this is the police officer we were told to expect.   Dorothy watched as his hunched shoulders visibly relaxed, but she was still not at all sure he was telling the truth and, concerned, she decided he needed a nice cup of tea.

"Ready for a cup of tea, Marjorie?"   The other woman was about to refuse when she saw Dorothy's furtive wink and the slight incline of her head towards the young man standing behind her.   Marjorie took a quick peak and quickly understood.   She nodded.

"Oh, yes, thank you, Dorothy, that would be very nice," she agreed a little too loudly.

"Tea, Sergeant Harte?"   Dorothy asked him.

Completely lost in thought, he appeared not to have heard and, after waiting a few seconds, Dorothy asked again, this time he responded.

"Oh, yes…yes thank you," he answered edgily.   "I'm sorry, I was miles away."

"Yes, I noticed."   Dorothy studied his face.   "Please forgive me, but are you sure you're alright?"

"I'm fine Mrs Renwick.   It is Mrs Renwick isn't it?"

"It's Miss Renwick, but you can call me Dorothy, everyone does."   Her warm smile helped him relax.

"Everyone but Ernie," Marjorie mumbled over her bowl of potatoes. "He calls her *dear*."

"Did you say something, Marjorie?"   A pink colour rose up Dorothy's neck to her cheeks.

"No nothing to worry about," Marjorie said quickly, "just said I wished Stuart was here."

Now he was in a safe environment, the banter between the two women provided John with a welcome respite from his fears and, in the pleasant surroundings he concluded it was time to put the scary interlude out of his mind for good.   For some reason his imagination had been playing tricks but he was on duty and this was not the time to worry about an imaginary bogeyman.

Dorothy poured out the tea and pulled up a chair, sitting opposite him at the long table.

"Harriet's writing some letters in the study, I'll take you up in a little while, but don't rush your tea, there's no hurry."

John smiled, gratefully sipping the warm reviving drink and looked around the big, cosy kitchen with the barrel-vaulted ceiling.   The warm, cheerful room and the happy chatter of the two women brought back his sense of reality, dispelling the remaining unease.

"This is a nice room," he remarked.

"We like it. It's our comfort room," Dorothy answered him.

He looked at his watch. It was later than he thought. Finishing his tea, he stood up. "Thank you for the tea ladies but it's time I saw Mrs Atkins."

Marjorie had continued working at the sink while Dorothy and John were chatting and, realising they were about to leave the room, she turned to give John one of her sweetest smiles. Unfortunately, as she had little practice or experience in smiling, it ended up as more of a grimace, causing Dorothy to rush the poor man out of the room before he received another fright.

"Through here," she said, quickly guiding John ahead of her through the swing door. "Is there any news about our night-time visitor, or what they were after?"

"No, we're no further on yet, but we'll find out who he is. He won't get away with it." A vision of Alison being pushed and falling on to the hard cobbles flashed into his mind. "Oh yes, we'll find out alright, you can bet on that!" He followed Dorothy up the three steps into the hallway and gave a long, low whistle of admiration at the exhibited weaponry and the two splendid crystal chandeliers.

"Wow! What a collection!" Dorothy waited while he took a good look around; she was used to first-time visitors reacting this way. "You know, I've been past the Manor a hundred times or more and never realised this was here." He stared open-mouthed, turning this way and that trying to take in the entire magnificent display.

"Most people think we keep these under glass for security and that's mostly true, but it's not the main reason from my point of view," she smiled at him, "it's just much cleaner. You don't get dust under glass, so it saves an awful lot of time. We're at the study and Harriet's waiting in here for you." She opened the door and stood back allowing him to enter the room, then went out closing the door behind her. Harriet was sitting at an antique writing desk by the tall window overlooking the front lawns. She stood up and extended her right hand in greeting.

"You must be Detective Sergeant Harte," she said, smiling warmly as she shook his hand. "I'm Harriet Atkins, please sit down." She indicated one of the cream sofas and sat opposite him on the other. Between them was a glass-topped coffee table upon which was a vase containing six sweet smelling red roses and six cream lilies. Close to the vase were some items that looked a little out of place in the uncluttered room; a gold jewellery box, a pocket watch and chain, a flexible steel-strapped watch, an engraved pewter tankard with dragon design, and what appeared to be a diamond pendant. John casually wondered why they were there, but did not ask about them as it was none of his business; he had enough to deal with but,

43

even with his untrained eye he could see they were nice pieces.

But the biggest surprise was Mrs Atkins herself and realised he was staring at her. He hurriedly took out his notebook. From the things he had previously heard about Harriet, with her being the wife of a man like Atkins, then shutting herself away from her family, he had thought he would dislike her, but this woman was completely different from the image he had built up. She was warm and friendly, not a bit like the cold, distant type he expected. Her face bore no trace of make-up and her red hair was tied back in a kind of knot on the top of her head making her appear younger than he would have thought. She was simply dressed in a black sweatshirt, blue jeans and trainers. But what struck him most, even with her youthful appearance, was that she looked awfully tired, her face pale with dark circles under her eyes.

Having a naturally kind personality, John saw every heartache Harriet had endured over the years etched in her face and felt an urge to protect her and her family from any further torment. After all, he told himself, it was only a few months ago she had been widowed, and now this.

"I'm sorry to report slow progress Mrs Atkins but we still don't know anything more about your intruder. The SOCO team are at the stables now and if there's anything to find, they'll find it. Their senior officer, Isabel McKenzie, is one of the best I've worked with, very experienced."

Harriet looked down at her hands then lifted her eyes to look at him. She spoke softly. "I must admit, it scares me to think someone's been hiding in our stables and no-one knew about it and, judging by the items found, this person seems to have been studying us," she looked down at her clasped hands, "…and our home. Do you think they were 'casing the joint', as they say, prior to breaking in?" She was calmer than he expected.

"No. In my experience, in this area, burglars are opportunistic mostly. I don't believe anyone would have spent as much time as we believe our intruder did up there, just to break in. Besides you're too well protected here. I've checked. Your security system's excellent."

"My thoughts exactly," Harriet said rising from the sofa and pacing in front of the fire. She stopped and turned, her green eyes coolly examining him. "So, tell me honestly, Sergeant Harte, do you think whoever this person is has some connection to my late husband? Please, if you know anything or think you do, don't keep anything from me. I found out a lot of things I'd rather not have known about the man I married since he died and there's probably not much that could surprise me now." John opened his mouth to speak but Harriet spoke again. "My concern is for my family and friends, which includes the people who are employed by us. Alison should never have gone through such a horrible experience and I want this person caught…before anyone else gets hurt."

"I assure you we're doing everything we can. Superintendent Smith asked me to tell you that when Ernie's on duty, he'll be mostly stationed here. Of course, if something urgent comes up, he might be called off for a while, but we'll do our best to have him here as much as possible and, when Ernie's off duty, we'll post another officer here, so there'll be someone about most of the time and, of course, now that Tom's back..." Harriet uttered a breathy sound, but John ignored it and continued speaking, "he can keep an eye out. We'll ask all your staff, whether inside or outside the house, to be vigilant. We will catch him…and soon. I can assure you."

"Thank you Sergeant. I feel better now and I know you'll keep us updated."

"You'll be the first to know Mrs Atkins, that's a promise." John realised the interview was over and stood up to leave. "There's just one more thing, Mrs Atkins. I said earlier that your security is excellent, but it's still open to human error. Please make sure your windows are shut and your doors are locked, especially at night, we don't want to make it easy for anyone to get in do we?"

"Definitely not! I'll make sure everyone knows what to do, thank you." Harriet opened the door into the hall, "You know your way out don't you?"

Before he could answer, a noise attracted her attention. "It's alright, Jonah," she called out, "you can stop eavesdropping. The officer's just leaving."

A teenaged boy with spiky dark hair and a small gold earring in his left ear poked his head around from behind one of the suits of armour at the bottom of the wide staircase. With a casual shrug, he ambled over, his wide grin revealing a wire brace across his front teeth.

"How did you know I was there?"

Harriet smiled indulgently, "I've learned what to expect from you. You're a little too predictable." She ruffled his hair affectionately.

"Sergeant John Harte of Wells C.I.D, meet my son, Jonah." As Harriet stood beside him, she had to reach up to put her arm around his shoulder as the boy was quite a bit taller than his mother, and John was surprised to find him so amiable. He had heard awful things about this boy, but here he was reaching out to shake hands, very politely. The stories had clearly been exaggerated or Jonah had undergone a personality transplant. John took the proffered hand, shaking it firmly.

"Is there any news Sergeant?" Jonah enquired. "I hope you find whoever it was. I like Briar, she's a great dog and Alison's pretty cool too."

John smiled. "Yes, she is, isn't she?" he said quietly, a dreamy look fleetingly appearing in his eyes. Harriet and Jonah looked at each other and Jonah smirked. He coughed and the policeman recovered himself with a

sheepish grin.

"Umm, right! Time I was going," John said, turning towards the kitchen door. "Bye Mrs Atkins, Jonah. I'll probably see you both again soon." With that he headed, along the hall and down the three steps into the kitchen. Dorothy was in the big green armchair, her feet propped up on the hearth, reading the newspaper. She looked up at the swish of the swing door.

"Oh, hello. Have you finished with Harriet?"

John nodded. "Yes, for now, thanks."

"Right then, I'll see you out." Dorothy made to get up, but John stopped her.

"It's OK, I can see myself out. Thanks again for the tea." He nodded a farewell to Marjorie who peered around the door of the walk-in larder.

"Bye dear, see you soon," she called.

"Bye dear." Dorothy mimicked, chuckling over the top of her newspaper. Marjorie sniffed, stuck her nose indignantly in the air, and returned to the larder.

In the vestibule, John put his hand on the handle of the outer door, but hesitated before opening it. Steeling himself, he opened the door. It was now around four in the afternoon and he wondered where the day had gone. Heavy grey clouds darkened the sky threatening an early nightfall. He pulled up the collar of his sheepskin coat and took in the gloomy scene. Stepping over the threshold, he felt the same unearthly chill he had experienced earlier. He weighed up his options and baulked at the idea of returning the way he had come. The thought of opening the black gate and facing whatever might be waiting for him in the field, in this dim light, did not appeal to him at all. He searched for a different exit and discovered a small path running along the back of the house that disappeared round the side of the building, and followed it down towards the front driveway, through an avenue of shrubs sprouting new spring growth. There was nothing here to give him the jitters. Emerging from the shrubbery, he crossed the drive and stopped by the fountain standing idle in the centre of the well-tended lawn. Taking out his force radio, he called to PC 742, Ernie Rogers. Through the crackling static, Ernie replied.

"Hi John, what are you up to?"

"Ernie, are you still at the stables?"

"Yep. Where else would I be?" A harsh whining sound almost blotted out Ernie's voice, but John was just able to make out, "some of us have work to do you know," and Ernie's chuckle through the high-pitched buzzing.

"Yeah, right," John answered good-naturedly. "I'm not reading you very well, Ernie, it must be the weather or something. Come and pick me up

will you? I've done enough walking for one day. I'm at the fountain in front of the Manor."

"What a young man like you, too tired to walk? Yeah, OK. I'll be there in five minutes."

John clicked off his radio, relieved not to have to go through the field again.

In the larder, Marjorie had been baffled seeing John go by the small frosted window, towards the side of the house.

"Dorothy, I think that young man's lost," she called out. "He's going the wrong way. Shall we check if he's alright, 'cos he's gone the long way round for some reason?"

So, partly to make sure he was alright, but more out of curiosity, they followed him.

"I wonder why he didn't go back through the field," Marjorie whispered. "He'd have got back in no time that way, and the gate's been left unlocked especially."

"No idea," Dorothy shrugged, "but he looked a bit shaky when he arrived, didn't...," Dorothy stopped, her eyes wide.

"What is it? What's the matter?" Marjorie asked.

I've just thought...you don't think he's heard those daft stories about the woods do you?"

"What a strapping lad like him, scared by a few silly tales? It's not likely," Marjorie scoffed.

"Oh well, I don't know," Dorothy shivered, "it would explain a lot though. Look at him now." She carefully moved a willow branch out of the way. "He's radioing for a pick up so he knows the walk will be too long." She shivered. "Well, whatever's up, it's none of our business. Come on, let's get indoors, it's got quite chilly out here now."

The two women headed back along the path, only too glad to get back into the warmth of the enormous kitchen. Dorothy lit the gas under the saucepan of potatoes whilst Marjorie took the chicken out of the oven and basted it.

"All the same though Marjie, he did look awfully pale, just like he'd seen a ghost."

Chapter Six

Helping Charlie to clear away after lunch, Sam told him about meeting Claptrap and Piggybait and Charlie immediately agreed he should stay overnight. Later, warm and comfortable in front of the log fire, Jane and Charlie watched the obligatory Bond film on the television while Steve slept, his head at an awkward angle, snoring softly and making odd little grunting and puffing noises.

"'E'll get an awful crick in 'is neck," Charlie remarked with an amused grin.

"Serves him right," Jane said, a little grumpily. "He shouldn't have eaten so much in the middle of the day, it always makes him sleepy."

Cathy had been determined to finish a piece of intricate embroidery while watching the film, but she too had dozed off, her chin nodding onto her chest.

"She never can stay awake after a glass of wine," Charlie chuckled. Trying not to disturb her, he removed the embroidery and needle from her hand and put them away in her work basket. For a while they sat in companionable silence, broken only by an increasingly noisy Steve.

During an advertisement break, Charlie brought up the subject of Sam staying overnight, as shouts and squeals of laughter came from the kitchen where Jenny and Sam were playing a computer game.

"Simon, tha's Jenny's brother," Charlie began, "was askin' if Sam'd loike ter go next door fer a game o' summat. I dunno, one o' them compooter games or such loike, later," he said casually. "If 'e does, 'e can stay 'ere overnight, and come 'ome after breakfast tomorrow."

Jane looked at her very large brother-in-law. "I don't see why not, but I thought Simon and Sam didn't get on?"

"Oh no! Twern't tha' Simon didn't loike 'im or anythin'. It were more, bein' that bit older, 'e didn't think they'd got anythin' in common."

"Well what's changed?" Jane asked.

"Simon's a nice lad, an' very fond of 'is sister an' Sam steppin' in to 'elp 'er when there was on'y one o' him an' four o' them, made Simon see

48

'im a bit diff'rent loike. 'E's got a lot o' respect fer young Sam now…an' so 'ave a lot o' folk 'ereabouts, especially seein' as 'e went back to 'elp Jonah when 'e could've got 'imself to safety. 'E saved Jonah from drownin' in that underground lake an' there's no gettin' away from it. Jonah'd 'ave died for sure, in the water or with the cave roof fallin' in. It were on'y through Sam's bravery Jonah survived. Everyone aroun' here knows that. Make no mistake, Jane. Your Sam's a bit of an 'ero around 'ere, although there's some'd rather Jonah hadn't survived o' course, but even they've 'ad ter think agen seeing 'ow the lad's changed since then." Charlie's eyes held a gentle smile. "Your Sam's a lad to be proud of m'dear. Cathy and me think the world of 'im."

"That's nice of you to say so, especially when you think of the hard time he gave you to begin with, and I know he's very fond of you both," she said softly. "Of course he can stay if he wants to. Steve won't mind and I certainly don't, not during the holidays. We'd have to be a bit stricter during term time, especially with exams coming up, but its fine at the moment."

Charlie gave a wide grin, "Good, tha's settled then. Oi'll pop up and get 'is room ready." On his way upstairs he made a quick detour to the kitchen.

"Sam, d'you want ter stay wi' us tonight, only Simon's wonderin' if you wanna game next door while Cathy and I are at church."

"Yeah, great," Sam said, his fingers furiously pressing buttons on the controller, not once taking his eyes off the screen. Jenny was working equally hard on the other joypad, determined to beat him but, from what Charlie could see, she had no hope.

After Jane and Steve went home and Cathy and Charlie headed off to church for the evening service, Sam and Jenny headed next door. Hearing voices at the front of Jenny's cottage they ran around the side in time to see a large blue car driving away.

"Ohhhh!" Jenny groaned. "I missed them!" Her parents were waving to the occupants of the car as it drove away.

"Missed who?" Sam asked.

"Helen and Ted Miller." Jenny seemed quite upset. "Helen's my Godmother. She and Mum have been friends since they were at school," she explained as she took Sam's arm and ushered him towards the back door. "They only live a few miles away so we see them quite often, but I hate missing them and you would have liked them."

Once back in their kitchen, Jenny complained to her mother about why she hadn't let her know about the visit.

"I didn't know," Sarah replied, slipping her arm through Jenny's. "They were passing and called in for a few minutes. They couldn't stay any longer as they've got new guests arriving and had to get back fairly

49

sharpish otherwise they'd have stayed longer."

"New guests?" asked Sam.

"Helen and Ted live at Godney, just outside Wells," Sarah began. "They've got a lovely guest house there. It's called Double Gate Farm, it's really pretty and you can see Glastonbury Tor from the back garden. It's a shame you didn't get to meet them, maybe next time."

Sam spent the next couple of hours playing *Amazing Spiderman* on Simon's PS4 with Jenny while Simon did some studying up in his room.

Not having played this game before, Sam was at a bit of a disadvantage so Joe Richards, Jenny and Simon's bespectacled father, tried dropping Sam hints, to Jenny feigned indignation. Although she accused him of cheating and called her father a traitor, it was all in good spirits and the cottage rang with laughter. Sam enjoyed the evening, even if his mind did stray from time to time. He kept wondering what Piggybait and Claptrap wanted. At nine o'clock, he thanked Jenny's parents for their hospitality, arranged to see Jenny in the morning and, on going back to Charlie's cottage, tried to sneak back in without the dogs hearing him. He did not succeed. Within seconds of creeping into the kitchen, both of them hurtled towards him barking excitedly, knocking him flying.

"Hey! Go steady!" Sam laughed, leaning against the wall. "You almost had me over."

"They're jest pleased to see you," Charlie grinned. "I'm about to take 'em fer their walk." He said loudly enough to make sure Cathy had heard. "D'you wanna come wi' us, Sam?" He took two heavy torches from the sink unit drawer.

"Yeah, that would be good. I'll get my jacket," Sam winked.

"Won't be long, Cathy," Charlie called, "but they've bin cooped up since lunch, so they'll need a good long walk."

"OK dear," Cathy replied from the sitting room, her feet up on the pouffé. She was working on the embroidery again and watching 'A Touch of Frost' on the television, Agnetha, curled up on the sofa beside her, purring softly as she snuggled in ready to sleep. Then, catching a glimpse of embroidery silk moving, all thoughts of a nap vanished as she pawed at the thread. Cathy chuckled as she gently moved the thread out of the reach of the sharp claws.

On their way out, Charlie locked the door for security's sake. "You can't be too careful, Sam. I wouldn't have bothered before Christmas, but we'd never had villains like the Atkins' gang around afore then," he said, handing Sam a torch. Although it was a hazy night, they could see several metres in front as they headed through the garden and out into the field before entering the trees at the woods edge. Benny and Bjorn walked steadily alongside them, ignoring the nocturnal bustle of the woods.

Switching on the torches, Sam and Charlie were able to see clearly as the pale yellow beams sliced through the darkness. A soft hooting caught Sam's attention and he shone his torch into the branches of the nearest tree, where its beam located a very indignant owl. He caught a glimpse of its heart-shaped face and golden eyes as they glared down at him, before it flew off with an angry screech, clearly resenting being disturbed.

"Looks loike you jest lost a frien'. Barney's never been keen on being near 'umans."

"You can drop the accent now Charlie," Sam grinned.

"Oh yes," Charlie laughed. "I'm in character so much I sometimes forget to be myself."

"Barney?"

"He's a Barn Owl, one of a number in these woods. He'll be off hunting for the night now. I've got to know a lot of the wildlife around here, right down through the generations. They know me, but it might take them a while to get used to you, especially if you're shining torches at them."

"Well I didn't know he was there," Sam protested. "I'll be more careful next time."

A shuffling sound in the trees to their left made Benny's hackles stand upright and he gave a low growl. Charlie held up a hand signalling Sam to stop as a large stag crossed the path in front of them, sniffing the air apprehensively. Bjorn nervously edged backwards, straight into Sam's legs.

Sam recalled seeing a stag testing the air on his first venture into the woods and wondered if it was the same animal. The stag stood still, warily eyeing them, but Charlie softly uttered something in a language Sam did not understand. Still rather nervous, the stag moved closer. Sam thought it looked ready to bolt at any moment.

Charlie took a step forward, still uttering soft syllables that made absolutely no sense to Sam, but seemed to calm the stag enough to let Charlie within arm's length. Sam held both dogs by the collar, keeping them still and quiet, a good few metres away from the stag. Slowly, slowly, Charlie reached out to the anxious animal and tenderly stroked its neck, whereupon the stag relaxed and nuzzled the man's hand. More rustling in the undergrowth nearby caught Sam's attention, and the stag's. He lifted his magnificent head and calmly watched as his herd emerged from the trees. Sam counted six females, which Charlie had said were called hinds and two fawns, and guessed this probably was the same herd he had encountered previously, only now they had young. The hinds waited docilely for the stag until he backed away from Charlie to lead his family further into the woods.

51

"That was cool!" Sam was completely overawed by close proximity to a wild animal. "What was it you were saying to him? He seemed to understand you, whatever it was."

"Nothing much. There's no magic language. Animals respond to kindness and calm and those were just nonsense sounds that Barron responds to. I've known him a long time too."

"Wow!" said Sam. "I love this life!"

Charlie put his huge bear paw of a hand on Sam's shoulder and they headed deeper into the woods, speeding up after the delay, eager to reach the elves' great chamber and about ten minutes later they reached the challim boulder concealing the entrance to the elves underground home.

The elves, needing to camouflage the entrances to their cave tunnel network from human eyes, had used a very light material that could look, or feel, like any natural wood or rock and named it challim after the brilliantly clever elf who created it. Charlie pushed the huge boulder aside and, once again, the tunnel expanded to allow them entry. Inside, Charlie told both dogs to lie down and wait, a command they obeyed immediately. Bjorn even closed his eyes and went to sleep. The dogs safely contained within the ante-chamber, Charlie led the way, his torch beam lighting their path as they headed along the narrow passageway avoiding tripping on the uneven, rocky floor. Again the tunnel stretched to accommodate his large frame and shrank to its original size behind Sam as they moved along; Sam no longer found this phenomenon at all unusual having seen it all before. A faint glow appeared in the distance, becoming brighter with every step, as they approached the elves cavern home just beyond the next turn. By then it was bright enough to turn off the torch.

The catastrophe just before Christmas had not only affected humans. The explosion reverberated through the caverns causing vibrations which Jimander, their elderly leader, had been unable to withstand. His old body suffered fatally from the shock and he died soon after Jeremiah Atkins. The loss to the clan was devastating and it took a group of three to replace him on the Council of Elders. Piggybait, Claptrap and Jerrill, did their best to follow Jimander's values and lead their people safely. It was they who waited at the mouth of the cavern to greet their chief and his nephew.

Piggybait and Claptrap had always been the clowns of the clan, but everyone knew that at times of trouble they could be relied upon to act responsibly and could command respect. Jerrill, on the other hand, had changed dramatically since Jimander's death. He no longer suffered bouts of nervousness and petulance, and had emerged from the tragedy, and Jimander's shadow, with dignified authority. This new Jerrill was a strong leader who exuded quiet confidence as he strode forward to greet Sam and Charlie. All signs of weakness in his face had disappeared, replaced by an

expression of pride and determination. As Charlie held out his hand, Jerrill grasped it with both of his own. He had developed a good solid grip.

"It's good to see you, Klaus, and you too, Sam."

Sam had paid many visits to the elves since Christmas. On his first visit, there had been considerable animosity from Claptrap, but that was a thing of the past and they were now good friends. Claptrap winked at him. Behind Jerrill stood his son Halmar, a quiet handsome elf, with shoulder length dark blond hair and deep blue eyes that radiated a reassuring integrity.

Standing beside Halmar, was Jimander's exquisite daughter Ellien, to whom Halmar was betrothed and Sam could not take his eyes off her. Her luminosity set her apart from all the other elves. On this day, she wore a golden-yellow gown with a collar, high at the back of the neck, coming to a point just below her throat. Her knee-length pale blonde hair was tied back at the crown, threaded with small white flowers, then allowed to tumble down her back in waves and, as usual, she wore no shoes, her tiny, perfect toes just visible as she moved. She too smiled a welcome to Charlie and Sam as she leaned against Halmar.

Firefly lanterns and torches illuminated the vast cathedral-ceilinged cave, just as they did when Sam first visited, but now the tubs of Christmas trees were long gone. They would return at the end of November but for now, in their place, were huge pots of teasels and grasses from the autumn, dyed in the bright spring colours of yellow, white and blue. As the elves walked on the reed and herb scattered floor, the strong sweetness of lavender and lemon verbena rose from underfoot releasing a light heady fragrance into the warm chamber. Long garlands of wild spring flowers, daffodils, bluebells and primroses hung across the chamber, high up on the walls. Sam loved this warm, wonderful, enchanting world. Gradually the great chamber filled as other elves streamed in from the many smaller rooms, or descended the stone stairs from the sleeping compartments above, and soon over one hundred elves had crowded into the chamber. Sam spotted Corporal, the elf with flat ears, two rows back.

"Will you have some dandelion beer or acorn wine?" Jerrill asked. "It's a cold night for this time of year, it'll warm you."

"Thank you. Maybe a small acorn wine for me and a VERY small dandelion beer for Sam."

As Halmia, Halmar's twin sister, rushed to fetch the drinks, Jerrill's face took on a sombre expression.

"We need to talk Klaus," Jerrill's tone was grave. Sam was surprised to hear Jerrill call Charlie, 'Klaus', just as Jimander had done before him, whereas before Charlie was 'Sir' or 'the Chief'. "But maybe not with an audience," he was concerned by the number of elves present. "I suggest we

adjourn to the meeting chamber."

Jerrill nodded to the Council members who broke away from the mass of curious elves and followed him into a smaller chamber under the stairway. Charlie beckoned Sam to follow. Once inside, two elves Sam did not know, barred the way preventing the others from following their leaders. Inside the smaller chamber was an oversized armchair, which Charlie made a bee-line for. Obviously it had been tailor-made for him as the rest of the furniture was far too small for his use. Sam sat on the end of a wooden bench, eager to hear what was considered to be so urgent the elves felt it necessary to call this unplanned meeting. Halmia, squeezed through the crowd waiting outside, entered silently, handed them their drinks and disappeared again without a word. Sam thought he heard a voice outside asking her what was going on, but she shushed whoever it was, and moved on. Just Piggybait, Claptrap, Jerrill, Ellien, Halmar with two older elves Sam barely knew were the only occupants of the small room.

"Klaus, Sam, we asked you here tonight because we are troubled by what happened at the Atkins stables yesterday," Jerrill began. "Have you heard anything about it?"

A noise at the entrance of the chamber disturbed the group as a large bird with blue-black wings flew in over the heads of the assembled elves, heading directly for Charlie's shoulder, where it settled contentedly, ignoring the rest of the company.

"Hello. Hello." The bird uttered in a rasping voice, its beak almost in Charlie's whiskery ear.

"Hello Mélusine. It's good to see you. How's your mistress?"

"Good." The bird replied.

"What's that?" Sam asked Piggybait.

"It's Mélusine, she's a raven. She and her mate are cared for by Mrs...um...a lady we know. "

"But how did she get down here?"

"Upstairs, where the sleeping quarters are, there are small windows hidden in the roots of an old tree and the birds get in and out that way. It's a bit of a squeeze for Mélusine and her mate Taliesin because of their size, but the smaller ones get in easily enough."

Charlie sat back with Mélusine happily settled on his shoulder and rested his elbows on the arms of the chairs, his chin on his clasped hands.

"Now where were we Jerrill? Oh yes, the stables. Do please go on," Charlie sounded casual, but Sam was not convinced.

"They had an intruder who actually injured one of the staff while trying to escape. Unfortunately he ran off into the woods and, as far as we know he's still about," Jerrill informed them.

Sam intercepted the worried look passing between Claptrap and Piggybait.

"Are you expecting trouble?" Charlie asked coolly.

"Perhaps," Jerrill replied. "We recently began transporting Christmas gifts again and, of course, there's the night patrol. We're just not used to humans wandering about here at night, not since Jimander scared off the poachers and that Atkins gang. "We must not put the...ladies at risk when they are exercised," Jerrill continued, "and it wouldn't be fair to keep them locked up all the time."

"I see what you mean." Charlie sat forward in his armchair and Mélusine shifted to make herself more secure, her feet digging tightly onto his jacket. Charlie looked around at the group of elves.

"So there's no question that this person is up to no good."

"No sir. None at all," Claptrap replied. "Piggs and I have been watching the stables. We keep an eye on anything untoward around the woods and the stables are teeming with Police. They're not happy, and neither are we."

"Played a good joke on one who went to the Manor though didn't we Claptrap?" Piggybait grinned.

Charlie raised an eyebrow at Piggybait who quietened immediately and slunk back into the shadows, wishing he had kept silent.

Claptrap continued, ignoring his friend's interruption. "From what we can gather, this person has been hanging around the stables for a while, in fact, since shortly after Atkins died. Now why would anyone want to live and sleep in an old hayloft during the winter months...," he waited for his words to sink in, "unless they had something to hide?"

"Perhaps he's just homeless," Sam commented.

"We checked that Sam," Jerrill answered, kindly, "but from what we've learnt, this person's more likely to be up to no good. He's been spying on the Atkins' family, so his being there seems more planned than just looking for somewhere to squat, but why, we don't know."

"You think he's spying on them?" Sam questioned. "Surely that's not likely. Maybe before when Mr Atkins was alive, I know he got up to some strange stuff and had even weirder friends, but I thought all that was over now."

"No, we're fairly sure we're right. The Atkins family are the target, but it's bound to have a knock-on effect to us," Jerrill went on. "Our first problem is the intruder himself. The dog chased him and he disappeared in our woods. We found the dog, hurt and almost unconscious, near the lightning tree clearing. We eased her pain and took her to where we knew she would be found and looked after but, by then the woods was thick with humans searching for them both."

During Jimander's leadership, a situation like this would have found Jerrill a bundle of nerves, but this time he was very much in control.

"Klaus, you know that anything posing a threat to our world, what we're here for or anything or anyone connected to us needs to be taken seriously, and at the moment we have no idea what we're dealing with, but these are our woods and I'm not going to wait until a calamity befalls us. Are you happy for us to deal with this as we see fit, or do you wish us to tell you if, or when, something happens and wait for your instructions?" Jerrill sat back awaiting Charlie's decision.

Before Charlie could answer, a commotion outside the room sent Piggybait dashing to the door.

"It's Rondo! Jossamel and Lommie are holding him back – we said we didn't want to be disturbed."

"We might as well have stayed in the great chamber," Piggybait whispered to Sam. "Anyone close to the entrance can hear what's being said anyway."

Mélusine, fluttered her wings in Charlie's face, but he gently pushed her aside and set her down on the back of the chair. "Let Rondo enter." His deep voice rang out over the din at the doorway.

Jossamel and Lommie released the struggling Rondo, who triumphantly straightened his jerkin as he strode into the room, a number of curious elves following.

He bowed first to Charlie, then to Jerrill.

"I apologise for interrupting the meeting, sir." Considering his insistence at being admitted urgently, Sam was surprised Rondo took the time to be so polite.

"Saldor and I were on night patrol..." Rondo glanced towards the throng looking for Halmia.

"Yes, what of it?" Jerrill's impatience was getting the better of him, but Rondo was clearly enjoying his moment in the spotlight and hoped Halmia had seen him. "What should we know?"

"Sirs, we thought there was one man in the woods we had to watch out for, but I have just seen another...and they don't appear to be together. More importantly, we think we recognised one of them and, you're not going to like it."

Chapter Seven

The next morning Sam returned home just after nine o'clock, and was stretched out on the settee dozing and watching a cartoon Spiderman television programme when the telephone rang in the hall. He got up to answer it but it stopped ringing just as he got there.

"Typical!"

"Who was it Sam?" Jane had been putting washing out on the line in the garden and had rushed in when she heard the telephone ring.

"No idea. They hung up just as I got there."

"Well try 1471, it'll give you the last number."

Sam dialled 1471. He immediately recognised the number and rang back.

"*Winterne Manor?*"

"Hi Jonah, its Sam. Did you just phone?"

"*Yeah, Meredith's offered us riding lessons, you, me and Jenny. What d'you think?*"

"Yeah, cool. When?"

"*This morning, if you've got nothing else to do.*"

"This morning? Well, yeah, cool. I've got nothing planned." Sam answered with nervous enthusiasm. "I'll call Jenny. What time?"

"*About eleven should be OK.*"

"Fine, see you then."

Jenny eagerly accepted the invitation and called for Sam half an hour later.

"You haven't been riding before have you, Sam?" she asked.

"No…why?"

"Well you'd better put on a pair of jeans instead of those soft jogging bottoms," she answered knowledgeably.

"Why…what's up with these?"

Jenny rolled her eyes. "Think about it. You're going to be on a horse for about an hour and your legs are going to rub against the horse all that time. If you don't wear something stronger…a thicker material, your legs might chafe."

Sam laughed, but Jenny kept a straight face, staring at him with a 'you'll see' expression.

"You're joking, right?"

"You stay as want, but if your legs get sore, don't come running to me," Jenny smirked.

A few minutes later, they walked along the hedge bordered lane, Sam having changed his jogging bottoms for a pair of jeans.   The light frost of early morning had disappeared in the warmth of the spring sunshine; the air was crystal clear. It was a beautiful day and it should have been a pleasant walk for the couple, but now Sam was finding it difficult to find something to talk about and they walked, side by side, in self-conscious silence, their fingers lightly touching. The occasional sighting of a rabbit or squirrel prompted a few words but Sam, uneasy in their new status, was confused about how to behave now Jenny was no longer just a friend. Jenny, on the other hand, was more comfortable with the situation as she had always known which way their friendship was going.

Beneath the hedgerows, wild spring flowers adorned the raised grassy verge while groups of sparrows chirruped and squabbled, in and out of the tightly packed foliage above.

"It's been ages since I went riding," Jenny broke the silence.

"You've been before then?" Sam was thankful for something to talk about.

"Yeah, a few times but not for a while…probably a couple of years. How come you never tried it?"

"Don't know. I suppose…well, I lived in a city didn't I? I just never got…round…to it.

Jenny noticed his hesitation and looked round at him but Sam was staring past her into the hedge. Through a small gap in the budding greenery, he had seen something moving on the other side. He put his finger to his lips to signal Jenny to be quiet, and tiptoed nearer to the hedge to investigate.

"What is it?" she whispered.   Sam gently shushed her and pointed beyond the hedge. Tiptoeing silently, Jenny joined him on the grass verge and they both leaned into the hedge to get a better view. Portia, Sam's cat, was crawling through the grass on her stomach, slowly creeping forward then stopping.   Her tail flicked irritably but her eyes were firmly fixed on something ahead of her. She skulked forward again, first one paw then the other, all the time staying low to the ground and close to the hedge.

"She's hunting," Sam whispered. "I've never seen her do that before." He craned his neck to see what Portia was watching so intently. "Oh no! Jenny, take a look at this!" Jenny squeezed herself a little way into the hedge and had to stifle a giggle at Portia's over-confident attempt at stalking. They both tried not to laugh when it turned out that her quarry was an enormous peacock that continued, pecking and scratching at the ground, totally oblivious to the cat sizing it up for dinner.

"If she does catch it, I'm not sure who'll come off worse," Sam whispered.

"Yeah, it's a bit big for her," Jenny replied. "D'you think we should break this up?"

"Wait a second. I want to see what happens. With a bit of luck Portia'll get a shock and leave peacocks alone in future, but I'll stop it before either of them gets hurt. Just look at her though…proper little hunter isn't she?"

Portia crept closer, her ears back, close to her head, her body skulking along the ground, as unaware of her audience as the peacock seemed to be of her. A flock of starlings, suddenly alerted to her presence, rose in the air at the other end of the hedge, and Portia's head darted up in surprise, but the peacock continued scratching at the ground undeterred and enjoying its moment of freedom in the meadow. Portia crawled closer to the bird, her underbelly now coated in dust and loose grass. The starlings gone, she turned her attention back to the peacock, hiding in the long grass close to the hedgerow, keeping her head low and crawling forward stealthily. The tension was getting to Sam and he was about to shout at the cat when she sprang. In a flash the peacock turned and spread its magnificently large eye-dotted tail, startling the inexperienced cat and, terrified, she dived under the hedge and fled down the lane, her tail fur sticking out like a bottle brush. The peacock, having seen off its enemy, lowered its tail and resumed scratching the ground as if nothing had happened.

"I hope she's alright," Jenny frowned.

Sam grinned. "All this is new to her still. She used to chatter at the birds at home, I mean in Nottingham, but she never tried to catch anything. I don't think she did anyway." Sam stepped down from the verge and held out his hand to help Jenny down. She took it and, this time, did not let go as they resumed their stroll towards the stables.

"Will she go home?" Jenny asked, watching Portia flee.

"Yeah, she's bound to. She's certainly heading that way. She knows her way about now and can get in through the cat-flap. Her basket's under the stairs and I bet she'll head straight for it. She always does when she's not happy."

When they arrived at the stables, they found Jonah waiting for them. Sam felt Jenny's arm stiffen.

"Hiya," Jonah grinned. He smiled a lot lately and Sam realised something was missing.

"Hey, where's the brace?" he asked.

"Jenny's Dad took it out a couple of days ago and replaced it with one I can take out. Whaddya think?" Jonah, clearly delighted, grinned widely. "And he says I won't need this one much longer, then no more metal mouth."

"It's worked though," Jenny said frostily. "Sam never saw what your teeth were like before." She turned to Sam. "Jonah's teeth were crooked and stuck out in front, y'know Bugs Bunnyish."

"They weren't that bad!" Jonah protested. "Anyway, that's enough about my teeth, let's change the subject." Jonah moved between Jenny and Sam and, ignoring her coolness, put his hands on their shoulders to lead them along. "Meredith waiting for us, she's got your hats ready."

"Hats?" Sam enquired.

"Yeah, it's a safety thing. You have to wear hard hats so when you fall off, your head's protected."

"Well, in your case, nothing vital would get hurt," Jenny muttered under her breath, spitefully. Jonah flinched. He had obviously heard her. Sam tugged at her arm and leaned closer.

"I know it's hard, but he's trying…give him a chance." He turned back to Jonah who looked a little crestfallen.

"Fall off?" Sam continued. "OK, so just how big are these horses?" Jenny turned her face away to hide her amusement, even managing a small grin at Jonah's conspiratorial wink.

"Oh they're pretty big, about eighteen hands, so your head'll probably be about seven feet off the ground," he said with such an expression of angelic sincerity that Sam almost believed him. Jenny struggled not to laugh at Jonah's teasing as he led them to the Tack Room where they kept the hats and other riding equipment.

Sam's feet were like lead. He could not back down now without looking like a wimp and, so far, none of the horses he had seen around the yard looked that big. He wondered how he could ask for one of the smaller ones.

"That one looks nice, "Sam asked thinly, pointing to a small dappled grey that was being saddled up by the mounting block. "Couldn't we have one like that?"

"No. Too small for you. You want a real horse." Jonah cast a sideways look at Sam and tried not to laugh as Jenny scowled at him. Meredith was leaning against a wall, talking to a young dark haired man.

"That's the C.I.D. Sergeant," Jonah told them, "DS Harte. You've heard about what happened here on Saturday night?" he said as they approached his sister and the police officer.

"Mum told us a bit about it," Jenny replied, "but what really happened?"

Sam feigned ignorance. "Yeah, what happened?"

They were now within earshot of Meredith, and Jonah, shaking his head said, "Tell you later."

"OK John, if you're sure there's nothing else you need," Meredith said as they approached. She nodded to Jonah and started heading towards them. "You'll keep us up to speed with what you find?"

The detective sergeant opened his car door. "No problem." He eased himself into the driver's seat. "As soon as we know anything we'll be in touch. SOCO are doing their stuff in the lab." He started up the engine and slowly edged the car forward. Winding down the window, he called out, "We'll get to the bottom of it soon."

He waved to Jonah and drove away slowly, taking care not to frighten the horses in the yard.

"Well, you lot," Meredith smiled, "you ready for riding?"

"Oh yes," Jenny replied enthusiastically. Sam nodded. He did not appear so keen.

"Something wrong, Sam?" Meredith asked.

"No...not really," Sam muttered. "I was just wondering how big our horses are going to be."

Meredith saw the unusually innocent expression on Jonah's face.

"Now, what have you been saying?" she asked her grinning brother.

"What me? Nothing much," he looked down at the ground and shuffled his feet. "I only said our horses were eighteen-handers." He struggled to keep a straight face.

"You didn't? No wonder Sam looks worried." She put her arm around Sam's shoulder. "You just ignore him. We never put inexperienced riders on the larger horses." She cast a reproving glance at Jonah who, having found the joke he had played hilarious, could no longer contain the giggles that had been threatening for a while. Laughter being infectious, soon everyone was joining in, including Jenny who appeared to have finally put her animosity put aside. Sam thought that was worth being the butt of the joke for.

"Take no notice of Jonah, Sam," said Meredith, "he's just being a pain." She scowled at her teasing brother before pointing to the dappled grey horse Sam had seen earlier.

"You see that one, Sam," he nodded, hopefully.

"That's 'Grey Cloud', she's being made ready for you and Jonah knew that all along."

Relief brought the colour back into Sam's face and, Jenny, finally realising how scared he had been, felt a little ashamed of laughing at him. Jonah, on the other hand, was still grinning widely.

"I'm gonna get you, Atkins!" Sam grinned, seeing the funny side and hugely relieved.

"Well, I thought you'd be a bit nervous, and if I said we were on the bigger horses you'd be a lot happier when you saw Grey Cloud, so really I was doing you a favour."

"Don't give me that!" Meredith said. "You were winding Sam up and you know it. Doesn't matter how you try and excuse it but enough of that now. They're all saddled up and ready so, come on, let's get you all sorted out. We're not busy today so Kelly and I will come out with you." Jonah pulled a face and pretended to put his fingers down his throat. He shook his head vigorously. "Aargggh! No, please, no! Not Kelly!" he whispered to Sam behind Meredith's back.

"I heard that, Jonah!" Meredith barked, without turning around.

The group watched as two other horses, one a reddish-brown and the other, a light cream colour, were saddled up.

"Oooh, can I have the pretty cream one?" Jenny asked eagerly.

"Yes, that's 'Mayo', she's for you anyway, and Jonah's riding 'Forest'."

"Mayo?"

"Yeah, she's creamy."

"I can't believe you said that!"

Meredith took them through basic riding techniques, and soon they were on horseback heading out into the quiet lanes of the woods, where dappled sunlight broke through the canopy of branches casting moving patches of sunlight on the ground. From the many hoof-prints in the dried mud and the occasional pile of horse-dung, Sam guessed this was a regularly used trail. There was barely a sound from the horses' hooves on the soft leafy floor as they moved in a slow walk in pairs. Meredith, on her own horse Angelo, rode in front with Jenny, followed by Sam and Jonah and Kelly bringing up the rear. The woods were peaceful and almost silent apart from the gentle rustling of leaves and birdsong. Those were the pleasant sounds but there was also the constant droning hiss emitting from Kelly's IPod and her tuneless humming which Sam and Jonah tried to ignore. Jonah had gone uncharacteristically quiet.

"Whassup Jonah?" Sam asked.

"Nothing… Oh hell!" Jonah's face was a picture of misery.

"Come on Jonah, what's wrong."

"I haven't been riding for ages," Jonah answered quietly.

"Why, did you have a fall or something?"

"No, nothing like that." Jonah struggled to put his thoughts into words and Sam not wanting to push too hard, changed the subject.

"Did you get your maths homework done? That algebra old Barnard set was horrendous!"

"Sam, can I talk to you?"

"Yeah, course you can," Sam replied warily, wondering what was coming. He pulled back on Grey Cloud's reins to slow her down a little, so Jonah could talk without Meredith or Jenny overhearing. Kelly would hear nothing over the noise in her earpieces.

"I've never told anyone else about this. Meredith already knows about it," he began. "It was three years ago when there was an accident at the stables...it was my fault." Jonah lifted his face to look at Sam. "Meredith's sort of forgiven me since...well since Christmas, you know, the explosion..."

"You don't have to tell me if you don't want to," Sam said, trying not to let his curiosity get the better of him.

"No, it's OK. I want to," Jonah insisted. "It might help explain some stuff." He glanced quickly at his sister and Jenny, but they were deep in conversation. Jonah turned in his saddle to see if Kelly was taking any interest in them, but her eyes were closed and she was happily mutilating a Rihanna song, wailing in a voice much louder than she realised. Sam wondered if the pained expression on Jonah's face was entirely down to his worries.

"Are you sure you're OK?" Sam asked.

"Yes, I'm OK and you're meant to be honest with your mates aren't you?" Jonah swallowed and gave a sad little laugh. "It's funny really. Here's me trying to tell you about something that just about everyone knows, but don't talk about anymore, but you might hear about it from someone else, so I'd rather you heard my side first." He inhaled deeply. "Things are a lot better between me and Meredith now, but we were really close once. We're OK now, but it's not the same and I don't know if it ever will be. In the early days, the trouble between our parents made us close. The worse things got, the more we leaned on each other, but then I blew it." He looked at Sam. "You know you scared me when you came to Winterne."

"I scared *you*!" Sam was taken aback. "You didn't exactly act scared, it looked like you hated me."

"Yeah, I did," Jonah said with a sad smile, but that's 'cos I was scared of you. I knew you were going to be popular, not like me. No-one liked me. Doesn't that sound pathetic? I knew you'd never let people down like I did. I'm sorry."

"But, that's in the past. We're mates now," Sam insisted.

"Yeah, I know we are now. You know I only ever had one close friend before...and I let him down, badly." Jonah looked really miserable. "This is the first time I've been to the stables in a long time. Meredith persuaded me...I'm glad she did...but it's brought back a bad memory and I'd like to get it out of my head. Are you ready for this, Sam?"

"Yeah, no problem, what are mates for?"

63

"I used to go to the stables a lot when I was younger...I liked helping out." Jonah smiled at the memory. "I fetched hay and water for the horses, mucked out the stables, that sort of thing." He paused to gather his thoughts. "Peter Wilkinson was my best friend. The only real friend I ever had...before you. Not like the others. They wanted to be with me because we had money and the big house. Peter spent most of his school holidays with us and Meredith let him help in the stables too. She was always going on about how we had to be careful around the horses, in case we frightened them."

It was quite warm in the shelter of the trees, but Jonah shivered. "We should have behaved better. God knows Meredith drummed it into us enough, but we were fooling about wrestling in one of the stables. There were two young horses in there with us. They'd only been with us a few days, so they were a bit nervous, skittish, and Meredith had already had a go at us a couple of times. She threatened to send us away if we didn't quieten down...we were on a final warning, but we forgot. I'd started putting down fresh straw when Peter dived on me and we started wrestling again...got too close to one of the horses and it...it panicked, reared up and bucked all over the place. It kicked out, caught Peter on the side of his head." Jonah lowered his eyes. Sam cast a glance in Jenny's direction, but she and Meredith were too busy talking to pay attention to him or Jonah. "The other one squeezed into a corner away from us...I remember its eyes...rolling. It looked terrified and...and I can still see Peter now," Jonah's eyes stared into the distance. "He was on the floor, unconscious...out cold. I didn't know what to do...I froze. The horse was panicking, trying to not to stand on him, but that just made it more frantic. They can't stand anything under their feet, it makes them nervous. Peter was lying face down directly beneath it, and the poor thing didn't know where to put its feet," Jonah shuddered at the recollection. When he spoke again it was as if he was in a trance. "I remember trying to hide in a corner. The horse was terrified and kept trying to manoeuvre itself away from Peter but there was no room...he was in its way...and then somehow...I still don't know how, it twisted awkwardly and hurt its back somehow. I didn't know what to do...for Peter or the horse...I felt like I was in a nightmare...but it was real. It felt like hours listening to the horse thrashing about and wailing. I panicked and ran," Jonah looked into Sam's eyes searching for accusation or rejection, but saw no judgement there.

"I left Peter and the horse and ran...without getting anyone, without trying to help. Two girls heard the noise. They saw me run away and told Meredith I'd caused the accident." He inhaled deeply. "It wasn't till I got to my room I realised what I should've done, but it was too late. The vet put the horse to sleep...he couldn't do anything else," Jonah fell silent, racked by guilt and remorse.

Sam waited until Jonah felt able to continue. He looked back to see if Kelly was watching but her plump round face was still tunelessly mouthing words to another unidentifiable song. Jonah heard and managed a grin. Without warning, Sam's horse swung her head into the hedge and chewed off some leaves. The sudden movement threatened to unsaddle him but Jonah quickly grabbed the reins and pulled her away from hedge. They moved on again with Sam feeling quite unnerved at how close he came to falling off.

"What happened to him?" Sam asked.

"Head injuries. He was taken to a specialist centre in Bristol and his parents moved there to be nearer. I tried to explain but, without Peter to back me up, I was blamed for everything. It was him who started the wrestling again...but he got hurt, and I didn't. Nothing was ever the same between Meredith and me after that. I even tried to run away...twice. The first time I got as far as Farnshall before they caught up with me, and the second time they found me sleeping in one of our greenhouses. Everyone blamed me for what happened...I blamed myself. I know Meredith felt responsible for Peter's injury and the horse dying...it was her little brother who ignored her instructions and then abandoned them...both."

Sam was confused...what was he supposed to say?

"I had bad dreams for months...kept seeing the horse rearing up and hearing..." Jonah shook his head as if trying to clear it. He looked sadly at Sam. "Well, what're you thinking?"

"Look, Meredith's forgiven you and, OK you ran, but you were only a kid. I'm sorry for your mate, but if he'd done what she said, it wouldn't have happened. Do you ever hear from him?"

"No, not until recently when Mum made some enquiries. They're still in Bristol and Peter goes to a special day centre. We heard he's better...but he'll never be...right again."

"It's not your fault Jonah...and you've punished yourself long enough. It's been...what, how long did you say, three years? It's time to put it behind you. You've got your mother and sister back and life's better now for all of you, except your Dad's gone."

"Yeah, but I hardly knew him, so life goes on like it did before as far as I'm concerned. Speaking of mum, she's asked me to take you and Jenny back to the house after."

"Why?"

"No idea...she didn't say. Just said it was important she saw you."

"That sounds scary." Sam looked worried.

"Nah...," Jonah seemed a lot more cheerful now, "don't worry, I heard her phone your folks and Jenny's to tell them you were having lunch here."

"Lunch at the Manor, eh," Sam laughed. "Going posh."

"Don't know about going posh, but you've gone round," Jonah grinned, "round in a circle…look we're back at the stables. We've done a loop." One of the girls Sam had seen before noticed them heading in and walked over to take the reins of their horses to lead them towards the mounting block where Jenny was already dismounting. Sam's legs seemed jelly-like when he stood on firm ground.

"Next time I'll show you how to dismount properly," said Meredith sliding deftly out of the saddle. Jenny pointed to a horse looking at them from its stable. "Hey, look at that beauty!"

Sam and Jonah turned to look. A magnificent grey horse with large dark eyes and ridiculously long eyelashes was studying them from over the stable door. She had a small head, in comparison with the others they had seen and a slender neck that arched down to a sloping shoulder.

"Isn't she a beauty? Come and meet Celeste," Meredith said.

As they approached the stable, the horse whinnied, tossing her head up and down as if in welcome. Meredith stroked her warm velvety muzzle as Sam and Jonah caught up with them.

"Celeste?" Jenny enquired.

"That's her pet name. Her racing name is Celestial Sovereign, but she can't race anymore. She was injured last season and I bought her to give her a good home. I like to exercise her myself when I can but most of the time, I'm too busy. When I do get a ride, it's usually on Angelo. Celeste's in foal so we're expecting the patter of tiny hooves, aren't we my girl? Angelo's going to be a father."

"Oh that's so sweet!" exclaimed Jenny.

Sam and Jonah exchanged a 'girls are weird' look.

"Right. Now I'd better get on. I don't get to stop for lunch, not like some people," Meredith smiled and headed off to the office.

"I hear we're going to the Manor for lunch," Jenny said. Sam nodded, still wondering what on earth Mrs Atkins could want with them. Jenny stopped to stroke Celeste, while the boys waited patiently.

"Well, I can't help it…she's just so gorgeous," Jenny giggled as she put her arm through Sam's.

Leaving the stables, they strolled through the tree-lined meadow toward the Manor, a pine-cone, a remnant from autumn, dropped very near Jonah, and a little further on another landed on his head.

"What the?" he yelled.

Looking up, they expected to see a squirrel, but they saw nothing.

"Must be a squirrel," said Jonah.

"Or a bird," volunteered Jenny.

Sam nodded in agreement, but was quite certain it was no squirrel or

bird above them. Without seeing the culprits, he knew exactly who they were. Scanning the branches above him, he dodged an acorn as it came hurtling down at great speed and looking up he caught a glimpse of something silvery moving along one of the lower branches. Claptrap's hair!

"Look over there," Sam said, pointing in the opposite direction. "I'm sure I saw a fox."

"Where?" Jenny and Jonah yelled in unison, turning to see where Sam pointed. With Jonah and Jenny otherwise occupied. Sam frowned at four small booted feet dangling from a branch. Dressed in shades of brown and green, camouflaged in the new leaves, there they were. Piggybait and Claptrap waved gleefully at him, throwing more acorns. They were at their rascally best, appearing not to have a care in the world, which was totally at odds with how they had been the night before.

"Can't see a fox anywhere," Jenny said. Jonah shrugged. "Perhaps we disturbed it."

Sam glanced up again, Piggybait and Claptrap had vanished. Under his breath Sam muttered. "It's not the only one that's disturbed."

"What was that?" asked Jenny.

"I said I'm sure I saw one," Sam answered quickly. "You're right though. Those squirrels are pests."

Chapter Eight

Dorothy chewed the end of her pen. The household accounts had become very muddled and she was finding it difficult to make everything balance. This was the one part of her job she did not enjoy.

From beyond her window, a peel of youthful laughter came from the direction of the back garden and, glad of the disturbance, she laid down her pen on the desk and waited for the back door to open. She glanced at her watch and wondered where the time had gone but was grateful for the distraction from the tedious paperwork.

"That'll be Jonah and his friends back for lunch, Marje. They'll be hungry after their ride."

Marjorie sniffed as tears seeped from her eyes and trickled down the side of her nose. The red-skinned onions she was chopping gave off powerful fumes making her eyes red and blotchy and she blew her nose noisily into a man-size tissue. "I hate onions! They're the bane of my life, I can't stand peeling onions."

The inner door flew open as Jonah, Sam and Jenny burst, giggling, into the kitchen.

"Where's Mum?" Jonah began.

"What? No hello or how are you this morning?"

Marjorie, too busy losing the fight with the onion vapours, missed Dorothy's conspiratorial wink as she dabbed at her irritated eyes with the end of her apron.

"What's the matter, Mrs Seymour?" Jonah asked politely. Marjorie's mouth dropped open in surprise; she still found Jonah's new-found geniality quite unsettling.

"Don't you worry about me, young man, you just get and see your mum. She's waiting for you in the study."

Jenny and Sam stood side by side, staring around the massive room. "This is a kitchen? I've never seen anything like it," Jenny sighed, captivated. "It's a good job my mum hasn't got a kitchen like this one. We'd never get her out of it."

"Er...excuse me, you two," Jonah prompted. "You know, just whenever you're ready..." He grinned at Dorothy. "I dunno. You'd think some people'd never seen a kitchen before," and he headed towards the swing doors. Jenny and Sam smiled at the red-eyed cook and the slightly scary housekeeper, and followed him through the door and up into the oak-panelled hallway.

"Wow! This is amazing!" Sam exclaimed as he entered the magnificent armoury in the hallway. He tried to look everywhere at once, pointing into the display cases. Jenny did not speak. She was too busy staring, but not at the weapons, she was open-mouthed, awe-struck by the ornate and elegant crystal chandeliers. "I've never seen anything like this, Jonah. It must be fantastic living here," she said.

"Yeah, I suppose so. It's always been here, so I guess I'm used to it." He shrugged. "But the cleaners are always complaining about having to keep the dust off them." He nodded towards the chandeliers.

A door on the right opened. "I thought I heard voices," Harriet Atkins said warmly.

"What do I do?" Jenny whispered out of the corner of her mouth to Sam.

"What about?" he whispered back.

"She's Lady of the Manor. Do I curtsey or anything?"

"No, she's not royalty."

A slight upturn at the corner of Harriet's mouth suggested she had heard their muffled conversation.

"We'll be having lunch in the conservatory, if that's alright with you both," she said looking directly at Sam and Jenny.

"Er, yes. Mrs Atkins, that's fine with us," said Sam.

Jenny said nothing.

"Isn't it, Jen?" Sam nudged her.

"Oh yes, fine," echoed Jenny, a little shyly.

"And, as I only live here, I don't get asked where I'd like to have lunch," Jonah grinned.

Harriet ignored him. "OK, follow me, Jenny, Sam. Jonah, pop down and tell Marjorie we're ready for lunch, will you?"

"I hear and obey, Mother dearest." Jonah headed back to the kitchen while Jenny and Sam followed Harriet Atkins round the side of the staircase and through a door which led them into a long, white-painted corridor and from there into a bright, airy conservatory that overlooked the tree lined lawns. Sam nudged Jenny again, this time he pointed out a peacock, accompanied by two rather dull-looking peahens, as they meandered in and out of the low hanging branches of a weeping willow. Sam, suddenly unsure of himself, continued staring out of the window, while Jenny looked around the room excitedly admiring everything.

"Your conservatory's much bigger than our sitting-room, Mrs Atkins," she said.

Harriet gave her such a warm smile, her green eyes almost shone. "I like it in here too. In fact I spend most of my times in this room and the study. We only use the drawing-room and dining room on formal occasions, and I have as few of those as I can get away with these days."

Jonah returned carrying a large wooden tray containing plates, cups, cutlery and glasses, closely followed by Dorothy, pushing a large trolley.

Sam jumped up. "Let me help," he offered to Dorothy, who looked surprised, smiled gratefully and declined.

"No it's easier for me to do it, but thank you." Pushing the trolley to the table, Dorothy mumbled, "Nice to see some young people have manners."

Jonah scowled.

Harriet helped Dorothy set out the lunch. Sam and Jenny watched in disbelief as the tablecloth vanished under plates piled with sandwiches, cheese, egg, sausage, bacon and ham, chicken legs, a small tureen of steaming tomato soup, a cheese and tomato quiche, pork pies, crisps, salad, apples, bananas, iced doughnuts, apple turnovers and Bakewell tarts. In addition, there was a pot of tea, fruit-flavoured sparkling water, orange juice and cola. As Sam sat down again, he and Jenny looked at each other; they would never finish all this lot in a month of Sundays.

"We don't usually get all this for lunch," Jonah said, reading their minds as he reached out for a party-sized pork pie. "They're only feeding me 'cos you're here. I'm lucky if I get bread and water normally." He pulled a face of wounded innocence.

Dorothy raised her eyebrows. "Yes, look at the poor thing…all skin and bone, isn't he?" she tutted and walked towards the door trying very hard to keep a straight face as she left the room.

Harriet sat on a chocolate coloured sofa, reading a farming magazine while the young people tucked in, only half listening to their conversation. Eventually, lunch over, she felt the time had come to explain why they were there. She put down her magazine and joined them at the table.

"Sam, Jenny, I asked you here for a reason."

This is it, Sam thought. Jenny looked uneasy.

"There's nothing for either of you to worry about," Harriet smiled at their puzzled faces. "Jonah, Meredith and I felt we should thank you for everything you've done for us."

"But we didn't do anything," Sam said, brushing Bakewell tart crumbs away from his chin, his eyes flickering between Jonah and his mother.

"You've done more than you know," Harriet continued. "Jonah is deeply sorry for all the hurt he caused you Jenny, aren't you Jonah?" Jonah

nodded and hung his head, the tips of ears a shade pinker than usual. "And he wants to apologise to you, Sam, for his behaviour when you first arrived here." Both boys were obviously embarrassed.

"But that's all done with now, Mrs Atkins," Sam told her.

"That's as maybe Sam, but you went through a horrid time at Jonah's hands and then you put yourself at risk to save his life." Her eyes glistened with tears and she swallowed, before blinking them away. Jonah looked away, ashamed of the obvious distress his past behaviour had caused.

"None of us will ever forget what you did," Harriet continued, her sorrowful green eyes clouded over with memories of earlier suffering. After a few moments where she appeared to be in a kind of daydream, she quickly recovered her more cheerful outlook. "Right. Now let's get on with it shall we?" She headed to the other side of the conservatory to a large Welsh dresser and pulled open a door. "Jonah's father, although I'm sure he didn't realise it at the time, put you both in danger. I'm convinced he had no idea you and Jonah were anywhere near but...his greed could have killed you both and, as his wife, I have to take responsibility for that. So, to you, Sam, with thanks for the life of my son and, to Jenny, in recognition of your friendship to him since, we would like to give you both a gift, even though it's nowhere near enough to express our profound gratitude." She took a large shiny black box out of the dresser and placed it on the coffee table. "Come closer," she urged. Jenny and Sam looked at each other; it was clear they both felt very awkward, and neither wanted to take the first step forward.

"There's no need for you to give us anything, Mrs Atkins," Jenny protested.

But Harriet insisted. "Yes there is, Jenny. Jonah had no friends. He had driven everyone away with his appalling behaviour. Not that it was entirely his fault. His father and I must share the responsibility in making our son what he was."

Jonah looked distinctly uncomfortable.

"You two turned things around and the other young people in the village have followed your generous lead. Our life is better now than we could've imagined just a few months ago, thanks to you."

"Mum wants you to look in the box," Jonah nudged them closer to her.

"Here, sit down beside me," Harriet patted the chocolate coloured sofa. Sam sat on Harriet's left and Jenny on her right. Harriet leaned forward and slowly lifted the lid of the box. Inside, Sam saw a tankard, something he thought might be a jewellery box and, craning his neck he glimpsed a couple a chains. He looked across Harriet to Jenny who shrugged. She was at a complete loss as to what to do next.

Jonah prompted them. "Mum wants you to choose something from the

box."

"But we can't do that! I'm sorry Mrs Atkins, but this doesn't seem right," Jenny said with a deep frown. "We're not friends with Jonah to get rewarded for it."

"Oh, bless you dear," Harriet laughed, I know that and that just makes your friendship all the more valued. This is just a little something to show the family's appreciation and especially to you, Jenny, for all you went through. You endured intolerable brutality and, although Jonah's my son, I cannot excuse that kind of behaviour. You could've had him charged with assault, if not worse, and I couldn't have blamed you if you had. He'd have deserved it."

Jonah squirmed.

"But you, and your family, were kind enough not to do that and kindness should always be rewarded. I'm now taking this opportunity to do just that. After all if you found something somebody had lost and handed it in to the police or back to its owner, you'd deserve a reward. In some ways you have 'found' Jonah for me, and this is my way of saying thank you. I'm touched by your reluctance to accept these tokens. It shows what decent people you both are but I spoke to your mothers while you were out riding and explained what we were doing and they are happy with it. So go ahead, choose your gift. Take your time, there's no hurry."

Sam picked out the pendant, intending to give his mother, but Harriet stopped him. "This should be for you, not your mum or Jenny or Cathy."

Sam put the pendant back. He had a wristwatch already and the tankard did not particularly appeal to him. His eyes fixed on the watch and chain and he carefully lifted it out of the box. Pressing the catch at the side, the front cover opened revealing a white watch face with gold coloured roman numerals. Between the centre and the number twelve, a crescent moon and six stars were inlaid in a gilt metallic material, into the white face. Jenny, Harriet and Jonah watched in silence as Sam studied the watch. It was not working. Harriet pointed out a button on the side. "It releases the back cover," she explained.

"The key to wind it up is inside."

With a tiny click, the back cover of the watch opened. Sam took out the key and began winding up the mechanism then he noticed a line of writing on the inside of the case, but it was too small to read clearly. He asked Harriet if she knew what it said.

"No, we wondered about that. The inscription's probably some sort of code meaning something to whoever originally owned it, but the only thing we can make out is the year 1888, sorry."

"That's alright, Mrs Atkins, I just wondered."

The hands on the watch started moving at a regular pace and Sam listened as it softly ticked, warming up in his hand as if coming to life. Delighted, he looked up and smiled broadly at Harriet. "Is it OK if I have this, Mrs Atkins?"

"Yes, of course, Sam. You've chosen well. Now what about you Jenny, what would you like?"

Before Jenny could answer, there was a knock at the door and a young, dark-haired woman entered. She cast a quick look in Jonah's direction, her expression a combination of fear, loathing and contempt. As she looked away and turned towards Harriet, Sam thought he saw her shudder.

"Yes, Peggy?" Mrs Atkins asked.

"There's a genl'mun to see you Miz Atkins, name o' Morriz Fisher. Shall I show 'im in?"

"Maurice Fisher? I don't think I've ever heard of him. Did he say what he wants?" Harriet looked puzzled.

"No, Miz Atkins, 'e never said, jest that he wanted to see you if you woz free." Peggy cast a quick wary glance at Jonah under her lowered eyelashes, before turning back to Harriet.

"No, Peggy, don't bring him in here. I'll see him in the drawing room...and ask Dorothy to come up as well please."

As soon as Peggy had gone, Harriet asked Jonah. "Does that name mean anything to you?"

"Nope, never heard of him either, but it won't hurt to make him wait, will it? He should have phoned first."

Still with a slightly puzzled expression, Harriet turned back to Jenny. "Sorry about that Jenny, but it's your turn now. Have you made your choice?"

"Grandma Richards left me some of her jewellery and I've never had anywhere nice to keep it. They're still in a drawer in my bedroom. I meant to get a jewellery box but never got around to it. This one's lovely."

Jenny lifted out the polished wooden box and opened the lid. It was lined with red velvet and inside the lid was a small ornate mirror. The body of the box comprised two sections, a lift out tray with two large compartments on either side of a slotted section for rings and, underneath, a large space for trinkets. Jenny noticed a small repair in the velvet in one corner, but was so pleased with the box that this very minor fault did not spoil her delight. "May I choose this please?"

"I hoped you'd choose the box Jenny, it's perfect." Harriet smiled. "Meredith, Jonah and I are delighted to do something for you for a change."

"Did you want me, Harriet?" Dorothy had entered the room unnoticed.

"Oh yes, Dorothy...sorry Jenny, Sam...will you excuse us for a minute?" She joined Dorothy by the door where they had a whispered conversation about the visitor. Sam saw Dorothy shake her head when

Harriet asked if she recognised his name. The two women talked in low tones for a minute or two while the three friends looked out of the window at the peacock family who were still strutting and scratching on the lawn beyond.

"I'm sorry," Harriet called over, "but I'm going to have to see this man, whoever he is, but thank you both for coming and I hope you'll be frequent visitors to the Manor...whenever you like." After shaking their hands, a formality which surprised Jenny, Harriet left the room to see her newly arrived visitor.

"I suppose I'd better go home," Jenny said, holding her newly acquired jewellery box. "Are you coming too, Sam?"

"Yeah, I guess so, but I was wondering about us going into Wells tomorrow or Wookey. I've only been to Wookey Hole once and it's cool, the caves are amazing. It'd be good to get out, all of us, before we go back to school."

"Nice one!" Jonah replied. "I'm up for it. I'll make some calls and see who's interested but it'll be quicker for you to get home if you go out the front door. It'll be much longer going right round the stable way," Jonah said, leading them back through the armour lined hallway. As they passed the drawing room, Jonah hesitated. The door was slightly ajar and they could just see Harriet's visitor. He had his back to them, so they were unable to see his face, but he was tall, wore a black pin-striped suit, and his dark hair was going grey at the side. That was about all they could see of him, but they could hear his voice. He spoke in a well educated manner with soft, rich tones that were easy to listen to. Harriet was facing him, so they could see her very clearly. From what Jonah could see she seemed quite impressed by him and was so enthralled, she failed to notice the three curious friends peeking into the room until Jonah waved to her.

"Excuse me a moment, Maurice." His eyes followed her as she walked to the door. On seeing them looking in, a flicker of displeasure crossed his features cancelling out the charming smile, that glided effortlessly back as she shut the door on them.

"I'm not quite sure that I like him," Jonah spat.

"Yeah, but it looks like your mum does. I thought he seemed a bit creepy though," Jenny volunteered.

After his friends had left, Jonah tiptoed back to the drawing room door. Unable to hear any of the conversation inside, he leaned closer, squashing his ear painfully against the cold wood. Thankfully, apart from Marjorie singing off key in the kitchen, the house was fairly quiet. Struggling to blot out Marjorie's drone, he heard a snippet of the conversation from inside the study that astonished him.

"What! That can't be right." He stuck a finger in the other ear to shut

out the noise from downstairs.

"What do you think you're doing?" Dorothy, had crept up behind him. Jonah's heart missed a beat.

"Whaaa!   Don't do that! Anyway shush!" he put one finger over his mouth.

"Don't you shush me, Jonah Atkins!"

"No, Dorothy, please be quiet. I'm trying to hear what's he's saying," Jonah whispered.

"Why, what's the matter?"

"I'm not sure I heard right, but I think he said he's a friend of dad's."

"What? No! Move over. I want to hear this."

Chapter Nine

As Sam and Jenny left the Manor, Jenny's grandfather, Arthur Sykes, was spring cleaning the dolphin fountain in the centre of the grass covered circular island in the driveway. He was spraying detergent around the bowl, cleaning away the unsightly green algae that had gathered during the winter months.

"Hey Granddad, look what I've got." Jenny ran across the grass to show him her newly acquired gift. He peered through rheumy eyes at the ornate patterns worked into the outer case, opened the lid and examined the inside for a few moments, before closing it and returning the box to her.

"Very noice my girl, you look after it."

"Sam got a present from Mrs Atkins too. Show him Sam, show Granddad your watch." Sam duly handed over the watch and chain for the old man to inspect. Arthur squinted as he studied the antique timepiece appreciatively.

"Well...my word. 'Tha's a noice piece o' workmanship from what my old eyes can see. You'd do well ter look after it my boy. It's a roight noice piece, is tha'," he said, handing the watch back. "So what're you two gonna be up to now?"

"We're on our way home. Tell Nan I'll pop round tomorrow if I can. See you later." She gave the old man a kiss on the cheek before joining Sam and heading off down the driveway.

"Isn't it time your granddad retired?" Sam asked.

"Don't let him hear you say that! He says he'll never retire. Anyway Nan's told us often enough she wouldn't want him under her feet all day." Jenny laughed and turned back to wave to the old man who was busy scrubbing the dolphin's tail and missed her wave.

"He probably wouldn't have seen me from this distance anyway," she shrugged. She talked animatedly about Mrs Atkins and the gifts as they strolled down the tree-lined driveway, but Sam was only half listening to her chatter. He was watching for movements in the branches overhanging the drive fully expecting to be pelted with acorns or pine-cones at any

moment.

Hiding in the trees, a thin sallow faced man, watched them head away towards the main gates. From his vantage point, he had a good view of the front of the Manor and all movements in and out of the front door. He was unshaven, with red rimmed and sunken eyes, surrounded by large dark circles and a haunted look about them. His stained and crumpled clothing was at least two sizes too big for him, and he frequently scratched at his unkempt, dirty grey hair which had obviously not seen a comb for months. He had been there for some hours leaning against a wide tree-trunk or sitting at its base and, a short while before, he had shrunk back into the undergrowth as a grey BMW car glided up the driveway. He struggled up from his uncomfortable tree-root seat and pushed aside an obstructing branch to get a better view. The driver emerged from the vehicle and nodded to the old man before knocking on the door. As his back was turned, the observer, unable to see the visitor's face clearly, shuddered as something about his height and the way he stood, struck an unnerving chord. He retreated further into the trees, appalled to see the newcomer admitted to the house. His hunger and cold now forgotten as a thought occurred to him. He prayed he was wrong. He saw the door open again and hoped it was the visitor leaving but was disappointed to see a young girl and boy exit the house. The girl called to the old man and ran over to him, the boy close behind her. She seemed excited about something and he watched as they handed something to the old man, who nodded appreciatively, then handed them back.

He screwed up his eyes trying to see what it was they had, but from that distance, was unable to make out what they were so excited about. There was a little more conversation before they left the old man to his work and walked away down the drive, the girl talking incessantly.

Once he was sure they were too far away to see him and the old man was engrossed in his task, he crept out of hiding and, using the cover of the trees, moved closer to the house where he thought he might be able to get a better view of the visitor when he eventually left. Concealed within the trailing branches of a weeping willow, he shivered and pulled his jacket closer. A tickling in his throat made him want to cough, but he forced himself to suppress it, fearing the old man would hear. A noise nearby made him jump and he ducked down behind the trunk of the willow. A girl's voice called out. She was near, too near. Peering from behind the branches, he looked for her but she was not within his range of vision. Instead, from around the side of the house a Dalmatian dog come into view. It was heading straight towards him.

"Not now! *Not yet*!"

He shrank back, praying the dog would not find him. He could hear it

panting. It was getting closer. If only he could have stayed in the barn. But he could never go back there now and being outside was so much more dangerous for him, with that damned dog and the police everywhere. He knew they had found his things at the stables, and now his only possessions were those he had on.

He longed for the comfort of the barn. It might have been a little damp, and the woodworm infested floorboards could be dicey, but if you knew what you were doing, it was safe enough, and his camping gear was there. Now his only shelter was the cave. Why had he been so stupid? If only he had not been so determined to go to the Manor that night he would not have been seen, the girl would not have got hurt and things would never have got this complicated.

"That blasted dog!" he said to himself. He hated having to hurt her. Had that girl called it Briar? If it had not chased him, he would not have had to defend himself. He had no choice. He had to get away. He looked down at the rip in his coat sleeve.

"Could've been worse I suppose," he croaked.

The dalmatian barked. He would be on him any second. He braced himself for discovery.

"Hey, Wilmot, come and get your dinner."

He could not have been more grateful for good timing. The girl had obviously said the magic word, as the dog ran off. He heaved a sigh of relief as it disappeared from view. The tickle in his throat returned, but this time he was unable to stifle a rasping cough. His chest heaved with the effort to get his breath as the cough abated.

"Even the dog eats," he gasped, leaning against the tree trunk for support while his heart beat returned to normal.

Finally, the wide carved oak door opened. The man shook hands with the red-headed woman and they walked together to the waiting car. He was concerned to see they seemed very friendly. At the car, the couple turned, and he had a clear view of the visitor's face. A chill ran down his spine which had nothing to do with the weather.

"I knew it!" His heart thumped loudly in his chest and his hands grew clammy. "Pull yourself together man. Don't give way now. You'll need your wits about you. That no-good swine might think he's on to a good thing, but not this time."

As the car drove away, he slunk back into the shadows of the trees, muttering obscenities.

But the observer was now the observed. Four pairs of eyes followed his progress through the trees towards the caves. As he forged deeper into the woods, first Jossamel, then Lommie stalked him. Shortly after, Rondina emerged from the bracken, taking her turn following their target. Rondo,

her brother, waited high up in an oak tree until their quarry came within view and, mimicking the harsh cry of a crow, attracted Rondina's attention signalling he would take over the pursuit, and she fell back to join Jossamel and Lommie. The three then headed for the elves cavern, leaving Rondo to continue the task until Halmar took over.

The elves were making it their business to keep an eye on this man. They were not comfortable having him within their territory in view of the recent occurrence at the stables. Like a gathering storm, trouble was in the air.

Chapter Ten

Sitting in front of the kitchen fire that night, Meredith and Jonah talked late into the evening, something they had not done for a very long time. Meredith, her legs curled under her, occupied the over-sized green armchair, while Jonah sat on the hearth rug with his arms wrapped around his knees. Wilmot twitched in his sleep at the foot of Meredith's armchair occasionally catching Jonah's foot with a jerky paw. Although the fire was dying down, it was still warm and reassuring. Jonah stared into the diminishing flames, sipping his mug of hot chocolate.

"I told Sam about Peter today," he said.

"Ah, so that's it." Meredith responded. "I wondered why you were so quiet. What did he say?"

"He said I shouldn't take all the blame myself...Peter was just as responsible."

"He's right and it was a long time ago. At the time, I blamed you because Peter was injured and you weren't. Running away didn't help, but I realised afterwards fear can make people do things they wouldn't normally do."

"I said we'd never got back to normal. Is that still right?" He looked up at her with eyes full of hope.

She reached out for his hand. "We're fine...things are different now. When you got caught up in that cave-in, I was worried sick and when you survived, I put the past in the past. You, me and mum, we're fine, a real family again, probably more now than ever before."

Jonah grasped her hand while he stroked Wilmot with the other. The comfortable dog stirred in his sleep.

"So. Tell me about our visitor today," Meredith said lightly.

"You heard about him then?" Jonah scowled.

"Yes, but who was he? What did he want?"

"I don't know." Jonah shrugged. "It's just...I'm not sure. He said he'd come to pay his condolences to mum, but there's something creepy about him."

"How d'you mean?"

"Well, that's the point - I don't know. I can't put my finger on it."

"You're sure you're not imagining things?"

"Maybe I am…I dunno…but Jenny thought so too. He said he'd been abroad for a while and only just read about dad's death."

"Well, perhaps he had. What's odd about that?"

"It's weird that's all." Jonah stood up disturbing the sleeping dog, and paced the length of the room, trying to put his thoughts in order. "Look, its four months since dad died, so how could he have read about it recently? Surely anyone who's been abroad doesn't go through four months' worth of newspapers to catch up, unless they know what they're looking for. Oh, I dunno, maybe they do…it just seemed a bit weird to me."

"How was Mum while he was here?" Meredith enquired.

"OK. Yeah, she seemed…almost as if she liked him."

"Hmm. But you didn't?"

"Nope."

"What about Dorothy?"

"No, she's a bit suspicious of him too. What was it she said? Oh yeah, "his clothes looked expensive, but his aftershave's cheap." Meredith chuckled. "That sounds like something Dorothy would say. Did Mum say if he was coming back?"

"No. No I don't think she did."

"Maybe it won't be a problem then, not if his call was a one-off."

"Yeah, well let's hope so."

"Anyway little bro', I'm off to bed. Dan's coming in early to check on Celeste and Briar."

"Have the police found anything else yet?" Jonah asked, draining the last dregs of his hot chocolate.

"No not yet. They've taken away everything they want, so the place isn't teeming with uniforms anymore and we can get back to normal, whatever normal is around here." Meredith laughed. Wilmot, groaned as Meredith moved her legs, then raised his head and yawned as she took the mugs to the dishwasher. Jonah banked down the fire and hooked the fireguard across the grate for safety's sake. His last chores were to make sure the back door was locked, and turn out the light before they headed up to their rooms with Wilmot padding alongside.

In the hall, one night-light remained constantly on, casting a shadowy illumination onto the oak panelled walls and bestowing a life-like glow on the suits of armour. Apart from their footsteps on the stairs and the creaking night sounds of the house settling down, everything was silent. Reaching the first landing, they stopped to look at the full moon through the unicorn and maiden stained glass window, her white robe glowed silver in the moonlight. Wilmot trotted up the stairs just ahead of Meredith, eager to get to his basket. When Jonah stopped at his door Meredith gave him hug. Wilmot whined until they said goodnight, then he bounded along the corridor ahead of her, obviously anxious to be off.

"Whatever's wrong with you, Wilmot?" she asked as they walked by Dorothy's room, where a snuffling snore could just be heard and then up a short flight of stairs to her rooms. Meredith turned off the lights in the hallway, opened the door and Wilmot threw himself down onto his bed with a loud grunt. Meredith laughed.

"Kept you up late did we?"

It had been a long day and Meredith suddenly realised how tired she was. Being up nearly all the previous night worrying about the horses and Briar had taken its toll. She got ready for bed and snuggled down, too tired to bother with the book lying on the bedside table. Turning out the lamp she was asleep almost as soon as her head hit the pillow.

Jonah, on the other hand, lay awake for a long time. Maurice Fisher kept stealing back into his thoughts. What was the man up to? His mother might trust him, but should she? He lay under the covers listening to an owl that sounded so close, it could have been on his window sill. He was still puzzling over what Maurice Fisher was up to when he dozed off to sleep.

Soon after midnight, a panel in the wall beside the unused fireplace clicked softly open and a thin figure cautiously emerged. A shaft of moonlight filtered through the gap in the curtains, giving enough light to define the features of the sleeping boy, his dark hair contrasting with the whiteness of the pillowcase. The man hesitated by the bed, watching Jonah breathing, but eventually he moved away and headed for the door. Silently exiting the room, he waited until his eyes became accustomed to the darkness then peered around the doorframe into the corridor before tiptoeing out of the room, carefully turning the handle to close the door without making a sound. Satisfied no-one was still wandering around the house and the only sounds were the occasional floor board creak, he was reassured he could move on safely.

He turned on a small torch, its beam sliced through the dark illuminating the portraits on the walls. He reached the stairs and stopped, listened for any sounds from the floor below, then descended the wide moonlit staircase. He paused at the dagger display cabinet, running his hand appreciatively along the glass top, before moving on towards the kitchen. Through the swing doors, he clicked off his torch and risked turning on an overhead light. Confident now he would not be discovered, he chanced making a huge mug of tea and cutting a chunk of bread and cheese, which he ate greedily before tearing into a cold chicken leg he had found in the refrigerator.

He eased himself into the green armchair and wept silently as he cupped his hands around the mug, grateful for the heat that spread through his hands. After finishing his hurried meal, and cleaning away any evidence he had been there, he dragged himself away from the retained warmth of the dying fire and the comfort of the armchair, ready to face the chilly evening air again. But first decided to see what else the well-stocked refrigerator had to offer.

He stole four cold cooked sausages, some sliced cheese, a plastic bottle of milk and two more cooked chicken legs. Then he turned his attention to the larder. Taking a large shopping bag from several hanging on a hook, he filled it with bread rolls, biscuits, a fruit cake and three cans of beer, then threw a few teabags in for good measure. They had so much food, he told himself they would never notice a few things going missing. Finished with the larder, he made a quick search of the sink unit drawers where he found a small knife, a can-opener that would also open bottles, and helped himself to a couple of forks and spoons. In another drawer, he discovered matches, a ball of string and, under the sink, a box of firelighters, which he wrapped in a carrier bag to contain the paraffiny smell, and a larger torch than the one he already had and put them all in the shopping bag.

Reaching up to the wooden rack, he helped himself to a small frying pan and one of the many saucepans hanging there and wrapped tea-towels around them to stop them clanking against each other.

Finally, he took a mug and a plate from the dishwasher. There was just one more thing he needed before he left. In the vestibule he looked through the coats and jackets and chose a dark blue waxed padded coat he knew would fit him. It was of good quality, which he expected, and he could not resist taking it, telling himself his need was greater than the owner's.

Now his stomach was full, so was his bag and he had a warm waterproof coat; a satisfactory haul. It was probably time to leave before he pushed his luck too far. Through the swing door, he listened carefully before venturing into the main living area of the house. He was about to ascend the staircase when he stopped at a door in the hall. Slowly turning the handle he entered the study and switched on his torch. A standard lamp stood beside the book-shelves in the right hand corner of the room; he turned it on, put down his bag and switched off the torch. Why waste batteries? He tried the drawer of the writing-desk, it was locked. He cursed angrily. A few minutes later, after searching the room thoroughly, he furiously moved behind the curtain to the left of the window. Hoisting his bag onto his shoulder, his hand lightly touched a small and almost barely discernible bump in the wooden panel beside the window. A concealed panel slid open. He had just stepped into the dark corridor

beyond when a thought occurred to him and he almost smiled. Swiftly retracing his movements, he closed the panel behind him and roughly pushed the curtain aside as he hurried back into the study, closed the door quietly and climbed the wide staircase again.

Back on the landing he put the bag down carefully and softly opened a door on the left at the top of the stairs. In the open doorway, he stared for a moment at the red-haired woman sleeping peacefully, completely unaware of the intruder. Stepping quietly into the room, he headed towards the large mirrored dressing table, where he slowly eased open the top drawer all the while keeping an eye on the sleeping figure who, luckily for him, made no move. He checked the contents of the drawer and, not finding what he was looking for, slowly slid it closed again and opened the one below, repeating the process. Unsuccessful, he decided to inspect the enormous carved wardrobe again easing open the doors.   It soon became obvious that whatever he was looking for was not in the wardrobe either.

"Damn!" he muttered under his breath. "Where the hell are they?"

The woman in the bed stirred and he darted behind the curtain until she settled again.

"What the hell have they done with them?" he whispered. He punched the wall in frustration and a sharp pain shot through his hand but he gritted his teeth. He could not make a sound. The woman sighed loudly and turned over her in bed.

"Gotta get outta here," he hissed, "but I'll come back. They're here. I know they are."

Keeping one eye on the sleeping woman, he tiptoed to the door and out onto the landing where he picked up his bag to head back to Jonah's room. A door on his right had been left slightly ajar. He pushed it open. It was large white-decorated bathroom with plush, dark blue towels folded neatly on rails. He stared at the bath and sniffed at his filthy jacket. It was pretty putrid. He felt a longing for hot water, bubble bath and shampoo. He stepped halfway into the room, remembered his dirty shoes and looked down. No, no muddy footprints, thank goodness. The dirt must have been wiped off earlier. He looked at himself in the bathroom mirror and wished he had not bothered. The face staring back at him was not his own. This unrecognisable creature had dirty, matted hair and a beard that belonged to someone else.

He looked down at his hands. His nails were filthy like the rest of him. What was he doing here? He opened the airing cupboard door, stole one of the larger towels and helped himself to a bar of soap, a sachet of shampoo and a razor from an open packet at the back of the cupboard. He had no idea how he was going to use them, but they smelled nice and the thought of a shave made him feel better.

It was time to go. Out in the hall, he left the door ajar, just as he had found it, then outside Jonah's door, he listened for sounds of movement inside, but satisfied all was peaceful, he pushed it open. Jonah slept soundly as his intruder made for the fireplace and pressed an almost undetectable button in the centre of a carved ivy leaf on the fire surround. A mechanism clicked softly and the panel slid open.

With one last look at the sleeping figure, he hoisted his bag over his shoulder and slipped back through the gap into the dark passageway just as the panel began to close behind him. Unfortunately, he was not fully through the doorway when the panel banged into the cumbersome bag, making the handles of the pans rattle together. He held his breath. But, after a few seconds, satisfied all was well, he clicked on his torch and shuffled back along the passage confident he had got away with his foray into the house undetected.

He could not know that, just as he turned away, Jonah had been woken by the noise and his eyes snapped open just in time to witness a foot vanishing into his wall and the panel closing. Frozen with terror, he stared at the wall, unable to move. With clenched clammy hands, he rose from his bed, switched on his bedside lamp and hurried across to the fireplace. Nothing seemed different. Switching on his main bedroom light, he went back and examined the wall closely. Even using the magnifying glass he kept in his computer desk drawer did him no good. There was nothing to indicate a hidden door.

"There's no break in the wallpaper, not even a crease," he said out loud. "I'm going mad, I must be! There's nothing…nothing." He ran his hand over the area carefully feeling for any slight crack. "Nothing! I imagined it. I must have done," he told himself, running his hand through his hair. "I'm having bad dreams. Dorothy said I shouldn't have cheese for supper. I'll listen to her next time."

Turning out the top light, he got back into bed, switched off his bedside light and tried to sleep but chaotic thoughts and worries about his weird dream kept him awake long into the night. He finally fell into a fitful sleep just as the night sky grew light.

Deep inside a concealed area of the house, the uninvited visitor, unaware of Jonah's turmoil, lowered the beam of his torch onto the damp, crumbling stone steps of an old spiral staircase. It was narrow and difficult to negotiate, but he knew where to take extra care, hampered though he was by his cumbersome bundle. Close to the bottom of the staircase was a narrow door with a small window. Through the door he found himself in a dark circular chamber and made directly for another door opposite, avoiding looking at the dark shapes standing motionless in the shadows. The second door lead into a dark, damp flag-stoned corridor with two low doors on either side, but he showed no interest in these or the enormous rat that scampered, squeaking shrilly out of his way. A third, wider door blocked his way, a large brass key still in the lock. Turning the key anti-clockwise, he opened the door into a wide earthen corridor, closed the door behind him, locked it again and placed the key on the decaying wooden doorframe above.

The damp earth floor rose in long roughly hewn steps, uneven and strewn with old stones and timbers from bygone days. Venturing along this underground corridor was hazardous. He had to stoop to avoid hitting his head on low sections of the tunnel roof, knocking spiders from their webs and avoid tripping over large blocks of stone and bones of who knew what...or whom...or rats as they scampered under his feet. Dank, fusty air triggered his cough again. Brushing cobwebs aside, he eventually reached the door leading out to the woods and, with the door open, he gulped in the good clean air.

When he had found the tunnel some years before, it had seemed a good idea to keep the knowledge of it to himself and now he was very glad he had. It was filthy, damp and some places held a foul stench, but it was useful. Before heading out into the woods, he stopped to leave his original torch in a small alcove behind the door, beside a small oil lamp and another torch. The torch, stolen from the Manor kitchen, he took with him.

Emerging from the tunnel, he brushed off the dust and cobwebs and stared up at the clear starlit sky. The bag was comforting. He now had food and the means to make a fire, but he still bitterly regretted leaving his sleeping bag behind in the barn. He shivered. The temperature had dropped again since he had entered the Manor. He pulled the waxed jacket out of the bag and put it on. It smelled of the stables, something he found strangely reassuring. Picking up his bag, he forged along a well-worn trail unaware of several pairs of elven eyes still watching his progress through the woods.

Reaching a wide stream, he negotiated the steep bank, grabbing hold the bushes whenever he felt he might slip down the muddy bank into the fast flowing freezing black water that disappeared into the hillside through a small tunnel obscured by scrubby clumps of foliage. Pushing aside a branch, he stooped under the slanting roof of the cave stepping carefully onto a small ledge running alongside the stream. Taking the torch out of the bag, he turned it on. The eyes of a rat reflected, brilliantly red, back at him before it scurried away to hide. Tackling the slimy, algae covered path was difficult, burdened as he was, but he was determined not to lose any of his precious new acquisitions. With his back to the wall, he carefully placed his feet on the slippery ledge. Slipping into the surging stream would surely mean death.

Soon, his back aching with stooping, he gratefully straightened up as the ceiling rose and the ledge widened out to form a wide rocky border of a circular, underground lake where the water gathered before exiting under the rock wall at the far end of the cavern. He stood for a moment, his torchlight shining on the glistening stalactites suspended from the ceiling, before staggering up a narrow rocky path that rose steeply from ground level and ended some twenty metres above the swirling water. At the top, a wide, dry sandy corner flanked by rocks that formed a dry, draft-free area with obvious signs of habitation. Newspapers, empty carrier bags, old biscuit wrappers and empty fizzy drink cans, were strewn about messily. He dropped to the ground, amongst the litter, trying to get his breath; his climb had left him breathless and panting. "I must do the housework." His rasping laugh ended in a spasm of harsh coughing. As the cough abated, he sprawled across the newspapers, unpacked his bag and took off his newly acquired jacket. He lit a small hurricane lamp, previously stolen from the Manor farm, turned off the torch, leaned back wearily against the cave wall and opened a can of beer. Now he had time to think, he remembered the man he had seen at the house earlier.

"There's only one reason that good-for-nothing slime-ball would come here," he spat. "What the hell have they done with them?" A deep frown creased his grimy forehead and he scratched at his greasy hair, kicking a plastic bottle against the ledge wall in frustration. Watching him, high above on another ledge, an elf accompanied by a grey wolf, its tongue lolling out of the side of its mouth, stared down at him. The wolf grinned, revealing two rows of strong white teeth, strings of drool hung from his jaw.

"Are you sure I can't eat him, Piggs?"

"No. No, probably best not to. He'd hardly make good eating these days and, anyway I don't believe it's in his destiny."

Chapter Eleven

On Tuesday morning, Susan Askam waited at the bus stop, butterflies flapping about in her stomach. She was going to spend one whole wonderful day with Sam. Granted, the others would be there, but she was certain today Sam would notice her. She woke early, spent hours with sprays and gel getting her thick auburn hair to behave itself, and was confident the full ponytail she had managed to achieve, looked good. She hoped she could return the khaki coloured top she had 'borrowed' from her sister, Rachel, before she returned from her shift at the hospital. With luck Rachel would never notice. Then she remembered the broken lipstick. Rachel would definitely notice that; maybe she could blame the dog! Her stomach rumbled. Perhaps she should have listened to her mother and had breakfast but she was too nervous to eat.

"You'd better eat something. It settles the nerves." Susan wondered if there was time to run indoors and grab a cereal bar or something, but then her mother might see she was wearing make-up, so she decided against it.

Spotting Jason across the green, she guessed the others were probably not far behind. The butterflies were now doing cartwheels. Sam would be along soon. She had tried several times to engineer a meeting with him and, on a couple of occasions had followed him on one of his trips into the woods, but somehow she always lost him.

Jason crossed the road, earphones in, listening to his Ipod. He sat beside her and began talking but could not hear her replies as he had not removed his earphones. Susan rolled her eyes. "Sorry Suze. What were you saying?"

But she was not looking at him. Her eyes wide, she was staring happily as two fair haired people approached, their bodies obscured by a hedge. Jenny and Sam were talking animatedly and laughing, which was not unusual as they were such great friends, but as they turned the corner and came into full view, Susan's eyes were no longer wide with excitement.

"Oh!"

They were holding hands. Jason saw Susan's shocked expression and understood.

"Oh."

Jason had always known Susan had a crush on Sam, but assumed that, like everyone else, she knew how things stood with him and Jenny Richards, but he realised now he was wrong. She struggled to blink away hot tears of disappointment and jealousy, but her misery was very evident.

Jenny, suspecting nothing, called out a cheerful greeting. She looked happy and suddenly Susan, one of her best friends since primary school, hated her for it. When Jenny had telephoned Susan the previous day to tell her about the planned day out at Wookey and Wells, she had given no inkling that she and Sam were together and Susan felt betrayed.

"It's alright for her to be cheerful," she muttered.

"Whaddya say?" asked Jason, pretending not to have noticed her animosity. He knew better. Getting between two girls fighting over a boy was a dangerous place to be.

"Nothing," Susan snapped, forcing a smile, but speaking in monosyllables and only when spoken to.

Jason, attempting to keep the conversation light, wondered where the others were.

"Hiya. The bus'll be here soon," he said as Sam and Jenny reached the bench.

Susan, her arms tightly folded, avoided Jenny's eyes. Sam noticed nothing unusual, but Jenny quickly sensed the chill.

"Hi Susan. You ok?" she asked in an unnaturally light voice. Susan pretended not to hear.

Sam, still unaware of the discord around him, went to sit next to Susan, but Jason quickly moved between them, forcing Sam to sit on the other side of him, while Jenny squeezed in at the far end of the bench, next to Sam. She knew exactly what the problem was with Susan and was grateful to Jason for his constant chatter, but even he was thankful to see Jonah heading to join them from the other side of the green.

"There was a time when I couldn't imagine I'd ever be so pleased to see him," Jason whispered.

"Yeah, I know, but he's really ok now," Sam replied still not having a clue what Jason really meant.

Jonah broke into a run, stopping only to allow a car to pass before darting over the green.

"You look tired," Jenny said, as he approached. Susan groaned sarcastically and raised her eyes to heaven. Jason nudged her sharply. She turned angrily. "Pack it up," he mouthed.

"Why should I?" she hissed.

Jonah, quick on the uptake, as usual, sensed the atmosphere and

concealed his amusement. Looking at the sullen girls he thought it might be a very interesting day.

"Yeah, I had a terrible night," he told Jenny. "You'll think I'm nuts, but I think I saw a ghost. Either that or it was a rotten nightmare."

"A ghost! What happened?" Jenny asked.

Susan sighed loudly. Jenny threw her an impatient glare before turning back to Jonah.

"Didn't you say the Manor had ghosts anyway?" Sam asked.

"Yeah so they say, but none of us have ever seen anything, until last night."

"Hey look at her!" Sam interrupted Jonah, pointing towards the centre of the village green where a tall, grey haired woman wearing a black raincoat and black Wellington boots walked briskly across the green. With her back straight and her head held high she swung her arms vigorously taking long strides, almost as if she was marching. Padding obediently behind her was a black and white collie, carrying a looped up lead in his mouth, and behind him, to Sam's astonishment, was a grey cat following along very contentedly, its tail high and curled around at the top.

"Haven't you seen them before, Sam?" Jenny asked.

"No never. Is that cat really following them?"

"Oh yeah, that's Bandit. He follows whenever Merlin's taken for a walk."

"That's amazing. Who's she?"

"That's Mrs Jenks. We don't see her very often as she keeps herself to herself pretty much. She's got a bit of a reputation. Some people say she's a witch 'cause she knows about herbs and stuff and she's really good with wild animals and birds."

"Yeah, I heard that too, but it's just stupid," Jonah remarked, with just enough of a sneer to recall his old unpleasant self.

"A witch! That's daft, everyone knows there's no such thing," Sam said with a forced chuckle but he recalled what Charlie had said about Mrs Jenks and was not so sure.

Striding briskly to the Post Office, Mrs Jenks seemed oblivious to the group watching her, but Sam was too intrigued to look away. After making sure no cars were coming, Mrs Jenks stepped out into the middle of the road and waited as first the dog, then the cat, crossed to the safety of the pavement before she followed them. On the kerb, to the surprise of their audience, the animals sat down to wait for her. Mrs Jenks had just reached the pavement when, quite abruptly, she stopped, stock-still, and fixed a disturbingly piercing, dark blue gaze on them, her eyes shifting from one to the other. The cat began to groom himself while the dog yawned and lay down resting his chin on his paws, wagging his tail gently. Finally, Mrs

Jenks' eyes rested on Sam. Jenny watched him squirm under the unrelenting stare. The others looked from the woman to Sam and back again. Jonah looked quizzically at Jason who shrugged. The cat stopped licking his tail and with half closed lids, he too fixed his round pale jade eyes on Sam, slowly opening and closing them, in what Sam hoped was a look of goodwill. Then, to his amazement, Mrs Jenks smiled warmly at him. Unable to force a return smile, he managed a barely perceptible nod, which seemed to satisfy the extraordinary lady who turned to join the waiting cat and dog, before heading into the Post Office.

"What was that all about?" Sam asked, totally perplexed by the incident.

"Not a clue mate," Jonah answered. "Not a flaming clue, but you'd better watch yourself. You never know what's going on with witches." He shook his head and drew a finger across his throat.

"Don't be stupid Jonah!" Susan said scathingly.

"Hey, just fooling, Sue. Chill!"

Sam grinned and took hold of Jenny's warm and comforting hand.

"Hiya." Ben and Ian had arrived, unnoticed during Sam's encounter with Mrs Jenks. Jason started telling them about Sam's unusual experience with Mrs Jenks when the arrival of the bus to Wells interrupted his story. They boarded, bought their tickets and walked along the aisle between the seats as the bus started up. Sam sat down by the window with Jenny taking the aisle seat next to him. Susan, still brooding, walked peevishly towards the back of the bus, but Jason grabbed her hand pulling her down into the seat beside him. He was not going to allow her to be seen sulking.

"Like it or not, Suze," he whispered, "you're going to enjoy yourself, or you'll look like you are, and that'll help you feel better. If it doesn't, it'll certainly make me feel better."

Susan managed a weak smile, her eyes glittering just a little too brilliantly as she turned away to look out of the window.

As they pulled away from the bus stop, Sam felt compelled to look back. Mrs Jenks was in the doorway of the shop smiling at him as if they were old friends, something he found very unnerving. But, involuntarily, his eyes were drawn away from her to the cat whose eyes seemed to increase in size and began spinning, changing colour until they became kaleidoscopic orbs. Feeling nauseous, he forced himself to break eye contact.

"Looks like you've made a friend, Sam," Jenny remarked in a brittle voice. He wondered what he had done to upset her, not aware that it was Susan's attitude that was annoying her. Having been friends for so long she did not want to fall out with Sue, but she would not give Sam up for anyone and hoped it would blow over soon. Watching Jason's efforts, Jenny wondered how long it would take Susan to realise just how much

Jason liked her. The sooner she did the better.

Beside her, Sam simply assumed she did not feel like talking and was soon caught up in his own thoughts. He wanted to tell Jenny about the cat's eyes but decided she would think he was crazy, so he said nothing as the bus drove away from the village.

Chapter Twelve

"Susan had a real strop on today, especially with Jenny," Jonah said as he and Meredith chatted over dinner with their mother that evening.

"Perhaps she's jealous," Meredith suggested.

"Jealous? What of?"

"You said before she had a bit of a soft spot for Sam and now Jenny and Sam are going out…"

"Yeah, but I'd have thought she'd be over it by now."

"Perhaps she's just good at hiding it," Harriet commented, cutting into a crispy skinned jacket potato. "Jonah, you look really tired, are you sleeping alright?"

Jonah had decided not to mention his dream, in case Meredith laughed at him. Now things were back to normal, she was enjoying teasing him again.

"No, I didn't sleep much last night. Probably the cheese sandwich I had for supper. Dorothy warned me not to, but I didn't believe her. I'm going up earlier tonight, without supper."

"Heard any more from that man, Fisher, Mum?" Meredith asked, spooning coleslaw onto her plate.

"Yes I have. I was going to tell you. He's coming here this evening."

"What again?" Jonah complained. "I don't like him. He's slimy."

"Slimy?"

"I know what Jonah means. I don't trust him either from what I've heard and I don't think Dorothy's too keen either," Meredith added.

Harriet put her fork down on her plate and looked quizzically at her children. "I thought he seemed perfectly pleasant. The only thing that concerned me was that he was an old associate of your father's and you know what some of them were like." Harriet looked thoughtful.

There was a short silence before Meredith said, "Isn't it just too coincidental that he turns up here soon after what happened at the stables. I hope the two aren't connected."

"Oh, I wish you hadn't said that." Harriet rose from the table and walked towards the window. She had a habit of looking out into the peaceful gardens when troubled.

Jonah and Meredith exchanged concerned looks.

"I had a little word with Ernie earlier," Meredith whispered to Jonah while Harriet's back was turned, "just in case he came back."

Jonah moved closer. "Why? What are you planning?"

Meredith winked. "Tell you later." Meredith left the table to join Harriet at the window.

"Come and finish your dinner, Mum," Meredith coaxed. "Don't worry too much, just be…careful. After all, we don't know anything about him, do we? He might drive an expensive car and dress smartly, but that doesn't mean he's trustworthy. What time is he getting here?"

Harriet looked at her watch. "In about half an hour."

"So soon!" Meredith flashed a worried look at Jonah. "Look I've got a couple of things to do, but I'll be back in a minute. I want to see for myself and anyway, you shouldn't see him alone." Meredith rushed out of the room.

"Whatever is she up to?"

"No idthea, but I'll thtay too if you want," Jonah said, cramming potato into his mouth.

"Oh no you won't!" Harriet replied. "Too many of us will make him uneasy and if he is up to something, it might put him on his guard. No Meredith and I can meet him."

Ten minutes later, the family were in the study preparing for Fisher's visit. Harriet plumped up the cushions on the sofas, while Meredith and Jonah huddled together by the fireplace, whispering.

"What's going on?" Harriet asked, walking slowly towards her children.

"Nothing." Meredith grinned.

"Nothing at all." Jonah said, trying to hide a smile.

The sound of a car heading up the drive sent them to the window. Harriet sighed. "He's here."

The grey BMW swung around the circular lawn and pulled up at the wide front door.

"Here goes." Harriet said, taking a deep breath. Jonah left the room with her and darted up the stairs, two at a time.

"Don't worry Mum, we're around if you need us." Harriet looked up to where he stood on the first landing. The last blood-red rays of the setting sun shone through the window onto his dark hair, streaking it with the brilliant colours of the stained glass unicorn and maiden.

"I've just realised how much I love this house," Harriet said quietly. "I was a fool to shut myself away for so long."

Meredith, who had just come out of the study, laid a comforting hand on her mother's shoulder just as the dragon's head knocker hammered loudly on the front door. Jonah disappeared around the bend in the stairs while Meredith picked up a book and stretched herself out on the sofa. Everything was staged to appear very casual for their unwelcome visitor.

"Good evening Mrs Atkins. Not too early I trust." He was overly polite but she noticed his smile did not reach his eyes; her family were right, there was no sincerity in him.

Knowing her family's attitude towards Fisher, Harriet made a point of studying him more closely than before. On closer inspection, she conceded that, if he was as successful as he professed to be, little things did not add up. His black shoes were clean and highly polished, but looked old and worn, his pin-striped suit was too shiny to be of good quality and his shirt collar was slightly shabby and frayed. Why hadn't she noticed these things before?

"You are a little early, but no matter, Mr Fisher. Come through to the study."

"Thank you so much, dear lady." Something about his manner made her skin crawl. As he strode past her, her nose was assailed by a very strong and very unpleasant aftershave. Cheap. Just as Dorothy said, Harriet thought.

"No servants tonight, Mrs Atkins?"

Fisher's fishing, Harriet thought. That's good. I must remember that one. "We don't have servants Mr Fisher. Mrs Seymour, the cook, and her son have been here for years. Then there's Peggy, of course, she stays with us because there's nothing else for her here in the village. Apart from that there's Dorothy, our housekeeper and my cousin, not my servant. She's visiting a friend this evening. But no, none of them are here, so we're looking after ourselves tonight."

Fisher gave a leering smile of satisfaction as Harriet led the way towards the study. "Of course, Harriet, I apologise if I offended you. I merely assumed they were paid staff. You have a superb collection of weapons, Mrs Atkins, very nice."

"It was a passion of my late husband's Mr Fisher," Harriet replied, trying to hurry him along. "I'm sure as you knew him so well you'll remember his fondness for them."

"Yes, yes, of course," he said, eyeing up a particularly attractive set of duelling pistols, "and my friends call me Maurice."

"We're in here, Mr Fisher. I have coffee prepared."

Meredith stood up as Harriet and Fisher entered the room. His smile vanished on seeing her, quickly followed by a flicker of anger, before it slid back into place.

"This is my daughter, Meredith. Meredith, this is Mr Fisher. He was an old friend of your father's."

"Pleased to meet you Mr Fisher," Meredith lied, holding out her hand.

"Delighted and enchanted, Miss Atkins," he said smoothly, limply shaking Meredith's outstretched hand. She felt the damp warmth of his palms and felt the urge to wash her hands, but could not leave her mother.

"Coffee, Mr Fisher?" Harriet obstinately refused to use his first name. She no longer had any intention of getting on friendly terms with this man.

"Yes, thank you. No milk or cream and two sugars, please."

The next hour was spent in polite small-talk, while Fisher regaled them with his recollections of Jerry in their early days. At one point, Meredith heard a noise outside in the hall and guessed Jonah was eavesdropping at the door. She forced a coughing fit to cover the sound. Eventually, Fisher steered the conversation around to investments he had supposedly made with Jerry. Now we get to it, Harriet thought.

"Can I get you a drink, Mr Fisher? A brandy...or something else?" Meredith asked, rising from the sofa and heading towards an elegant rosewood cabinet at the far end of the room.

"Well I'm driving, but maybe a very teensy brandy. That'd be most agreeable, thank you."

Meredith opened the cabinet and found the brandy. "Mum, how about you?"

"I'll have a small sherry please, dear."

Meredith took out three glasses, poured one brandy, one sherry and a diet cola, but just as she was about to put the bottles away, she reached into the back of the cabinet and pressed a button on a tiny recording device, then closed the cabinet and handed out the drinks.

"Yes, of course Jerry and I made lots of investments in the old days," Fisher continued smoothly. "Money was no object when we had the housing development business. We even invested in South African diamonds, but of course you'll know about that."

"No! No I didn't, Mr Fisher," Harriet said, astonished. "I had no idea Jerry had anything to do with diamonds. He never mentioned it."

Her shocked expression seemed so genuine, Fisher could not doubt her sincerity, but that posed a problem and he had to think fast. If the diamonds were not part of Jerry's estate, where were they? He concluded they must still be in the bank security box where Jerry had secreted them. He knew which bank, but how was he to get at them? And what had Jerry done with the key? His thoughts raced. Jerry would have made a note of the box number somewhere, and, in case anything happened to him, knowing his fixation with security, he would have kept the number and the key separate. He had assumed Jerry would have made sure his wife would have known about it. Now he was not so sure. It had begun to look as though he would learn no more from the Atkins woman, he looked at his watch.

"My goodness Mrs Atkins, I hadn't realised how late it is and I've got to drive to Bristol tonight, so I really must get on my way, so if you don't mind perhaps I won't have that brandy after all."

"No, not at all, Mr Fisher. Perhaps you'll call in on us again," Harriet said, ignoring Meredith's wide-eyed look of incredulity.

"Oh, I certainly intend to do that, dear lady," Fisher replied. Meredith thought she detected a note of concealed threat in his voice.

"Let me see you out," Meredith volunteered, casting an anxious glance at her mother.

She had only just closed the front door behind Fisher, when Jonah burst into the study, making Harriet, who had been deep in thought, jump in surprise.

"Well, what was that all about?" he demanded.

"I thought you'd gone to bed."

"Of course he hadn't," Meredith grinned as she re-entered the room. "He was eavesdropping weren't you little Bro."

"Yeah. You didn't think I was going to stay upstairs while he was here, did you? Anyway what *was* that all about?"

"I'm not sure," Harriet replied, "but I'm quite sure he's up to something and it's good we're on to him."

"Perhaps more than you think Mum." Meredith lifted the cushion from where she had been sitting a little while before and produced something small and round from behind it. "Wonderful little things, these bugs!"

"What on earth is that?" Harriet stared in astonishment at her secretive offspring.

Jonah smirked. "Nice one!"

"Will someone please explain?"

"I just thought we needed to be prepared," Meredith grinned triumphantly. Returning to the rosewood cabinet, she produced a small electronic recording machine and removed a tiny cassette. Smiling, she walked back and handed the machine to Harriet.

"We didn't tell you in case it made you nervous," Jonah told Harriet. "It was better you didn't know."

"But is it legal?"

"Shouldn't think so," he laughed, "but I doubt Fisher's playing by the rules either."

"Ernie lent it to us, but we didn't exactly tell him the truth about why we wanted it," Meredith admitted.

"You got Ernie involved!" Harriet looked shocked. "No…no, don't say anything else. I don't think I should know any more." She walked towards the fireplace, shaking her head, attempting to appear disapproving of her scheming children. "I have to admit though you were all quicker on the uptake than me over our fishy Mr Fisher. Jonah, pop down and let Dorothy know it's alright to come up. She's probably dying to know what's been going on, and she must get this back to Ernie," she looked down at the recording device in her hand.

As Jonah left the room, Harriet turned to Meredith. "I think we should speak to Sergeant Harte, but it'll keep till tomorrow." She checked the time on the mantelpiece clock. "But it's not too late to call an old friend." She picked up the telephone and dialled a number.

"Hello Chris, its Harriet."

Meredith hovered nearby intrigued by what her mother was up to, and when Jonah returned with Dorothy, she put a finger to her lips to shush them.

"Who's she talking to?" Jonah whispered.

Meredith shrugged her shoulders, "Don't know."

"...and Julie and the children are well?" Harriet continued.

Jonah leaned in towards the telephone, but Harriet gently pushed him away. He winked at Meredith.

"Listen Chris, I know it's a bit late, but I need a favour. You have a prisoner by the name of Jake Rumpsall." She paused for the reply, and put her hand over the mouthpiece, laughing at Jonah's puzzled expression. Dorothy looked equally perplexed, but Meredith stared in dawning admiration.

"That's right he was in Jerry's um...gang...been with Jerry for years seemingly. Yes, yes, I understand that Chris, but I'm trying to find an old family member of Jerry's from the East End regarding his Will and Jake may remember his last address. We've had problems trying to trace this relative, and it's very possible Jake could help us. You know I wouldn't ask if I wasn't desperate, but it was Jerry's last wish you see. Would it be possible for Jake to give me a call? I know prisoners are allowed telephone calls."

Apart from the muted, tinny voice at the other end of the telephone, the room was hushed.

"Oh, thank you Chris. That's wonderful. I know Jerry's cousin will be pleased to hear from us. Yes...give my love to Julie. Tell her we must meet up for coffee sometime. I haven't seen her for ages. Bring the family out to the Manor. The girls would love the stables. Oh good. I'll look forward to it. So I'll hear from Jake tomorrow?" While Harriet listened to the answer, she grinned at her family who were watching her, their curiosity evident. "Yes, thank you so much, I really appreciate it. Bye Chris."

She put the phone down and looked at her astonished family with a wide, satisfied smile. "What?"

"Well, what are you up to?" Dorothy had her hands on her hips and a worried look on her face.

"What I'm up to Dorothy dear, is finding out what Jake Rumpsall knows about Fisher. Chris Robertson's an old school friend of mine, who just happens to be Governor of Bristol Prison, where Jake is serving time for his part in Jerry's last venture?" Harriet looked very pleased with herself. "You have to fight fire with fire."

"But you said you were looking for one of Dad's cousins?" Jonah cut in.

"You don't always have to tell the whole truth, do you?" Meredith beamed.

"I never knew you could be so scheming, Mum," Jonah said, seeing his mother in a new and delightfully devious light.

"I've been learning from my children," Harriet gave a smug smile, looked down at her clenched fist and opened it. There, on her flat palm sat the tiny device. "Clever," she said.

Chapter Thirteen

It was around ten-thirty on Wednesday morning when the telephone rang.

"Winterne Manor. Can I 'elp you?" Peggy adopted her best telephone voice.

"*Yeah. Is Mrs Atkins there?*" *said a gruff cockney voice.*

"Whom shall I say is callin'?"

"*Jake Rumpsall. She's expectin' me.*"

"If you say so. Jest a moment, I'll enquire as to 'er whereabouts." Peggy put the telephone down on the hall table with a look of disgust. The caller did not sound at all like the kind of person Mrs Atkins would talk to. She was tempted to tell him her employer was out but, on the other hand, if Mrs Atkins was expecting a call from this…this person. She knocked on the study door and entered without waiting.

"Miz Atkins. There's a bloke on the phone sez you want ter speak to him an' you're expectin' 'im."

Harriet looked up from the letter she was writing. "Did he give his name?"

"Yeah. It was Rumple or Rumsill, or summat, but 'e don't sound very nice Miz Atkins. Not your sort at all."

Harriet hid her smile. "That's alright Peggy, put the call through please."

"Well, alroight, Miz Atkins, if yer sure."

"Quite sure, Peggy. I've been waiting for this call. Thank you." Peggy sniffed loudly to indicate her disapproval before heading back to the hall telephone.

"Are yer there?"

"*Where else am I gonna be?*"

"Miz Atkins will speak to you."

"*Told yer.*"

Peggy ignored him. "I'm jest gonna put you through."

The line went dead for a moment.

"Jake, it's good of you to call," Harriet began.

"Well, I never 'ad much choice did I?"

Harriet ignored that.

"Jake, I need to pick your brains. You knew Jerry a long time didn't you?"

"Yeah, all in all abaht firty years. What's all this abaht Mrs Atkins. The Guv'nor said yer lookin' fer a lost relative or somefink."

"Um, well I'm afraid I didn't quite tell the truth there, Jake. You see, I've had a couple of visits from someone who says he's an old colleague of Jerry's. His name's Maurice Fisher. Have you ever heard of him?"

"You bin lyin' to the Guv'nor? You'll get me shot if 'e finds out this ain't on the level." Harriet heard a loud grating noise in the background and, for a moment, Jake stopped talking. The noise stopped and he continued with what he was saying. "I'll 'ave me privileges took away."

"I'll take full responsibility. I don't want to get you into trouble, Jake, but I really need your help. I think Fisher's up to something, but not knowing much about Jerry's past, you're my only hope. I'll sort things out with Chris...I mean the Governor, if there's any trouble."

"You'd better be as good as your word, lady."

"Don't worry, Jake. I just need some information from you."

"Maurice Fisher you say. Sorry, but that name don't mean much to me. I knew most of the types Mr Atkins mixed with, right back to the Ginger Osgood days, but the name Fisher don't ring no bells. What's 'e look like?"

"Well...he's quite tall with greying dark hair. He's been here a couple of times...wears pin striped suits and very cheap aftershave, I might add."

"Well, that's not really enough to go on. Anythin' else?"

"He drives a BMW, if that's any help...and he has a very smooth...easy to listen to voice."

"Yeah, well, don't make things easy will yer, Mrs Atkins?"

"I'm sorry Jake. I don't...oh, yes, he mentioned something about investments he'd made with Jerry. All sorts of investments...and diamonds, South African diamonds."

"Diamonds! Well why didn't you say so. There was only one bloke around like that when Mr Atkins started lookin into buyin' diamonds, but 'is name weren't Maurice Fisher. It was...wait a minute. It'll come ter me. Just can't think of it."

"So you think you know him? You remember him?"

"Gimme a minute. It's on the tip of me tongue." Harriet heard a deep voice mumbling quite close to the telephone. "No! Yer can flamin' well wait till I'm done." Jake yelled to someone unseen. "Take yer turn like everyone else."

"I beg your pardon!"

"No, not you Mrs Atkins. Just tellin' this lot 'ere. There's a queue fer the phone, but I 'ad ter wait, so they can too."

"Do you want time to think about it and call me back later Jake?"

"No, no I've got it...Farrow, that's right. Now what was 'is first name? I think that began with an M an' all. Farrow...Farrow. Got it! Malcolm, Malcolm Farrow. Nasty piece of work 'e was. Bit of a bully-boy too, 'e was as I remember. It was 'im used ter fake surveys on the 'ouses what Mr Atkins wanted ter sell. But 'e got greedy an' Mr Atkins didn't want 'im aroun' no more, so 'e closed up the business, gave Farrow 'alf of it and they parted company."

"A nasty piece of work Jake?"

"Yeah. Farrow'd sell 'is own granny for a fiver in them days an' I can't imagine 'e's improved any since. If you've got dealin's wiv 'im, then watch out fer yerself Mrs Atkins. Get shot of 'im, sharpish."

"How much longer have you got to serve Jake?"

"Um...yeah, well...wiv good behaviour, I could be aht in abaht eighteen monfs. Why?"

"Well, behave yourself and come and see me when you get out. You never know, I might be able to help you out with a job or something. I owe you a favour. Write to me when your release is near."

"Well, fanks Mrs Atkins, I'll do that. I don't never intend to find meself back in this sorta gaff again. I've 'ad enough; I'm gettin' too old."

"Good to hear it Jake. And thanks very much for your help, it's appreciated."

"Don't forget what I said. Steer clear of Farrow. Bye Mrs Atkins."

"I'll try. Bye Jake and thanks again."

"Oh yeah, one more fing, Mrs Atkins."

"Yes?"

"Mr Atkins did get 'old of some diamonds but 'e never said where from. To be honest, I'm not sure whether they was on the level or not, the only fing I do know was that 'e bought 'imself a watch, a fob watch, you know, one o' them antique types, on a chain, at the same time."

Harriet gasped.

"Are you alright Mrs Atkins?"

"Yes fine, I'm fine, please go on."

"Mr Atkins kept it wiv 'im all the time to begin wiv, then 'e put it away somewhere, in a security box in some bank, an' I seem to remember 'e 'ad the box number engraved on it. It looked like a date, y'know, a year. 'E said it'd be easy to remember like that, but no-one'd know what it was. It was eighteen summat I fink."

That was just the breakthrough Harriet needed. Now she knew what they were up against. But how she was going to deal with it was something else. "That's very helpful, thank you Jake. Is there anything else you can remember?"

"No, not right now. Oi! 'Op it will yer! I'm talking to a lady an' I'll finish when I'm ready."

"What was that?"

"No, sorry Mrs Atkins, not you. There's a bloke 'ere wants the phone so I'd better go. Don't forget, don't you 'ave nuffin' to do with Farrow if you can 'elp it. If I fink of anyfin' else, I'll call you again. Yeah, yeah, alright I'm done. 'Ere, you can 'ave the flamin' phone."

The line went dead. Harriet put down the telephone and stared out of the window at the beautiful morning. For a moment she watched a family of magpies playing on the lawn, but her head was spinning. She now had the information she needed but how was she to use it?

Chapter Fourteen

Shortly after Harriet received her telephone call, Piggybait and Claptrap looked down from the tunnel mouth onto the empty bedding strewn with empty beer cans, crumpled newspapers and carrier bags. They were surprised to find the makeshift dwelling deserted. Shafts of dazzling sunlight streamed in through two natural chimneys onto the creamy-coloured pillars of limestone deposits and the crystal, turquoise waters below.

"I said someone should've watched him," Claptrap complained, climbing down to the ledge. "Now we've no idea where he is."

Piggybait was equally exasperated by their 'quarry's' disappearance and, being peevish, took it out on his friend. "There you go again! Negative! Alright, so he's not here, but there are enough of us to pick up his trail and it's still early. He won't be far away. He'll be back, his things are still here."

Claptrap looked as if he had been slapped, making Piggybait regret sounding more abrasive than he had meant. "Sorry."

"You hope he'll be back," Claptrap muttered.

"What was that?" Piggybait snapped, his impatience again getting the better of him.

Claptrap turned his pointed nose in the air. "Nothing. Just clearing my throat."

A heavy silence hung between them until Claptrap broke the tension.

"You know Piggs, I wish Jimander was here. I miss him more at times like this. He would've known what to do. "

"I know," Piggybait replied in a kinder voice. "I keep wondering what he would've done too and not just about this, about everything." Sitting down on the warm sandy floor, Piggybait dangled his legs over the ledge, and stared down into the crystal blue, watery floor of the cave seeking inspiration.

"The police still don't have a clue who he is," Claptrap said, sitting down beside him. "It's a pity we can't help."

"Hmm. I've been thinking about that too." Piggybait rested his chin on his upturned palm and dropped rocks into the icy water watching for the small splash. Then, taking Claptrap completely by surprise, he sprang to his feet and dashed towards the bedding.

"What ARE you doing?" Claptrap shouted after him.

"Trying to do what Jimander would have done and move things along a bit." Piggybait hurriedly searched the abandoned bag and soon found what he was looking for.

"Yes! This will do very nicely."

Claptrap, swung his legs back onto the ledge and, curious to see what Piggybait had found, walked over to join him. "What've you got there?"

"Just a handkerchief," Piggybait carefully put everything back into the bag in the same order he had taken it out.

"OK. I give up. You don't have a cold...so why the handkerchief?"

"Claptrap old friend, watch and learn. It's time we got involved rather than just observing. I'm tired of doing nothing and our woods could do with one less uninvited human intruder. Come on. Let's go before he comes back."

Piggybait took off his brown wool cap, stuffed the handkerchief inside the rim to keep it safe, and put it back on before making the short easy climb back to their tunnel entrance, with Claptrap following close behind.

Soon after, in the elves cavern, Piggybait explained his plan to Jerrill, who gravely agreed to it. Claptrap, sitting on the other side of Jerrill, listened intently, certain there must be some flaw in his friend's scheme but unable to come up with anything better. There were some curious stares from elves working nearby, and Claptrap noticed Primola edging closer as she swept the floor.

"Alright Piggy," Jerrill said watching his son, Halmar at work. "Do what you can."

Jerrill smiled at the intense look of concentration on his son's face. Halmar had a notable talent for working with wood and, had become known for his delicate touch with carving. Right now, he was working on an arch of oak under which he and Ellien would marry. His determination to create something beautiful was etched on his handsome young face.

Sitting cross-legged on the floor near to Halmar, evidently enthralled by his skill, was the childlike Saldor, who clapped his hands and uttered appreciative comments at regular intervals.

Jerrill turned back to the waiting Piggybait. "I want this problem over as quickly as possible," Jerrill continued. We could really do without this danger to the clan and Klaus wants it brought to an end quickly as well. Go ahead Piggy. Do what you think necessary."

Primola stopped sweeping and several pairs of eyes followed Piggybait as he left the chamber, but there were no comments. Whatever he was up to, they had no doubt he knew what he was doing. Outside, the sun was high in a cloudless blue sky, so Piggybait, stayed concealed by keeping to the bracken undergrowth. A small herd of red deer paid no attention to him as he passed them, but a surprised pheasant flew out of the ferns just in front of him, its alarm scaring a flock of sparrows into the air. Other than that, his short trek passed incident free.

On approaching the stables, he kept low, crawling from bush to tree where the foliage was sparse and eventually hid behind a holly bush where he could see clearly into the stable yard.

A young woman, her wrist in plaster, leant against a stable door talking to the man Piggybait recognised as the one he and Claptrap had frightened in the meadow. He grinned at the memory; discovering the man was a police officer only made their prank more enjoyable. Beside the woman a German Shepherd dog lay resting, her right leg strapped up in a blue elastic bandage. Piggybait watched sympathetically as she tried nibbling at her sore injured leg through the bandage, but her owner was keeping a watchful eye on her and gently stopped her before she could do any harm to the dressing.

"So Briar's here," Piggybait smiled. Having her here would make things easier than he could have hoped. The woods contained many varieties of trees and Piggybait looked for a Sessile Oak knowing that, this early in the year, it would have enough leaf cover for him to hide in. He found what he was looking for, close enough to the stables to be suitable for his purpose. Nimbly shinning up to a lower branch, he found a position with a good view of the yard and made himself comfortable. The couple were still talking when a slightly stout lady in a white coat joined them. Beyond her, a movement drew Piggybait's attention to a young man who was staring wide-eyed at the trio from behind a tall stack of straw bales at the other side of the yard. His curiosity aroused, Piggybait watched him as he stared fearfully at the policeman.

"I wonder what he's been up to," Piggybait said to himself. "You don't look that guilty unless you've done something wrong."

The man obviously wanted to avoid the group and darted behind the wall of the stable block. Although Piggybait watched for him to reappear, he did not see him again. A few moments after the anxious young man had left the scene, the trio broke up and the young woman, Briar limping alongside, headed off towards a group of stable workers.

A man whose daughter had been due to have a riding lesson complained loudly at being told by Alison Pembury that the lesson could not take place. His daughter wailed even more piercingly and stamped her foot in anger. Her father was somewhat placated when Alison pointed out the police officer and the woman in the white coat and she gave him his money back.

But his daughter was not to be so easily mollified and was dragged away emitting ear-splitting shrieks. Waiting until father and daughter had left the yard, Alison then went to speak to the four stable girls who were waiting for her instructions. After talking to them briefly she called the limping Briar to her side, then they both disappeared inside the office. The girls took the reins of one or two horses each and led them back to their stables where they removed the tack and bolted the lower half of the doors before gathering in a group waiting as though they were expecting something to happen.

Piggybait saw the policeman and the woman in the white coat talking and, closing his mind to all other sounds, concentrated his exceptional hearing on them.

"...no Izz, we're still no further on and, I can't help feeling we're missing something."

"Aye, an' I canna mind a time when there's been no wee bit o' evidence tae go on like this."

So they're still stuck for clues, thought Piggybait. It's a good job I'm here.

The policeman turned towards the trees where Piggybait was hiding, but swung round as two white police vans pulled into the stable yard. "Good, they're here."

Several policemen and their dogs got out of the vehicles. The dogs excited barking disturbed the horses and Piggybait now realised why they had been stabled. The men and dogs gathered in a circle around the Detective Sergeant.

"OK. Now you've all been briefed." DS Harte told them in a voice loud enough for the entire team to hear. "We've already searched the area but we're no nearer an answer than we were before. I want you to spread out around a mile or so from the stables and then move back in. Let's see if the dogs can pick anything up. Bag anything you find and give it to either Miss McKenzie or myself. She'll be staying here, but I'll be out with you. OK, let's go."

Leaving the yard, the handlers and dogs spread out through the trees, some of them passing right under the branch where Piggybait sat watching. One dog looked up as it passed and whined, but Piggybait put his fingers to his mouth. "Shusshhh."

The dog paused for a moment, tilting its head from side to side, but a gentle tug from its handler moved it on. After the group moved away, Piggybait, ensuring no-one could see him, slipped back to the ground. Taking the handkerchief out of his cap, he tucked it under a raised up tree root, then shimmied back up the tree to await the outcome. He made himself comfortable, resting his back against the trunk, and laughed as a

surprised squirrel almost bumped into him on its way back to its drey. Chattering shrilly, it scrambled higher up the tree and out of his way. It was a beautiful day, pleasantly warm, and without the usual activity in the stables, very quiet, the only sounds were birdsong, the buzzing of insects and the occasional far off barking of one of the police dogs. Piggybait's eyes felt agreeably heavy.

"So! Sleeping on the job, eh!"

"Whasss? Oh it's you."

Claptrap looked delighted at having caught Piggybait napping.

"What're you doing here?" Piggybait yawned.

"I thought you might be lonely and wanted to keep you company. I didn't expect to find you snoozing."

"I just shut my eyes for a minute. Wasn't asleep," Piggybait protested.

"Oh yes you were! I've been here an hour and you were snor…"

"Listen!" Piggybait interrupted.

The deep, throaty bark of an excited dog sounded quite nearby, quickly answered by another.

Piggybait pushed aside a small branch and spotted a dog and its handler, just a few metres away. "They're coming back. Let's hope they find the handkerchief."

"Where did you put it?"

"Just down there, under the roots."

"What! This tree?"

Piggybait nodded, gleefully.

Claptrap removed his monocle and peered down at the ground. Protruding from under a thick root, he spied the tip of the handkerchief.

"I suppose it had to be that close, did it?" Claptrap whispered, nervously watching the policeman and his dog walk by right below him.

"Of course. I didn't want to miss anything."

"Well, by Alfheim, you've taken a risk," he said, shrinking back against the wide tree-trunk. "Let's hope they don't find us too."

"It'll be fine. You worry too much."

The sound of cracking twigs and barking grew ever closer and, on seeing more returning policemen, the two elves moved a little higher where they would be better concealed. They watched the man and his dog enter the stable yard where the woman in the white coat looked at him hopefully.

"Anythin'?"

"No, nothing."

"Och, weel, there's a brew in the office an' that pair wee dog'll be wantin' some watter. Ah'm waitin' here the noo."

Another officer approached. He was struggling with a very excited dog that was panting heavily and pulling on its lead.

The woman laughed.

"Ye'll need tae get that young'un calmed doon a wee bit mair afore he's any real use, Andy."

"I know tha' Miz McKenzie, but 'e's still trainin'." The officer smiled fondly as the dog played tug of war with its lead. "Tis only 'is second toime out. 'E'll be alroight wi' more 'sperience. Anyway, where's tha' tea? My tongue's jest about stuck ter the roof of me mouth."

Isabel pointed to the office and chuckled as the patient handler walked away with the excitable young dog still tugging at his lead.

Two more officers, one with a dog, arrived at the yard and nodded to Isabel, closely followed by DS Harte. "What a waste of time, Izz!"

"Aye so it seems. Still there's a few mair to come in yet. Come on, John, I've been waitin' fer yeh to go for a brew."

They were followed towards the office by another officer and his dog who arrived just as they turned away. They were almost at the door when a shout halted them. John darted at full pelt back to the entrance.

"That'll be us havin' tae wait fer oor tea then!" Isabel McKenzie had no intention of running at her time of life, and took a much more sedate pace to see what all the noise was about. A dog was barking and jumping up at his handler as John approached. "What've you got, Phil?" The officer was putting something into a plastic bag.

"Yeah, well done Bruno, well done, boy," the policeman said, patting the delighted dog.

"It's a handkerchief, Guv. Bruno found it just in amongst the roots of that big oak over there." He pointed to the tree. Piggybait and Claptrap crouched low on the branch.

John knelt down and hugged the dog.

"I don't know if it's anything useful mind," Phil went on.

"At least it's something. We've had nothing else. Good boy, Bruno. Remind me to get you a doggie chew," John said, ruffling the dog's neck.

Isabel caught up with them, she was puffing. "You need exercise," John teased.

She threw him a scathing look. "Ok, what've we got?"

John held up the plastic bag to show her the dirt covered, grass stained white handkerchief. She stared at it for a moment and held it up to the light.

"Ah can see what looks like the remains o' embroidered initials. It could be quite a find ye ken." She went quiet for a moment. "John, ah've an idea. When the team's gone, I want tae try somethin'. Are yeh wi' me?"

John nodded as two more dog handlers returned to the yard.

"There's tea for you and water for the dogs at the office, fellas. Find anything?" John asked hopefully.

"No nothing, Guv," replied one of the officers. "Still, it beats doin' paperwork." They followed the others to the office.

"There's only two more of the guys to go, Izz. What're you up to?"

"Ye'll see when they're all away. Be patient." She winked at him and headed to the office, desperate for that cup of tea. Soon after, the search team were all accounted for and back in the vans ready to leave. John thanked them for their efforts, closed the van doors and banged on the side to let the drivers know the dogs were all safely in their cages and they were alright to start up. The vans left the yard leaving Isabel and John alone.

"Now then Izz, what are you up to?"

"Ah'll need Briar to have a sniff o' this. Ah'll no take it oot o' the bag 'cause o' contaminatin' the evidence, but wi' the bag open she may get enough o' the scent tae recognise it."

"I get it. If there's enough of the initials left to make anything out, we may have our man."

"Mah thoughts exactly. Yoor no sae daft airfter all!"

Alison smiled a welcome as John entered the office followed closely by Isabel. Isabel caught the fleeting look that passed between them. So that's the way of it, she thought. Aye, weel it's time he settled doon again.

"Alison, we've found something that may be of use in this enquiry," John explained, "we wanted to see if Briar recognises the scent on this handkerchief."

Alison looked sceptical. "Yes, yes I suppose so, if you think it'll work." She took the open bag to Briar's blanket bed under the desk, where the injured dog struggled to rise but once she was up, apart from the limp she moved quite easily. Alison held the bag close to her nose. "Here girl, take a sniff at this," she said, stroking Briar's head.

Her instant reaction took them all by surprise. The hair on Briar's neck stood upright, her ears went back, almost flat to her head, and she bared her teeth in a vicious snarl. Alison fell backwards in shock and John rushed forward to help her. But Briar growled and edged backwards away from the bag, clearly distressed.

"Briar!" Alison moved towards the frantic dog, but John held her back.

"Careful!"

"It's OK, she won't hurt me."

Alison called Briar's name, repeating it softly, moving closer step by step. Her gentle tone relaxed the dog and she crept back into her bed where she shudder until Alison moved close enough to stroke her, then she lay down, whimpering.

"She's alright now." Alison turned too John. "I don't know why she reacted like that but you've proved your point. I've never seen her behave that way before."

"Aye. Ah'm sorry we had tae dae it, Miss Pembury, but it's answered oor question. If your dog has nae reacted like that before, it stands tae reason she does nae like the scent an' it's my guess this belongs tae the pairson who hurt her. Ye get ma drift?"

"Aye. Sorry, I mean yes."

"Alison, we'll leave you to settle Briar down again, and I'm sorry we had to do this. I'll give you a ring tomorrow, if that's alright," John said, concerned about how badly Briar had reacted.

"Yes, of course, and don't worry, she'll be OK. She's calm now."

Isabel and John left the office and walked out into the sunlight.

"Well, what d'you make of that Izz?"

"Dinna call me Izz!"

"Yeah, yeah," John grinned. "So what now?"

"D'you ken what those initials look like to me John?"

He shook his head.

"Weel, if ye turn the bag on its side an' hold it up tae the light, you'll see what ah see."

John did as Isabel suggested. Holding the bag up to the sunlight he could see where initials had been embroidered, but the stitching had long since worn away. All that was left were tiny holes. He screwed up his eyes, and soon saw an outline of initials.

"No! This can't be right."

"Och ye see it, do yeh?"

"Yes, I see it, but I don't believe it. It looks like 'JJA', but that's not possible."

"Aye, it's nae possible, but it canna be anythin' else. Ah'll need a saliva swab from the Atkins boy tae confirm it, but I think oor intruder was the late Jeremiah Atkins."

"But Atkins is dead...the cave-in...at Christmas!"

"Aye mebbe so, but remember, there was nae body found an' that pair wee dog only moved here airfter. She'd never met Atkins, neether had she ever reacted like that afore today. Ah'm convinced she reacted tae the scent of the pairson who hurt her an' Alison. Airfter all this time, all we needed tae dae was ask the dog."

"But how? Why?"

"Och! Ah dinna have all the answers. That's your job. Mah gut feelin' is that Atkins was hidin' here an' got caught oot, but yeh'll need tae find oot why. Ah'm off tae the big hoose to see the laddie."

"What are you going to say when they ask why?"

"Ah'll think o' somethin'"

John scratched his head. "I don't know how I'm going to explain this back at headquarters."

"Och, dinna fash yersel'. Ye'll think o' somethin' too."

From their oak tree hideout, Piggybait and Claptrap watched them leave.

"Yes! It worked!" Piggybait declared. They slapped each other's right hands in a 'high five' salute.

"They'll find him soon and it'll be one less problem for us." Claptrap said, as they climbed down from the tree. "Jerrill can relax a little now. One down, one to go."

Chapter Fifteen

A car drove slowly onto Winterne Manor land by a small back road beyond the stables. Malcolm Farrow knew luck was with him when he found this small lane. He had one heart-stopping moment when a security light flashed on as the car glided by the stables, but no-one appeared, so he continued unheard and unnoticed, to a rough track behind the cottages. He took a good look around before stopping. Considering the amount of police activity in the area, he was fortunate to have got this far undetected.

Satisfied the car was well hidden from the lane and cottages he opened the door, got out and looked around, listening carefully, but all he heard was the hoot of an owl. Softly clicking the door shut, he took a pen-like torch from his pocket, turned it on and checked his watch. It was five minutes to midnight.

Reassured no-one was about and the nearby cottages were in darkness, he decided it was safe enough to go ahead as planned. Earlier, in his shabby room at a small motorway services hotel, he had chosen his clothes carefully; black jeans, black polo neck sweater and hat, and packed them in a bag intending to change somewhere quiet, somewhere he would not be seen.

Finding a suitable spot in a lay-by close to the woods, he made a quick-change and stared at his reflection in the rear-view mirror, steeling himself for the job ahead. Casting a final look around, he cautiously left the cover of the trees and crossed the lane, following the line of the tall hedge, his breathing shallow; his heart beating so fast he could hear the pulse in his head.

Finding a spot where the hedge was weak, he forced his way through to the lawned area that led up to the house. The night was cool with a big pale moon and, if he had taken the time to notice, Malcolm Farrow might have appreciated what a beautiful night it was, but he had more urgent things on his mind.

There were still lights on at the Manor, so he kept close to the surrounding hedge or stayed low as he ran between the trees. On his visits to the house, he had only been through the front door, but suspected he might find a weak spot in security at the back, and was about to put his theory to the test. If he could just get inside, he might be able to find what he needed to get hold of Jerry's diamonds. After all, he reasoned, Jerry had no use for them now, and his widow knew nothing about them, so why shouldn't he, an old friend and colleague who was now in trouble, have the benefit of them, rather than leaving them forgotten in a bank. He knew where they were. He just needed the box number and the key for them to be his.

In the back garden, concealed amongst the shrubbery, he crept to the back door, watching the windows where lights still showed. From the cover of the bushes, he skulked between a large maple and a weeping willow, diving within its trailing branches when a dog barked inside the house. The sound seemed to come from a room at the right hand corner of the house and, sure enough, the curtains at a window opened and a young woman looked out. She opened the window and leaned out to look around.

"You silly dog, Wilmot."

The head of a dog appeared beside her at the window. It barked again, more insistently.

"Come on. Get down! You'll scratch the windowsill with your claws. There's nothing there, see. Are you satisfied now?"

The dog disappeared and he heard the young woman say, "It's probably an owl and nothing to worry about." The window closed and the curtains were closed again.

Farrow, the blood thumping in his temples, waited until all was quiet before skirting the bushes, until there was only moonlit lawn between him and the house. He crouched low and scuttled to the back door.

"Damn!" His theory was wrong. The door was secured by a mortise lock which he could not pick. In frustration, he kicked out at the wall, but only succeeded in hurting his foot. Leaning against the wall, he rubbed his sore toes, visualising the inside of the house, trying to find an alternative to his failed scheme. He paced up and down, alternately swearing at the pain and the Atkins family. It was then he discovered the larder window. It was not big by any means, but, at a push, he guessed he could wriggle through. It appeared to be single-glazed and the frame was worn and rotten in places. Maybe his luck was in after all. Taking a brown leather pouch out of his pocket, he chose a small chisel-like tool, but before sliding the tool between the window and the frame, he turned on the torch and shone the beam around the window looking for burglar alarm wiring. He saw nothing. Forcing the implement into the crack between the wood surround and the frame, he tried to prise the window open. Nothing happened. He tried again, but only managed to splinter a small piece of the frame.

114

"Damn!"

Praying no-one had heard the noise of the wood breaking, he stopped and listened. No-one appeared. Again the chisel slid into the wood. He pushed. This time, with a horrible cracking sound, a chunk of the frame broke away. The dog barked again and Farrow huddled close to the wall. He heard the girl telling the dog to be quiet. As Farrow examined the damage, his hopes were shattered. The window needed no electronic security. It had a metal grille across it that would stop anyone breaking through. What a waste of time this night had been! From the woods a night bird called. It sounded to Farrow as if it was laughing at him.

"If I wasn't so bloody annoyed, I'd laugh too!" He snapped bitterly, before retreating into the shelter of the trees, his objective thwarted. Having no reason to remain, Farrow wanted to get away fast. Still aware he was trespassing, he remained cautious as he headed back to his car. He would have a lot of explaining to do if he was discovered, especially dressed the way he was. He found the gap in the hedge, squeezed through and pushed the two ends together to hide the break. In daylight someone would notice it, but by then he would be long gone. Someone was bound to see the damage done to the window as well. Moving warily, watching and listening for signs of life, he jumped as an owl hooted from somewhere nearby. He crossed the lane and plunged into the undergrowth, fishing in his pocket for his car keys. He reached the car, put the key into the door when he sensed a movement behind him that made the hair on the back of his neck stand up. A shudder ran down his spine. When he heard the voice, his blood turned to ice.

"Malcolm, what are you doing here?"

He knew who it was instinctively, even though the voice was harsh and grating. A master of the art of deception for a number of years, Farrow formed his features into a look of delighted surprise and turned to face a 'ghost'.

"Jerry! How wonderful," he lied through gritted teeth. "You're alive. I heard you were dead!"

Even in the pale moonlight Farrow could see the terrible condition his former partner was in. His thin, ravaged face appeared spectral and gaunt. "But you don't look at all well, my old mate."

"Oh, don't let a little weight loss fool you, Malcolm." Atkins gave a hoarse chuckle. "I'm still *fighting* fit." Farrow thought that sounded like a threat and desperately wanted to get away, but Atkins blocked his way. Jerry, however, seemed in no hurry to move.

"Well, we really must catch up sometime soon, but I really must go. It was good to see you," Farrow said, just a little too cheerily.

"Oh, Malcolm, must you go so soon," Atkins growled. "We've only just

met up again and, there's so much catching up to do."

Atkins moved closer. Farrow felt sick. "After all these years, how strange to find you here at Winterne?"

"Just a courtesy call on your nearest and dearest, old mate," Farrow lied, his voice shook. "I read your obituary and wanted to pay my respects. Nothing sinister,"

Atkins moved closer. In the moonlight, Farrow could see cold bitter hatred reflected in his eyes. "Don't give me that, you slimeball!" Atkins spat. "You're after something! It's a bit late for social calls and what are you wearing? Fancy dress, is it? Come as your friendly neighbourhood burglar." He was now just a metre away from Farrow whose palms grew clammy with fear. His mouth was so dry it felt as it was full of cotton wool.

"I saw you call on my wife. Now, what could you possibly be after?"

"No, no you…"

"No, no, I what?" Atkins spat. "Just shut up, I need to think this out." Atkins paused, walking around Farrow's car. "You and I haven't seen each other for years, so you'll have no idea what I'd been working on since we parted company." He stopped to look at Farrow. "Am I right so far? Please feel free to correct me any time you want." Atkins gave a bitter gravelly laugh and continued pacing the length of the car and back, never taking is eyes off his adversary. The moon emerged from behind a cloud giving his face a ghoulish appearance.

"Yes," Farrow replied weakly.

"So logically, you're interested in something from before we split. Am I right?"

"Yes, um…no. But…" Farrow looked around for an escape route.

Atkins held up a hand. "It was rhetorical! I didn't actually expect you to correct me and I'd rather you didn't interrupt. That was always a bad habit of yours as I recall." He took a pace to the left, turned and walked a few steps to the right, then stopped in front of Farrow.

"I also recall we split the money and the property from our venture equally, so technically you should be quite well-off. I take it that's not the case?"

"No Jerry, I…"

"You need money?"

"Er…yes."

"Well as I'm legally dead I can't give you any and there's little likelihood Harriet would. She doesn't know you from Adam, so you'd have to steal it. All correct, yes?"

"Yes. Well no...not to begin with." Farrow gave a nervous giggle. "I thought I could make her believe I have a right to a fifty percent share of the diamonds, that we made the investment together."

The flash of a toothy smile caught Farrow off guard before Atkins rounded on him.

"Harriet's not that stupid! She wouldn't play ball would she?" Atkins gave a gruff chuckle that ended in a throaty, rasping cough. "If she had you wouldn't be skulking around here at night, dressed like a comedy burglar and anyway you'll get nothing. A half share...of *my* diamonds! You're mad! You put nothing in. *It was my money, not yours! I paid!* And I'm still paying," he added quietly. Atkins stared at the ground and shook his head sadly, before turning back to his one-time partner. "You get nothing, understand...nothing." His voice was heavy with contempt. "Just get out of here."

"But Jerry, I need to get out of the country in a hurry. The Benson brothers are..."

"Ha! Now we get to it. The Benson's! Well, not my problem my old mate! Your problem! Now go...leave my family alone. D'you understand?" He poked Farrow hard in the chest, pushing him back against his car. For all his wasted appearance, he was still surprisingly strong. "Now get in your car and go, before I do something I won't regret."

"Before I do Jerry, I have to know. How did you get out of the cave? Everyone thought you'd died in there."

Atkins gave a low chuckle. "Oh yes, my...resurrection."

Farrow leaned against the car door.

"It had all been planned so precisely, down to the last detail. Nothing should've gone wrong." Even in the dim light, Farrow saw a wild look in Atkins eyes. He looked unstable.

"They thought they'd fool me, but I saw the way things were going with those wasters. The boy, Mikey's brother, was useless and scared. I should never have taken him on. He was a weak link." Atkins seemed to be talking to himself, almost as if he had forgotten Farrow was there. "They were all jumpy," Atkins continued. "I knew I couldn't trust them, any of them...not even Jake. Mikey poisoned him against me...even Mikey let me down," his voice cracked.

While Atkins was talking, Farrow's right hand reached slowly behind him to the car door handle; if he could just get it open. But Atkins had seen. With a sudden lunge, Atkins slammed the door shut. Farrow froze, but Atkins went on talking as if nothing had happened. "That first night I went to the cottage, I made a stop on the way at the tunnels where they would be working and set explosives in case anything went wrong. I knew those tunnels inside and out." Atkins teeth flashed white in the moonlight, as he gave a cold smile. "D'you remember, in the old days, I never got into anything I couldn't get out of, did I? Well I found a pothole, it ended in a massive cave with a small lake at the bottom. The water flowed out from there under the rocks. This pothole came out above a ledge that sloped all the way down to ground level and I could get out through the stream entrance. It was very good escape route." Although he faced Farrow, he seemed to look straight through him. "So I was ready when they turned against me. Everyone thought I used the dynamite they'd brought with them, but no…I was already at the other end of the pothole when I remotely blew the second charge. I was nowhere near when it happened. Clever eh?"

Farrow nodded his head vigorously.

"So, just as I planned, everyone believed I was dead and buried under the rocks. There was no way I was going to prison. I'd planned to get to the cottage, take the silver and disappear but that's when things went wrong. When I got there the Police were already there."

"And now you're back for the diamonds?"

"Correct! That means I get them, you don't. Time to leave, old friend," Atkins said, sarcastically.

He opened the car door and tried to push Farrow inside, but Farrow caught him off guard, landing a hard blow on Atkins left cheekbone, cutting the skin. Atkins stumbled backwards and Farrow, taking advantage of surprise, flew at him. They crashed to the ground grappling and punching, their battle vicious and brutal as they rolled around the dirt track. Farrow was taken by surprise at Atkins strength, considering his condition, and it dawned on him he was losing the fight. Summoning up all his strength, he forced Atkins off him, managed to get up and made a dash for the car. But Atkins was right behind him and a hard rugby tackle brought Farrow down, pinning him to the ground. Atkins eyes radiated a cold malevolence in the soft moonlight.

"I spent too many wasted years damaging my family and it's only now, now I can't go back, I finally understand what they mean to me," he panted, "but it's too late for me now. And you…you're going nowhere near them. You'll leave Winterne right now or by God you'll have worse than the Benson brothers to worry about."

Farrow nodded, terror in his eyes. "Yeah, OK I'll go. Don't worry Jerry. Let me up and I'll leave, I won't ever come back." He knew Jerry meant every word.

After a moment, Atkins got up and stood back to let Farrow get to his feet. He wiped his bleeding cheek with his hand. He was still looking at the smeared blood on his hand when Farrow, using the advantage of surprise, clasped his hands tightly together and lunged at Atkins with a double handed punch to the side of his head. Atkins fell, pole-axed, to the ground. Farrow grinned.

"That'll teach you not to watch your enemy," he snarled. Before turning away to his car, he took a last look at Atkins still lying on the track. He started up the engine and began reversing towards the lane. Without warning Atkins threw himself at the driver's door, trying to stop Farrow getting away, but Farrow drove on, Atkins overbalanced and slid to the muddy ground. A few metres away, Farrow stopped the car. He looked in his rear view mirror at his enemy who was struggling to his feet. Farrow knew he had to end it, tonight. "No more Jerry. No more."

Putting the car into reverse, Farrow drove at speed directly at Atkins who had just managed to stand up. Seeing the car hurtling towards him, he twisted out of the way but, his foot caught in a rut and, as the car hit him he fell with a hideous thud, cracking his temple against a large rock as the car reversed over him. Farrow stopped the car and stared at the motionless body in the road ahead of him, feeling strangely detached, his breathing rapid and shallow.

In the dark silence, he thought he heard a groan. He panicked. Putting the car in gear and his foot hard on the accelerator, he drove at speed over Atkins' body again, ignoring the bump and the crunch of bone. It was not until he was a few miles along the road that it dawned on him the groan may have been in his imagination. Sickened, he disappeared into the night.

At the precise moment Jeremiah Atkins died, Wilmot howled balefully. It took Meredith almost thirty minutes to quieten him, but he trembled for most of the night.

Chapter Sixteen

Thursday morning arrived bright and beautiful, promising warmth and sunshine. Meredith's bedroom window was slightly open allowing in the fresh air and a jubilant dawn chorus of birdsong that eventually awoke her. Wilmot was sleeping soundly in his bed near the door, his paws occasionally twitching as he chased dream rabbits.

After the upset of the previous night, Meredith was worried about how he would be this morning, but he seemed to be himself again. When he had howled so pitifully the previous night, she thought he might have been in pain and had been about to call the vet, but the lament ceased as suddenly as it had begun, taking them all by surprise. Harriet's rooms and Marjorie's bedroom were too far away for the sound to have disturbed them, but, Jonah, closely followed by Dorothy a few minutes later, had arrived to see what was going on. Mystified by Wilmot's behaviour, they tried everything they could think of to calm him down. Meredith found his favourite ball, which he had hidden underneath a chair, Dorothy rushed down to the kitchen for doggie chews and Jonah tried rubbing his belly and shaking his paw. Eventually distracted, Wilmot sloped away to his bed where he stayed, quietly shivering in his sleep, for most of the night.

After Jonah and Dorothy had gone, Meredith eventually fell asleep and slept surprisingly well. Having reassured herself that Wilmot was none the worse for his ordeal, she turned sleepily and watched the specks of dust floating in the sun's rays as they came through the gap in her curtains. Wilmot opened one eye lazily and scratched an ear with a back paw.

"Morning Wilmot. You'll be tired this morning."

He yawned and flicked his tail a couple of times in a sluggish sort of wag by way of reply, but Meredith decided to keep a close eye on him during the day. She looked at her alarm clock. It was only six o'clock, but it was too beautiful a morning to waste.

"OK, lazy. It's time we were up."

Swinging her legs out of bed, she put on her dressing gown and went to the window. Wilmot stood and stretched his legs, before padding across to the window where he jumped up and rested his front legs on the window sill, watching the birds as they flew close to the house. He wagged his tail excitedly, turning his head from side to side, giving snuffling little woofs. Meredith watched him and, to her great relief, thought that he seemed to be his old, cheerful self.

"No, you can't chase the birds but I think we could do with a walk so we'll go and fetch the papers. I'll be ready in a few minutes."

By her reckoning, she could pick up the papers from the village shop, get back, feed Wilmot, shower, grab a cup of tea and a slice of toast, and still be at the stables by seven o'clock. That meant she would have time to check on Celeste before going to the office and still get a good start on the day.

"Right, so that's the plan," she told Wilmot as he dropped back down onto the floor.

Ten minutes later she emerged from her bathroom in a tee-shirt and jogging bottoms, and her hair tied back in a ponytail. She reached under the bed for a pair of trainers and after tying up the laces, took out a hooded sweatshirt from her wardrobe, putting it on as she headed for the door where Wilmot waited expectantly. She picked up his lead from on top of a chest of drawers and put it in her pocket.

"OK, let's go!"

Wilmot barked.

"Shhhhh! You daft animal! Dorothy and Jonah are still asleep."

Darting through the door ahead of her, Wilmot scampered down the steps and had disappeared before she reached the red-carpeted landing. He was waiting for her, wagging his tail eagerly, between the suits of armour as she went down the stairs.

"Alright, alright I'm coming. Don't nag."

As she reached the bottom of the stairs, he scuttled off towards the front door impatient to get outside. The air was clean with a fresh crispness and Meredith smiled with delight on seeing butterflies and bees for the first time since winter. It was a glorious day and she felt glad to be alive as she jogged down the long driveway with Wilmot running alongside. At the end of the drive she pressed a button on the honey coloured stone gatepost and waited for the electronic gates to open. With a click they glided apart while Meredith reached down to attach Wilmot's lead to his collar.

"Got to keep you safe on the road, haven't we?"

The walk into the village was quiet, just as she had expected it to be at this time of the morning. She waved to Frank Perkins, the postman as he drove by and caught sight of Dr Brownlow heading towards his surgery, but he did not see her. At the village store, Mrs Jenks' collie and her strange, but beautiful cat sat outside waiting patiently. Merlin edged away as the cat, sneakily, edged closer. Mrs Jenks was obviously inside and the cat was taking the opportunity to tease. Merlin stood up as Meredith tied Wilmot's lead to a metal ring in the wall, and the dogs eyed each other suspiciously. Wilmot's hackles stood up stiffly, but Bandit remained completely unruffled and moved between them, his tail twitching crossly. Meredith was so enthralled by the interaction between the animals, she was completely unaware of Mrs Jenks standing behind her, watching and waiting for the outcome. For a few seconds the cat out-stared the dogs, first one then the other. Then, as if obeying a silent command, both dogs lay down and ignored each other. Mrs Jenks smiled at the grey cat indulgently.

"Merlin always does as Bandit tells him. I see he has the same effect on your Wilmot."

Meredith jumped and, scarcely believing what she had seen, was lost for words. But then anything was possible when Mrs Jenks was around. After apologising for startling her, Mrs Jenks said goodbye and Meredith watched as, first the dog then the cat, fell in line behind the very upright elderly lady and headed across the green.

A few minutes later, as they walked home with the newspapers a jeep drove up behind them and braked. Meredith smiled at the driver, a large man with collar length grey hair and a bushy grey beard.

"Ow's it goin', m'dear?"

"Good, thanks Charlie. Isn't it a lovely morning!"

Wilmot jumped up at the door of the jeep and seemed to smile as he stared into the big man's kindly face.

"It's a good'un. It'll be loike this fer a few days yet, but we're due fer some spring rain." He looked up at the clear blue sky.

"You know that for definite do you, Charlie?"

"I've 'ad it on very good authority, Meredith. The woodland folk 'ave told me."

Meredith smiled. She had heard Charlie speak of the little people who lived in the woods before and she, like others locally, indulged Charlie in his little fantasies. He was a nice old man, always willing to help anyone who needed it, very knowledgeable about the woods and local wildlife completely harmless. So what if he was a bit eccentric?

"Nice to see you Charlie. Give my love to Cathy, and can you tell her mum wants to speak to her about a mural she'd like to have on the wall in the new nursery, if Cathy's got the time that is."

"Oi certainly will. Give our regards ter yer mum an' all. See you soon m'dear." Meredith smiled at him as the engine rattled into life. But, quite unexpectedly, his expression changed and he looked at her with eyes full of pain, almost as if he had just heard some terrible news. She shuddered.

"If you need any 'elp," he said gravely, "if there's anythin' Oi can do, you jest gi' me a call. Cathy an' me'll be there fer you if you need us." It sounded like a warning.

"Thanks, Charlie, but I'm fine," Meredith replied, now a little frightened and confused.

"Oh I know, but jest don' you ferget m'dear, we're 'ere if you need us." He drove away leaving her with a feeling of impending trouble, as if a dark shadow had come between her and the sun. Wilmot whined and tilted his head to one side questioningly.

"Oh, come on boy. The sun's still out, the sky's blue. It doesn't look any different now than it did a few minutes ago, so I'm not giving in to imaginary misgivings."

At the Manor gates, she had just pressed the button on the side of the gate post again, when another vehicle slowed down and stopped.

"Hi Meredith. How are you?" Dan Hedges, the vet, stepped out of his car and walked towards her, smiling. She liked his smile. It made her feel better. Wilmot, clearly delighted to see him, wagged his tail wildly, bounding around the young man. Dan was very tall (he towered over Meredith) and so thin, people said a puff of wind would blow him over. He had an angular face with slightly crooked front teeth, which only added to the charm of his friendly smile, and his mop of pale blond hair fell across his deep set blue eyes. He brushed it away.

"I'm fine, but something was wrong with Wilmot last night. He began the strangest howling that went on for ages. I almost called you out, but then he stopped and seems OK now. So how are you? Where are you off to?"

Dan crouched down and felt around Wilmot's head and neck and opened his mouth to look at his teeth and throat.

"Well, he seems OK but if it happens again pop down to the surgery or give me a call, anytime."

He said the last word looking directly into her eyes making her blush. There was an awkward silence for a moment, before Dan recovered the situation.

"Umm…I'm on my way over to Ben Bragg's. One of his pigs isn't eating and then I'm seeing Briar again. You're up and about early aren't you?"

"It was such a lovely morning I thought I'd get the papers then sort myself out and make an early start at the stables." She looked at her watch. "But seeing the time now I think I'm going to head straight up to the stables. Jonah can collect the papers from me later."

"So you'll be there for the rest of the morning then?"

"Oh yes, at least until mid-afternoon."

123

"Right. I'll stop by for a coffee after I've seen Briar. It should be a bit quieter then."

Meredith smiled. The day had just brightened up again. "Fine. I'll see you later."

Dan waved as he drove away, and Meredith watched him go from inside the gates. She removed Wilmot's lead and let him run free until he reached the bend in the driveway where he stopped and waited for her, unsure which way to go, home or stables?

"Stables, Wilmot, stables," Meredith commanded.

Wilmot bounded up the lane that would take him by the cottages and on to the stables and farm buildings. He was a good few yards ahead of Meredith and quite close to the cottage where Arthur and Gwen Sykes lived, when he came to an abrupt halt. He howled loudly and his hackles rose stiffly. Meredith, thinking this was a recurrence of his problem the night before, ran to him. Wilmot did not move. His howl became a whimper as he stared at a heap of old clothes lying close to the grass verge.

As Meredith moved nearer, a cold fear clenched her stomach and she forced her unwilling feet to move. She already knew what she was about to see, but prayed she was wrong. She didn't notice the newspapers slip out of her hand onto the muddy lane. Wilmot crawled, low to the ground, very close by, making snuffling, whimpering noises.

Horrified, she realised it was the body of a man. His head was turned away from her, the face obscured by a large rock. Her first thought was to turn him over, but she could not bring herself to touch him. Her stomach churned, her head spun, she fell to her knees and retched. After a moment the spasm ended and she staggered to her feet not knowing what to do next. She had to get help! Forcing her reluctant feet to move she fled to the nearby Sykes' cottage, Wilmot running alongside, never taking his eyes off her, he seemed to understand it was not a game this time. Shouting and banging on the door, she almost collapsed when Arthur opened the door.

"Why Miss Meredith! Wha's the toodoo?"

"Arthur, call the Police. There's a b-body in the lane…over there." She pointed a shaking hand in the general direction.

"A body! Whose? You sure?"

"Yes, I'm sure. It's a…man…I can't look. Please Arthur, phone the Police."

"Yeah…yeah, it's alright…Oi'll call 'em. You jest get yerself insoide."

Meredith, leaned against the wall in the hallway, Wilmot followed, not leaving her side and Gwen, hearing the commotion from the sitting room, helped Meredith into the cosy sitting room and settled her in an armchair.

"You poor dear. You jest sit yerself' down 'ere an' Oi'll mek you a noice cup of sweet tea. Nasty shock you've 'ad. Them Police'll be 'ere in

a minute. You jest sit down there quietly."

Wilmot trembled as he lay on the floor close to Meredith, his head on her feet. After finishing the telephone call, Arthur disappeared. Meredith was vaguely aware of his voice in the hall, but paid no attention. She just stared blankly out of the window. Gwen hovered closely nearby, concerned at the girl's vacant expression. She waited for Arthur to come back, and soon heard a siren someway off, the sound grew louder as it approached. Arthur appeared in the doorway and beckoned to Gwen. Keeping a worried eye on Meredith, who was still staring, unblinkingly, ahead, Gwen joined her husband in the hall.

"What is it?" She kept her voice low.

"I jest 'ad a look at that body. You ain't never gunna believe this." He peered around the doorway to see if Meredith was listening, but she was absent-mindedly stroking Wilmot and in no state to pay them any attention.

"What? Don' keep me in suspense."

"Well you'll think Oi'm goin' daft, but Oi'm telling' yer that body is Jeremiah Atkins."

"Can't be you old fool! You bin on the cider agen? 'E's already dead, everyone knows that."

Arthur rolled his eyes. "Yeah. Well we all know tha', 'cept mebbe no-one told 'im."

A car pulled up outside the cottage. The driver got out and walked towards the corpse. Kneeling down, he pulled the body towards him slightly to see the face. Arthur saw the doctor's look of disbelief as he stood up. He shook his head as he walked over to join them.

"Better let Meredith know the Doc's 'ere, Gwen, an' come ter think on it, you'd better gi' 'er mother a call an' all. She still don't know wha's 'appened do she?"

As Dr Brownlow entered the room, Wilmot left Meredith's side and padded over to the small, grey-haired man, then returned with the doctor following. Gwen and Arthur watched from the doorway.

"Meredith, I came here to help the police, but I told them I was going to see you first. I didn't want anyone asking you any questions until I was sure you were able to cope. How are you, my dear?" The local GP, Dr Brownlow had known Meredith most of her life. He always talked about retiring, but kept putting it off because he could never trust anyone else to look after his patients as well as he did.

Meredith gave him a shaky smile. She looked deathly pale. "Oh I'm OK, Doctor. It was just such a horrible shock."

"Yes, it must be. I'm so sorry you had to be the one who found him. It's awful for you."

Arthur coughed a warning, shook his head slightly to signal the doctor not to say any more. Dr Brownlow gave Arthur a puzzled look. "You'd be better at home, Meredith, amongst your family."

Gwen moved over to help Meredith up, while Dr Brownlow joined Arthur in the hall. They walked towards the still open front door, their voices low.

"I thought she knew, but I take it that's not the case?"

"Thass roight, Doc. Seems she never looked too closely loike, an' it weren't till she were inside I took a look fer meself. Roight shock it were too, I can tell yer."

"I can imagine but you look a bit peeky yourself, Arthur, are you OK?"

"Me! No, Oi'm alright. No need ter worry 'bout me, I seen worse than this afore. You jest tek care o' that poor girl."

Two police cars sped up the lane and braked sharply, coming to a halt close to the cottage.

"'Bout toime they got 'ere," Arthur muttered.

Two uniformed officers stepped from the first car and made straight for the body, while Ernie Rogers and a plain clothes officer emerged from the second. The plain clothes officer walked towards the doctor and the old man.

"That's Detective Sergeant Harte," Dr Brownlow whispered to Arthur. "I met him the other night, at the stables."

"You don' think this 'as anything' to do wi' that do yer?"

John Harte joined them before the doctor could answer. "Hiya Doc. What d'you make of this, then?"

"No idea, John," the doctor replied.

"Beats me," said the old man.

"John, this is Arthur Sykes. Mr Sykes recognised the body. The deceased's daughter's inside. She found him, but didn't see his face, and we haven't told her."

The detective nodded gravely. From the doorway, the three watched as a cordon of yellow plastic ribbons was hastily arranged around the dead man. John's force radio crackled into life.

"Tango Four. What have you got?"

Arthur leaned closer to the policeman, but was unable to make out much. His hearing was not what it used to be, and static did not make eavesdropping any easier.

"That's interesting," John commented.

Arthur and Dr Brownlow exchanged looks. Arthur shrugged. The doctor nodded, unable to understand very much either. The only thing he heard for sure was "*BMW*" and "*Cairnstow.*"

"OK, we're on our way. Has anyone notified Isabel's team yet?" A voice answered over the buzzing.

"Good! Get the car picked up and bring it in. Any idea who it's registered to?"

Dr Brownlow clearly heard the name, '*Foster*'.

A third car drove slowly towards them, and stopped behind the other two police cars. A tall, balding man in a dark raincoat and carrying a well-worn trilby hat emerged from the passenger seat. He hunkered down to examine the scene for a moment, then stood up, saw John Harte with Dr Brownlow and walked over to join them. John made the introductions. "Arthur Sykes, this is DCI Cromwell. Guv, this is Arthur Sykes, he lives here. You know Doc Brownlow, of course,"

"Yes, hello David, good to see you again," the DCI said, "Dr Brownlow and I are old friends, John. I thought I'd get involved with this one myself as there's been so much activity here recently. Our friend here," he pointed his thumb towards the body, "would have some explaining to do if he could."

"It's come as a complete shock to all of us." Dr Brownlow replied. "Look Tony, Meredith Atkins is inside, she still doesn't know who it is, even though she found him. OK to take her home?"

"Yes, of course, but she doesn't know? Didn't she recognise her own father?"

"Poor lass weren't there long enough to look," Arthur cut in. "An' Oi weren't gunna tell 'er."

The senior detective nodded gravely.

"Has her family been told anything yet?" Dr Brownlow asked the Detective Chief Inspector.

"Only that a body's been found and we're shutting off the lane for forensics. There's some fresh tyre tracks and we'll need to get an impression, amongst other things. If you want to take her home, you'd better do it now, before the team get here. She won't want to be here then and the lane will be closed for a couple of days, at least."

"A couple o' days!" Arthur protested. "Ow am I ter get ter the village if your lot's closed the lane?"

"Sorry Mr…"

"Sykes," John reminded him.

"Yes, Mr Sykes. As I was saying, sorry but it can't be helped. I'm sure you can use the back road."

"Well, yeah. I suppose so, but it ain't so quick, 'specially on these ol' legs."

"Don't worry, Arthur." Dr Brownlow cut in. "The police won't take any longer than necessary." He turned to the senior detective. "I take it you'll be calling at the Manor soon Tony, so I'll wait with the family until you get there. It should really be the Police who break the news. They'll be looking for answers. Do you have any?"

DCI Cromwell shook his head. "No, not yet. Who does? It's beyond me! But, yes, I'll be up soon, I just need to sort things out here. I'll be along in about half an hour."

Minutes later, Dr Brownlow helped a shaken Meredith out of the cottage to his car. Wilmot trailing along behind, jumped on to the back seat of the car the instant Dr Brownlow opened the door. He lay down quietly, his head on his paws. Meredith averted her eyes as they drove by the body, now screened behind a police car. She gave an involuntary shudder and turned to the doctor. Tears seeped from her closed lids and slowly trickled down her face.

"Doctor Brownlow?"

"Yes my dear?"

"Why did my father have to die twice? Didn't we go through enough the first time?"

Dr Brownlow braked so hard that, even at that slow speed, only the seat belts prevented them from hitting the dashboard. "We thought you didn't know."

"Did you think I wouldn't recognise my own father?" she said in a far-away voice. "He didn't look the same, but I knew."

"Oh, my poor girl, what a shock! And just as you've come to terms with....with...it all...come on, let's get you home. You need your family at a time like this. You'll need each other."

Just as the doctor's car reached the end of the lane and turned into the driveway, two small figures emerged from behind the hedge.

"I hadn't anticipated this," Piggybait said, watching the car disappear around the corner

"I know you hadn't. I hope our...or rather, your interference didn't make things worse."

"Thanks Claptrap! All I was trying to do was make sure he got caught," Piggybait retorted angrily. "I thought the police would get him. What I did couldn't possibly have affected the outcome!"

Visibly outraged, Piggybait barged through the hedge with Claptrap following meekly behind, clearly regretting not choosing his words more carefully. "Well, all I meant was..."

Piggybait spun round. "Yes...and just what did you mean? We know Atkins was no good. We know he should already be dead but he wasn't. He even fooled us and we're supposed to know everything that happens here. We now know he faked his death, and destiny has a habit of catching up with people who try and play tricks with it. *That* has nothing to do with me...us!"

Claptrap shrank back. "Sorry Piggs. I suppose I'm a bit upset with him dying like that...again. I mean that poor girl. You have to feel sorry for her."

Piggybait calmed down. "I do feel for her. I feel for all of them, even the boy, but someone else caught up with him and I'm guessing it was the other man that Rondo saw. I'm sure he's responsible for this and he's got to be stopped before he causes more trouble. Come on, Jerrill and the others don't know what's happened. There'll be even more police activity around here now. Oh, I'm glad this isn't around Christmas time. With so much activity, maybe we should stop the night patrol." Piggybait continued mumbling as they headed into the shelter of the undergrowth. "Oh, and by the way, you're forgiven."

Chapter Seventeen

About forty minutes later, DCI Cromwell arrived at Winterne Manor. Getting out of the car, he stood for a moment absorbing the now faded grandeur of the magnificent building.

"How the other half live eh?" he muttered.

A young, dark haired man was already at the open front door. The Detective Chief Inspector noticed he appeared ill at ease, but police officers used to this reaction when a suspicious death was being investigated.

"DCI Cromwell to see Mrs Atkins, she's expecting me."

"Yes, she is," the young man answered stiffly. "The family's in the study, follow me please." He seemed to be avoiding eye contact and in an apparent haste to get away.

"Don't I know you?" the detective asked. "What's your name? I'll need it for my report."

"It's Seymour, sir, Stuart Seymour and no, I don't think we've met before, sir," Stuart answered politely, but the DCI made a mental note to check on him later. "The family are in here, sir." Stuart opened the door and stood back to let the policeman in.

DCI Cromwell was convinced he heard a sigh of relief, as the door banged shut behind him.

Harriet was standing by the window, staring out into the garden when the door opened, her stance tense, shoulders high. Meredith was sitting on a cream sofa sobbing softly into a handful of tissues and a woman, very like Harriet Atkins but a little older, was sitting beside her, her arm around her shoulders. On the opposite sofa, a morose dark haired boy, in his early teens, sat cuddling a dalmatian dog, who growled at the arrival of the newcomer. Dr Brownlow was standing by the fireplace, his expression grave. He looked relieved at the Detective Chief Inspector's arrival.

"David! I'm glad you're still here," the DCI said, reaching out to shake his hand. Harriet Atkins moved towards the doctor.

"Harriet, this is Detective Chief Inspector Anthony Cromwell," Dr

Brownlow began.

"Yes, I know." Harriet reached out to shake the policeman's hand. "We met after a talk the Detective Chief Inspector gave a couple of years ago at Jonah's school and it's a shame we have to meet again under these circumstances."

DCI Cromwell studied Harriet for a moment, surprised at her composure. He recalled hearing of her reclusive reputation and expected someone much more fragile.

"Please sit down Detective Chief Inspector."

"Thank you Mrs Atkins. Unfortunately, I have some bad news for you."

"It's alright, we know it was Jerry. Meredith told us she knew who it was immediately. What we don't understand is how or why?"

Meredith's distressed sobbing became louder, and Dr Brownlow urged her to leave the room. He wanted to give her something to help her rest, but Meredith shook her head and insisted on staying.

"No...not yet. I want to hear...everything."

"I'm sorry Mrs Atkins," the DCI continued, "but we don't know anything yet. Like you, we believed your husband was dead. How he survived we won't ever know, now."

Harriet sat down next to Jonah, gently pushing a reluctant Wilmot off the sofa. "Very recently our cook, Marjorie Seymour, mentioned some food items and a few utensils had disappeared from the kitchen and there has been some damage done to a small window in the larder but I'm afraid I was too caught up in meetings and Manor business to take much notice. I did wonder about the coat going missing though..."

"And you thought I'd had a bad dream when I said someone had been in my room the other night," Jonah interrupted quietly, "but then, so did I," he ended lamely, staring into the cold fireplace. Jonah had eventually told her and Meredith about the incident that night but they were convinced he was dreaming.

"Oh yes, of course," Harriet exclaimed, "I'd forgotten about that. I suppose it must have been Jerry." She stood up and went to sit beside him, taking his hand in hers. "It's awful to think of him wandering about the house at night and we had no idea." Harriet put her arm around her son who leaned in towards her, slow tears escaping from his tightly shut eyes. "Although, how I would have reacted, I really don't know. To be honest, I thought it was Stuart helping himself to the food; nothing more sinister had occurred to me, even though things have gone missing before."

DCI Cromwell felt admiration for Harriet Atkins. Her strength of character would see her family through this second ordeal.

"Mrs Atkins, we'll do our best to get to the bottom of this as quickly as we can. I'll send DS Harte up to take a statement from Meredith when she's feeling up to it." He gave Meredith an enquiring look. She nodded her agreement.

"We'll need to talk to all of you, of course," he went on, "but first, there's some news we can give you. It may be unpleasant, but you said you wanted to know everything. I can tell you that, on examining the corpse," he looked at Harriet apologetically, "sorry, your husband's body, we discovered he'd been struck with some considerable force and subsequently hit his head on a rock but, at this stage, we believe he would have survived that. The pathologist will confirm how he died but it's likely the car was actually the murder weapon. His other injuries were consistent with being hit, at speed, by a car and there were paint particles on his coat which we believe came from the vehicle. DS Harte put out a call to look for any abandoned cars in the area. It's unlikely our man would stay with a suspect vehicle for long, and would want to dump it and I can tell you that just such a car, hired by someone…by the name of," he took his notebook out of his pocket and flipped through a few pages, "…Foster, Michael Foster, has been found abandoned…near… Cairnstow. I understand it was a grey BMW…"

Harriet gasped.

"Mrs Atkins?"

"A grey BMW! Maurice Fisher's car."

"Maurice Fisher?"

"We recently had a couple of visits from a man who wanted to pay his respects to the family. He said he was an old friend of Jerry's and had been out of the country for a while. He'd only recently returned and seen Jerry's obituary notice in the papers."

"See! I was right! I didn't like him right from the start, I told you there was something about him," Jonah said, sullenly.

Meredith looked up through swollen eyes. "Mum thought he…he seemed OK to begin with," she sniffed, "but…but there was something nasty about him. We took a re…recording of him when he c…came here the second time. I know we probably shouldn't have, but we didn't t…trust him."

DCI Cromwell's eyebrows shot up. "You recorded him?" There was more to this family than he thought.

"I'm afraid we did," Harriet confessed. "There were certain things about his first visit that made the children suspicious. I'm sorry to have to admit it, but they were quicker on the uptake than me. He had me fooled, to begin with anyway. We knew he would be back, so we…umm…made a few preparations."

"But where did you get the recording equipment from?" the DCI wanted to know

Harriet flicked an uneasy look at Jonah.

"Sorry, but I'm not really at liberty to tell you that," she said. "It might get someone in trouble. We only borrowed it...we didn't think what we were doing might be illegal. You do understand, Chief Inspector...we were...desperate," Harriet coaxed. She joined the doctor near the fireplace, appearing the not the least bit concerned by what they had done, quite the reverse in fact, she looked quite pleased with herself. "You see we wanted to make sure, if he incriminated himself somehow, we had some evidence. I'd been warned about him...let's just say by an old colleague of Jerry's, but it seems his name isn't Maurice Fisher and he's used the same initials again so don't know if his real name is Fisher, Farrow or Foster or something else completely."

Dr Brownlow stared in open admiration at her. She had just been told her husband had turned up again, dead after all, having believed along with everyone else that he died four months ago. She was supremely self-possessed, playing detective and calmly providing the police with information that might help them piece together the puzzle.

"Malcolm Farrow...Malcolm Farrow," the DCI repeated. "The name doesn't mean anything to me, but I can check all his aliases."

"Sorry Chief Inspector, I interrupted you. It was hearing about the car, I'm afraid I stopped you before you could say what was significant about it."

Not looking at her, replied, "I was coming to that anyway, Mrs Atkins. The reason we're interested in it, is that it'd taken a bump to the nearside rear lights, and there's some deep scratches in the paintwork and mud on the tyres. We'll take an impression of tyre tracks found in the lane, and if they match the BMW tyres, and, if the flakes of paint on the victim's coat, sorry... your husband's coat, match. I'm sorry to have to say it, but we have a murder on our hands, we'll analyse the mud too. If the mud on the tyres comes from around here, then there's no doubt. Farrow or Fisher, whatever his name is...or Foster, will have to be found, quickly. This is a murder case."

Meredith, who had stopped crying, burst into loud sobs again. Dorothy, feeling totally inadequate to help the inconsolable girl, shook her head sadly, and Jonah reached down for Wilmot, pulled him back up onto his lap and cuddled him tightly.

"Come on, sweetheart." Dorothy gently helped Meredith to her feet, "I'm taking you upstairs." She turned to the doctor and mouthed, "Have you got anything to help her sleep?"

The doctor nodded and mouthed back, "My bag's in the car."

Harriet watched her daughter being led from the room with the doctor following. "I'll pop up to see her soon," she told Dorothy.

Jonah, too, stood up. "If you're alright, mum, I think I need to get out of here. I need some air."

But Harriet, still pre-occupied worrying about Meredith, did not respond.

"Mum? Are you alright?"

"What?" She turned. "Oh, yes, sorry Jonah. What were you saying?"

"If it's OK, I think I'll go and find Sam."

"Is it alright for Jonah to go out, Chief Inspector?" Harriet asked with a worried frown. "I mean if Fisher, or whatever his name is today, is still at large, are we safe outside?"

"With caution, Mrs Atkins, yes," came the guarded reply. "You don't have to shut yourselves up in here or anything, but be careful. Don't be alone too long," he addressed this last part to Jonah. "We'll find him. I'm confident we'll make an arrest soon." The Chief Inspector rose to leave. "That's all for now and I *will* keep you updated."

"Before you go, Chief Inspector, your Forensic Officer took a DNA test from Jonah. What's happening with that?" Harriet enquired as she walked him to the front door, Jonah following along behind.

"I think that's a little academic now Mrs Atkins. It was definitely your husband at the stables. We just can't fathom out how he got supplies in or moved about the yard without being seen. We think someone was helping him, someone who would fit in, not look out of place."

At the front door, the Chief Inspector shook Harriet's hand, said goodbye to Jonah and turned to leave. Then he remembered something. "About that recording Mrs Atkins, you'd better let me have it. It's not admissible as evidence, but it might prove useful."

Harriet walked briskly back to the study, returned with the mini cassette and handed it to the Chief Inspector.

"Thank you. I'll look after this." He put the cassette into the inside pocket of his raincoat. "And, in future Mrs Atkins, please don't make any more illegal recordings."

"I sincerely hope I won't have to," she replied, solemnly.

Chapter Eighteen

Sam woke late that morning with a horrid sinking feeling; the exams were imminent. Although Mrs Wilkinson and Mrs Tansley had coached him, he was worried whether his school move would have a harmful effect on his education. Soon after breakfast, he left the cottage to pick up some groceries from the village shop for his mother, and was trying to remember the names of people who had made significant developments in medicine, starting with the ancient Greeks when, turning a bend in the lane, he saw a number of policemen grouped together near two police cars. A plump, uniformed policeman, with bushy sideburns, barred his way.

"D'you wanna go through 'ere lad? 'Cause you can't."

"What…um? Sorry…I," Sam stuttered, finally noticing two more men, dressed in plain clothes, near a small white tent. He recalled hearing sirens earlier, but had not thought too much of it at the time. Now he was interested, now it looked as though the sirens and what was going on here were linked. "What's going on?"

"Sorry Sonny, if I told you that I'd 'ave ter kill yer." The policeman chuckled.

Having heard that particular phrase shortly before Christmas, Sam wondered why the older generation of men in the village found it amusing. "I can't go through this way then?"

"Tha's roight, m'boy. It'll likely be tomorrer or per'aps the day after, afore the lane's open agen. I'd cut across the fields if I was you, Sonny."

"Yeah. I'll do that. Thanks," Sam replied, bristling at being called 'Sonny'.

Someone at the door of the ambulance called the policeman and held up a large steaming mug.

"Coffee up, George."

"'Bout toime," the policeman mumbled, trudging away from the barrier. Sam intended to leave, but his curiosity aroused, he could not drag himself away, he was gripped. A number of officers in protective clothing were on their hands and knees, painstakingly inspecting the ground. Nearby a young, dark-haired man and an older woman, both wearing white overalls talked animatedly as they pointed to what Sam guessed must be tyre tracks and the woman was holding what Sam thought looked like a dark blue waxed coat. He recognised the man. He had been at the stables talking to Meredith on Monday.

Just then the man looked over in Sam's direction. He said something to the woman then hurried over leaving the woman to examine the coat. The back door of the ambulance opened. There was some obscured activity then the doors were banged shut again.

"I saw you the other day at the stables, didn't I? D'you live near here?"

"Yeah, just round that corner." Sam pointed up the lane.

"What's your name?"

"Sam Johnson, why?"

The ambulance engine started up.

"Pleased to meet you Sam Johnson. I'm DS Harte. Did you hear anything last night…maybe a car late on, voices, anything else?"

"No…not that I can think of. Why, what's going on?"

"Well, I can't say too much, not until the family's been told, but it'll be public knowledge that we've found a body soon enough, so there's little point in trying to hide it."

Sam shot a look at the canvas sheeting and a sickening chill ran through his body. "What! That's raw! Is it still there?" he asked quietly, staring at the canvas.

"No, the ambulance is taking him away to the mortuary."

"It's a man! Do you know who it is?"

The detective looked very uncomfortable. "We know who it is, but I'm not at liberty to say until we've had a chance to speak to the victim's family."

"Victim! So it's a murder?" Sam's eyes were as round as saucers.

"I didn't say that," DS Harte snapped. "Stop putting words in my mouth." He seemed irritated. "You'd better head off to wherever you were going but I may need to talk to you again later. For now, though, you're not to say anything to anyone. You understand?" He held up a finger at Sam, as if to emphasise the point. Sam nodded and turned away.

DS Harte called him back. "Just a minute Sam. How old are you?"

"Nearly fifteen. Why?"

"Do you go to St Merriott's?"

"Yeah. Why?"

"Do you know Jonah Atkins?"

"Yeah. Why?"

"Nothing."

Sam watched as the detective walked away to join his colleagues, leaving him thoroughly intrigued and desperate to tell someone what had happened even though he had promised not to discuss it. Turning back, he ran home and charged through the front door, eager to find his mother, convinced she would be exempt from the promise he had made.

Portia, panicked by his loud and unexpected entrance, darted under the sideboard and hissed angrily as he darted past her bolt hole.

"Mum, you'll never guess what's happened."

Jane Johnson was in the hall. She had just put down the telephone.

"A body's been found in the lane," she said coolly.

"Aw, rats! How did you know?"

"Marj Seymour's just phoned. Harriet asked her to tell me not to go up to the house today. Seems the police are there now. She'll phone me when they've gone."

So desperate to tell someone about what he had seen, Sam didn't take in what she had actually said. "I wonder who it is. Maybe it's someone we know. Hey cool!"

"Why do teenagers have to be such ghouls?" Jane said irritably.

Sam grinned. "It comes automatically on the first double figure birthday."

"Well that's enough for now. If you haven't been to the shop yet, I suggest you go now and stop getting under my feet."

Unable to use the lane, Sam cut through the trees, all thoughts of medicinal masterminds now put out of his head he looked out for Charlie or the elves. Spring flowers, daffodils, bluebells and primroses carpeted the woodland floor, and warm sunlight flooded in between the tall trees. A small frightened rabbit scuttled out of his path into the undergrowth, and bird song rang out from every tree he passed by. Thinking of the dead man, Sam suddenly felt glad to be alive, but his high spirits quickly gave way to an overwhelming pity. It was a terrible time to die, just as the world was coming to life again. Perhaps his mum had been right, he had sounded ghoulish. He said a silent apology to the man's spirit, whoever he was.

Near the village the trees thinned, and he found himself beside a tall hedge surrounding the garden of an old farmhouse cottage. It was the only one for miles that still had a water-tower, leftover from bygone days when cautious farmers stored rainwater to use in time of drought, but it had long since gone out of use. Sam suddenly realised where he was and shuddered. This cottage was owned and occupied by Mrs Jenks, the 'crazy cat lady'. He sped up hoping she would not see him. But luck was not with him. Unfortunately, as if thinking about her could conjure her up, the gate opened and there she was, beckoning to a very apprehensive Sam.

"Sam, so glad I caught you," she said as if they were old friends. "Come in, quickly," she urged.

This is freaky, Sam thought. How does she know who I am? Confused, and more than a little panicky, Sam backed away, which Mrs Jenks seemed to find amusing.

"Don't be silly," she giggled. "There's no need to be scared of me. I'm not going to turn you into a toad and we actually have more in common than you know." She ignored his eagerness to get away. "I'll explain everything soon, but do come in. We have things to discuss after what's happened." She fixed him with a steely look and powerless to do anything but obey, he found himself following her towards the back door of her cottage. Merlin rushed to meet them wagging his tail and barking amiably as Bandit climbed through the open window and sat regally on the windowsill, keenly observing Sam as he approached.

"Look, I know you think I'm scatty, or worse, but I've some friends inside I think you'll be glad to meet." Mrs Jenks bestowed one of her warmest smiles on him and stood back to let him go first into the dark porch. Any thoughts of shopping or revision were now completely forgotten. On entering the low-ceilinged dark hallway, his nostrils were assailed by the strong smell of herbs and the dry dust falling from cobwebs hanging from the corners of the ceiling, made him sneeze.

"She needs a cleaner," he muttered softly.

"I'm sorry the place is in a bit of a mess, I keep meaning to sort it out, but I never find the time."

She heard me. How did she hear me? She must have the hearing of a bat, Sam thought.

"Yes, I always had a fondness for bats."

Sam's blood ran cold and he desperately tried not to think.

Merlin followed them inside and Sam jumped as the back door clicked shut of its own accord! Now he was really nervous. He felt in his jeans pocket for his mobile phone and slid it, unobserved, into his hand, hoping she would not see. He looked down. There was no signal! He had never had a problem anywhere in the village before. Now he was getting nervous.

"Oh, your phone won't work in here Sam, there's no signal." Mrs Jenks smiled as she filled the kettle at the sink.

"Er...look, I've got to go, Mrs Jenks," Sam said nervously. "I've got to go to the shop."

"That'll wait, dear boy and don't worry, I won't keep you long." She put the kettle onto an old round stove with a rickety chimney, all the time laughing softly, which made Sam feel even more on edge. He had never seen anything like this house except in pictures of fairy tales. Everything about the room was peculiar. There were more books than Sam had ever seen outside of a library, the walls were hung with dusty, faded tapestries, dried plants and a clutter of grimy ornaments filled every spare bit of shelf space and it was warm, very warm. In the grate, burning pine logs sent up a wonderfully fresh smell that lifted the stuffiness a little, but Sam still found it pretty stifling.

On the sink worktop, Sam saw a saucepan with a burnt and blackened bottom sitting on the draining board. Mrs Jenks noticed Sam looking at it and her dark blue eyes crinkled into a smile.

"Not one of my successes, I'm afraid. I got distracted and it burnt, but the potion eventually got made anyway."

Sam's curious gaze took in the charts and diagrams on the wall, and the peculiar cards set out on the table but, not wanting an in-depth conversation, he said nothing. He wished Mrs Jenks would get on with telling him what she wanted with him or who he was to meet, but she seemed not to be in any hurry and continued pottering about. Bandit jumped onto the table near to him. He stared intently at Sam for a moment, before breaking into a loud purr. Sam was very grateful his eyes refrained from going kaleidoscopic again.

"Good. He likes you. You obviously pass the test. Now we…"

"You know I really…"

"Nonsense, dear boy, this will only take a minute…you'll see things more clearly when you meet my friends. Ah, here they are now."

A door at the far end of the kitchen opened revealing, to Sam's surprise, Piggybait, Claptrap and Jerrill. Mrs Jenks took several cups from the cupboard near the sink.

"Hi Sam. Bet you didn't expect us?" Piggybait jumped onto a chair, grinning broadly and sat down on the table next to Bandit whose mouth curled in an aristocratic smile at his newly arrived friend.

"We've got some explaining to do boys," said Mrs Jenks, cheerfully. "Sit down Sam, make yourself comfortable."

Claptrap, a folded newspaper under his arm, stretched out on a small floral-patterned sofa, his legs on the armrest and stuck his nose into the Elfland Chronicle. "You must excuse me Sam, we've been so busy I haven't been able to catch up, Piggy's had me chasing about all over the place. You do understand." Without waiting to see whether Sam understood or not, he disappeared behind his paper. Jerrill pulled up a stool near the fireplace and settled down facing Sam, he smiled.

"Are you alright Sam? Have you had a bit of a shock?" he said, amused by Sam's bewilderment. Sam struggled to remember if he had ever seen Jerrill smile before. It looked so odd it was obvious it didn't come naturally to him and Sam was unsure whether it actually suited him. He was still thinking about it when Mrs Jenks handed him a mug of tea, passing smaller cups to the elves.

"Herbal tea Sam," she explained, as Sam's nose twitched at the strange aroma.

"Try it. It's not poisonous, you know and you might like it."

"Got anything stronger, Armie?" Piggybait cheekily enquired. "Maybe a nice glass of dandelion beer perhaps?" He sat back, smiling hopefully and patted his round tummy.

"Not until after dark Piggy, no." She winked at Sam as he took a sip of his tea. It was not at all to his liking; it tasted as he imagined rusty nettles would. He put the cup down on the table hoping Mrs Jenks would not be offended if he left it, and looked up to see Piggybait grinning at him, knowingly. As Mrs Jenks walked by the table, Bandit ran across it and lightly sprang up onto her shoulders where he draped himself, like a shawl, purring contentedly.

Merlin snoozed under the table, resting his chin on his forepaws and snoring softly. Mrs Jenks stood over Claptrap, waiting for him to make a space for her. When he ignored her, she pushed his feet off the sofa and sat down next to him without disturbing the settled cat. Claptrap gave her a scornful look through his monocle, but winked at Sam with the other eye.

"Now then, firstly Sam, I must apologise for the scare I gave you the other day," Mrs Jenks began while Claptrap continued reading his paper. "You must have wondered why this batty old woman was staring at you like that."

"Well yes...I suppose I did...not that I thought you were batty, of course," he added quickly.

"Goodness me, young man," she replied briskly. "Don't tell me fibs. Of course you did! I would have, if the situation had been reversed. No suppose about it, young man, the expression on your face said it all. I had hoped to meet you for the first time in more...appropriate surroundings."

"She means our cavern," Piggybait interrupted.

"Don't interrupt old boy. It's very rude," Claptrap commented, not taking his eyes off his paper.

"Don't you start..."

"That's *enough!*" roared Jerrill. "By the Lords of Alfheim! You two have been at it all day, bicker, bicker, bicker. I could bang your heads together. You're worse than a pair of elflings."

Claptrap looked over his paper at Jerrill and winked at Piggybait, who winked conspiratorially back. Mrs Jenks chuckled. Bandit opened one eye, closed it again and went back to sleep, still perfectly snug across her shoulders, although Sam thought they were beginning to droop a little under the cat's weight.

"Now then, where were we? Oh yes, I did mean the cavern. I'd hoped we'd meet up before this, but it didn't happen."

140

"Why did you want to meet me anyway, Mrs Jenks?"

"Why, bless you, Charlie told me all about you. He's a dear friend who I've known through all my incarnations." Sam tried not to appear sceptical. "He, of course, stays just as he is, whereas I'm mortal. I always pass on, but I'm reborn, my spirit has returned many times through the centuries and we always recognise each other immediately. It's a great comfort to know I'll always find someone who knows me, whoever I am." She looked at Sam with understanding. "My dear boy, this must be terribly difficult to take in."

He felt more comfortable with the elves there, especially when the bickering began, but all the same, it was becoming quite bizarre. "It would've been a couple of years ago, even just a few months ago I wouldn't have believed any of it, I'd have thought you were crazy, but I'll believe anything now, even if you told me Bandit can talk."

Hearing his name, the cat opened one jade-coloured eye and mewed.

"See what I mean!" he laughed and reached out to stroke the handsome cat.

Mrs Jenks laughed. "I can see why Charlie is so fond of you."

"I'm sorry but I have to ask," Sam began. "Charlie said you were hanged as a witch once. Cathy and I thought he was kidding and he laughed it off, but he was telling the truth wasn't he?"

Mrs Jenks face took on a grave expression. "Yes, it's true. Witches were executed by fire, water and rope, mostly rope."

"Sorry?"

"I'll explain. The old belief was that witches couldn't drown, so the witch-hunters tied you to a chair and dunked you in the river. If you drowned you were innocent. If you survived it mean the Devil was protecting you so you were hanged. I lost a lot of friends both ways over the years."

"But could you do spells and things?" Sam was fascinated.

"Bless you, no, nothing like that! None of us did. All it took to be accused was to have an expertise in healing, be good with herbs or animals, or it could be something as trivial as a neighbour didn't like you, to have the accusations flying. Superstition was rife in those days, and it still is in some places even today."

"How d'you mean?" Sam asked.

"I have a number of books on witches and their persecution, if you're interested I'll lend them to you. The kind of thing blamed on witches was for instance, if a farmer had sick cattle or his crops failed, he needed someone to blame. If your face didn't fit for one reason or another, you'd soon find yourself with a noose around your neck, or worse. You see Sam, ignorance begets ignorance."

"In what way?"

"The average man, a couple of hundred years ago, living in a rural community like this, would probably be one of many children. Families were larger then, there was little education, high infant mortality and people had larger families to work to support everyone. Working from dawn to dusk left no time to think, so children learned from their parents. Whatever belief the parents were brought up with would be passed on to the children. They were too busy surviving and weren't encouraged to question the teachings at the time. And they were too frightened of eternal punishment in the next life so they did as they were told. If they were lucky, they grew up, had their own family and the cycle went on." Mrs Jenks said sadly. "

"Yeah, I can see that," Sam looked thoughtful. "It must've been a rotten way to live if you were a bit...different."

"Yes, sometimes, but I'm painting a very bleak picture, it wasn't all bad all the time. I still had my friends here and Bandit and Charlie."

"Bandit?"

"Oh yes, he and I have been together, in one form or another, through the centuries. Just like Charlie and me, we always find each other." She stroked the purring cat. "Of course, herbs are popular now, but my interest in them got me into trouble lots of times."

Sam smiled, "At least you won't get arrested for knowing about herbs these days," he said, looking at the huge amount of plant pots crowding the shelves. "Are all these used in cookery?"

Mrs Jenks followed his gaze around the room. "Some of them, some are for healing and some can be used for both." She was delighted at his interest.

"Talking about food and dunking, got any biscuits Armie?" Piggybait grinned, batting his long eyelashes at her cheekily.

"You and your stomach! Alright, help yourself, you know where they are, dear," she smiled indulgently.

Jerrill tutted as Piggybait jumped down from the table.

"Get me one, Piggy old friend, will you?" Claptrap murmured from the sofa.

"Lazy gnome! Get it yourself," he said, passing Claptrap the biscuit tin on his way back to the table.

"Can we get back to explanations?" Jerrill snapped. "Sam, our clan has known Armistice about five hundred years now..."

"Speak for yourself old boy," Claptrap cut in. "We're not *that* old, yet!"

"As I was saying," Jerrill sighed. "We have been close to her through her many lives. She told us she had recognised in you a kindred spirit." He turned to Mrs Jenks, who took over the conversation. "I couldn't talk to you with all your friends around, but I wanted to warn you."

"Warn me?"

She sat forward, making Bandit dig his claws into her cardigan to secure his hold. "The cards told me something awful was coming and now a man has died and...well...I have seen you getting caught up in this."

Sam was horrified. "Me? How? All I've done is to get stopped by a road block. What've I got to do with it?" he asked, nervously looking from Mrs Jenks to Jerrill.

"No, no...I didn't mean with the man's death, Sam. No, don't get me wrong. You'll be caught up in the aftermath."

"But how?" Sam's face was a peculiar shade of grey.

Mrs Jenks' deep blue eyes glazed over as she stared towards the cards laid out on the table. Piggybait and Jerrill waited, watching her closely. The atmosphere in the room grew tense, everyone was silent. The only sounds were the crackling of the fire in the stove and Merlin's snuffling snore.

Mrs Jenks snapped back from her daydream. "I seem to have a knack of worrying you, don't I, Sam? It seems you're involvement will be to help solve this terrible puzzle."

Merlin sneezed, rose from his rug under the table and went to her side, laid his head on her knee and stared up at her through deep brown, adoring eyes. She stroked his head absent-mindedly.

"You know who it is, don't you?" Sam asked, looking at Piggybait.

As if seeking consent, Piggybait looked first at Claptrap who was so engrossed in an article about arguments within the higher ranks of the Pennine elves, he had not been following the conversation, then to Mrs Jenks and lastly, to Jerrill, who nodded agreement.

"It was Jonah's father, Jeremiah Atkins," Piggybait said.

Sam laughed. "Now I know you're having me on! He died months ago, we all know that!"

"That's what everyone thought," Jerrill said. He had begun pacing up and down in front of the hearth. "He even fooled us for a while, but his body was never found, was it? It seems he had planned everything down to the finest detail for his escape. When he realised his men were going to let him down, he faked his own death rather than get caught. It looks as if he'd been using the stables for weeks, probably since he '*died*' the first time, but even we didn't realise he was around until he fled to the cave."

"But how do you know all this?"

"Been watching him," Claptrap said, without looking up from his paper. "Recently, anyway."

"Well some of us have," Piggybait retorted. "Nice to see you're still with us Claptrap."

Claptrap made what Sam guessed was a rude gesture for an elf.

"So how did he die…this time I mean?"

"It was murder," Jerrill replied gravely. "You remember Rondo said there were two men. One was Atkins. We know little about the other one except that he killed Atkins and we're not sure why, yet. But we'll find out"

"Blew in with the east wind," Mrs Jenks commented.

Jerrill looked at her but made no response. "He's dangerous, and now he's killed Atkins he might be desperate. Keep a watch on Jonah, Sam. He'll need your friendship more than ever."

Sam slapped his forehead with the palm of his hand. "I'm so stupid!"

Claptrap looked up from his paper, finally. Everyone looked at Sam.

"What's wrong?" Piggybait spun on the table, almost knocking a pile of magazines onto the floor.

"When that policeman said they had to inform the family first, it never occurred to me he meant Jonah's family. That accounts for Marj Seymour phoning mum." His expression changed. "Aw…Jonah. Imagine, your dad's dead, then he turns up again, but really dead, all this time later? It's horrible." Sam's stomach churned. "That's rotten."

"They do know now. The Detective Chief Inspector was almost there just as you were stopped in the lane," Mrs Jenks said in a distant voice, her eyes fixed on the cards again.

Sam thought the people in this new world he found himself in were very strange, but very cool. They had a unique understanding of the world in which they lived, and it occurred to him just how very fortunate he was to be part of it.

Chapter Nineteen

Having left the crime scene, John returned to the stables, telling himself that seeing Alison was necessary for his investigation. In the yard, two girls leading a pair of horses headed his way. They stared at him as they walked by and one leaned closer to the other and whispered something to the other, who burst into a fit of giggles. He ignored them, eager to find Alison, but felt a strange uncertainty about seeing her again.

Tom Pembury, wide-eyed and haunted, glowered at him over a stable door, but as this seemed to be Tom's perpetual state, and seeing Alison waiting for him at the office door, he ignored Tom too.

Alison, however, looked very pleased to see him. "Morning, John. Coffee?"

"Thanks, I could do with one."

Following her into the small shabby room that served as an office, John found himself lost for words, suddenly shy, something he rarely experienced. Uncertain how to break the silence he concentrated on the framed photographs adorning the once white walls. Running his eyes over the numerous pictures of horses and riders, some holding cups or rosettes, he recognised Alison in two of them and thought he saw Meredith in one, but the girl in the picture was so young it was difficult to tell.

Grey patches of wall showed where the top coat of paint had flaked off, and holes in the threadbare blue paisley patterned carpet revealed the concrete floor underneath. In the far corner, a portable gas heater threw out just enough warmth on a cold day to make the room comfortable; it was adequate.

Alison switched on the kettle, spooned coffee into two chipped mugs, and wondering about his silence, turned to see what John was doing. She followed his gaze around the photographs.

"Where's Briar? I didn't think you two could be separated," John asked, finally finding his voice.

Alison gave a soft laugh. "She's at home. After yesterday I wanted her to have some peace and quiet."

"Hmm, yes, I'm sorry about that. We didn't realise she'd get that upset, but it gave us some answers."

"No, it's alright, honestly. I do understand but I just wanted her kept calm today. Anyway, excuse the mess, it's a bit tatty in here I'm afraid, with all the mud and hay we walk in, we don't really bother with it all that much."

"No, no it's fine. Ours is the same, but we don't have horses and hay as an excuse," John's laugh sounded a little forced. "I was just looking at the photos. I take it that's you?" He pointed to one that clearly showed Alison. She moved closer.

"Yes, that was at Burghley. That's 'Doughnut'. We got a Second in the show-jumping that year. He was fantastic. He knew exactly where I needed him to be every time, wonderful pacing, step by step. He was very special. He's retired now."

"I bet it wasn't all the horse," John smiled. They turned towards each other at the same moment and their eyes locked for just a second longer than necessary. The atmosphere was strained and neither of them knew what to say. It was Alison who broke the silence.

"Take a seat," she said, pointing to the only chair in the room, which was situated behind a small, much-used desk, which was practically hidden under overflowing filing trays, newspapers, a saddle, three rosettes and several riding hats.

"No, it's OK, I'll stand, thanks."

While Alison made the coffee, John leaned his elbow on an old dented grey filing cabinet without realising it was not as sturdy as it seemed; it tilted unsteadily pitching him off balance. Alison giggled and John smiled breaking the awkwardness between them.

"D'you take sugar?"

"No thanks. Not for me."

As she handed him his coffee, he noticed her wrist was still strapped up.

"I'm sorry I clean forgot. I could've made the coffee."

"No...no, it's OK. I can manage."

"How is it?"

"Not bad. It throbs a bit sometimes, especially at night but it's getting better. There are worse things," she said, looking up at him with a frown. "How's everyone at the Manor? Meredith?"

"The doctor's seen her and she's resting, Mrs Atkins seems to be holding things together, but Jonah's gone."

"Gone?"

"I don't mean it like that...he's gone out." John took a sip of his coffee. "He said he was going to see a friend, Sam Johnson, I think. It wouldn't be fair to coop him up in the house all the time but I hope he's careful. We recommended none of the family went out alone."

"Why? Isn't it all over?"

John shook his head. "No, not yet, there's still the car driver to be found. You know Meredith discovered the body and who it was?"

Alison nodded, "Yes, Dorothy told me. Imagine how awful it must have been to find him like that."

"We're not sure how long he'd been in the hayloft, but it's possible he'd been hiding up there since…" But Alison was prevented from hearing any more when the door burst open, revealing a shaking and ashen-faced Tom, his eyes glassy and red-rimmed, his features contorted with misery.

"It was me!" he screamed. "I did it!"

Alison ran to him. "You did what, Tom? What's the matter?" She turned to John. He was as puzzled as she was. She guided Tom to the chair and helped him sit down. He seemed unable to manage it unaided. She crouched down to look up into his distraught face and spoke quietly. "What is it Tom, what have you done?"

His head low, his hands covering his face, Tom spoke, so quietly, it was no more than a whisper. "I hid him…I let him stay here."

"I can't hear you, Tom. What was that?" Alison moved closer.

*"I said it was me…*I let him stay. It's my fault you got hurt."

"Tom! What are you saying?"

The door was still open. John saw Kelly watching them from the yard eager to find out what was going on. He walked over and closed it, watching her until she disappeared behind the stable block. Tom was still staring at the floor, struggling to find the right words to explain. Alison looked over his head at John, before turning back to grip her brother's cold and shaking hand.

Tom remained stonily silent, his hands gripping the side of the chair. He was unmistakably scared. "Tom, I…" Alison began, but John interrupted her.

"Give me a minute with him, Alison." He gave her a supportive smile and sat on a corner of the desk in front of her brother. Alison nodded, moving quietly behind Tom. "OK, so what's this about?" John began.

Tom looked up, but could not meet John's eyes. "I'm s…sorry. I didn't mean Alison to get hurt."

Alison gasped, "What are you talking about?"

"That man, I let him into the stables. It's my fault…it's all my fault!" He burst into shuddering sobs.

"OK Tom, let's start at the beginning," John kept his voice low and sympathetic, now that Tom had begun his story, he did not want to scare him into clamming up. "Take your time…there's no hurry. Start with how you met him."

Agonizing sobs prevented Tom from speaking as he released his pent-up guilt. John turned to see sympathetic tears trail slowly down Alison's face and, at that moment, a forgotten emotion rocked him. He absolutely knew that, for the rest of his life, he would make sure nothing ever hurt her again. He was in love. She looked up and smiled gently at him as if reading his thoughts and he forced himself to break eye contact with her. He had a job to do, they could talk romance later. No-one spoke until Tom calmed enough to catch his breath.

"Are you OK now?" John asked Tom gently, remembering he sometimes needed an inhaler.

After a few convulsive sobs, Tom controlled his tears. "He…he started hanging around here in January…I thought he was homeless." He raised his eyes to look at John. "It was so cold you see," he gave a gulping cough.

"Have you got your inhaler, Tom?" Alison enquired, but he waved away her concern.

"He asked me if he could stay in the barn. I told him it was locked and dangerous, but he said it didn't matter, it…was better than what he had. I…I thought he just needed a roof over his head," he paused, "I found out later who he was and why he was there. He said he needed to find something…something that would help him get away and start a new life. I believed him."

"He told you?" John could not believe his ears. "Why on earth didn't you tell anyone?"

"I know I should have, but I felt sorry for him. He was…thin and dirty but…somehow…he sort of…reminded me of dad."

Alison's eyes glittered brightly and she wiped the tears away with the back of her free hand. "It's alright Tom, go on. What was it about him that reminded you of dad?" she asked quietly.

He shook his head. "I don't know. He didn't look like him." He took a deep breath. "But I couldn't help dad. I couldn't help mum either, but…I could…help him. He just wanted to disappear, that's what he said."

"You've heard what happened earlier today?" John asked.

"Yes. Kelly told me. A man's body was found in the lane." His eyes opened wide as he looked at John questioningly. "Oh no! Don't tell me…"

"It was Jeremiah Atkins."

"No!" Tom was so clearly shocked John could only believe his reaction was genuine.

"H…h…how?" He began trembling violently. Alison put her arms around him to comfort him.

"Shhh, Tom. It's alright. John doesn't think you had anything to do with it. Do you, John?"

148

"No, but we'll need a statement from you." John walked to the window. It was dirty. He wiped a small area with his hand and peered out looking to see if Kelly was still hanging around but there was no sign of her or anyone else in the yard. "It must have been hard finding out you were...helping the person who hurt your sister."

"I didn't mean for that to happen!" Tom swung round to face his sister. "Honestly Alison, I never thought you'd be hurt. I just wanted to help him out."

"It's alright, it's alright," Alison soothed. "I know you wouldn't want anything to happen to me or Briar."

"Poor Briar. She was only protecting you. If only I hadn't been away that night," he ended bitterly. "I'd have stopped you going out."

John walked back from the window. "OK, Tom, I want you to think back to your talks with Atkins. When did you find out who he was?"

"It was about three weeks ago."

"Don't forget John," Alison interrupted, "we didn't come here until after he was supposed to have died and we'd never met him. Tom wouldn't have known what he looked like."

Yes, I understand that, but how did you find out?"

"I'd been at the pub one evening, and just got to the yard when I saw him going into the barn. I heard him cursing...he sounded really angry. I went into see if I could help. He had his back to the door and didn't see me come in. He had some papers and photographs in a plastic carrier bag, but it had broken and they were strewn about everywhere. Thinking I was helping, I picked some up for him. Every photo was of the Atkins family and the housekeeper, whatever her name is..."

"Dorothy, Dorothy Renwick," Alison said. Tom nodded.

"He went ballistic when he saw me...started shouting, saying I should mind my own business. I told him I was only trying to help, but he snatched them out of my hand...I think one got ripped. Then he screamed at me to leave, or else."

"So what did you do?" John asked.

"I left. What else could I do? He was furious for some reason - I didn't stick around. I'm not really built for fights these days," he gave a kind of grimacing smile.

"Then what happened?" John sat on the edge of the desk.

Tom shrugged. "It was odd really, I'd just left when he called me back and apologised, said I'd taken him by surprise...he looked a bit, well...mad, I suppose. I asked about the photos, that's when he told me who he was. He said he hadn't meant to scare me, especially as I'd been so good to him. I used to leave him bits of food, you know, bread, fresh milk, stuff like that, in a safe place when no-one was around."

149

"So that's how he got his supplies," John said.

"Yes, some of them, anyway. Sometimes, he'd go out during the night when the stables were closed, so I guess he got some stuff for himself." He turned to Alison. "That's probably what he was doing when you went out that night."

"That'll do for now. Come by the station tomorrow and we'll sort out that statement? But now you can stop worrying so much." John stood up and moved towards the door.

Tom's shoulders dropped, his tension eased and he gave a half-smile. "Yes, yes of course. How did he die?"

"It looks like murder. Someone ran a car at him. He wouldn't have stood a chance."

"Oh how horrible!" Alison exclaimed.

"What a horrible way to die," Tom sighed.

Alison sat down on the corner of the desk and Tom looked up at her and then to John. "I hope you get whoever did it. Mr Atkins was looking for something he needed to start again. I asked him once why he didn't tell his family he was alive."

"What did he say?" John asked

"He said they deserved some peace and it was time for him to move on, he'd done them enough harm and it was better they believed him dead. He seemed quite sad when he said that."

"Did he tell you what it was he was looking for?"

"No. He said he would go abroad, but didn't say much more. I only remember him saying when he had…whatever it was, he could start a new life under a new name. But whatever it was, he couldn't leave without it."

"Well it looks like whatever *it* was, there's someone else looking for it too, which is probably why he was killed. Anyway, it's time I got back," John said.

"But aren't you going to arrest me," Tom stood up.

"No, not right now," John smiled, heading towards the door.

Tom sat down again, obviously relieved.

"But," John turned back, "I'd rather you didn't discuss this with anyone. There'll be gossip enough. I'll see you at the station tomorrow morning, Tom. About ten OK?"

Tom nodded.

"He'll be there," Alison confirmed.

John closed the door behind him and was heading back across the yard when he heard running footfalls behind him. It was Alison. He waited for her to catch up.

"How hard will they be on him?" her golden-brown eyes sought reassurance.

"Oh, I doubt they'll throw the book at him." His levity went unappreciated. "Seriously? He'll probably get a Caution. He withheld information regarding a fugitive and, of course, there's wasting police time." He smiled down at her. "But don't worry too much, with everything you've both been through and," a thought occurred to him, "he's never been in trouble before has he?"

"No, never. Why?"

"He has no previous record, so I doubt it'll get too far. I'll put in a good word for him anyway."

"Would you?" Alison looked hopeful.

"Yeah, of course. Umm, if you've got a minute, why don't you walk with me to my car?"

"I'd like that."

Chapter Twenty

"Mum. Mum!" Jenny thundered down the stairs carrying the gold coloured jewellery box under her arm. The back door was open; her mother was in the garden pegging out washing. Impatient, Jenny ran out to join her in the garden. "Mum! Look at this."

"Jutht a mimute." Sarah removed the pegs from her mouth and fastened a shirt to the line. "Now then, what's up?"

Jenny held out the open box.

"Yes, what about it?" Sarah said impatiently. "It's a family heirloom or something. You were lu…"

"I know, but never mind that now, Mum," Jenny said excitedly. "Look, look at this." She pointed to the repaired tear in the red velvet lining.

"Yes, but it was a gift, Jenny, you can't complain if it's not perfect."

"Aaarggh! No. You don't understand." She rolled her brown eyes, shooting an exasperated look at her mother. "Look, I was just putting Granny Richards jewellery in it and I knew about the rip, but it didn't matter and it's not that I'm talking about. It's what's underneath. Look…there. There's a lump under the lining."

Sarah ran a finger along the inside of the box near the repair and, sure enough, there was something stuck to the inside of the box hidden by the lining. "You're right. Perhaps we should tell Mrs Atkins and give her the box back. I don't like to be too nosey, 'cause if it turns out to be something important…"

"No, please don't give the box back. Why can't we just return whatever's inside?"

Sarah hesitated, unsure what to do. She thought about phoning her husband and asking him, but Joe had a full clinic that morning at his dental practice, so he'd be busy. Decisions, decisions!

Curiosity getting the better of her, she strode back indoors, Jenny following closely. In the kitchen, Sarah found a tiny pair of scissors from the 'bits and pieces' drawer and carefully snipped away the small stitches in the lining.

"Oh, come on, Mum, you're so slow," Jenny urged.

"You just hold your horses my girl! If you want it to look halfway decent when I'm done, then I've got to be careful, I'm not rushing it."

Jenny plonked herself down in a chair, tapping her fingers while Sarah painstakingly cut away enough stitches to give her room to push a finger through the hole she had made in the velvet.

"Well? What is it?"

"I'm not sure yet…but…it feels like, yes, it's metal. I think it's a key."

"A key! What's a key doing hidden in there?"

"How on earth would I know that? I didn't put it in there, so how should I know why whoever did, did it?"

"Can you get it out?"

"I'll have to cut some more of the stitching," Sarah replied, gently tweaking at the repair. "It feels like it's stuck somehow…I can feel sticky tape. This is weird and no mistake. Why hide it so well?" Carefully Sarah cut away a few more stitches until the hole in the lining was big enough to get at the key. "I wonder how long it's been in here." Using a small tweezer Sarah eased the tape away from the box. To use force would have meant risking more damage to the lining. Slowly the key slid away until she was able to ease it out of the lining altogether. "Finally!" She handed the key to Jenny who pulled off the remaining brown tape.

"What sort of key is it, Mum?" Jenny turned it over in her hand. "I mean what's it for? It's too long and thin to be a normal door key."

"I've no idea, but probably Mrs Atkins will. I'll phone her to tell her we've found it." Sarah headed towards the hall, but Jenny called out before she could pick up the telephone.

"D'you think that's a good idea mum? I mean…at the moment…with everything going on. I can't imagine she'll be worried about a key right now?"

"Good point. Maybe not," Sarah hesitated by the telephone, unsure what to do next.

"No, I think I will phone. I was going to pass on my condolences anyway, so I can kill two birds with one stone. Oops, probably not the best choice of words under the circumstances. Not really appropriate at the moment is it? I'd better choose my words a little more carefully, considering."

Chapter Twenty One

While Piggybait and Claptrap waited inside the cottage arguing over who was going to have the last chocolate biscuit, Sam leaned against the garden gate waiting for Mrs Jenks to emerge from the garden shed. When she did finally appear, her head and shoulders were almost completely obscured by a large, glossy blue-black bird perched heavily on her forearm. The bird stared keenly at Sam through black intelligent eyes.

"Say hello to Mélusine, Sam. Ravens are one of nature's most wonderful assets and much maligned," she stroked the bird's head tenderly.

"I've seen her before, at the cave. She came in with a message from you when Charlie and I were there the other day." Sam eyed the bird warily. She was beautiful alright, but that beak looked deadly.

"Yes, of course she was. How silly, I'd completely forgotten. She passes on messages for me regularly. Ravens are fantastic mimics, she memorises everything, as long as I keep it brief. If it's a long message I write a note and tie it to her leg. She doesn't mind it, but her mate's not so keen."

"Piggybait said there was another one."

"He's around somewhere, probably raiding some farmer's free-range chicken eggs if he can find them. He only takes one though. He knows I don't approve of him stealing more than one at a time."

Mélusine flapped her wings as Mrs Jenks softly spoke to her in a language totally unintelligible to Sam.

"She's quite a weight, I can tell you," Mrs Jenks supported her arm with her other hand. "I've asked her to look for Charlie. She'll find him in minutes. Do you want to wait or will you come back?"

"I can wait, but not too long, I still haven't been to the shop, but I'd like to see him."

"Here, hold her for a minute will you?" Mrs Jenks offloaded the bird onto Sam's arm. "Ooh, that's better, she's heavy."

Sam took the bird nervously. "Does she bite...I mean peck?"

"Bless you, no. Although I can't speak for her namesake, she used to bite as I remember."

"Another raven?"

"No. This Mélusine really was a witch and a very good one. You didn't cross her...oh no. A bit wild, she was," Mrs Jenks thought for a moment. "I knew her in a previous incarnation. She became quite famous eventually. French you know."

The raven began walking up Sam's arm and he looked distinctly uncomfortable as he tried to keep his face as far away from her large and sharp beak as he could.

"She was quite a character," Mrs Jenks continued, "and very pretty when she was young but she grew very, very old and life was hard for her. She lived in a cave too, deep in a wood in the middle of France...sixteenth century if my memory serves me right, I've lived so many lives I can't always remember dates. Strange creature though. At a guess she must have been at least a hundred and fifty years old when she disappeared or died. No-one's quite sure what happened to her. Of course I'd passed on again by then."

Sam's recent experiences had shown him that life could be so much more intriguing than he had ever realised, but some concepts were still far too mind-boggling to take in. Convinced this time Mrs Jenks was barking mad, he tried not to laugh out loud, but made a sort of snorting sound, which prompted a snooty 'kronking' response from the raven, whose beak was just a little too close to his face now for comfort.

"You think I'm having you on, don't you?" Mrs Jenks asked.

"No, well, no not really," Sam flustered under her stern scrutiny. "It's just that everything's so fantastic. I don't know if there's anything I *can't* believe in anymore. If you said trolls and dragons live just round the corner, and that Doc Brownlow's really Dracula, I probably wouldn't question it now. Everything's just been so weird since I moved here!"

Mrs Jenks looked at him pityingly.

"Don't get me wrong, I think it's amazing and I wouldn't change it now, even though makes things awkward."

"How does it make things awkward?"

The raven stepped further along his arm towards his shoulder, and Sam turned his face away from her, holding his head at a painful angle keeping as much distance between her beak and his eyes as possible.

"I can talk to Charlie, Claptrap, Piggybait and the other elves, and now I can talk to you, but my girlfriend and my parents know nothing about...anything. I have to watch everything I say. I can't talk about the cave or the reindeer with anyone close to me. I'm positive Cathy knows more than she lets on, but she never says anything about it and I'm scared I might let something slip accidentally."

"Poor Sam. I can understand how it must feel but thankfully Charlie

155

and I are considered eccentric anyway, so we don't have that problem. Not that that helps you."

"I still love being part of all this though."

"Of course," Mrs Jenks warned, "if anyone did find out about Charlie or the elves, you know how catastrophic it would be." Bandit strolled over and Mrs Jenks picked him up, cradling him in her arms.

"Yeah. I know that. Don't get me wrong, Mrs Jenks. No-one will ever find out from me. I'm really made up to be a part of all this, it's just that I know Jenny would be too."

Bandit looked up into Mrs Jenks' eyes and miaowed softly. She smiled down at him. "No Bandit, sadly I quite agree." Turning sympathetic eyes to Sam she said, "Well, you never know. Perhaps one day. Anyway enough talking, it's time Mélusine was on her way." Putting Bandit back down on the ground, Mrs Jenks took the raven from Sam, much to his relief; her weight was making his arm ache. She stroked the bird's proud head, speaking softly to her. Bandit gave the bird a look of disdain and, with his tail held high, he trotted back to the house. Merlin stayed outside, rolling around on his back in the grass.

"OK, Mélusine, go and find Charlie." They watched the raven fly over the trees, towards the caves before disappearing from sight. "There, that should bring him here sharpish. Now how d'you fancy another cup of tea while we wait. I've made a fruit cake if you'd like a piece."

Recalling the untidy and probably unhygienic state of Mrs Jenks' kitchen, Sam refused the cake. "Thanks very much, but I still have to get to the shop for mum. She'll be wondering where I am."

"As you please, young Sam. As you please."

Bandit was grooming himself on the sofa when they returned to the kitchen. Rising from the sofa he sprang onto Sam's shoulders and stretched out comfortably, purring loudly in his ear.

Jerrill, having tired of the constant bickering of his companions, had left sometime before, saying he had far too much to do to be wasting time with a pair of elflings, and stalked off muttering something about 'not growing up'. Not the least bit bothered by his exit, Claptrap was still reading his paper and Piggybait, at the table, tried to read his future with the unused Tarot cards. "It's no great surprise he's taken to you," Piggybait told Sam, looking at Bandit. "He knows you're one of us."

Mrs Jenks made more tea while Sam wandered around the room looking at the books with Bandit stretched across his shoulders. He knew he should leave but was unable to drag himself away.

"Oh good, here's Charlie," Mrs Jenks called out. "I knew Mélusine would find him."

"What's the...ouch!!" In his hurry, Charlie forgot the lower than usual

ceiling and banged his head on a beam, uttering a stream of bad language of which his alter-ego would have never approved. Piggybait winced, but chortled at Charlie's misfortune, and Sam was certain Claptrap was struggling not to snigger.

"Are you alright, Charlie?" Mrs Jenks asked. "It's about time you remembered those beams, they've been here a long time. For goodness sake, sit down before you do yourself more harm." Mrs Jenks turned the sturdy rocking chair around for him to sit on.

"I'm fine, Armistice. Don' you worry about me none, but Mélusine said you needed to see me." Charlie rubbed his forehead where a large red mark was beginning to appear.

"You'll need Arnica for that," Mrs Jenks told him briskly. Searching in a sink unit drawer she found a small blue tub of cream and handed it to Charlie.

"I was working near the stream when she found me, she said it was urgent." He looked a bit annoyed. "Anyway, what's up?" He spotted Sam and his mood lifted. "Hello, Sam. What're you doing here?" Charlie dropped his local accent.

"Hiya Charlie. You've heard about Mr Atkins haven't you?"

Charlie nodded, "I knew before he was found."

Sam did not question this statement. It seemed perfectly logical for Charlie to have known before anyone else except, perhaps, the elves.

"I'm hungry again Armie," Piggybait interrupted.

"When are you not? You've got the biscuits, help yourself, and there's a fruit cake in a tin on the shelf too." She raised her eyes to the ceiling. "I don't know…it's no wonder they call you Piggy."

"Thanks Armie." Piggybait jumped down and, as he headed for the cupboard, he realised everyone was watching him and had gone quiet. "Sorry, didn't mean to interrupt. Go on with what you were saying."

"Thank you so much," Mrs Jenks said loftily.

"Charlie, Jonah told me he'd had a nightmare…like he'd seen a ghost his bedroom," Sam began, "but I don't think it was a dream. If it'd been anyone else they'd found I wouldn't have thought about it, but maybe it was Mr Atkins Jonah saw. If there's a way to get into the Manor without anyone seeing, that is. Do you know if the Manor has secret passageways?"

Charlie rocked creakily in the chair and smiled. "Of course it has. Most houses that old have secret passageways. With all the raids in Tudor times or during the Civil War, or back as far as Viking times, folk were mindful of their safety. Many houses were built with passageways, hidey-holes and tunnels, some had them put in after the original house was built by losing a little space off the rooms, but Winterne Manor had a good many secrets built into it, and there's more than passageways in that building."

"Wow! So he could have got in and out without anyone knowing."

"If he knew about them, then yes, very possibly he could, and it's very likely he did know."

Claptrap and Piggybait had been sitting quietly in the background, gradually working their way through the biscuits while listening to the conversation.

"We found where he stayed when he left the stables," Claptrap put in. "He left everything behind when he rushed off that night and wasn't able to go back for any of it. To re-stock he took stuff from the Manor."

"But what could he have been looking for?" Sam asked no-one in particular. "What was it that kept him here?"

"There's something specific he was after," Charlie replied. "Otherwise, why risk discovery going upstairs if he only needed food, especially when he could have stolen that elsewhere. No, you're right. There's something in the Manor that was worth him taking a big risk for."

"Yeah, but like what, Charlie?"

Mrs Jenks, Piggybait and Claptrap followed the conversation while the clock on the mantelpiece ticked softly in the background.

"No idea, but it was obviously worth killing for." The shopping forgotten, Sam walked around the room, Bandit clinging indignantly onto his shoulders, while he tried to think up an answer to the puzzle.

"Surely some hidden passageways inside the house would lead outside as well, especially considering why they were needed in the first place," Sam suggested looking at Charlie, whose face now had a meaningful expression. "You know where it is, don't you, Charlie. You know a way in."

Charlie inhaled long and deeply and stroked his thick, grey beard. "Yes, yes, I do," he boomed. "I'd take you but I'm too big to get through some of it and it doesn't expand like some others we know," he chuckled. "D'you know the big dead oak in the clearing?"

Sam nodded. He avoided the clearing when he was in the woods; it had a weird atmosphere. "You mean the one that got hit by lightning?"

Charlie nodded, "The very same. Stand facing the split side, about…four metres away from it and enter the trees to your left and you'll see a path, follow it for about half a mile it and you'll see the ground slopes upwards. Stay on the lower level and you'll find yourself at the side of a small hillock with a mass of ivy cascading from the top. Take a look underneath. You'll find a door."

"The ivy's growing over it," Piggybait broke in again.

Charlie frowned. "Thank you Piggy, would you like to take over?"

"Thank you sir," Piggybait missed the irony altogether. "The ivy's very thick, Sam, so the door's completely camouflaged. You'd have to know it's there 'cause you'd never see it. Inside, the tunnel ceiling's quite low and it's very dark and damp, but it slopes right down into the house. As far as we know the passageways run all round the house. Priests had hiding places in there, one of them was forgotten about after one raid and he's still supposed to roam the house," Piggybait explained.

"What like a ghost?" Sam asked wide-eyed.

"No. Not *like* a ghost. He is a ghost. Spooky ain't it?" Piggybait pulled a horrible face, making his eyes bulge.

"You look just like that ugly pixie, Garrak, when you did that," Claptrap shuddered.

Piggybait grinned maliciously.

"Jonah never mentioned a ghost. Well, not until now." Sam said, ignoring the remark about Garrak.

"Yes, but look how he used to be, Sam. Do you think any self-respecting ghost would want to appear to him?" Claptrap asked.

"But he's not like that now," Sam defended his friend.

"Maybe so, but that piece of news might take a while to get around the spectral community."

"I'm going to have to tell Jonah about the tunnel, but how do I explain how I know about it? I can't say you told me, can I?" Sam said glumly.

"You can't tell him about Piggy or Claptrap," said Mrs Jenks. "But there's no reason why you can't say Charlie mentioned it. He works in the woods…and knows it like he knows his own home. There's no-one more knowledgeable…except me, perhaps. Jonah wouldn't question anything Charlie told you about the woods."

"True, Armistice, very true," Charlie agreed. "Yes, tell him I told you about it. It's not like it leads to the elves home, so it can't do any harm. One word of caution though, keep a watch out for the stranger. I don't want you lads putting yourselves at risk. Promise me."

"Yes, Charlie, I promise. We'll be careful." Sam crossed his fingers behind his back.

Chapter Twenty Two

Word of the murder spread like wildfire through the village, even though the police tried to keep it low key. Susan and Jason avoided talking about it as they sat together on the bench overlooking the green. It was just too horrible.

"You know, you're a lot nicer than I thought, Jase," Susan smiled shyly. Over the last half an hour they had slowly inched closer and now their hands were just a fraction apart, but they were still too timid to touch.

Having known her nearly all his life, although he really liked her, Jason had never thought that Susan would ever see him as anything other than one of the group of friends, but everything changed when she found out about Sam and Jenny.

Like everyone, except Sam, Jason had known about Susan's crush and understood how much of a disappointment it had been seeing them both together. To keep her occupied, and to prevent her tearing Jenny's hair out, Jason had stayed close to Susan all through their trip to the Wookey Hole Caves, keeping her busy talking about the colours of the rock, the icy crystal blue water inside the caves and telling her of his ambition to become a diver carrying out underwater exploration through the underground streams. They laughed in the Hall of Mirrors and the Mirror Maze and he took photographs of her in the Dinosaur Valley, all the time making sure that she and Jenny never got within spitting distance of each other.

Later, at the cinema, he bought her a huge carton of popcorn and a cola and chose seats at the other end of the row from Jenny and Sam. Thanks to his efforts, she no longer seemed concerned about Sam and Jenny, and Jason was trying to pluck up the courage to ask her if she would go out with him. He almost managed it twice, but something very large and lumpy stuck in his throat and choked him each time he tried, so he remained tongue-tied.

"There's Jonah." Susan pointed across the green.

"I'm not sure what to say to him," Jason said, kindly.

"I know. Mum told me about it. She knows everything before it's happened and loves spreading it around the village. We don't need newspapers here, she could just stand on the corner of the street and shout," Susan said scathingly.

"Yeah, she can talk a bit can't she?"

"She gossips for England. But never mind her, let's go and meet him."

Jason saw the misery in Jonah's eyes. "I'm really sorry, mate. I don't know what to say."

Susan gave Jonah a hug. "It must be awful for all of you. How's your sister?"

"Yeah," Jonah answered softly, avoiding her eyes. "You know about dad then?"

They both nodded.

Jonah shrugged. "I just feel completely numb, but that just makes it worse. I feel like I should be more upset, but I'm not, and it feels wrong."

Susan held out a hand to Jonah. He gripped it. "It's too soon, Jonah, it won't have sunk in yet. Come on," she coaxed, as the trio turned back to the bench. An elderly couple walked by, saw Jonah and crossed the road, speaking in hushed tones. Mr Driver, the vicar, cycled by on the other side of the green, but seeing Jonah, he doubled back and stopped, shaking his head sympathetically. Jonah let go of Susan's hand.

"My dear boy, I'm so sorry for your trouble. Please pass on my condolences to your dear mother. Tell her I'll call by in the morning to see if there's anything I can do."

Jonah nodded miserably, not knowing what to say.

"Right oh! Must dash," he said, looking rather ill at ease, "parish work to do, but I'll probably see you at the Manor tomorrow." He nodded to Susan and Jason, got back on his bike and hurried off along the Glastonbury Road.

"So everyone knows then?" Jonah observed grimly.

"Yeah, we were just talking about that." Jason and Susan exchanged glances.

"Look at it! The sun's shining, the sky's blue and I feel like running away. I suppose I'd have been better staying at home today, but I just had to get out of the house for a while." He looked around. "Have you seen Sam?"

"No, not today," Jason replied.

"Or Jenny?"

Susan flinched. Jason caught the movement and, screwing up his courage, he reached out to take her hand. She took it and held on. Jonah was too pre-occupied to notice.

"No. I haven't seen her either."

"Shame," Jonah sighed. "I could've done with seeing him."

"Look, Jason, if you and Jonah want to find Sam, it's OK. I've got homework to finish anyway. I'll see you later," Susan volunteered looking at him over Jonah's forlorn head. He gave a small nod and silently mouthed 'see you later'. Susan nodded back. "Phone me," she whispered.

161

"Come on Jonah, let's go for a walk," Jason suggested.

"See you later fellas." Susan headed home and the two boys walked back towards the Manor. They were almost at the driveway, when Sam emerged through a gap in the hedge behind them.

"Hiya Jason. Jonah, how are you?"

"You know then?"

"Yeah, look if there's anything I can do…"

Jonah looked up at Sam, his eyes glittering. "D'you know the numbers of times I've heard that today?" he snapped, then immediately regretted his outburst. "Sorry, mate. I didn't mean that. The police said dad was murdered…it looks like it was that Fisher bloke we saw the other day who did it, but it's a bloody nightmare. First he was dead, then he was alive, but we only found he'd been alive when he was dead." He looked from Sam to Jason and back, his eyes heavy with pain.

"I heard something that might help, but no promises mind," Sam volunteered warily.

"Dad been sending messages from the astral plane, has he? I don't think anyone can help, not unless Mrs Jenks holds a séance and gets in touch with him."

"No, listen, you don't understand. Charlie told me earlier about a secret door into the Manor…it's near that dead oak, the one that got struck by lightning…it's hidden by ivy."

Jonah looked up from the ground. "Are you serious? How does he know?"

"He's worked these woods for years…if anyone knows its secrets it's Charlie," Jason pointed out.

"I don't know if it'll help you find what you're looking for," Sam broke in, "but surely its worth…hey wait a minute. Wait for us! You don't know where it is."

Jonah had broken away and darted through the hedge into the meadow. "Don't be dim," he barked, "of course I know where the lightning tree is," Jonah called back.

Jason turned to Sam. "Well, what's he got to lose? Come on let's go." They finally caught up to him just as he was about to enter the trees.

"It's this way," Jonah shouted excitedly. Jason seemed reluctant to follow and slowed his pace.

"Well, come on, what are you waiting for?" Jonah thundered through the bracken, terrifying flocks of birds into taking flight and disturbing the busily chatting squirrels.

"What's the matter, Jase?" Sam asked the troubled Jason.

"I…I'm not sure about going in there, Sam," his fear evident. "You know what they say about these woods."

Sam grinned, "I know, I've heard the rumours, but d'you think Charlie would let me go in there if he thought there was something wrong with the place?"

Jason shook his head. "I hadn't thought of that."

They ran through the ferns to catch up with Jonah who was now some way ahead. Blindly hurtling through the undergrowth at a rate of knots, he missed seeing a raised tree root and fell with a crash onto the pebble and rock strewn mossy path.

"Rats!" He pulled himself up and looked to see what damage had been done. His jeans were ripped from the knee to the ankle and, as he held the two edges open, they saw a nasty cut to his shin and his knee looked badly grazed.

Jason looked down at the wound and whistled. "That's some mess Jonah. You've got to go back, it needs cleaning up."

Jonah looked down at his wounds. The cut was bleeding quite badly and the graze was oozing blood through bits of leaf, moss and dirt that had stuck in it. "No." he protested. "Not yet. It's my own stupid fault. I should've looked where I was going."

Propping himself against a tree trunk, he dabbed at his injuries with the sleeve of his sweatshirt. Blood trickled down his shin and into his trainer. "I've got an idea." Taking off his sweatshirt, he pulled off his tee-shirt, put the sweatshirt back on, and ripped the tee-shirt into three pieces and gave Sam and Jason a piece each.

"Can you tear those into strips for me while I hold this on? I'll get it cleaned up later."

"But what if it gets infected?" Jason asked, tearing the cloth into several strips.

"I'll worry about it if it happens. Right now I want to find that tunnel."

Folding one section of the tee-shirt into a makeshift pad, Jonah laid it over both wounds. Then using their torn-up strips like bandages, he bound it securely around his leg, knotting the ends at the back. The blood had stopped flowing freely, but seeped inexorably through the material. He frowned at the make-do dressing. "Well, it'll have to do for now. If it keeps bleeding, I'll borrow a tee-shirt from one of you," he said, not bothering to ask. "OK, I'm ready. Let's go." Reaching out for their hands, he struggled to his feet and gingerly tested his weight on the injured leg.

"Arggh! That's sore."

"Are you sure you're OK to keep going?" Sam asked. The dressing had slipped a little exposing the top of the graze, but Jonah had tied it too tightly above the calf muscle for it to slide any further down, so the worst of the injury remained covered.

"Don't fuss!" Jonah snapped. Jason and Sam exchanged a 'just put up with it' look which Jonah intercepted. "Sorry, I didn't mean that."

"Yeah, we know," Sam grinned. "Come on, it's not far."

Their progress through the woods was much slower than before, with Jonah limping and swearing under his breath, but soon they stood before the twisted carcass of what was once a magnificent oak, that now stood isolated and splendid. The tree, over two hundred years old, had grown proudly until its trunk had been sliced through during a major thunderstorm some forty years before. The hollow, distorted shell, with bent and withered branches, towered several metres above them, forlorn and lifeless except for the many insects that made it their home. The boys stared at it, silenced by the change in atmosphere. In the woods there had been bird song, leaves rustling in the trees as the breeze played through them, the reassuring sounds of life but, here in the clearing, there was no sound. No birds flew over the scene. It was as silent as the grave.

"Some people say it takes on strange shapes in the moonlight," Jason broke the silence.

"Yeah, yeah, and *they* reckon the woods are haunted, Jase," Jonah said sarcastically. "You'll be agreeing with the nutters about little people in the woods next."

Sam turned away to hide his smile, but caught Jason's wounded expression and put his hand on the sensitive boy's shoulder as Jonah limped away.

"Forget it Jason, he didn't mean it. He's sounding off, his head's all over the place right now."

"Yeah." Jason gave a weak smile. "It's just a bit hard to take his mouthin' off sometimes."

"Come on, what are you waiting for? Christmas?" Jonah yelled, forging ahead of them. Within the trees, again, Sam was relieved to hear sound. Everywhere birds sang and leaves rustled as the breeze drifted through the trees. Jason rolled his eyes upwards as they hurried to catch up with the impatient Jonah. Soon after, Sam knew they had reached the slope Charlie had described. Growing down its side was a mass of ivy. He was sure this was the right place. A tingle of excitement ran through him. "Jonah! Jason!"

Jason ran and Jonah hobbled over to join Sam, watching as he struggled to move along under the heavy swathes of ivy searching for the door. Jason moved closer to help him, recklessly tearing away clumps of foliage. Sam shouted at him to stop. "No Jase! Be careful! If there is a door here, there won't be enough ivy left to cover it up. The way in has to be our secret?"

"Oh yeah. Got a bit carried away. Sorry."

"It's here!" Jonah shrieked, his voice echoing around the trees sending more birds into the air. Sam and Jason hurried over to find him struggling

164

with a thick growth of ivy with one hand, and trying to push open an old wooden door that refused to budge, with the other. "Here, quick. Give me a hand with this, it won't open."

Jason held back the heavy, woody-stemmed foliage while Sam, leaning forcefully on the door, twisted the circular handle but only managed to move it a centimetre or so. "It's moving!"

"Here let me help," Jonah squeezed in next to Sam and they both pushed, but even with their combined strength, the door refused to budge any further.

"Your uncle didn't say how to move this thing did he?" Jonah asked, panting heavily as he leaned against the wall.

"No…no, he didn't. I don't understand. There must be some way to get it to open."

Jason, still half hidden by trailing ivy, was pushing and prodding anything that appeared remotely suspicious or prominent, to no avail. Eventually, he gave up and emerged, hot and sweating with ivy leaves and dirt in his hair. "I give up. I…need a breather."

Jonah plonked himself down on a mossy mound under the trees, and inspected his injury, carefully pulling at the tee-shirt padding. "It's stuck!"

"Don't pull it. It'll soak off in the shower," Sam said, lying down beside him. Cupping his hands behind his head, he stared at the sky through the branches of a larch tree. Something silvery-white moved swiftly through the leaves. Claptrap!

"Er, I'm going to have a look from the top. I might get a better view up there…I won't be long."

"You won't see anything to help from up there, it's too far up," Jonah sneered.

"I'll come with you," Jason volunteered.

"No!" Jason's puzzled expression meant Sam had to think quickly; he had been too quick to refuse his company. "No, Jase, I need you down here. If I see anything, I can direct you to it."

"Oh yeah…didn't think of that. OK, I'll wait by the door."

With Jason placated, Sam was free to find out why Claptrap was here. He walked back to where the ground began sloping upward. Piggybait and Claptrap were waiting at the top. Claptrap grinned. "I knew you'd seen me. I was willing you to look up. I told you it would work Piggy."

"I didn't say it wouldn't," Piggybait retorted.

"You did! You said telepathy wouldn't work on Sam."

"I said nothing of the sort!"

"Stop arguing you two!" Sam glowered. "No wonder Jerrill gets fed up. We're here to find out how to get through that door, alright?"

"It might be," Claptrap sulked.

"Now don't start again," Sam said impatiently. "We've got enough to deal with. Jonah hasn't got a clue what's going, his head's all over the place and I'm trying to help him sort things out. Your squabbles can wait until this is over. That girl and her dog got hurt, now Jonah's Dad's been killed, so this is not the time for a strop. Are you going to help me or not?"

Claptrap and Piggybait looked at each other shame-facedly before Piggybait pulled his brown wool cap down completely over his face making Sam laugh.

"Idiot!" Sam chuckled.

"Made you laugh though," said Piggybait pulling his cap back into place.

"What's the matter with his leg?" Claptrap jerked his thumb in Jonah's direction.

"He tripped over a root. He's got a nasty cut and his knee's grazed. We tried to make him go back and get it seen to, but he's too stubborn to go."

Claptrap stared down at Jonah, who was still trying to peel the padding away. It was coming away gradually, but began bleeding again at each pull.

"Tell him to leave it alone, Sam. It'll be alright if he leaves it alone."

"Jonah, *leave it alone!* It'll get worse if you pull at it like that," Sam called down.

Absorbed with inspecting his wound, Jonah jumped at Sam's shout. "OK, OK." He folded the material back over the injury, securing the strapping tightly.

"Good, that's sorted out." Claptrap screwed his face up in concentration, looking intently at Jonah.

Sam recalled hurting his hand the night he had first met the elves. They had healed that wound too, but it had never been discussed.

"Now, if you've quite finished with the walking wounded, perhaps we can get on," Piggybait snapped. "Sam, lie down, close to the edge, same side as the door, and look over," Piggybait began.

"Just by that holly bush and look straight down," Claptrap added.

Piggybait's eyes flashed angrily. "I was telling him."

"And, as usual, taking too long about it," Claptrap retorted.

"Wasn't!"

"Not again! Pack it in, both of you!" Sam hissed.

"Sorry Sam." Piggybait looked very contrite.

"Yes, sorry," said Claptrap, looking so apologetic, Sam almost laughed out loud.

"Right, can we get on with it! I haven't got long or they'll be wondering what's going on ."

As if to reinforce that, Jason called up. "Hey Sam, what you doing?"

"Just looking around…won't be long," Sam shouted back. "OK, so what have you got for me?"

"Lie down Sam, just there," Piggybait indicated the spot.

"You're having me on?" Sam queried, looking over the steep drop.

"No, I'm not. Do you want our help or not?"

Sam did as he was told and hung his head, uncomfortably, over the edge.

"Now look straight down, near the door. There's a rock sticking out to the left of it, the one a bit triangular shaped. See it?"

"I think so. What about it?"

"Just underneath, within easy reach, is a clump of moss. If you lift it up, you'll find a small lever hidden underneath…it releases the mechanism that allows the handle to turn and, just inside the door is a small alcove where Atkins kept a couple of torches."

"Hey, Sam!" Jonah was getting impatient. "Find anything? You've been up there forever."

"Yeah, maybe. I'm coming down." He turned to the elves. "Gotta go. Thanks for your help guys."

"See you later, Sam, and don't worry about the other human, we've got the woods covered." He pointed into the branches of the larch tree. At first Sam could not to see anything unusual, and then he spied Rondo high up in the tree, his leggings and jerkin exactly the colour of the leaves and his shoulder length blond hair caught up in a cap. His camouflage was perfect. Sitting next to him and waving happily was Saldor. Sam thought it probably made a change for him to get out in daylight. Something moving in the bracken behind Jonah caught Sam's eye as Rondina, half concealed in the undergrowth, smiled in greeting. He was a little surprised she was there. He had only ever seen the male elves away from the cavern and then, just as he was about to move away, the leaves of a large fern near to her moved aside revealing Lommie and Jossamel.

"Cool!" Sam grinned, delighted with their elven bodyguard. "Looks like you've got things covered, but why's Rondina here?"

Piggybait rolled his eyes. "Don't get him started," he said, nodding over at Claptrap.

"She keeps going on about women's rights," Claptrap said belligerently. "She says females are as capable as we are and should have the right to take night patrols and carry out Christmas duties," he sneered. "It seems she's too good to cook and weave for *we* inferior males. She even had the nerve to say females would be more efficient. Can you believe that?" Claptrap glowered at Rondina, who in turn, glared back at him and poked out her tongue.

"Human women already have that sorted," Sam said, struggling not to laugh, but Piggybait caught his amused look and winked at him.

"Seriously though Sam," Piggybait broke in. "No-one's getting through without us knowing. You're safe enough while we're watching."

"Come on, Sam. What're you playin' at?" Jonah called, completely unaware of the elves concealed behind him.

Rondina giggled and Jossamel covered her mouth with his hand. "He'll hear you!"

"You took your time," Jason commented, as Sam rejoined them.

"Yeah, but it was worth it. Follow me."

Back at the doorway, Sam pushed aside the ivy and Jason held it back for him while he felt around for the moss covered lever. On the mound, Jonah was irritated by an itchy sensation in his knee and began rubbing at it gently.

"Hey!" Sam cried triumphantly. "Here, look I found something!"

Jason moved in closer, letting go of the mass of ivy which flopped down on to his and Sam's heads. Scattering earth, leaves and the odd insect disturbed from its otherwise peaceful home.

"Thanks for that, Jason," Sam complained, brushing an orangey-brown centipede from his arm. Jonah hobbled over to join them and brushed a group of grey wood-lice from Jason's shoulder with his hand.

"Ugh!" I hate bugs," Jason whined. Sam grinned.

"You're going to have a great time in there then," Jonah nodded towards the tunnel door. "You sure you want to go in?"

Jason hesitated. "No. But I will. I have to now I'm here."

Jonah laughed. "You're my hero." Turning to Sam, Jonah said, "OK, so what have we got? Have you found how to open it?"

"Yeah. Look at this." He took hold of the bottom of the patch of moss and lifted it to reveal a small lever. Jason and Jonah looked at each other in amazement.

"How did you know about that?" Jonah asked. Admiration clearly shown on his face.

Sam shrugged. "Guessed. I saw a bulgy bit sticking out from up there and wondered why it stuck out and decided to check it out." He tugged the lever downwards. "We have...lift off!"

After a brief moment when nothing seemed to happen, they heard a grinding noise from behind the door, then when he turned the handle there was a loud click and the door swung open.

"You've done it!" A heavy smell of damp earth and stale air almost overwhelmed them.

"Aw, that's putrid!" Sam exclaimed.

"It smells like someone's died!" Jason declared, but seeing the expression on Jonah's face, he apologised. "Sorry, Jonah, I...didn't think."

168

"Nah. It's OK. I know you didn't mean anything by it." Jonah peered into the gloom of the pitch-black tunnel. The light from the open door allowed them to see just a few ominous metres ahead.

"It's no good Sam, it's too dark in there," Jason shook his head. "We'll have to go back and get some torches later. I suppose we should have thought about that before."

But Sam had already taken a few steps inside. "Wait a minute," he said, looking behind the door, "maybe your dad left something we can use, Jonah. Have a look round, Jason. See if you can find anything that might help."

Jason, pinching his nose to lessen the awful stale stench, disappeared into the tunnel and felt his way around behind the door.

"Ow!" Jonah held his now throbbing knee.

"What's up?"

"My leg's really sore. Maybe I should have got it looked at but it's too late to worry about it now, now that we've come this far. I'll see to it later."

"You can go back if you like. Jason and I can do this."

Before Jonah could reply, Jason called out. "Good guess Sam, there's a ledge with two big torches."

"Are you sure you're alright to go on?" Sam asked Jonah again.

Jonah nodded. "Too right I am! Come on, let's go." He limped past Sam into the tunnel and waited while Jason switched on both torches. The vivid beams cut through the darkness. Jonah took one and went ahead while Sam, taking a last look into the trees saw Claptrap and Piggybait watching him from the undergrowth. Claptrap gave him the 'thumbs-up' sign.

"The leg will heal." Sam did not exactly hear Claptrap speak; it was more as if he felt the words in his head. He turned to see Jason and Jonah heading away. He had to catch up before they got too far ahead of him. Giving a quick wave to the elves, he closed the door shutting out the comfort of the daylight. He did not see the swathes of ivy move back, shrouding the door from view. From the outside no-one would ever know the three boys had been there.

Chapter Twenty Three

Once the door was closed and the daylight gone, Sam experienced a moment of panic, but forced himself to follow the torch-lights and soon he caught up with Jason. The claustrophobic atmosphere of the passageway made his head reel at first but he soon became accustomed to the smell of decay and was able to breathe without wanting to be sick.

Jason, held his breath for as long as possible before necessity forced him to take another deep lungful of the mouldy air. Jonah alone was breathing normally, seemingly too intent on what lay beyond to worry about the assault to his sense of smell.

The earthen tunnel was wider than Sam had expected, at times allowing all three of them to walk comfortably side by side. Shining their yellow torch beams around the walls and above, they discovered the low, uneven ceiling was supported by fragile, rickety wooden beams and sinuous tree roots.

"You don't think this lot'll collapse do you?" Jason's voice was shaking and it made Sam feel much better not to be the only one who was scared.

"I sincerely hope not," Jonah replied, thankfully sounding just as tense.

Sam made a weak attempt at bravado. "It's probably been up for a couple of centuries, so it should stay up a few more hours," he replied, brushing aside a thick, sticky cobweb. "Just try not to bump the sides."

"A few more hours! I didn't think we'd be in here that long!" Jason exclaimed. "I can't take this mucky air all that time!"

"Hold your nose. You can't smell it so much if you breathe through your mouth," Sam advised.

"But then I'll probably get poisoned or swallow some disgusting bug or worse!" Jason's voice was muffled by the hand he had clamped over his mouth.

"Jonah, why do we always end up in tunnels?" Sam asked trying to keep the atmosphere light.

"Just lucky I guess," Jonah smiled, his face ghostly as he held the torch underneath his jaw. "As I remember it though, it was me who followed you into the tunnel before, not the other way around."

"How's the leg?" Sam asked, stepping over a piece of rotten timber.

"Yeah, it's alright. It's weird, but it doesn't hurt at all now."

Sam smiled. Claptrap had obviously been at work again.

Jason, now a little ahead of them, suddenly let out a loud juddering groan. "Aargh! The floor's not where I thought it was."

"What? Are you alright?" Sam and Jonah both spoke at once.

"Yeah, the floor drops down here. I wasn't expecting it. Jarred my leg a bit, but it's OK."

Sam remembered Piggybait saying the tunnel sloped downwards."

Jason had discovered the first in a series of long shallow steps leading downwards. They lowered their torch beams to see the steps more clearly and Sam moved closer to Jason. He had no intention of falling and needed to see where he was going. At the bottom of the steps they came across a number of large square rocks strewn around the muddy floor.

"These must be some of the original stones used for building the Manor," Jonah said. "Hey, look at this!" His torch beam had settled on something long and white jutting out from underneath.

"They're not human are they?" Jason asked, his voice brittle.

One large bone, very like a human femur, protruded from under one of the blocks. A second similar bone lay alongside the block.

A horrible image came into Sam's head and he shuddered, quickly forcing himself to think of something else, but he wondered what had happened to the rest of the skeleton. "No, it can't be human. What would human bones be doing down here? They must be from some animal."

"But how would they get in here?" Jason questioned, still breathing behind his hand.

"No idea, mate. Come on let's go."

Sam reached out for Jason's torch and shone it directly ahead. He soon had his answer about the rest of the bones. Scattered around the tunnel floor were several separate and broken bones; ribs, collar bones, shoulder blades and with the torch beam directed straight ahead, Jason failed to see where he was placing his feet and tripped over something embedded in the earth. Steadying Jason, Sam pointed the torch downwards. A skull, that judging by its shape and size could only be human, with a clearly visible straight and deep cut on the crown.

"Jonah! Come and take a look at this," Sam called, his voice echoed along the tunnel.

Jonah retraced his steps to join them and hunkered down to inspect the bones. "There's only one way this fella died. This was murder." He stood up and all three boys stared down at the sad remains. "I wish I knew what happened here. I might be able to find out if I get a chance to check into the history of the house but, come on. We've gotta get on."

The boys walked on in silence and Sam's heart sank when he shone the torch ahead. There was no end of the passageway in sight.

It already felt as if they had been in there for hours and the upsetting discovery of the skull had disheartened them. The dank air felt warm and heavy, and Sam, listening to Jason's laboured breathing, sensed he was starting to panic. "Come on let's speed up," he suggested giving the torch back to Jason to give him something to do. "We'll get to the end soon and fresh air."

Eventually, after what felt like another hour, the earthen floor became flag-stoned and the tunnel narrowed but they found the way blocked by a locked heavy wooden door.

"Now what?" Jonah groaned.

"We'll have to go back!" Jason muttered.

"No wait!" Sam was not going to give up yet. "We can't have come this far just to go back. Your dad used this way to get in and out of the house, Jonah, so there must be a way to get through. There has to be a key somewhere."

"Maybe he kept it with him," Jonah sighed.

"Yeah, but maybe he didn't," Sam replied, convinced Charlie would have said something if they were not going to get through.

Jason and Jonah shone their torches on the walls and the floor around the door, while Sam checked the lintel above the door.

"Yeuk!" His hand had plunged into an old sticky, dusty spider's web and the remains of it clung to his fingers and fell into his hair. He pulled it off his fingers, brushed his hands down his trousers and then through his hair to get rid the repulsive black web. Suppressing his disgust, he forced himself to run his hands along the top of the door frame again and, this time, found a key. "Got it!"

Jason and Jonah waited impatiently while Sam put the key in the lock and turned it clockwise. Nothing happened.

"Oh, what?" Jonah groaned.

Sam tried it anti-clockwise and the lock clicked open. "Let's not make anything easy, eh?" He pushed the door and held it back as it slowly swung open on its groaning hinges.

"You need to get some E45 on that lot Jonah," Jason said.

Sam chuckled.

"Don't you mean WD40?" Jonah smirked.

"Yeah, whatever. It's all cream innit?" Jason said defensively.

"You try using WD40 on your spots," Sam laughed.

The vaulted corridor they entered was wide and flag-stoned with two low doors on either side. An old worm-ridden stool with a broken leg lay on its side beneath a large ring that was riveted into the wall where several

large metal, dust-covered keys hung on a hook. They were the biggest keys Sam had ever seen and they reminded him of some of the old films he had seen when jailers kept prisoners in castle dungeons.

"Phwoar! It stinks even worse in here!" Jason cried, holding his nose.

"Yeah, it's pants," Sam agreed. "What is this place?"

"The dungeons. It's the dungeons!" Jonah was too excited to be bothered by the smell. "I've heard they were here but Meredith and I could never find a way down. This is cool!" He shone the torch through the small metal grille of a cell door. From behind came a squeaking and scampering noise prompting Jason to squeeze past Jonah for a better look.

"Hey rats, look!" Jason shouted. Jonah recoiled in fear.

"Jenny'd love this, I don't think. She hates rats," Sam said.

"Hey yeah. You could bring her down here for a romantic date and play the hero again," Jonah said, "saving her from the howwible nasty wats!" Tongue firmly in his cheek, he gave Sam a playful punch to the shoulder.

"Yeah, well they're prettier than some of the girls I've seen you with," Sam retorted.

"How about we get out of here," Jason prompted, but the way was blocked by a second heavy wooden door. Jonah joined him. "I hope this one isn't locked," Jonah said, trying the handle. This time, luck was with them and it opened stiffly, with loud creaking noises and, pushing Sam in front, they entered a large damp circular room where thin shafts of dim light filtered down from three small grilles in the roof, revealing thick, heavy cobwebs that hung from the ceiling, some long enough to reach the dust covered floor.

Sam noticed a shallow channel cut in the floor that divided the room and briefly wondered what it was for, but soon forgot it when he spotted a dilapidated wooden table with barrel-like structures at either end in the middle of the room. In the centre and on one side only, was a large wooden wheel that would not have looked amiss on an old pirate ship. It had timeworn frayed, brown stained ropes attached to it and, his imagination told him that these were dried blood stains but, not wanting confirmation, he said nothing to his friends. Chains were hung from one barrel to the other and then to the wheel. As he stared at it, a chilling thought crept into his head.

"Jason, you're the shortest, do you want us to help you grow a few inches?" he said with a nervous laugh, hoping a little humour would alleviate his own distorted sense of fear.

Jonah, examining chains and manacles hanging on the wall, turned to Sam. "What's the matter, you sound scared?" Jonah chuckled.

"Er...no, not really, but even you've gotta find this place a bit weird, Jonah."

"Yeah and you don't have to sleep upstairs from it, do you?" Jonah chuckled, strolling over for a better look at the rack.

"What's that in your hair?" Jonah asked.

"What?" Sam's hand flew to his hair and he frantically ran his fingers through it. A large black beetle that had probably landed in Sam's hair during investigation of the door frame fell onto the floor, along with a ton of dirt, and scurried away to safety.

"That's gross!" Sam exclaimed as Jonah chuckled.

Jason, meanwhile, had switched on his torch and wandered over to the darker section of the room. The beam sent spiders, not used to the light, scurrying for cover as it glided over them. Moving through the murky corner, something bright caught his attention. A tall, coffin like box stood upright against the far wall looking a little like an upright sarcophagus. He tried to open it but the door would not budge, so he felt around the side of the box until his fingers found a button and pushed it. The door clicked open and he sprang back as a number of long spikes came into view on the inside of the door.

"Hey! Look at this. It's an iron maiden!" Jason stared open-mouthed at the horrific contraption. Jonah and Sam joined him. "You know what this is? It's a torture chamber...how cool is that?" Jonah was delighted at their discovery, but Jason was already mooching around in another part of the room. "Not many people have a rack and an iron maiden in their basement," Jonah said, "and I think I've figured out what that long groove is."

"I wondered about that, it runs into a drain over here?" Sam pointed towards the outer wall.

"Yeah, I know. Look, this floor's stone and it's a torture chamber...they had to have somewhere for the blood to wash..."

"Here look! Look at this!" Jason's torch beam had landed on a human skeleton propped up against the wall near the iron maiden. The yellowed bones were intact, but the ankles were manacled and chained to the floor. On closer inspection, Sam saw a few long wispy hairs still attached to the skull and it had a sizeable hole just over the ear which he pointed out to Jonah.

"I wonder who he was," Jonah said quietly, shining his torch onto the pathetic bones.

"And how he ended up like this?" Sam added. "Hey! Look at his mouth!" A large, thick coin protruded between the teeth, resting on the bottom jaw. As Sam hunkered down to get a better look at the coin, Jason moved nearer and when Sam reached out to touch it, Jason pushed his hand away.

"Don't do that!"

"What?"

"Don't take it out of his mouth," Jason looked down at the bones, a mingling of pity and fear in his eyes. Sam and Jonah exchanged quizzical looks and Jason, tearing his gaze away from the skeleton, realised they were staring at him and looked a little embarrassed.

"What's the matter, Jason? I was only going to have a look."

"No-one should move it, Sam. It's there for a purpose," Jason stated firmly.

"What purpose?"

"It keeps the devil away," Jason mumbled.

"It does what?"

"It keeps the devil away," he repeated, more loudly this time. He stared down at Sam resolutely. "Don't you town folk know anything?"

"Surely you don't believe in that old rubbish?" Sam asked, incredulously.

"I didn't say I believed it, it's…it's tradition that's all." Jason seemed very unnerved at the thought of moving the well-preserved coin.

Sam looked up to see Jonah grinning at him.

"Have you heard these traditions, Jonah?" Sam asked him.

"Oh yeah, but I don't believe them and a few months ago I wouldn't have cared, but you'd better not touch it Sam, it might bring bad luck…we've had enough of that lately. Mind you it looks like our friend there," he pointed to the skeleton, "had just about all the bad luck he could take. He didn't chain himself up and put that coin in his own mouth!"

"Alright Jase, you win," said Sam standing up. "I just wanted to check it out and see how old it was." Jason looked relieved.

"Hang on, what's that?" Jonah reached down between the hip bones of the skeleton. He had seen something glittering in the torchlight. He picked it up.

"What is it?" Sam asked as he and Jason moved closer. Jonah brushed off the dust.

"It's a ring…with some sort of crest on it," Jonah said. "Here Sam, hold the torch. I want to have a better look."

The ring was wide, seemed to be made of solid silver and depicted a wolf between crossed lances with a dove hovering above on a square blue background.

"It's pretty old and that's definitely a crest. I think I've seen something like it in the house somewhere," Jonah said. "It's a bit worn but I'm positive I've seen it before. I'll have a look later."

"Hang on!" Jason exclaimed. "That crest's on the church window, the stained glass one by the altar."

"Yeah, you're right. I'll going to keep this." Jonah put the ring in his back pocket and, taking the torch back from Sam, examined the black chains binding the skeleton. Jason watched him resentfully, unhappy about anything being moved away from the room but it was Jonah's home, and he had never heard of a tradition about a ring on the floor keeping the Devil away, so he said nothing.

Sam borrowed Jason's torch and headed towards a third door at the other side of the room, with the beam directed onto the floor, Sam noticed lines of disturbed dust. There were two lines with smudges at regular intervals leading from one door to the other.

"Jonah, come here! Look at this!"

Jonah put down the manacle he was holding and went to join Sam as he ran the beam along what was obviously a pattern of footprints in the dust. Jason dragged himself away from the skeleton and joined them.

"What've you found? Oh!" Jason looked at Jonah, who had gone very quiet. The footsteps could only have been made by Jonah's father.

"Are you alright, Jonah?" Sam asked.

Jonah hunkered down and laid his left hand on one of the dusty footprints.

"It had to be Dad, didn't it? It couldn't have been anyone else. I don't think anyone else has been down here in a century or more, but he somehow found the way. Why didn't he tell us?" He stood up and ran his hand down his jeans to brush the dirt off.

"It's weird, but...well, being down here helps me feel closer to him but, the more I know, the more secretive he becomes and the less I know. Does that make sense?"

Sam had no idea how to answer him. Nothing he had done before had prepared him for this kind of situation. Jason struggled for something to say, but gave up and shrugged his shoulders.

"Come on, let's go," Jonah said, sadly.

Reaching the door, Sam wiped the grime off the tiny round window with his fingers, trying to see through, but it was so dark on the other side, cleaning it did not help. He tried the stiff round handle.

"Hey! Stairs!" Shining his torch up into the dark winding staircase, Sam observed many of the steps were broken and uneven. "I'll go first," he said. "Watch where you're putting your feet, they don't look very safe."

With Sam taking the lead, Jonah went second carrying the other torch and Jason followed close behind to make sure he could benefit from the light from the torches. They climbed the perilously winding stairs for what felt like an age.

"Look on the bright side, at least there's no rats," Sam joked.

"No, but there's spiders," Jonah groaned, brushing a cobweb away from his face.

"My knees are giving out," whined Jason.

"Is it tomorrow yet?" Jonah wheezed.

"Never mind your knees, Jase, how's your knee Jonah?"

"Its fine, but my lungs are gonna give up."

On reaching what appeared to be a small landing, Sam came to an abrupt halt. "Hear that?"

"Hear what?" asked Jonah.

"Hear what?" echoed Jason.

"Shhh! Listen!" Sam hushed them, pointing at the wall. Leaning against the cold stone, he could hear voices on the other side. "Hear them?"

"I hear something," Jason agreed.

Jonah pressed his ear hard against the wall. "It's Dorothy and Marj! They're just on the other side of this wall. If we can hear them, they might be able to hear us, so keep quiet. We don't want to advertise we're here, do we? We must be near the fireplace, the wall feels warm. Come on, let's keep going."

With Jonah now in the lead, then Sam and Jason following closely, they continued in single file up another flight of narrow, dusty stairs until the next turn brought them finally to the top of the staircase.

"At last," Sam gasped as they found themselves in a narrow stone passage with a low, arched ceiling.

Within a few minutes, Sam had stubbed his big toe on a raised flag-stone and Jason had a lump where he had banged his head on a metal torch sconce on the wall, so they kept one torch trained on the floor and the other on the ceiling. Jonah had managed to avoid further injuries since entering the Manor. After brushing aside cobwebs and spiders, he came across what looked like a rope of twisted metal. "I wonder what this does." He listened against the wall for a moment before pulling it.

Sam and Jason held their breath. Slowly and surprisingly quietly, a section of the wall slid away revealing a wooden panel with a very narrow slit at eye level. Jonah peered through.

"It's the…study!" Jonah began loudly, then remembered where he was and lowered his voice. "The window's on the left so where we are is the gap between it and the curtain. It's only a narrow gap so there would only be room for one of us to squeeze through at a time. This is fantastic." He moved aside to let Sam and Jason peer into the room but they were unable to see much because the curtain blocked their view, but they were very impressed.

"Come on, let's see where else the passage goes," Jason urged.

"No, wait a minute," Jonah said. "There must be a way in here. There's levers and things everywhere else…so why not here." He felt around the stonework and finally located a button. He pressed it and jumped out of the way as the wooden panel slid silently open, allowing them entry to the study, hidden by the curtain. Thankfully, the room was empty.

"I'm gob-smacked! Absolutely gob-smacked! This is amazing. I've lived here all my life and I never knew. If you think I was bad before, just think what I could have done if I'd known about this. What a waste!"

"Yeah, good job you didn't, you're an angel these days aren't you?" Sam joked, just as they heard approaching footsteps outside in the hallway beyond the study. "Someone's coming. Come on, let's go."

Pulling Jonah back into the passageway, Sam pushed the button and they watched as the panel glided back. They had to jump out of the way as the section of wall slid back into place.

"They move really quietly. Your dad must have kept it all in good nick," Jason said as they continued along the dark corridor and within minutes had located another metal rope, this time they entered the oak-panelled dining room. Jonah was overjoyed. "This just gets better and better."

At the end of the corridor they discovered another winding staircase. Up and up they went.

"How long have we been in here?" Jason asked.

"No idea," Sam replied, "but I bet Mum's gonna be mad with me. I was supposed to get some stuff from the shop and it feels like I've been out for hours. She'll kill me when I get back without them."

"Don't worry, Marj's always got loads of stuff in the larder, so you can probably help yourself to what you want if you can't get to the store in time," Jonah volunteered. "OK, there's another of those pull things. We're obviously upstairs and we might be near Meredith's room. The Doc was going to give her something to help her rest, so we'd better be quiet. I'm not really sure where we are." He pulled on the metal rope and took a deep breath.

The wall slid back, revealing another panel. Jonah listened. Everything was quiet on the other side, but this time there was no slit to see through. Surprisingly, this panel opened outwards and, to his surprise, he walked out into his bedroom. Sam and Jason followed close behind, utterly dumbstruck.

"So that's how he got in!"

Jonah suddenly darted back into the passageway leaving Jason and Sam perplexed. With his voice faint and echoing, he called out. "There must be something that opens the panel on the inside, probably on the fireplace somewhere. I guess it lines up with the chain thing in here. If you stand about half a metre from the end of the fireplace, there should be something about shoulder height. Can you see anything?"

"Just flowers and plants," Sam replied, carefully examining the

carvings.

"What sort of plants?"

"Oh, I dunno, what do I know about plants? And how come you don't know? It's your room. There's some here looking like ivy leaves, there's some…"

"Ivy leaves!" Jonah shouted. "That'll be it. Like at the door in the woods. Try pressing one."

Using both hands, Sam pressed every ivy leaf he could see. Nothing happened. "No nothing."

"Try again." Jonah was convinced they were looking at the right place. After pressing several ivy-looking leaves, Sam found the right one and Jonah sprang behind the panel as it swung shut on him.

"That's the one then," Jonah's muffled voice came from behind the wall. The panel opened again and he stepped back into the room. "Which one?"

Sam showed him, and Jonah pressed it. The panel swung back leaving no trace of its existence.

"Clever, very clever," Jason said, clearly impressed.

"OK. I'm going to get this leg sorted out and get changed. I won't be long. Help yourselves to a game or something. There are plenty of them about, but keep the noise down 'cause Meredith's room's just up from here." He took the ring out of his pocket and stared down at the crest.

"Hmm. Not sure what to do with this yet," he said, putting it away in his computer desk drawer. "I'll check it out later." Then he headed to the bathroom. Soon they heard water running from the shower.

"Those pads'll take some getting off. They'll have dried onto the cuts," Jason said as he and Sam searched through Jonah's collection of games, but Sam thought otherwise.

"Hey! Look!" Jonah called loudly, clearly forgetting about disturbing his sister. He was standing in the doorway of the bathroom, water dripping from the ripped leg of his jeans, the tee-shirt padding in his hands. "I don't believe it. This was completely stuck on, so how?" Jonah ended weakly, staring down at his leg. "I thought it would take ages to get it off let alone clean up but…look. I just don't get it."

No trace of dirt or leaves remained and the wounds were healed. Sam's acting deserved an Oscar as he tried to keep a straight face. "No idea. Perhaps it wasn't as bad as it looked," he suggested. "Now that it's been cleaned up."

Jonah looked sceptical. "Well I dunno what's going on and things are freaking me out but one thing's for sure, we need to keep these tunnels to ourselves. Agreed?"

"Agreed," Sam and Jason said together.

Chapter Twenty Four

A little after nine-thirty the following morning, Meredith, huddled in her dressing gown, sat in her favourite place of relaxation, the big green kitchen armchair, staring vacantly into the fire. Lying on the hearthrug, Wilmot stayed loyally by her side, occasionally whimpering, his chin resting on her feet. He looked up as Dorothy approached with a mug of tea for Meredith which she took absent-mindedly, without looking away from the fire.

Marjorie went about her usual chores, refraining from her normal chattering or tuneless singing while Dorothy sat down near to Meredith, watching over her.

"I'm going to put the washing out," Marjorie whispered to Dorothy.

"Take Wilmot with you, Marjie, he could do with a run, he hasn't been out today," Dorothy whispered back. Marjorie nodded, and clicked her fingers for Wilmot to follow her. He looked up, torn between staying with Meredith and obeying a command, but eventually rose from the hearthrug and followed Marjorie outside. Once through the backdoor, he darted about the garden barking, chasing butterflies from the bushes and then darting off after the birds on the lawn.

"Pack it up you daft animal," Marjorie laughed, "they're not doing you any harm."

Wilmot, as expected, ignored her and, satisfied at having seen off anything with wings decided it was time to investigate the bushes and darted in and out of the shrubs, his tail wagging furiously.

"If you catch a bee you'll know all about it!" Marjorie chuckled.

Leaving Wilmot free to charge around the garden, Marjorie put down the laundry basket, hung the peg-bag on the line and reached down for a pair of pillow cases. She breathed in a deep lungful of fresh spring air. "Another beautiful morning," she said out loud.

"It certainly is," answered a gruff voice behind her.

Marjorie spun round. She did not really see the man because the gun he was pointing at her captured her attention: she could not take her eyes off it. At that moment nothing else existed - just the man and the gun until Wilmot flashed into her mind. She quickly scanned the garden looking for him, but to her relief he was nowhere to be seen. She was convinced he would be shot if he appeared.

"What do you want? What are you going to do to me?" she heard herself saying.

"To you, nothing. Nothing at all, just as long as you do as you're told. I know the housekeeper and the girl are in the kitchen but who else is in the house?"

"Mrs Atkins…she's in the study."

"What about the boy and the other one…the dark haired bloke?"

"My Stuart? No. He's in Bridgewater on business for Mrs Atkins and Jonah's out somewhere."

"Good, so much the better. Now get inside." He waved the gun towards the house.

There was still no sign of Wilmot. He would still be chasing insects somewhere in the garden. Marjorie wasn't worried about him. The garden was secure so he could not run off and get lost. She just wanted him to stay out of the way for a while; long enough to keep him safe anyway.

"What do you want with us?"

"What makes you think I want anything with you. Get inside, now," her captor barked.

Desperately trying to find a way of escape, she thought of slamming the door in his face and bolting it quickly, but he pre-empted her. Moving ahead, but still pointing the gun threateningly in her direction, he pushed in front to enter the lobby before her.

"Now lock it, properly," he snarled. "The bolts, key, everything. Good, I like people to do as they're told. Keep it up. You're doing well."

Marjorie did not feel as if she was doing well. She wanted to run but her feet wouldn't let her.

"Keep going on like this and no-one will get hurt. Now get through there." He indicated the kitchen door.

"You were…quick." Dorothy, sitting opposite Meredith, turned as the door opened. Farrow, at first obscured by Marjorie, appeared from behind her.

"Fisher! What do you want?" Dorothy stood up, rousing Meredith from her trance-like condition. "It's Farrow actually, Malcolm Farrow. I thought I'd pay Harriet another visit. Am I not welcome?"

"Get out!" She looked as if she was going to spring at him.

"Don't Dorothy, don't upset him," Marjorie shrieked through chattering teeth. "He's got a gun."

"You! You murderer!" Meredith screamed. "Was my father not enough for you? Are you going to kill us too?"

Dorothy rushed to calm and comfort the emotionally fragile girl who burst into tears. "You've hurt this family enough. Why don't you leave us alone?" Dorothy spat.

"I'm surprised you found out about that so soon. It seems the police were quicker than I thought they would be," he said, quite cool and unruffled, "but never mind that now. And I will," he answered with a cold smirk, "I'll leave you completely alone...when I've found what I'm looking for." He smiled smoothly, his voice harsh. "Now *sit down* and don't move!"

Dorothy pulled her chair nearer to Meredith.

"Better, much better. Now you!" He pushed the terrified Marjorie onto a wooden chair on the other side of the table.

Still holding the gun and facing the women, Farrow took a large tea towel from a drawer and wrapped it around Marjorie's mouth, tying it securely at the back of her head. Dorothy, appalled, hoped for an unguarded moment when she could try to overpower him, but realised he could shoot before she could get to him. The risk was too great. Never taking his eyes off them, Farrow searched the sink unit drawers and found some spare lengths of washing line which he used to bind Marjorie's hands behind her back, before tying her to the chair. Opening the larder door, he dragged a moaning and muffled Marjorie, lashed to her chair, inside, closed the door and locked it. He flexed his arms. She was a heavy woman and it had been an effort.

"Now for you two."

Throwing Dorothy a length of washing line, he ordered her, at gun point, to tie Meredith's hands and feet and then bind her to the armchair. Dorothy shot him a look that would stop a clock. "You won't get away with this you know!"

"Just get on with it." Farrow looked at his watch.

"Where's Wilmot?" Meredith cried out. "What have you done to him?"

"Wilmot? Oh, the dog." Farrow smiled what he thought was one of his more charming smiles. "Nothing, I've done nothing at all to him, so I assume he's quite safe."

Meredith's worried face relaxed a little. "Thank Heaven!" she whispered to Dorothy.

"That's enough," he growled. "No more talking. Here!" He threw Dorothy another large tea-towel.

"What am I supposed to do with that?"

182

"What d'you think," he rolled his eyes. "Gag her, of course. I need some peace to think."

"You mean you haven't planned everything already? That really wasn't very clever of you was it?" Dorothy goaded.

"Shut up and get on with it!" he snarled furiously.

Dorothy apologised to Meredith as the put the tea-towel in her mouth, and peered through lowered eyes at Farrow. His hands were shaking, he was nervous. She wondered how far she could push him.

"Quiet!" he snapped.

"My turn now is it?" she sneered. "Oh, goody!"

"You're very mouthy for someone with a gun pointing at them," Farrow declared, throwing a washing line at her. "Now tie your legs to the chair."

Dorothy obeyed but as she straightened up, Farrow threw a length of line around her chest and arms, pinning her tightly. He roughly seized her left arm and pulled it behind her before grabbing the right arm. With her legs tied together, her body securely roped to the chair and her hands tied behind her, Dorothy was helpless and she felt her courage ebbing away. A tea towel was roughly thrust into her mouth. His cheap aftershave was rank and made her feel nauseous.

"That'll shut you up." He yanked the tea-towel tightly into a knot behind her head. "Not so full of yourself now."

Ensuring her binding was secure; he stopped at the swing-door to brazenly wave at her before disappearing into the hallway. As soon as he had gone, Dorothy tried using her tongue to push the tea-towel out of her mouth, but it would not budge. She struggled to find a way to loosen her bonds, but she was tied fast. Meredith's terrified eyes met hers. They could only wait anxiously for the outcome. All Dorothy could do was hope Harriet would come to no harm.

Harriet was at the writing desk in the study when the door opened. She did not look up. "Dorothy, ask Marjorie for some coffee when you go back down, please?"

"I think Marjorie's tied up at the moment."

Recognising the voice, Harriet's first instinct was to run, but he was between her and the door. Steeling herself, she stood and turned to face the man she knew had killed her husband. She walked towards him, cool and unflustered as ever, so calm and composed; it was he who was unnerved. He had expected tears and pleading, but her courage intimidated him. It would have pleased him had he known her smile masked her abject fear.

"What do you want Maurice? Or is it Malcolm or even, perhaps, Muchael?" She flinched on seeing the gun. "Do we really need that thing?"

"Yes, I think we do, especially as you know who I am. If nothing else, you'll know I mean business."

"I don't give a damn what your name is. What have you done with my family?" She stood facing him, brazening it out.

"They're OK. Your daughter's comfy in the armchair downstairs but she's a bit tied up at the moment, just like your housekeeper and cook, but they'll be alright when I get the diamonds."

"Diamonds? What diamonds?" Harriet was either a good actress or she genuinely knew nothing about them.

"No more games. Jerry got hold of a load of diamonds years ago." Farrow made himself comfortable on a cream sofa and crossed his legs. "We were partners then and I want my share." Without warning his self-control slipped and he sprang up from the sofa, his face a hairs-breadth from hers, his face creased in anger. "*I need them*!" She flinched as his spittle landed on her cheek. She wiped it away with her hand, never lowering her defiant eyes. It was he who broke eye contact.

"Let's not fall out any more than necessary, my dear." He had regained his composure. "I need to leave the country and the diamonds will give me a way out, just as they would've done for Jerry…if…if he hadn't."

"Hadn't what?" she said coolly.

"Never mind!"

Harriet knew very well what he had been about to say. "I don't have them," she answered calmly, "and I certainly don't know anything about Jerry having any diamonds. So I can't help I'm afraid."

"Oh I think you can," Farrow sneered. "I know where they are, I've done my homework, you know. They're in a safety deposit box in the Somerset, Avon and Devonshire Bank, Main Street, Bristol. They were in London, but Jerry moved them. He had the box number engraved inside an antique watch as a reminder. It looks completely innocent, like a date."

Harriet gave an involuntary gasp, remembering the engraving she had seen inside the watch she had given Sam.

"So you *do* know something about it. Where is it?"

"I don't have it any more. I gave it away." She walked over to the window, her back to him.

"Who to?"

"A friend of my son's…I can't ask for it back now, it would look…suspicious."

Farrow thought for a moment. "Yes, I agree, but we only need the number. Phone them. Ask for the date, tell them it's something to do with insurance, they won't know any different."

Harriet, realising she had lost this point, said, "It's alright, it's come back to me. It was 1888." She walked to the window and looked out across the lawn, not wanting to look at him.

184

Farrow smiled. "There, that was easy wasn't it? All we need now is the key and we're all set and get over here away from the window," he ordered.

Harriet reluctantly did as she was told. "What do you mean by *we*? I don't give care about the diamonds. It's you who wants them, so why include me?"

"Because, my dear, you're going to the bank to get them."

"I'm doing nothing to help you!" Harriet snapped, defiantly.

"Don't forget the people downstairs who will suffer if you don't." He waved the gun close to her face.

"You wouldn't!"

"Normally no, I don't like violence, but I've had a falling out with the Benson Brothers from the East End of London. They're really not very nice people, and I'm scared enough of them not to care about hurting anyone who gets in my way. So you see, I'm desperate, and desperate people do things they wouldn't normally do." He looked genuinely scared when he mentioned the Benson's. She had no choice. She would do what he wanted and he knew it.

"What about the key?" I don't have it."

"I suppose you're going to tell me you gave that away too."

"Yes, I did."

A look of cold, hard fury crossed his face. He moved towards her menacingly, his fist clenched. "Don't forget the people downstairs. They'll suffer for your stupidity. You'll get that key back. *Now*! Call whoever's got it. In two minutes you will call whoever has the key. I'll be listening on the kitchen extension. Any mistakes and, someone gets shot. Understand?"

"Yes." Harriet's voice shook.

Farrow was about to leave the room when she said, "I do have the key."

"What?"

"It was hidden in a jewellery box I gave to one of Jonah's friends and they found it. The girl brought it back in case it was important."

"Why didn't you tell me before?"

"I don't know," Harriet said dejectedly. Her last bluff had been played.

"You'll drive to Bristol now," he barked. "I'll give you three hours. That should be enough time. Don't speak to anyone. If I get any idea something's wrong, your family will be in danger. They'll come to no harm as long as you do as you're told. Understand?"

"*I'm not stupid!*" she cried out. Then regaining her self-control, she said quietly, "What if I have problems at the bank? It was Jerry's box, not mine."

"That won't be a problem. You're his widow which means everything's yours and, by the way, he is definitely gone…this time." He smiled cruelly

as Harriet blanched. "Take identification with you and Jerry's death certificate, the original one, just in case. The bank won't know anything about...about, let's just call them...recent developments."

From a drawer in the writing desk, Harriet took out a small silver key with a long shaft. She put it in her handbag, together with her passport and some papers which she took from a larger drawer.

"Just a minute," Farrow said, reaching for the bag. "I'll keep this." Removing her mobile phone, he put it on the coffee table. "Just to make sure, you understand."

She shot him a contemptuous look.

"Your family are safe for the next three hours, but beyond that who knows. That's all up to you, my dear." He gave her a malicious grin.

"I really hope they get you."

"I'm sure you do," he said, still smiling. "But I'm not going to make it easy. I have no intention of getting caught by the police so when I leave I'll take your car. You won't need it as you'll be tied up with the others. It should give me a good start."

"Who said I was talking about the police?"

It was Farrow's turn to blanch. If the Benson's found him his life would be over.

Just over an hour later Harriet left the Somerset, Avon and Devonshire bank with a pouch of diamonds in her handbag. She felt conspicuous, as if she had a huge sign on her head telling everyone what she was carrying. At the car park two policemen walked by and she fought the urge to run up to them and tell him everything, but she could not endanger her family.

Jonah! What if Jonah had gone home? She prayed he would stay out for the morning, or longer. She looked at her watch. It was only eleven o'clock. How life had changed in just a couple of hours.

Back at her car, she turned the key in the ignition. What would she find when she got home? Her stomach churned. Were they all still safe? Would Farrow leave with no further trouble? Later, she had no memory of the return journey; how she got back safely she had no idea. The only thing she remembered was her anger, anger at Fisher, or Farrow, as she now knew him, and anger at Jerry for putting them in this situation. If he had not been dead this time, she felt she could have killed him! She was only vaguely aware of pulling up outside the Manor and felt as if she was in a dream as she walked into the house to find Farrow waiting by the front door with the mixed emotions of panic and delight on his face. Seeing him brought her crashing back to reality.

"Are they, is everyone...?"

"Do try not to worry, my dear, frowning ages you," he said spitefully, snatching the pouch from her hand. "They're just fine. You made very

186

good time. I trust you spoke to no-one." He waved her towards the study. "You'll join your family shortly, but first I want to see what you've brought me. Let's go to the study. After you, my dear."

Chapter Twenty Five

At the precise moment Farrow forced his way into the Manor, a rattling noise woke Sam from his sleep. He rubbed his eyes and peered at his bedside clock. He had slept badly dreaming of beetles and skeletons chasing him with keys up a spiral staircase where the steps crumbled under his feet.

He had slept late, but, as he had no plans until later, he closed his eyes and hoped he would have more pleasant dreams. The noise came again

Springing out of bed, he pulled back the curtains to be greeted by a very ill-tempered and precariously perched elf, on the window ledge.

"Finally! Let us in," Piggybait mouthed at the closed window. "We've been tapping for ages."

"What are you doing here?

Claptrap, balancing nimbly on the guttering, was making his way towards them.

"Piggybait hopped agilely over the windowsill, and looked back to see how Claptrap was getting on. "Come on, slow-coach. Hurry up."

Claptrap repeated a gesture Sam had seen him make when they were at Mrs Jenks, but this time it resulted in Piggybait turning his back on him. "I was about to help him but, after that he can do it himself!" He grinned. "So what happened with your mum about not getting the shopping yesterday?"

"It was alright. She guessed I was with Jonah and knowing what had happened, she didn't mind, but shhh…" Sam listened at the door. He did not want his parents hearing noises in his room and coming up to investigate. He could have done without these surprise visitors at home.

"Don't worry," Piggybait reassured him. "Your dad's at work and your mum's on her way to the village. She's gone to get the shopping you forgot yesterday-y-y-y," he said in a mocking, sing-song voice.

"We made sure of that before we came up, didn't we Claptrap?"

Claptrap, his face a picture of unlikely innocence, nodded as he hoisted himself over the window sill and into the room.

"Delighted you could join us," Piggybait said a little sarcastically.

"Your fault!" Claptrap sulked. "If you hadn't held me back like that, pushing in front, I'd have been here before you."

"*Enough!* Now what's up?" Sam was fast losing patience with his argumentative visitors.

"Oh yes." Piggybait pulled himself onto Sam's unmade bed. Scruffs, Sam's toy bear was perched on the headboard. "Nice Teddy," Piggybait grinned, picking 'Scruffs' up.

"Yeah, alright!" Sam, slightly embarrassed, snatched the bear back and laid it on his pillow. "Well?"

"Oh yes. Where was I?"

"At the Manor...the man Halmar saw, remember?" Claptrap reminded him irritably.

"What man?" Sam demanded.

"This morning, it was Halmar's turn to watch the Manor. You know Halmar...he's marrying Ellien..."

"Of course he knows who he is, Piggy, now please get on with it," Claptrap butted in.

"I was getting there! Anyway," Piggybait flashed Claptrap an indignant look. "Anyway, this morning, just a short while ago, Halmar reported seeing a man heading for the back garden of the Manor. He's convinced it's the one everyone's looking for and he followed him."

Sam sat back down on the bed, listening intently. "What happened then?"

"That big woman, the cook, went into the garden to hang out the laundry. Well, it's such a beautiful day...for those of us who are up and out of bed anyway."

"Piggy!"

"Oh yes, sorry, went off the point again, didn't I? Anyway, Halmar saw him get out a gun and point it at her."

"A gun?"

"Yes Sam, you know what a gun is," Claptrap took over. "He ordered her into the house and bolted the door."

"I was telling the story!" Piggybait barked.

"Yes, but not quickly enough, so it's my turn," Claptrap argued.

Piggybait stormed off, plonked himself down on the carpet and sulked.

"Do you know what happened next?" Sam asked.

"Halmar managed to get a look through the kitchen window. The cook wasn't on her own, the housekeeper and the Atkins girl were there too. Anyway, he tied up the cook, dragged her into the larder, and made the housekeeper tie the girl up then he tied up the housekeeper himself. They're gagged as well aren't they Piggy?"

189

Piggybait nodded but remained tight-lipped.

"This is bad, I mean really bad." Sam stood up. "Do you know where Jonah is now?"

Claptrap hung his head. "He went out earlier and we kind of…lost him. I don't know whether he went home or not. To be honest, it wasn't until after Halmar told us what had happened, we realised none of us had seen him for a while. We hoped he was with you."

Piggybait stood up and moved closer. "Of course, there's one possibility, somewhere we haven't looked." Piggybait stared at Sam waiting for the penny to drop. It did.

"Of course! The dungeon! That's where he'll be. I'd bet my Chelsea scarf he's down there exploring again. I'll need to find him." Sam darted out of the door, and had just reached the bathroom when he turned and ran back to his room.

"Do you know where Charlie is?" he asked.

"Yes, of course we do. We always know where the Chief is," Piggybait answered in a voice that implied Sam was being stupid for asking.

"OK. I'll call Jason and get him to meet me at the tunnel then we'll find Jonah. It's likely Jonah doesn't know what's happening, but if he's there he's in the right place for us to see what we can do. You find Charlie and get him to call the police. Tell him what Halmar saw and what I'm doing. Tell him he's got to say it was him who saw this bloke and he thought it was suspicious."

"Why should he say that?"

"Isn't it obvious? What are the police going to say if he says an elf told him…derrrrrr!"

Piggybait thought about it for a second. "Oh yes, of course…how silly of me."

"But Sam, what are you going to do when you get into the house?" Claptrap asked.

"I really don't know yet, not until we get inside and see what's happening. But at least we can get in without being seen and that gives us an advantage…maybe Mrs Atkins will be able to help."

"But she's not there Sam."

"Not there! Where is she?"

"We didn't get round to telling you about that," Piggybait began. "Just after Halmar reported in, Claptrap and I headed to the Manor to see if we could find anything out. We saw Mrs Atkins in that big room she works in, you know the one on the corner."

"The study?"

"That's the one. Anyway, she was talking to the man and he was pointing the gun at her."

"She must have been terrified."

"Well maybe, probably...but she didn't look it. She seemed more annoyed than anything, but so did he. Soon after, we saw her get in to her car and drive away. We guessed he was sending her off somewhere. She didn't seem to want to go and I can't imagine she willingly left her family unless she had to."

"Not with him having a gun," Claptrap put in.

"Exactly," Piggybait added.

"I need to think...and I need to get dressed." Sam remembered he was still in an old tee-shirt and pyjama bottoms. "Right outside you two! You need to find Charlie for me, quickly."

Piggybait and Claptrap headed for the door.

"Oh no, you don't! You got in through the window and you can go back the same way. I'm not having you bump into mum at the front door. She'd have a fit if she found a couple of elves in the hallway!"

The elves grinned at each other, clearly imagining the fun they would have surprising Sam's mother.

"No! Absolutely not! That's the way out." Sam pointed towards the window, giving the roguish elves no choice other than to do as they were told. First Claptrap, then Piggybait clambered back through the window, but just before he began the climb back down, Piggybait turned back to Sam.

"Once we've found the Chief, we'll head back to the Manor to see if there's anything we can do. You never know the odd bit of elfish...um...influence might not go amiss. Be careful."

"Thanks Piggy, we can do with all the help we can get. See you later."

Sam headed off to the tunnel having arranged to meet Jason at the entrance. For once Sam moved hurriedly through the trees, this time not noticing the sights and sounds around him. He had more important things to deal with.

On reaching the hillock, Sam pulled back the overhanging ivy, found the door and the triangular rock. The mossy pad was standing almost upright, a clear indication someone had been there and forgotten to cover their tracks. Sam was certain he had laid it flat when they had left the tunnel the day before. It had to be Jonah. Apart from him and Jason, surely no-one else knew about the door, except Charlie and the elves of course, but as Charlie had said he could not get through there and it wasn't the elves.

A rustling in the bushes made him shrink back close to the muddy wall, trying to hide under the dense, trailing foliage. With all the recent disturbance many of the insects had found other, less disrupted places to live.

"Sam? Sam, are you here?" It was Jason.

"Yeah, I'm here," Sam called from under the greenery.

Jason grinned. "What're you doing in there?"

"Waiting for you, what else? But there's no time to hang about talking." Sam grabbed hold of Jason's arm and pulled him towards the door. "It looks like the bloke who killed Jonah's dad's got inside the Manor."

Jason froze. His mouth dropped open. "What?"

"I'll explain as we go, but now we've got to find Jonah. I think he's in the dungeons and probably doesn't know what's happening. We've got to find him, then get inside the house."

"What about calling the police?"

"That's being sorted out. Charlie's calling them, but we'll be on the inside. Come on let's go."

Jason grabbed hold of Sam's sleeve, holding him back, his face white with fear. "But what are we going to do when we get inside?"

Sam had not had time to be scared but, seeing Jason's fear, he realised the danger they may be facing.

"I s'pose we'll find that out when we get there. Come on, let's go."

Sam pressed the lever down and, sure enough there was only one torch on the ledge. "Jonah must be here, he'll have the other one." Jason clicked on the torch and closed the door behind them before they set off down the long, smelly, cobwebby tunnel; somehow this time the smell was not as bad as before. Reaching the building blocks seemed much quicker this time and they trod respectfully over the scattered bones. Soon they came upon the sudden drop where the steps began, and soon after the tunnel widened as they approached the door to the dungeon corridor. It was slightly ajar and a strand of flickering light showed under the door beyond.

"I really hope that's Jonah," Sam whispered to Jason.

"It'd better be," Jason whispered back, his voice hoarse with tension.

Edging forward, their hearts hammering in their chests, Sam and Jason reached the door to the torture chamber. The handle gave a loud creaking groan!

"Who's there?" Jonah's shaking voice told them how scared he was.

"It's only us," Jason called out.

"What are you doing, scaring a person to death?" Jonah groaned. "And how did you know I was here?"

"We guessed. We've been trying to find you," Sam told him.

"Why, what's up?"

They told Jonah as much as they knew of the events since he had left home that morning. Obviously Sam left out the bit about the elves. It would only complicate things.

"You mean Fisher's up there now?"

"Yeah, and your sister and aunt are tied up."

"She's my cousin not my aunt...and Fisher's got a gun?"

"Yeah. So we heard."

"OK! Let's go...we've got to try to rescue them." He made a dash for the door, but Sam grabbed him and held him back.

"Hang on a minute, Jonah. Charlie's getting the police and we need to think out what we're going to do. If he's got a gun and we don't go carefully, someone might get shot," Sam reasoned.

"I don't care as long as it's Fisher," Jonah barked.

"Yeah, but it might not be. Best take it careful, eh."

"Yeah, you're right Sam, again. And I've just remembered, the DCI said his name was Farrow, not Fisher. Anyway, got any ideas?"

"No, not yet, but we've got surprise on our side. No-one knows about the tunnels so we need to keep quiet and watch out. Like I said, Charlie's phoning the police and they should be here soon."

"Now would be a good time," Jason said,

"Yeah, but they're not here yet and we are." Jonah led the way up the spiral staircase and along the corridor by-passing the kitchen.

"Listen!" Jonah held up his hand. From somewhere far off they heard frantic barking and whimpering.

"That's Wilmot!" Jonah frowned. "It sounds like he's outside, but I can't worry about him at the moment. At least if he's barking, he must be OK. Come on."

Stepping silently along the corridor, they reached the place where the wall felt warm.

"Meredith and Dorothy are just the other side," Jonah said wistfully. "I wish I could break through here and untie them." He leaned against the wall and pressed the side of his head against the warm stonework, listening for any signs of life on the other wide, but there was nothing to hear.

"I can't hear them," he whispered. "I hope they're alright."

Sam was relieved. If Jonah had heard crying or shouting, he might have been tempted to do something rash, which would draw attention to them and probably ruin their plans.

"They'll be OK," Jason sympathised.

"Come on, Jonah, we'll have them free soon." Sam tugged at Jonah's sleeve, still convinced staying silent and secretive was the best course of action. Moving on they soon arrived at the next set of steps.

"Jonah?" Sam tapped Jonah on the shoulder.

"Yeah?"

"Your mum uses the study most of the time doesn't she?"

"Yeah. Why?"

"Then the chances are that's where they'll be and it's easy to get in. The study's our best bet to get this bloke."

"Yeah, I was thinking that too."

From behind the panel, they heard the study door open and Harriet and Farrow, enter the room. Tentatively Jonah pulled on the metal rope and held his breath as the section of wall glided silently aside, thankful his father had maintained the mechanism so well. Through the slit in the wall, he peered into the study but was unable to see beyond the curtain and a lull in the conversation stopped him from pressing the panel release button in case it was heard in the silence. Then his mother spoke.

"There! There's your precious diamonds. Now get out of my house and leave us alone!"

"Ha! Brave words from the merry widow!"

That remark made Jonah's blood boil. Whose fault was it she was a widow? Furiously, his hand shot out for the button, but Sam grabbed his wrist.

"Not yet!"

Harriet must have appeared shocked by Farrow's last remark because Jonah heard him say. "Don't tell me you actually liked your husband. I'd have thought you'd be pleased to see the back of him, after all I understand he didn't treat you or your brats very well."

"Whatever Jerry did wrong, he didn't deserve what you did to him."

Farrow laughed scornfully. "You must forgive my amusement, my dear, but you obviously aren't aware of Jerry's more unpleasant activities so I'll let that one pass but, in the meantime, I quite like the Manor...no-one knows I'm here and it wouldn't be a bad place to lay low. So I might just stay for a while. Not for long of course, just long enough to see if you have anything else I might find...useful."

"No. It's out of the question. *I got you the diamonds, now leave!*" Harriet's courage was failing and Farrow knew it. Jonah's heart pounded. His mother's voice held an edge of desperation. She needed his help. He realised that, even though the panel had swung open quietly before, it might still make enough noise to alert Farrow to their presence and an argument may be just the thing he needed.

"Go on, Mum, wind him up," Jonah silently urged.

"I know I did," Farrow replied smoothly, "but I'm a bit of a villain and we villains rarely tell the truth."

"What are we going to do when we get in there?" Jason whispered.

"Not a clue," Jonah whispered back, "but Sam knows Kung Fu."

"It's Aikido and I haven't used it for ages," Sam whispered a protest.

"Yes you have, you used on me...twice and it hurt," Jonah grinned.

"And I saw you, in the locker room," Jason added. "Pretty smart that was. You're good."

Jonah flinched recalling how Sam's had rescued Jenny from his bullying some months before.

"Yeah, well don't expect too much, I'm a bit rusty." When they made themselves known to Farrow, he would have to use whatever skills he had; there would be no choice.

"Get ready!" Jonah signalled. He pushed the release button. The panel glided noiselessly aside. The boys crept out of their hiding place and waited, holding their breath, behind the floor length curtain. Jason glanced behind him to find their reflections could be seen in the window. He nudged Sam and nodded towards it. Sam nodded back, signalling he too had seen the images and held up crossed fingers. With luck Farrow would continue looking in the wrong direction. Jonah took a careful peek around the curtain. Thankfully Farrow still had his back to the window, so they were safe. Harriet, though, was facing their direction and saw him. Thinking quickly, she lifted her hand to her forehead as if feeling faint and sank onto the sofa. Looking through her fingers she knew she was holding Farrow's attention and watched the curtain waiting for Jonah's move.

"Not weakening are we?" Farrow sneered. "I thought you were made of stronger stuff, my dear."

"You won't get…" Harriet was cut off in mid-sentence.

"Now!" Jonah yelled. They sprang at Farrow taking him completely off guard.

As Jason dived at his legs in a flying rugby tackle, the gun flew out of Farrow's hand and landed in the fireplace. Jonah and Sam made a grab for his arms, trying to pin them to his side. Farrow fell forward catching his forehead on the coffee table. The impact sent the vase of roses and lilies crashing onto the carpet; water sprayed everywhere and the vase and flowers lay strewn about on the carpet. The leather pouch containing the diamonds flew into the air and ended up behind the sofa. Farrow desperately tried to regain his balance, but with the combined force of the three determined boys, he lay prone on the floor where, ignoring his protests, Jason sat on him.

With Farrow disarmed and immobilised, a shaking Harriet picked up the gun carefully, took it to the drinks cabinet and locked it away just as the door burst open.

Detective Sergeant Harte and Ernie Rogers stood on the threshold unable believe their eyes. All three boys were breathing heavily and grinning from ear to ear. Jonah and Sam stood over the defeated Farrow, who struggled to wriggle out from under Jason who was still sitting on him.

"Hi Ernie. What time do you call this?" Jonah joked, leaving a dejected Fisher to the uniformed police officers. He looked triumphant as he put his arm around his mother's trembling shoulders. Harriet, on the other hand, seemed unsure whether to laugh or cry.

"Well, well. What's been going on here, lads?" Ernie scratched his balding head.

"We came out of..." Jason began.

"We were in here waiting for mum," Jonah broke in, casting a quick conspiratorial glance at Jason and Sam, "then we heard *his* voice," Jonah sneered as Farrow was being handcuffed. "So we hid behind the curtains, didn't we fellas? Just like this." He moved quickly towards the windows, concealing himself behind the curtain.

Sam, realising Jonah was about to close the still open panel, had a sudden coughing fit just in case there was any sound.

When he returned from behind the curtain, Jonah winked at Sam before dropping to the floor to pick up the scattered diamonds. Amongst a number of smaller white stones he found a large and stunning yellow stone that even a non-expert in precious jewels could see was very valuable. He handed it to Harriet who held it in the palm of her hand admiring its shape and lustre. It was a magnificent gem.

Sam gave Jonah a hand searching the thick carpet carefully to make sure they had not missed any. Satisfied, they had them all, Sam handed his haul to Jonah who put them in the pouch.

Ernie suspected the boys had not been entirely truthful with their version of events, but decided that, having captured Farrow and saved the family, however the boys had become involved would probably make no difference to the outcome of the investigation.

But one thing still puzzled him. He could not figure out why it had been so easy for them to gain access to the kitchen. When they freed her, Dorothy told them Farrow had locked it...and bolted it from the inside, but when they tried it, it was unsecured and opened with a slight push.

When Charlie Nowell told them someone had been seen hanging around the back garden of the Manor, John had radioed Ernie arranging to meet him for a silent approach. Ernie suggested they meet at the back door, but John seemed reluctant to go along with that suggestion for some reason.

Arriving at the stables, Ernie found John talking to Alison and a surprisingly cheerful Tom. Within minutes, another police car with two armed officers and a paramedic arrived.

Crossing the meadow, Ernie sensed a tension in John but assumed he was concerned about what was ahead of them. Ernie was worried sick at the thought of Dorothy being in danger, but he had a job to do and had to be professional.

At the back gate Meredith's dog, Wilmot, ran at them, barking excitedly. The poor dog had probably been outside for ages and was

196

desperate to get in. Somehow dogs knew when danger threatened. Unbeknown to Ernie, it was at this precise moment, Jonah, Sam and Jason were behind the kitchen fireplace listening to Wilmot's bark. Ernie was very relieved to find Dorothy and Meredith unharmed and, Wilmot bounced around Meredith barking frantically as they were being untied. Dorothy told Ernie that Marjorie was locked in the larder and soon she too was released but in a state of nervous collapse which the paramedic dealt with. Soon she felt much better and spent the next fifteen minutes telling the paramedic what her Stuart would do to 'that awful man'.

Unaware of what had been going on upstairs, Dorothy told Ernie and John she believed Harriet was in the study with Farrow. After making sure all three women were taken care of, and forcing a reluctant Dorothy to remain downstairs, Ernie and John, with the two armed officers walking ahead, crept silently to the study. John listened at the door. He heard voices, quiet at first, but then Harriet's angry voice, followed by a commotion, told him the time was right to move in.

The four officers burst through the door to find Farrow lying face down on the floor, being sat on by one of the lads, Harriet on the verge of hysteria, and the boys looking very pleased with themselves.

The uniformed officers pulled Farrow to his feet, handcuffed him and read him his Rights. Harriet, who had not looked at him until he was about to be taken away calmly faced him. For a moment Ernie wondered what she was going to do and, judging by the look on John's face so did he.

Fury glinting in her green eyes, she raised her right hand and slapped Farrow so fiercely across his face, his head was forced sideways. "I'm sorry the police have arrested you."

Farrow looked at her, a resigned expression on his face as white finger-marks appeared on his reddened cheek.

Jonah looked at her admiringly. "Way to go, Mum!"

Looking at Farrow Ernie thought he probably already knew what was coming.

Harriet glared directly into Farrow's eyes and, when she spoke it was in a harsh, distant tone. "After the suffering you've caused my family, I would far rather the Benson's got you first. Prison's too good for you."

Farrow nodded. "I suppose I deserve that," he said submissively. "Better take me away, officers."

Harriet looked at Ernie. "I suppose you'll need to arrest me, Ernie. I'm sure that constitutes an assault."

"What does, Mrs Atkins? I didn't see anything. Did you John?"

John smiled, "See what?" He walked towards the boys. "Um…I'll take that, if you don't mind," DS Harte reached out to take the pouch from Jonah. "Evidence!"

Chapter Twenty Six

The Easter school holidays were officially over but St Merriott's had an Inset Day. For Sam and his friends it meant another day of freedom. It was fine, cloudless morning holding a promise of warmth and at the Manor, Sam and Jonah battled each other on a computer game while Jenny, stared contentedly out of the window watching her grandfather weeding flowerbeds. Remarkable though he was for his age, she wondered whether it was time he considered retiring. She could see the bending and digging were becoming more difficult and it upset her to see him stop to lean on his spade every few minutes. No matter what he told the family, the signs of age were showing. She made up her mind to speak to her grandmother about him.

A peacock, his magnificent eye-dotted tail folded and trailing, accompanied by his two less showy peahens, was busy scratching at a section of the lawn where Mrs Seymour had thrown out some cooked rice for them earlier that morning.

"Did your mum get in touch with the Coroner's office about that skeleton?" Sam asked Jonah while trying to concentrate on the game controls.

"No, she...arggh! I should have got that one...not yet. She's found out it's the museum people she needs to speak to...yay...got it...but she wants to wait...*NO!*...missed it again...where was I? Yeah, she wants to wait until we find the original way...down...there must have been one. She's got a friend who does up old houses...and will keep the secret...for us. Umm...get your piggin' fighter outta there...this bloke'll open up the steps down but keep the passageways into the woods to himself."

"She's got a lot of useful friends, hasn't she?" Jenny said.

"Always comes in handy to have friends in the know," Jonah answered.

"Why...does she want the tunnels kept quiet? Ggrrr!" Sam shouted. Jonah was winning.

"When I...when I showed her the way we got in, she decided she wanted to keep it our secret. She loves all the mystery."

"Will she be able to?" Jenny asked him, from the window.

198

"Yeah, prob...bably," Jonah replied distractedly. "Friends in the right places..."

"But if this bloke...uh...does find the way down to the dungeons and the chamber, surely the museum people will want the rack and other stuff when they take the skeleton," Sam said, struggling with the controller.

"Yeah, that's what she thinks. They'll probably want to take them away and she thinks she'll probably have to let them. So she's either got to turn this place into somewhere for the public to visit or let them display the torture stuff at the museum and she'd...rather we didn't have to open our home to the public. The tunnel's not wide enough to take the rack and things through."

"How's she going to hide the doorway through to the woods tunnel?" Jenny asked.

"Hang on...Jen...I'm about to slaughter your boyfriend here," Jonah said, with a look of smug satisfaction. "There, got ya!" Jonah grinned at Sam.

"Yeah, well you get more practice than I do," Sam replied, looking a little narked.

"Not like you to be a bad loser, Sam," Jonah smirked, "but these games bring out the competitive streak in everyone. We'll have to play more often." He winked at Jenny and, Sam, realising how foolish he was being, regained his usual good nature. "If everything's taken out, you could turn it into a games room," he suggested.

"I'd rather keep the torture chamber," Jonah smirked.

"You're sick," Jenny commented.

"Have you shown her that ring yet?" Sam asked.

"What ring?" Jenny questioned, her curiosity aroused.

"No, not yet," Jonah replied. Opening the drawer, he took out the ring and showed it to Jenny. She turned it over in her hand.

"This is beautiful. Why haven't you told her about it?"

"She likes secrets, and so do I." Jonah replied, with a straight face. "No, just joking. I will tell her but I want to check it out first. I'm sure I've seen it in the house somewhere and Jason thinks it's on the window at the church. It's worth investigating."

Jenny returned the ring then went back to the window while the boys put the game they had been playing away and started on another one. Her grandfather was on his way back to the house, probably for a cup of tea in the kitchen. He looked up, saw Jenny at the window and waved up at her. She blew him a kiss and waved back. His slow walk and stoop worried her; he looked so old. She was torn between talking to her grandmother and letting him continue doing what made him happy. She couldn't bear to make him miserable. What kind of life would that be for him? She just wished he would decide for himself when it was time to start taking things easier. She had completely switched off from the boys and their game and was so absorbed with her thoughts she was unaware of Sam sneaking up behind her. When he grabbed her shoulders, she jumped out of her skin.

"Don't do that! You made me jump."

Sam gave her a hug, as much to stop her playful slaps as from affection.

The telephone rang. Jonah answered it. "OK, down in a minute." He put the phone down. "Come on, Marjie's got tea and biscuits for us in the kitchen."

"How's Meredith now?" Jenny asked, as they the room.

"She's OK. Doc Brownlow thinks keeping busy will help, so she went back to the stables a couple of days ago. Celeste's foal is due any time and that's helping to keep her mind off things, but there's the funeral to arrange and it'll churn everything up again, so will Farrow's trial, but for the moment she's OK."

"Have they said how long it will all take?" Sam asked.

"We can't arrange dad's funeral until the police release his body. I know mum hopes it will be soon but they've said the court case won't happen just yet so probably it'll be a few months until everything's finished."

"Are you coping alright?" Jenny asked.

"Not bad. I'm luckier than Meredith I suppose. Dad wasn't around much when I was growing up so I never really got close to him...but then, if I had, I might not be handling this so well. He was just someone I knew...not even as close as a family friend," Jonah ended quietly.

A heavy silence fell as they descended the staircase until Jenny stopped at the unicorn window.

"This window always knocks me out. It's fantastic!" she said, breaking the gloomy atmosphere. "It's a bit special isn't it?" Jonah agreed, before they ran down the short flight of stairs, into the kitchen where Sam's mouth dropped open in surprise.

"Dad! What are you doing here?"

Steve Johnson was sitting at the table opposite Harriet Atkins and they both seemed incredibly cheerful.

"I came to give Mrs Atkins some news," Steve beamed. Harriet hurried over to Jonah, put her arm through his and led him to the table. Puzzled, Jonah allowed himself to be guided to the chair beside her, while Sam sat next to his father and Jenny pulled up a chair next to Sam. Marjorie busied herself with making tea and coffee and kept out of the way.

"Well, what good news?" Jonah bristled with curiosity.

"It makes a change for us to have some good news doesn't it?" Harriet began, smiling at her son. "Help me out here, Steve. You tell him, I'm too

flustered."

"OK, if you're sure."

Harriet nodded quickly.

"Jonah, the diamonds Fisher…"

"Farrow," Jonah and Sam said together.

"Yes, Farrow, thank you boys. Well we assumed they were, let's say not altogether…legitimate."

"You thought dad stole them," Jonah broke in, stony faced.

"Yes, we did. There's ways of stealing without breaking in somewhere and thieving. We, your mum, the police, all of us really, considering his background, thought they might be 'hot'."

Jonah frowned. "And are they?"

Steve laughed. "No. No, I'm very pleased to say they're not."

Jonah's face was a picture. He looked open mouthed, from Steve to Harriet, then to Sam and back to his mother. Marjorie burst into loud blubbering tears, and her hands shook worryingly as she carried the tray of mugs to the table, Harriet hugged Jonah, and Sam and Jenny grinned at each other.

"How d'you know they're legal, Mr Johnson?" Jonah asked, rescuing the tray from Marjorie, he put it on the table.

"As you know I used to work in South Africa, in the diamond business." Steve helped himself to a mug of coffee while Harriet handed the other mugs around. "I still have some contacts there and made a few enquiries. It seems your dad made a *genuine* investment a few years ago, and the stones have increased in value. The only one there is a problem with is the big yellow one. We know that was stolen and where from, strange as it may seem, my work colleague and I were chasing the thief when we had our car crash. That one will have to go back to the mining company but the value of the others, the legal diamonds, is more than enough to make your family very wealthy."

"We think Jerry bought them in case things went wrong and he needed something to fall back on," Harriet explained.

"Diamonds are a good investment, Jonah, and small enough to conceal easily," Steve added.

"Like in a security box," Jonah put in.

"Like in a security box, yes. When your mum went to the bank she only took out the diamonds…"

"I wasn't thinking clearly," Harriet cut in.

"Not to be wondered at, at a time like that?" Marjorie said, leaning against the back of the green armchair.

"But what she missed was the envelope underneath the pouch," Steve continued. "Inside was the Proof of Purchase. We wondered whether they

201

were fakes but they're not and everything's in order. Your mum, as your Dad's widow is the beneficiary of his Will and inherits everything, including the diamonds."

"WOW!" Jonah exclaimed wide-eyed.

"Maybe I shouldn't ask as it's none of my business, but how much are they worth?" Sam asked.

"Sam!" Steve glared furiously at him. "You're right. It *is* none of our business! You shouldn't ask a thing like that."

"No it's OK, Steve," Harriet said. "There's nothing wrong in Sam asking. He was instrumental in solving this family's problems often enough, so I've no objection to him knowing. Go ahead and tell him."

"If you're sure," Steve nodded. "The purchase price was five hundred thousand pounds..."

"Bloody hell!" Jonah exclaimed.

"...but in today's market," Steve went on, slowly. "They're worth close to four million pounds."

"*Bloody Hell!*" Jonah repeated, staring at Sam, wide-eyed and incredulous. "We're rich!" He sat back in his chair looking very pale and slightly exhausted.

"Steve, once everything's sorted out," Harriet said solemnly. "I'm putting some money into a Trust Fund for Sam, Jenny and Jason to help with their further education."

Sam and Jenny could not believe their ears.

"What! You can't do that Harriet, it's far too generous," Steve protested.

But Harriet was insistent. "Sorry, Steve, but with that amount of money I can do what I want and these young people have done so much for us, I want to assure their future and this will help. And, there's something else, Jonah. I intend setting up a fund for Peter and children like him. I've no idea how your father would have used the money..."

"I can make a guess," Jonah said coldly.

"...and, frankly so can I, but I want to use it well." Harriet continued. "We were fairly financially comfortable before anyway and I've been thinking about what we can do to give something back to the village."

"You do whatever you think is right, Mum."

Harriet smiled warmly at her son. "I thought you would agree. Is there any more coffee, Marjorie? I'm parched after all this talking."

So it was a very cheery group that a smiling Dorothy joined a short while later.

"Where have you been? You're looking suspiciously pleased with yourself, Dorothy Renwick," Harriet said, flashing Marjorie a knowing smile.

"Helping Ernie choose new curtains and carpet for his front room." She seemed to be in an exceptionally good mood.

"See, I told you." Marjorie smirked. "I knew he had a soft spot for her."

"Yes alright, Marjorie, don't go on," Dorothy blushed. "Changing the subject, I just saw two friends of yours, Jonah."

"Who was that?"

"That nice boy Jason and guess who was with him?"

"No idea, give us a clue."

"She's got red hair and her parents run the Post Office." Dorothy seemed to find everything amusing.

"Not Susan?" Jenny said, delightedly.

"The very person, Jenny, and they were holding hands. Isn't that lovely?"

Jenny smiled wryly. "Perhaps she'll leave you alone now," she whispered to Sam. It took him a moment to understand why she was so pleased.

"What? You mean she fancied me?"

"As I said Sam, for a bright fella, you're a bit slow on the uptake!"

The telephone rang and Dorothy, who was the nearest to it answered.

"Hello Meredith. What! That's wonderful! I'll tell her. I'm sure she'll be right up." Dorothy beamed as she replaced the receiver.

"Celeste's had her foal. It's a filly and they're both fine."

"Wonderful!" Harriet jumped to her feet, knocking over her half empty coffee mug. "I'm going up there, anyone coming?" Marjorie rushed off to get the kitchen roll and began mopping up.

"No, I'll head off home," Steve said.

"OK, Steve. Thanks for everything and tell Jane there'll be lots of work for her soon. Something tells me we'll be busy over the next year or so."

"I'll tell her. Are you coming or are you going to the stables?" Steve asked Sam and Jenny.

"Stables?" asked Sam.

"Stables," Jenny replied.

"See you later, Dad."

"OK, behave yourselves, see you later."

Steve disappeared through the swing doors to leave by the front door, while everyone else trooped out the back way, through the garden and out into the meadow. Sam kept a wary eye out for Piggybait and Claptrap, and was not sure whether he was relieved or not when they did not appear.

"You'll need to stay calm and quiet around the foal and Celeste," Harriet said as they were halfway across the daisy strewn meadow. "They need peace and quiet right now, but it'll be OK if we're all quiet," Harriet warned.

Meredith and Alison were waiting for them at the yard, and they had company.

"What are you doing here John?" Harriet asked. "No offence, but I thought we'd seen the last of you for a while."

"None taken Mrs Atkins, this is purely a social call." He smiled at Alison, who smiled shyly back and moved closer to him.

So that's it, thought Harriet. Well, it's time she had some happiness. "So where's our new babe, Meredith?"

"Over here, Mum. Dan's still with them."

"Why? Is anything the matter?" Harriet enquired, concerned.

"No, no problem, they're both fine. He's got a quiet morning and wanted to stay on."

Dan's head appeared over the closed lower half of the stable door. "She's a beauty, Mrs Atkins. Come and look."

Meredith joined Dan in the stable with the new mother and foal, while Harriet and the others squashed into the doorway, all trying to get a peek at the new arrival who was standing on shaky legs, leaning against her mother who licked her tenderly.

"See, she's just like Angelo, same colouring and everything. The only difference is that white lozenge-shape blaze on her forehead." Meredith stroked Celeste's neck and talked softly to her, telling her how clever and beautiful she was.

"Have you named her yet?" Harriet asked.

"No not yet. I've been trying to think of something matching her mother's name. Monarch or Empress, you know, something that'll go with Sovereign or with stars or heaven, but we haven't thought of anything yet, have we, Dan?"

"How about Queen of Heaven," Jenny suggested.

"Does anyone know what the Arabic is for Princess?" Dan asked.

"Estella's nice," Dorothy suggested, "and stellar's to do with stars."

"How about Queen of Diamonds," Jonah suggested.

"I always liked the name Cassiopeia. She was a queen in Greek mythology and there's a constellation named after her," Meredith said.

"That's a nice one," said Dan with a gentle smile, "and it would fit."

Kelly Jones, who had wandered up to join them, said she thought 'Twinkle' sounded nice, but she was completely ignored.

"How about Queen of Diamonds," Jonah said, a little more loudly.

Soon everyone was offering suggestions. Pete Hallett joined the group along with several of the stable hands, and a general hub-bub followed with everyone talking at once.

"*How about Queen of Diamonds!*" Jonah yelled over the din. The buzz of talk ceased and as everyone turned to look at him. He shrank under their

collective gaze. "And I thought we were staying calm and quiet around the foal," he added quietly.

Harriet took a peek over the stable door. "She doesn't appear to have come to any harm for all our noise, she's too busy feeding." She turned back to Jonah. "So you wanted Queen of Diamonds, did you Jonah?"

"Well yeah. I just thought with that sort of shape, mark, on her forehead and with everything that's gone on, it would be a good name."

Harriet smiled warmly and reached out to ruffle his hair, but he ducked out from under of her hand.

"It's a great name, Jonah, well done. What do you think Meredith?"

Meredith hunkered down to eye level with the newly born foal as she nestled closer to her mother for security. Celeste nuzzled the foal with her nose and softly whinnied.

"What do you think little one? Is it Queen of Diamonds?" Meredith asked the foal.

A loud neighing came from the next stable and Meredith laughed joyfully for the first time since finding her father's body. "Well, Angelo seems happy with it, so that's her name, Queen of Diamonds."

Chapter Twenty Seven

Mrs Jenks was picking leaves in her herb garden, with Mélusine firmly perched on her shoulder while her mate, Taliesin paced up and down on the thatched roof, as if on guard while Bandit stretched out lazily in the sun. The wind had changed direction and Mrs Jenks looked up at the sky. With a satisfied smile

"It's time to close the cards, Bandit."

Picking up her wicker basket she went back into the cottage, Mélusine flapped her wings in rhythm with the walking motion. Bandit rolled over, yawned and followed them into the cottage and Taliesin flew down from his lookout post to hop through the open window into the kitchen, where he stood guard on the windowsill. Merlin, asleep on the floor in front of the fireplace, stirred as Mrs Jenks entered the room, raised his head but did not move from his comfortable position. Taliesin gave a loud 'kronking' noise and hopped down onto the sink unit, accidentally knocking an empty bottle into the sink with his flapping wings.

"Careful now Taliesin, don't be so clumsy," Mrs Jenks chided, putting the bottle back in place. "What's got you so excited?"

She leaned forward to encourage Mélusine onto the worktop as her shoulder was aching from the weight of the heavy bird. As soon as Mélusine had stepped down to join her mate, Bandit sprang onto the table, where he waited for Mrs Jenks to join him.

"Good, I'm glad you came in too." She stroked the purring cat that stretched his neck to rub his head against her hand. "Are you ready?" The cat mewed and swished his tail.

The nine Tarot cards lay undisturbed, waiting for the closure.

"So much has happened in just a few days." Bandit moved closer. "Oh no, my dear," Mrs Jenks began, stroking him. "You're not to climb up yet. I've only just got rid of one weight and my shoulders need a rest." Bandit eyed her sulkily.

Mrs Jenks turned towards the window. "That's why Taliesin was jittery, Bandit. We're about to have visitors."

The backdoor opened and Piggybait, accompanied by Claptrap, entered the kitchen, squabbling as usual, which Mrs Jenks chose to ignore.

"Oh good, I'm glad you're here. You're just in time for the closing of the cards."

Piggybait clambered onto a chair and stared down at the cards while Claptrap wandered over to Merlin who wagged his tail in welcome. Piggybait stroked his chin, a newly acquired habit that reminded Claptrap of Jimander, who constantly stroked his chin when he had a problem to solve and he smiled sadly at the memory of their dear friend and leader.

"You're right, Armistice," Claptrap said. "There doesn't seem to be anything left to do. Atkins is definitely dead, Farrow's in custody and neither of them can do any more harm."

"And the wood is at peace again," Piggybait added. "I really believe this unpleasant episode is finally over."

Taliesin called again from the window.

"Another visitor," Mrs Jenks remarked.

"Shall we disappear?" Piggybait asked.

"No it's alright, it's only Charlie."

The door opened and Charlie entered the kitchen, remembering this time that he needed to stoop to avoid the low ceiling.

"Mornin' Armistice, how are you today?" His deep rich voice boomed loudly and the ravens flew out of the open window. "Something I said?"

Mrs Jenks chuckled. "They don't like loud noises Charlie," Mrs Jenks teased, "but I'm glad you're here. I'm just about to close the cards. Piggybait and Claptrap agree it's time. What do you think?"

"I don't see why not. The wind's changed direction bringing change. I think it's safe to go ahead."

"I'll do it at mid-day when the sun's at its zenith, but you didn't come here about the cards, Charlie."

"No, Benny's cut one of his paws again. The pad's cut quite deeply and I wondered if you'd look in on him. We've sorted it out for now, but one of your poultices would help."

Mrs Jenks' eye twinkled and she grinned slyly. "You'll get me into trouble with that new vet. He'll be getting fed up with me treating his patients but yes, of course I'll come round. It'll take about an hour to make something up for him."

"Sorry to interrupt, sir," Claptrap said from the hearth where he sat with Merlin, "but the bookings for visitors to Lappland are coming in. Do you want to see them yet? And Donner's arthritis is playing up again. Shall we train Rudolph up to take over, or bring another reindeer over as an understudy? Wolf needs time to get used to newcomers."

Charlie leaned his elbow against the mantelpiece. "OK, I'll call in later

when I walk Bjorn and take a look at the bookings, but you'd better arrange for another reindeer to be brought over, just in case Armistice can't heal Donner in time."

Mrs Jenks nodded. "I'll do what I can, but it's best to be prepared, she's getting old now and she's made a lot of flights."

"She'll be heartbroken if we have to retire her, but Piggy'll make sure Wolf behaves, won't you Piggy?"

Piggybait, flicking through a book on herbal poultices, had not really been paying attention, and suddenly heard his name.

"Sorry, what am I going to do?"

"Make sure Wolf behaves himself if we bring over another reindeer."

"I can't promise that," Piggybait grinned. "He's still disappointed he couldn't eat Atkins."

"Oh, how could you!" Mrs Jenks exclaimed.

"Your sense of humour will get you into trouble one day," Charlie chuckled. "Anyway, I've got to go. I won't stay for the closing of the cards. You don't need me as well. So thanks, Armistice, Cathy and I'll see you later." Charlie turned back to Piggybait and Claptrap. "The woods and the caves provide good hiding places for fugitives, but they don't know the clan. Farrow never stood a chance. It's a pity humans can't know about you, the world would be a better place if they did."

"They're still too closed minded to believe sir," Claptrap said sadly.

"Maybe it's just as well, we can do more when we don't exist," Piggybait added. "Being invisible provides us with the freedom to act as we see fit."

"And you remain one of life's splendid mysteries," Charlie replied, ducking under the doorway.

"Not to all of us though, eh," Mrs Jenks smiled at her small visitors. "Bye Charlie. See you later."

"I like getting involved with humans, they're so…unpredictable," Piggybait said thoughtfully. "It's a pity we can't mix with them more." He sat down on the chair he had previously been standing on.

"What about a nice cup of tea Armie? While I tell you how I finally perfected Jimander's trick of sliding bolts and turning keys?"

"It was very handy," Claptrap chortled, "after all the times you got it wrong before, it was brilliant getting it right just when it was needed."

"That's probably why you got it right, knowing what was at stake made you concentrate more," Mrs Jenks observed.

Piggybait looked very pleased with himself. "The police were surprised to get in to the manor so easily. You should have seen their faces, especially that John, but he's easy to wind up anyway."

"Don't be so mean, Piggy. Anyway he's got other things on his mind

now," Mrs Jenks said knowingly. The clock on the mantelpiece chimed twelve. "Right. Let's get to it. It's time." Walking over to the table, with her hand lightly hovering above the tenth card, she closed her eyes and silently mouthed some words but still she did not pick it up. A few moments later, she opened her eyes and looked down at again. "The tenth card closes the reading," she said, more to herself than to her companions. Piggybait helped Claptrap up onto the chair and they leaned on the table, as Mrs Jenks finally turned over the last card placing it across the existing central card.

"The Fool, upright! Oh, that is a good omen. New beginnings, happiness and optimism. What a wonderful card to close with!"

Piggybait and Claptrap smiled broadly. "Thank Alfheim," Piggybait sighed. "Now that's done, how about that tea Armie…got any biscuits?"

Bandit arched his back and with an elegant stride, jumped gracefully from the table onto Mrs Jenks' shoulder before draping himself around her like a shawl and purring very loudly in her ear.

Acknowledgements

Acknowledgements in this second book, will not vary a great deal from those in 'Silver Linings' because I am still so very grateful for the support that Helen Hollick, Cathy Helms of Avalon Graphics, Daniel Cooke, the Managing Director of New Generation Publishing, my daughter, Rachel Littlewood (AuthorPress Editing), Nottinghamshire authors Nicola Monaghan, Elizabeth Chadwick and Stephen Booth, experienced and popular Nottinghamshire journalists Jeremy Lewis and Dawn Bond, and Daniel Medley, Director of Wookey Hole Caves and his team. All these wonderful and inspiring people have done so much for me over the years. Their continued support is very welcome and much appreciated.

This time as well though, my thanks go to my son Greg and his fiancée, Kayleigh Hawksworth – who is incidentally a terrific singer and does a great Katy Perry tribute. Greg and Kaylie have been a tremendous help over the last year or so with the technical side of the events I organise for New Writers UK. It's wonderful to have their know-how when staging the book festivals.

Special thanks, as always, go to my husband, David, who not only spots all my typos, but continues doing most of the housework giving me the time I need for event organising and writing. Thank you for everything, my darling, and I know you'll be delighted to hear that I'll be working on the third book, 'Fool's Gold' very soon.

Jae was born in Isleworth, West London then lived in Essex and Suffolk before spending the rest of her childhood in Sherborne, Dorset, close to the Somerset border. During those happy years, a visit to Wookey Hole caves and an inspiring History teacher at her school, Gerald Pitman, sparked her interest in the facts and myths that surrounded the Mendip Hills. Another teacher, Anne Osmond, was equally inspiring with her love of literature and encouraged Jae in her first attempts at writing.

In her early teens Jae moved back to London and began writing her first book – a story set in Ancient Egypt based on the life of Queen Hatshepsut – it was never finished!

As the years went on and career, marriage and children became her priorities, Jae forgot her writing but never her love of reading and almost always had at least one good book on the go; in particular, historical or fantasy novels.

Years later she moved back to the West Country to the village of Butleigh in Somerset, just four miles from Glastonbury and seven from Wells and fell in love with the area all over again, but this was to be a short stay.

Later, Jae met and married her second husband, David, and lived in Dumfries for six years. Then in 1996, the family moved back to England settling in Nottingham where they have lived ever since. Jae's children, Rachel and Greg, are now grown up and she has two grandchildren, Erin and Finn.

Having originally written 'Silver Linings' in 2005 and self-published in 2006, Jae met two other self-published authors and together they attended book festivals and other literary events and met a number of other self-published authors, all trying to find their way through the world of bookstores, journalists, publishers and agents.

In 2006 she founded not-for-profit New Writers UK and organised their first book festival in November that year. Participating were just eight very local authors. Having invited the Lord Mayor of Nottingham the Chairman of Nottinghamshire County Council, the Mayor of Gedling and a number of local journalists, New Writers UK was on its way.

NWUK now has well over one hundred members throughout the UK and overseas, runs an annual Creative Writing Competition for Children and Young People of Nottinghamshire and last year created a 'Silver Scribes' short story competition for people aged fifty-five. Both competitions are entirely free to enter.

Since writing her books and the formation of New Writers UK, Jae (under her given name of Julie Malone), is a regular on local radio, writes articles for newspapers and magazines in the Nottinghamshire area and for the New Writers UK quarterly newsletter.

In February 2015, Jae (as Julie) was thrilled to be presented with the 'Pride of Gedling' Award in the Public Servant category in recognition of all her hard work in running creative writing classes, creative writing competitions and organising the Gedling Borough Council Book Festivals.

For more information on New Writers UK please visit www.newwritersuk.co.uk.

'Queen of Diamonds' is the second book of the Winterne Series. The first and third volumes are 'Silver Linings' and 'Fool's Gold', all three were originally written under the pen-name, Karen Wright, and received excellent reviews. The fourth book, working title 'Avaroc Returns', is well underway.

For further information about Jae please email her at jaemalone.author@gmail.com or contact her through Facebook or Twitter

Fool's Gold

Chapter One

'Papa! Papa Gabriel!'

The old priest had dozed off over his newspaper and woke with a start at the shout and the urgent loud knocking on his window. The newspaper slid to the floor as he stiffly rose from the comfort of the armchair and opened the slats of the window blind to find nine-year old Marisol Vasquez, clearly distressed and waving frantically at him. He had never seen her in such a state, her red-rimmed eyes pleaded with him for help and, having secured his attention, she rushed off towards his front door.

'Is there no peace?' he grumbled, forcing his creaky knees to move. 'I've been sitting far too long.' He shuffled slowly along the dim hallway as Marisol called and hammered incessantly on the door.

'Alright, alright child!' he shouted. 'Have patience!'

On opening the door, the sunlight dazzled his eyes, blinding him momentarily. Before he could see what was happening Marisol pounced forward and grabbed his hand. 'Come, Papa Gabriel! Mama needs you!'

He pulled away. 'What is this? What is the matter with you?'

But the girl was insistent. 'No time, Papa. Mama sent me.' She wiped away her tears with dirty fingers. 'She needs you. Now!'

'Wait, wait, Marisol, I must get my sandals.'

'No! There's no time for that, Papa Gabriel. Bare feet do not hurt.' She pointed to her own small dirty, unshod feet. With a resigned grunt, he reluctantly allowed the child to drag him along, cursing under his breath as he tripped on the hem of his robe scraping his toes on the stony dirt road. The sun reflected on the whitewashed walls of the one-storey houses, it hurt his eyes, his head began to throb and perspiration ran down his face. He hated the early afternoon heat and avoided going out until the cooler evening if he could. He thought resentfully of the sheltered comfort of his home situated as it was behind the church and in constant shadow but, once again, the Vasquez family were in trouble. There was always one or more of them in some kind of mess. Life was hard for Raul and Inéz Vasquez with a family of ten children, but then life was hard for many families in this backwater village. He shaded his eyes with his free hand.

Marisol, unusually unkempt and agitated, let go of his hand and ran along ahead of him, urging him to hurry when he stopped to get his breath. She ran back to him and reached out. 'Don't stop, Papa Gabriel. Come on!'

He pulled away from her grasp. 'Marisol. What is this? Why does your mama need me?'

'No time Papa Gabriel,' she urged. 'Come, come,' she pleaded again and clutched at the sleeve of his robe, tugging frantically. He gave in grudgingly and allowed himself to be pulled along by this determined child. Doors opened and sleepy-eyed villagers, disturbed from their siestas by the noise, began milling about in the street. Even black-garbed Rosa, snoring in her rocking chair in her doorway, managed to get to her feet.

Father Gabriel shouted at them to return to their homes. 'There's nothing to see. What do you want here? Go home!' he shouted but to no avail as the mob refused to budge. Soon a column of curious villagers had formed behind pursuing them through the narrow winding streets.

The Vasquez' home was at the end of an alley which afforded some shade from the intense sunlight in the shadow of its walls and Father Gabriel was able to stop squinting. The door opened and little Dolores Vasquez tearfully ran to join her sister. They grasped each other's hands tightly. The sight of a second crying child made the old priest wonder if he should have taken the time to fetch his Bible. Once inside the tumbledown house he closed the door shutting out the nosy villagers and found Inêz Vasquez carrying six month old Alejandra, pacing back and forth across the wide, square area that served as a kitchen, living room and bedroom for the older boys. She turned as he entered the room with the two little girls. Her face drawn, her eyes puffy and red, she appeared defeated, beaten. 'Father Gabriel, thank you for coming,' she said quietly without ceasing her pacing.

'My child, what's happened? The children didn't tell me.'

'It's Elêna, Father. She has vanished.' Alejandra, far too young to comprehend what was happening, tugged at her mother's hair. Inêz gently released the baby's grip and, with one hand, threw a bundle of brightly patterned tourist-aimed shawls piled on the bench to the floor, so that the old priest could rest while his heart rate slowed and his lungs could breathe easily again. Father Gabriel grabbed her hand and pulled her down on to the bench beside him.

'When?' Apart for the little girls, she was alone. 'Where is Raul? He should be here with you.'

'He and the older boys are out searching for her. Sandro and Hector are with my sister, Juana.'

Through the open window, the sound of the ever increasing crowd grew more raucous. A few were whispering but most were talking loudly, too loudly; their speculation causing added suffering. He heard a few sympathetic comments but some were obviously enjoying a good gossip, theorizing on what could have happened to the Vasquez family this time. It

was distracting and his head throbbed painfully. He went to the window and closed it, ignoring the inquisitive eyes and craned necks as the curious neighbours tried to get a better view. The noise lessened a little. Inéz cradled the gurgling baby, her eyes glazed and staring at the door while Dolores clung to her and Marisol stood behind, her arm resting on her mother's shoulder in a mature and loving gesture of comfort.

'What happened, Inéz?'

'We don't know, Father. She went to collect wild papaya...and cucumber from the lower hills early this morning...she should have been back after an hour or so,' she gulped as tears brimmed. 'Father...what am I to do...my girl has not returned?'

'Could she be at the ruins?' He knew Elêna spent as much time as she could spare in the ancient temple.

'No Father, Raul has already been there. There was no sign.' She looked down at her youngest child and tears dropped onto the baby's face. 'He and the boys have gone to look in the places where she usually goes to find fruit for us.' Inêz fell silent.

Father Gabriel stood up and groaned. He flexed his knees until they stopped creaking before he went to the window and pulled down the raffia blind shutting out the prying eyes.

Fourteen year old Elêna was his prize pupil at the village school, where he was the only teacher. She was not his favourite, she was too distant, too cold, but she was keen to learn, extraordinarily keen, and soaked up any knowledge he wanted to impart. She never forgot anything and always did as she was told without fuss or comment. Her intelligence and ability to absorb set her aside from the other pupils; intelligence and the most remarkable eyes he had ever seen. They reminded him of ice cold emeralds.

Green eyes these days were virtually unknown but, in this area, there were many people with Aztec blood and, if the stories he read were true, green eyes although unusual, were not rare and Elêna had been fortunate for that gene to show up again in her. She certainly showed an interest in legends of the Ancients. He realised that the only time he ever saw any genuine animation in her face was in their shared interest in local mythology and archaeology. Like many others who heard the calling to the Church he had been fascinated with the old deities, indeed this had been his first love although now he served God. But Elêna's absorption in the subject was almost an obsession. Few people called her friend and she showed little emotional attachment to her siblings or parents.

A shout outside caught Father Gabriel's attention. He lifted the blind and saw the crowd part as Raul and the four older Vasquez boys elbowed their way through. Inêz extricated herself from Dolores and handed

Alejandra to Marisol. The baby had fallen asleep and she whimpered at being disturbed. Inêz ran hopefully to the door as Raul, her husband and their sons Pedro, Jorge, Esteban and Emilio, their ages ranging between 13 and 10 years old, entered the room. Raul's hands were hidden behind his back. Jorge, Luis and Emilio stayed close to their father, their sorrowful faces clear evidence of misery, only Pedro stayed in the doorway. There was something almost like relief in his eyes. He saw the priest watching him and lowered his eyes hastily.

'Thank you for coming Father,' Raul's right hand gripped the priest's, the left stayed behind his back.

'Raul?' Inêz looked into his eyes, her question plain to see.

He shook his head sorrowfully. In his left hand he held a dirty, badly torn wicker basket with what appeared to be dried blood stains. Elêna had tied a number of ribbons to the handle some weeks before but now only a few tattered shreds remained.

'It must have been a jaguar or a stray wolf,' he struggled to speak, his voice grated harshly.

'*No!*' Inêz screamed and clung to her husband as he and the priest stared at one another in shared grief over her head. Father Gabriel broke eye contact first, miserably aware of how inadequate he was to help this despairing family, he laid an unacknowledged hand on Inêz' shoulder in an effort to console her, her heartbroken sobs pierced his soul. The girls wept with their mother while the boys stood in wide-eyed silence, attempting to hide their emotions. Grown men did not cry. Their self-control was agonizing to watch, except for Pedro who showed no emotion.

Inêz screamed. 'Father, she is dead. My Elêna is dead!' and she collapsed at his feet. The old priest lowered himself painfully to kneel with her, took her hands in his and prayed.

Lightning Source UK Ltd.
Milton Keynes UK
UKOW02f0054051016

284449UK00002B/116/P